The Resurrection of Nat Turner, Part 2: The Testimony

"Sharon Ewell Foster has . . . unearthed the *truth* about Nat Turner, rather than rehash and revisit the lies and distortions surrounding one of the most important people in American history. This is a liberating book, both psychologically and historically. Read it, read again, and then pass it on to someone who thinks they know who the real Nat Turner is."

—Raymond A. Winbush, author of *Belinda's Petition*

The Resurrection of Nat Turner, Part 1: The Witnesses

"Fast-paced . . . riveting and expertly told." —*Publishers Weekly*

Abraham's Well

"Innovative and intriguing. . . . This is the rare historical novel that both entertains and educates." —*Publishers Weekly*

"This is simply told and moving, Foster's best work since her groundbreaking first novel, *Passing by Samaria* (2000)."

—*Booklist* (starred review)

"*Abraham's Well* . . . [an] impressive, impeccably researched novel that deserves to be widely read; highly recommended."

—*Historical Novels Review*

"Sharon Ewell Foster merges little-known history with fiction to pen another amazing novel with *Abraham's Well*. . . . [It] is hard to put down. Definitely, one of the best reads of the year!"

—Victoria Christopher Murray, author of
Temptation and *Truth Be Told*

Passing by Samaria

"A sensitive, thoughtful look at a revolutionary time in American history. Foster's characters are unforgettable; full of life and unhesitatingly charming, they drive this powerful book."

—Kweisi Mfume, former NAACP president and CEO

"A rhapsody in prose. For a religious novel to simmer in the African American religious tradition, yet carry a universal message is a rarity. Readers will be thankful for this rare and splendid work."

—Dr. Barbara Reynolds, *Reynolds News Service*

"In this first novel, Foster's poetic telling is soft enough to capture and sharp enough to cut as she evokes the strength of faith needed to survive when all seems lost. This unique addition to the Christian fiction genre is highly recommended for all collections."

—*Library Journal*

"*Passing by Samaria* is a rarity in Christian fiction: it features an African American heroine in a kind of female *Black Boy*. . . . This is a fine first novel and most welcome."

—*Booklist* (starred review)

Ain't No River

"Foster's ears and pen are tuned to the rhythm and pace of small-town African American life, from the barbershop to the beauty parlor, from the church to the basketball court, and her dialogue sparkles with a memorable concreteness."

—Andy Crouch, *Christianity Today*

"This book is one more piece of evidence that Christian publishers are getting serious about producing literary fiction. Foster's prose is often evocative and eloquent . . . a rewarding read from an author to watch."

—*Publishers Weekly*

"Foster, one of the brightest lights of evangelical fiction, turns in a nuanced, often amusing tale."

—John Mort, starred review from American Library Association

Ain't No Mountain

"There's a reason the Christian publishing industry sat up and took notice when Sharon Ewell Foster's first book was released several years ago: She's good, very good, and with *Ain't No Mountain* she proves that she has staying power."

"Foster wants her fiction to entertain and uplift. She achieves both goals with this sassy, funny, heartfelt tale of women looking for love and themselves in contemporary Baltimore."

—Borders' Best of 2004/Religion & Spirituality

Passing into Light

"To me, she is one of America's best-kept secrets—but not for long! Sharon writes for those of us who want more than just words on a page, but pictures painted on the canvases of our minds. She has proven to be 'the Picasso of the pen!'"

—Bishop T. D. Jakes

"The name Sharon Ewell Foster is fast becoming synonymous with quality African American inspirational fiction."

—Pam Perry, Ministry Marketing Solutions

Ain't No Valley

"Foster makes ordinary lives seem exceptional through lively, lovable characters. She whisks us into drama and beautiful settings, using the Bible stories of Ruth and the prodigal son to frame the work and take readers to a deeper level of truth."

—*Ebony*

"Sharon Ewell Foster is a beautiful fresh voice in today's world of fiction. Her compelling stories draw us to a place where we somehow feel we belong, a place we want to visit again and again."

—Karen Kingsbury, author of *One Tuesday Morning*

Previous Works of Fiction by Sharon Ewell Foster

Passing by Samaria
Ain't No River
Riding Through Shadows
Passing into Light
Ain't No Mountain
Ain't No Valley
Abraham's Well

The Resurrection of Nat Turner, Part 2

THE TESTIMONY

Sharon Ewell Foster

HOWARD BOOKS

A Division of Simon & Schuster, Inc.

New York   Nashville   London   Toronto   Sydney   New Delhi

Howard Books
A Division of Simon & Schuster, Inc.
1230 Avenue of the Americas
New York, NY 10020

First Howard Books trade paperback edition February 2012

HOWARD and colophon are trademarks of Simon & Schuster, Inc.

For information about special discounts for bulk purchases, please contact Simon & Schuster Special Sales at 1-866-506-1949 or business@simonandschuster.com.

The Simon & Schuster Speakers Bureau can bring authors to your live event. For more information or to book an event contact the Simon & Schuster Speakers Bureau at 1-866-248-3049 or visit our website at www.simonspeakers.com.

Designed by Davina Mock-Maniscalco

Manufactured in the United States of America

10 9 8 7 6 5 4 3 2

Library of Congress Cataloging-in-Publication Data
Foster, Sharon Ewell.
    The resurrection of Nat Turner, part 2 : the testimony / Sharon Ewell Foster.—
1st Howard Books trade paperback ed.
        p.   cm.
    I. Title.
    PS3556.O7724R474 2012
    813'.54—dc23   2011029148

ISBN 978-1-4165-7812-3
ISBN 978-1-4516-5692-3 (ebook)

Scripture quotations taken from the King James Version of the Bible. Public domain.

For Darlene, Mary, Harriet, Easter, Nancie, and all the mothers who have lost their sons. For all the sons who have lost their way. You are welcome. Come home.

There is nothing covered, that shall not be revealed; neither hid, that shall not be known. Therefore whatsoever ye have spoken in darkness shall be heard in the light; and that which ye have spoken in the ear in closets shall be proclaimed upon the housetops.

—Luke 12:2–3

For God shall bring every work into judgment, with every secret thing, whether it be good, or whether it be evil.

—Ecclesiastes 12:14

Contents

Prologue

Minutes stretched into hours, hours into days, years into decades—time seemed bitter, thick, and useless like overboiled stew cooked to scorching. Afework counted the leaves, the pages, in her book of remembrance. There were thirty-two of them, one for each year since the theft of her child, her daughter, Nikahywot.

A month after the night of the theft, a night that sent the women fleeing into the darkness, her husband, Kelile, had found her in the Christian section hidden among the tens of thousands in the great city of Gondar. A family there had taken Afework and her granddaughter, Ribka, in. While there, the women had told her stories of other children—sons and daughters, brothers and sisters—stolen away.

The Arabian Peninsula was less than a mile across the Red Sea from Ethiopia. Ottomans, she had heard the women whisper, Arabs, Berbers, Turks, corsairs, Barbary pirates. The women spoke of Yemen, Hijaz, Cairo, Tripoli, and Tunisia. The thieves stole Christians to ransom and sell, the women whispered to her. They stole Christians from Ethiopia, from Sudan, and from as far away as Italy, Spain, Bosnia, and even beyond, where all the people were of white skin. They transported them to slave markets, even as far away as Morocco across the great Sahara. They sold them as slaves, carrying them back across the Red Sea, up the Mediterranean Sea. Stolen boys might be turned to eunuchs, the women wept for their stolen sons—there would be no generations to follow. But the young men might become guards, soldiers, or even well-paid officials. Their daughters, however, would most likely become concubines or even part of a harem. Some of the mothers dissolved into hysterical tears at the thought, but as they cried they overlooked the tears of the weeping servants who walked among them. But Afework could not shake the feeling that the slavery that had gripped Nikahywot and Misha was but an echo of that practiced in her own land.

Even in her own family, it was slavery that insisted that some family members were favored while others were born to serve. Some were blessed to be masters, *chewa*, while others were cursed to be slaves, *barya*. It was ancient slavery and deeply rooted. Afework worried that the slavery within her family displeased Egzi' abher Ab, God, the Father of all. They had failed to free Misha and her family, and now there was a family debt they owed. Now Nikahywot had been stolen and bound in slavery, or worse.

"Forgive us, Egzi' abher Ab," Afework whispered.

In the time it took him to find her, Kelile's hair turned gray. He took Afework and Ribka back home to the family farm. They would wait there for Nikahywot and her cousin Misha to return. But years passed and there was no word of their beautiful daughters.

Over time, Kelile lost all taste for farming and raising livestock. There was no one to help him—Josef, Nikahywot's husband, and Misha's husband had perished the night of the raid, the night before Misha and Nikahywot were stolen.

The land was raped of the young—the childbearers, those who carried truth and hope forward—and it suffered. The sky was brokenhearted and ran out of tears to cry so that each year the land grew more parched and cracked.

Before Afework's eyes Kelile seemed to shrivel like a gourd abandoned to the sun, drying up like the land that grieved for the stolen lives. Ribka cried every night.

They sold the farm and all their possessions and used the

money to travel to slave markets they learned of, like Zanzibar. They hoped to find Nikahywot and Misha, to ransom them, to purchase them back. But the two were nowhere to be found.

With the little they had left, what was left of the family had moved to Aksum. There were many mothers and fathers there also weeping for stolen children.

Now Ribka had become one of the shrouded women, living in a cave, swallowed in the ashen cowl of her grief. Each day she walked to stand outside the cathedral. She sang sorrowful psalms and offered prayers. Kelile found work sweeping the cathedral steps and doing other odd jobs. Afework spent her days in prayer and song, rehearsing the holy stories she had learned from her mother, reciting them aloud as though, far away, she hoped that Nikahywot would hear and remember.

Afework prayed day and night. The sun still shone in the sky over the highlands of Ethiopia like a gold coin against a curtain of blue silk with yellow and red ribbons. Birds like jewels still flew overhead. The water still roared off the edge of the Tis Isat Falls, but all that Afework could see was scorched brown grass. On her knees, her head bowed, she prayed that Egzi' abher would help her eyes and ears to remember that she was still in *ghe net*, paradise. She prayed to Iyyesus Krestos to help her to love and not hate—to remember that even those who stole and ruined so many lives were still Abraham's children, and that it was only the greedy ones who used the name of Mohammed to cloak their theft.

Afework turned on her knees to face the Cathedral of Maryam of Zion. Beneath the sun, and at night the moon and stars, she prayed that God would stir a strong wind that would blow her child back home. "Blow Nikahywot and Misha home." She prayed that the strong wind would destroy the chains and set all the captives free. She prayed that it would blow the dust of ignorance from the eyes of the captors. She prayed each day, but only soft winds and gentle storms arose.

Cross Keys Area, Southampton County, Virginia
1856

NATHANIEL FRANCIS USED the money he was paid to start over. Taking advice he got from slave traders, he now shackled the boys and men in the barn at night. There was no need to chain the women and girls; they would never leave the men, never leave their families. He was finally able to sleep comfortably at night.

Twenty-five years ago he had lost his brother, Salathiel, and his sister, Sallie, to the brutal insurrectionists. A quarter century past, as a young man of twenty-four, Nathaniel Francis had gotten his revenge. He looked back at his home—it had grown at least three sizes. With more money, money from the slave trials—Sam, Hark, Dred, Tom, Davy, Moses, Nat Turner—he was now a respected man, one of the elders of Southampton.

His wife, sweet Lavinia, had returned from her father's home in Northampton County in North Carolina and bore him many children.

In 1838 Nathaniel Francis became senior trustee at Turner's Meeting Place. He had the deed reviewed and the property surveyed: He believed in doing things in decency and in order. No nigger would ever be trustee.

Nathaniel rubbed his hand over the leather belt he still wore. Some had made wallets from Turner's hide. He had even heard of a lamp shade, but Nathaniel's trophy was a belt. It was a fine belt, a fine, fine belt.

He rarely saw his friend Levi Waller now, only occasionally, staggering drunk down the road. Thomas Gray had drunk away the money he earned from sales of *The Confessions*. He had lost his wife and, because of his inability to provide for her, his daughter was taken away. Gray no longer practiced law. Nathaniel Francis had seen him last crying and wallowing in the mud, begging for alms. Gray needed to pick his friends better. It was his just reward.

Trezvant no longer held public office. But Nathaniel Francis had done right well.

In all, Nathaniel Francis earned almost three thousand dollars for the lives of eight slaves, more than any other slave owner. He was not paid for Wicked Charlotte because he shot her. Nor was he paid for Will; the boy's body was never recovered.

Nathaniel Francis compulsively fingered his leather belt. Long ago, in 1831, he had dyed it dark brown. A fine belt indeed. He took it off only at night or to show his grandchildren when he told them the story of Nat Turner.

Nathaniel Francis wasn't afraid anymore. He had enough money that the lights in his home were always on.

Jerusalem, Southampton County, Virginia
1856

WILLIAM PARKER'S HAIR had grayed prematurely.

The Cross Keys bunch. Rowdies from the area just outside Jerusalem. Troublemakers. William Parker did not want to be one of them.

He had a recurring dream about a man he had seen when he was a boy, in a slave pen in the nation's capital. The man was dressed and shined like a new wagon waiting for a buyer. But there was something in the man's eyes—something sad, something broken, something angry. William Parker drew closer to his father's side, squeezed his hand.

When he awakened he could not remember if he saw the man's eyes in his dream, or if he had awakened during the night and seen the man's eyes staring at him in the darkness.

He did not make the system, William Parker had told himself for years. He did not make himself white. He could just as easily have been born black. He was one man; he could not change the world. He tried to do good in the spot that was his. He was as much a victim of fate as anyone, he told himself. He had no choice but to live out the life he had inherited.

William Parker had to live the life that had been given to him. He did not want to be one of them, but he was only one man.

Since the slave trials, William Parker hardly ever slept through the night. When he did sleep, he dreamed and saw their faces. There were so many innocent men hanged, and he felt powerless to do anything about it. So many women and children killed and so many families tortured.

Everything was in shambles. The little that still remained was crumbling around him. He dreamed over and over again that there was a decomposing corpse in his cellar and he did not have the courage to bring it out. William Parker had been praying since Nat Turner's hanging about what he should do. He prayed that God would make it all go away.

He remembered visiting Nat Turner at the jailhouse. He could still see the man's battered face. Nat Turner looked up at him from the bench where he sat chained. William had cleared his throat. "I'm sure that they are not going to allow me to put forth the evidence that you are a free man." It was impossible being the Negro's defense attorney. "In some ways it would only make matters worse. They are angry that you . . . They are angry at who you are and they do not want their beliefs challenged. I don't think there's much I can do." William Parker realized after he spoke the words that he had come seeking absolution.

"You owe me nothing," Nat Turner said. "What you do in the courtroom tomorrow, do for God."

William Parker had expected the next day's trial to be open-and-shut. Levi Waller would testify, some version of what Waller purported to be the truth. He had already testified six times and each time altered his story. But Waller's testimony was good enough; Nat Turner would hang.

Then on November 5, 1831, things in the courtroom had taken a turn. Maybe Waller was overconfident, or maybe he had taken a cup too much of the fruits of his still. Perhaps it was the hand of providence.

Waller stumbled during his testimony, the perjury so great the whole courtroom had gone silent. And against his better judgment, William Parker had pressed Levi Waller further.

"My question is this. Where were you, Mr. Waller? You testified you were in your home, and then you were hidden in the weeds. Now, today, you tell us you were hidden in the swamp. Is there a swamp close to your house? Where were you, Mr. Waller?" William Parker plunged in the blade. "You mentioned some other place I've never heard you mention before. Where was it you said you were?"

Waller hung his head. "My still."

"That just seems peculiar to me. Insurgents are coming, your family is threatened, and you have them loading guns. Your wife and children must be out of their minds with fear. They must have been terrified." William Parker withdrew the bloody blade and plunged it in again. "Where were you, Mr. Waller? And please say it loud enough that all the people can hear. Where were you after you learned the insurgents were coming?"

William Parker heard his own heart pounding. "Tell us the truth, Mr. Waller. You didn't see anyone, did you? You have no idea who was or wasn't there. The British? Nat Turner? Sam? Daniel? When your family was insane with fear, when your family was killed, where were you, Mr. Waller?"

Waller whispered his confession. "My still."

That was twenty-five years ago. Nat Turner had hanged. But the lies, the truth, still nagged at William Parker. A few had lied; many had hanged.

There was no doubt that Levi Waller lied. So had Mary Barrow, John Clarke Turner, Jacob Williams, and Nathaniel Francis— the whole Cross Keys bunch. But they were not forced to take their own medicine—there was no rack for them, no beatings, no burnings, no torture to make them confess.

Would there ever be a way to make it right?

Nat Turner/
Negasi

Chapter 1

Cross Keys Area, outside Jerusalem, Virginia
Christmas 1830

Nat Turner felt in his pocket to be certain the gunpowder mixture was still dry. He knew exactly the time and place he would use it. He had been planning for months. He was on his way to meet the others.

It had been a cruel winter. Snow in Virginia was most often one or two fingers deep or none at all, but this winter it had been heavy and so cold that the top of it was frozen. When he stepped, for an instant he stood above it. Then, shoeless, he was calf-deep again in the icy powder. At first cold pain shot up his knee and through his body with each step he took. Soon his feet were frozen and he numbly made his way past isolated farms and houses where he smelled the aroma of meat roasting outside. But he could not breathe deeply; the frozen air stung his lips, the membranes of his nose, ached his teeth.

The snow had snapped the brittle backs of withered corn plants. It covered the roads like a thick blanket so he barely recognized the fences and places he knew. The trees were his guide.

The trees were in the beginning and they had witnessed it all. They had seen husbands and sons dragged from their homes, castrated men dripping from their branches. They had seen women torn from the breast of their families and raped underneath the moon and stars. They had seen them beaten, burned, starved, and mutilated. The trees had witnessed it all. Their arms had borne the weight of the tortured.

He followed the trees, each one a signpost and a threat. Past sleeping apple trees—their feet and hair covered by the snow blanket—he ducked under leafless boughs and touched aged trunks covered with bark, rough even against his numb, bare hands. The trees were black and crooked against the snow's stark white. In warmer times, their hands and arms gave fruit and all the while told stories of death, strange fruit dangling from their limbs.

If the trees held the land's memories, then his mother held his. "You are a man of two continents," she had told him. "Your father is a man of America. They are the people of justice. An eye for an eye. At least that is what they say. But I am African. Ethiopians are children of mercy. It does not yet appear which will be strongest in you."

Ethiopian memories were rich, ancient, and deep. The images went back, his mother told him, before the *ferengi*, the foreigners, began to count time.

His mother told him that her mother's mother had told her that the Ethiopian highlands were waves, disobedient waves that had come crashing too far inland from the sea. The wayward waves had been abandoned by the others who returned to their watery home. Those left behind dried out and hardened, blanketed by green grass. But if you looked closely, you could see that the mountains were really only waves who'd gone too far and lost their way, his mother said. Heathen strangers.

Most of what he knew about life his mother had taught him. He had a grandmother who had helped raise him, but she was not really his grandmother. She was the old woman who tended all the slave children too old to nurse but too young to work, while their parents slaved in the fields or kitchens. But it was his mother who had taught him most about life, teaching him to honor his elders.

"They carry the wisdom and history of a people," she told him. "In Ethiopia they teach us the elders have learned to live a long time, and if we honor them they will teach us the way."

Ethiopia was a great nation—armies with twelve hundred

chariots, threescore thousand horsemen, with a host of a thousand thousand—and at her name other nations quaked.

He was born of a nation of great warriors; the world's first warriors—men who possessed the bravery of lions. Birthed from a nation of warriors who were also holy men, leaders at the world's great councils of holy men. She told him of the warrior priests and saints, like St. Moses of Ethiopia.

From the beginning, she told him, Ethiopia had God's favor. They were not rich in currency, but they were wealthy in greater things. There were great cities like Lalibela, Gondar, and Aksum. The spirit of God hovered over Ethiopia, and God had given Ethiopia's people to Maryam, the Mother of God, as a precious gift. The proof was in the emerald hills and the ruby valleys; the golden lions and leopards dotted with onyx; exotic birds of topaz, amethyst, and sapphire. The proof was in God's choice of Ethiopia as birthplace of the majestic Nile. God had crowned her with rainbows like jewels.

She told him the Nile's names—Blue and White—and as a child he had tried to imagine how the water divided into two colors, separated one from another. When he told her, she laughed and told him that in the old language the word for *blue* was the same as *black*. The color was not important. What was important was generosity: It was Ethiopia's gift to Egypt, birthed from Ethiopia's Lake Tana. It was the gift that gave Egypt her beautiful flowers.

From the beginning Ethiopia had been part of God's Great Church. She told him of the paintings, Bibles, and crosses that dated from the earliest centuries. She told him of Masqal-Kebra, the beautiful and merciful Ethiopian saint and wife—a great queen who advised her husband, good King Lalibela, on issues of state, with gentleness and mercy.

She told him the story of Moses and his Ethiopian wife and of the Ethiopian who rescued the prophet Jeremiah. Yes, there were Jews in Ethiopia, she told him. Families, thousands and thousands of them, who had been followers since the time of Solomon, Candace, and Menelik—and there were also others who followed the new religion, Islam. But all were brothers, Abraham's children, she reminded him as her mother had reminded her.

She shared the story of the Ethiopian Jew who, while reading Isaiah, had met the apostle Phillip and carried the good news of Iyyesus Krestos back to Ethiopia. His mother told him of the ancient bond between Egypt and Ethiopia—holy men had traveled the Nile, the Red Sea, and the Sahara for aeons between the great nations.

She shared stories of the great churches of Antioch, Alexandria, Rome, Armenia, and India—all sisters to Ethiopia and part of God's Great Church. She told him about the Ethiopian priests and their families. She told him about the wise men, *shimaghellis*, who lived their lives to serve the people—about people whose prayers awoke thunder and storms thousands of miles away.

She told him how St. Frumentius, a fourth-century Greek from Tyre—the Kesate Birhan, the "Revealer of Light," and Abba Salama, "Father of Peace"—brought Ethiopia the sacraments and helped spread the glory. She taught him of castles, palaces, and of Ethiopian cathedrals carved from stone. His mother whispered to him of the Holy Ark of the Covenant. "It rests in the Cathedral of Saint Maryam of Zion in the great city of Aksum," she told him.

The Ethiopian people believed in God and in miracles, in His mercy and in His love. What kind of person could look at the sun, the moon, the stars, the water, and not believe? she asked him. Only a fool of the worst kind would think himself greater than all the wonder and not believe, she said. God was a spirit and all mankind—all nations, and kindreds, and people, and tongues—were made in His image. God dwelled among His people and He was to them all things: Father and the Many Breasted One.

Nat Turner continued following the trees. Cold shot up his shins like steel spikes.

His mother told him that God heard prayers and always answered; He was not bound by space or time. God spoke to people now as He had spoken to their forefathers more than a thousand years ago. God spoke to King David, to the prophets Daniel and Jonah, and they were no different from the people of today. She shared stories of how God had answered prayers in her family's life and in the lives of others. "If you open your eyes and your heart, you will hear Him. If your heart is honest and humble, you will understand.

"God always answers, but He does not always say what we desire." Her hope and prayer had been to stay in Ethiopia with her family. She had prayed to never leave. "If God always speaks what you want to hear, then you only speak to yourself!"

She always frowned then. "I did not want to leave." His mother told him the stories over and over and she always sighed. "I did not want to leave." But other people had prayed and their groans and cries reached God's ears. "They were captive Africans, like us, taken from their families." God had heard and sent her in the belly of a ship on a journey, like Jonah, to plead with the captors to free the captives and repent. His mother had been stolen from Ethiopia. She often cried when she told him of the rapes, the humiliation, and bondage, and of Misha and of her baby floating to their graves.

She could not bear to speak of her daughter, the sister he did not know, the little girl she had left behind, could not speak his sister's name. "Sometimes the things we must do for others are more important than our own lives." Her eyes seemed focused on a place far away that he could not see. Then she shrugged and came back to him.

"Egzi' abher needed you born here—he needed me to be the ship that carried you." He was born to be a deliverer, a prophet, a man of mercy. "God is lover of us all, the oppressed and the oppressor."

She told Nat Turner—the son she called Nathan, secretly calling him Negasi, her prince—that he was a living answer to the captives' prayers. It was a heavy burden for a little boy to bear. But he was born to it.

It was a family debt he owed.

Nat Turner brushed past a clump of barren trees. Not far away he saw a squirrel scurrying, desperately scrambling for food. Nat Turner's stomach rumbled. He had not eaten since early the previous day. His mother's stories helped fill his stomach and his heart. He felt in his pocket again. He must keep the black powder dry.

He was born of men who possessed the bravery of the lion, his mother said. They were men who would give their lives to protect their families or their country.

She told Nat Turner he was born of a nation of beautiful people—women so beautiful that Moses, running in fear, stopped and fell to his knees before the lovely Zipporah. Moses was captivated, as King Solomon was taken by the Queen of Sheba.

She told him of the Empress Berham Mugasa Mentewab, whose name reflected her beauty. She told him of the brown-faced Maryam cradling her holy son, Iyyesus.

His mother told him of Ethiopian men browned by the sun and more handsome than eagles in flight. She told him of the paintings and crosses that dated from the earliest centuries.

He was descendant of a nation of people who were readers and writers, thinkers and builders, she said. The Americans believed no Africans read, wrote, or had language. So, it was Nancie and Nathan Turner's secret that before he could read English, she taught him to write and read Amharic—printing out the words on precious scraps of trashed paper. Pages were called leaves, she told him. When there was no paper, she used a stick, drawing the letters on the ground. She had taught him what she could remember of Ge'ez, the holy language. He had taught himself English.

She taught him the prayers. She told him about the great church at Gondar with the brown-faced angels in the ceiling.

Nat Turner was a child of rape, the child of two peoples locked in struggle, and the seed of revolution burned in his belly. He was his mother's shame and her glory, and the weight of it sometimes seemed to crush him. When he looked at her, he saw the affection she had for him, the hope that was so much more than love. He was the hope of her triumphant return to Africa. He was the hope of his mother's village. He was the hope and dream of all the captive people. She told him she saw her father and her grandfather, and strangely even glimpses of her Ethiopian husband, in him.

Nathan Turner was born in Southampton County, without her it was all he knew. His mother was his memory of Ethiopia— the shepherds, the lambs, and the tall lion-colored grass. His mother was his Ethiopia. He saw it in her eyes. After more than thirty years, her tongue still lived in Ethiopia, her English still broken—it was her revenge on her captors. But her Amharic, when they were alone, flowed like the Nile he imagined.

When he was a boy he had dreamed a dream. He had dreamed of a family, of a simple farm, and preaching God's word. He dreamed a dream of Africa, of returning to his homeland, the highlands of Ethiopia. But the One God had spoken to him and now he knew in this lifetime he would never journey there.

His mother had taught him the story of his African forefathers and taught him to number the generations. "King Solomon loved the Queen of Sheba and she bore him a child, Menelik. Solomon begat Menelik, Menelik begat Menelik the Second." She counted on her fingers. "And then Meshech begat your grandfather. . . ." He numbered them until she was certain he remembered.

"We are the people of the spirit, the people of God," she told him. "It is our inheritance." The roots of the faith, she told him, were buried in love. "If you have and your brother has not, you must share. To do otherwise is a sin, my Negasi."

Sometimes when they were alone, she asked him to whisper her Ethiopian name, so that she would not forget. "You are Nikahywot," he would answer. "Nikahywot, my source of life," he reassured his mother.

"A man of two continents," she would repeat. "One foot firmly planted in mercy and the other in judgment."

Nat Turner followed the trees—the oaks, the pines, the

cypresses, and the slumbering fruit trees—to a small cabin on a far patch of Nathaniel Francis's land. Smoke curled from the chimney. He heard people inside talking and laughing. He felt in his pocket again for the gunpowder. He knocked and then stepped inside.

He looked around the room.

They were all heroes.

Nat Turner had heard the word of God: This would be his last Christmas.

Harriet

Chapter 2

Andover, Massachusetts
Spring 1856

Back from Philadelphia, upstairs in her Andover home, Harriet Beecher Stowe sat at her writing desk. She looked around the room, then toward the streetside window that gave the room light. She imagined all the many people who had been welcomed in her home—pastors; professors and friends of her husband, Calvin; their families and his students. Among the visitors were some of the most well-known and notorious names in America—her brother, pastor and abolitionist Henry Ward Beecher, abolitionist William Lloyd Garrison, abolitionists Sojourner Truth, Harriet Tubman, and Frederick Douglass.

Like the home of her childhood, the Stowe household was a meeting place of sundry people, a home of hospitality and vigorous debate. Harriet smiled, then grimaced to think of the scandal her guest list might cause. Those who championed slavery—or even those who simply limited themselves to living bland monotone lives—would balk at the idea of blacks and whites mingling, conversing, breaking bread, or sharing in healthy debate as equals. Sometimes it amazed her.

Calvin, her professor husband, had encouraged her writing. "It is your fate," he told her. She could never have imagined, years ago, that her writing would take her before royalty like young Queen Victoria and the Duchess of Argyle, would have her name on the lips of politicians, would send her on national and international speaking tours, or would lead her to conversations and even friendships with fugitive slaves—friendships that others found shocking.

If the Beecher home, her childhood home, was a hearty meal, then the Stowe home was a feast, a banquet.

Her new life had its challenges, but she could not imagine going back to a more ordinary life—a life where she only read books written by women or by whites, a life where she attended church with members of only one hue. It would be as bland as a self-imposed diet of only one kind of food, or limiting oneself to see and smell only one kind of flower.

God had created and invited us to a banquet hall, to a wedding—full of sights and smells, of exotics and domestics. It was the worst kind of ingratitude to refuse His invitation, the worst kind of meanness to snub or belittle His creation, to refuse the feast, to refuse the bouquet.

Now, having tasted the richness of a life full of people like Sojourner Truth, Henry Bibb, Frederick Douglass, and Josiah Henson, it was hard to remember what might have kept her locked into a less colorful world. Proximity? Complacency? Fear? Laziness? Dullness? Now that she had participated in the feast, she would never turn back. And perhaps there was more to do—to add shades of brown, yellow, and gold, autumn colors, to her life.

Harriet looked at the papers on her desk, notes from her Boston meeting with William, a runaway slave, and her Philadelphia meeting with Benjamin Phipps, a resident of Virginia's Southampton County. Both of the meetings focused on Nat Turner, a slave from that same county. Among the notes was an anonymous letter.

Labeled a murderer, a fanatic, and an insurrectionist by his own confession to his attorney Thomas Gray, Turner had led an 1831 insurrection that killed more than fifty white people and resulted in his hanging.

Now, her brother Henry and Frederick Douglass insisted that she give Nat Turner's story a new telling. They had insisted that she meet with William and Phipps. Her own handwritten notes of those meetings covered her desktop—though it was difficult sometimes to tell where recollections from her dreams, still dreams of resurrection, left off and their stories began.

Before her were the witnesses of Sallie, Nancie, and Easter, provided by Will. Phipps had provided her the witnesses of Nathaniel Francis and William Parker.

The notes and the names swirled in her mind—Francis, Trezvant, Waller, Turner, Gray. The published confession penned by Thomas Gray had been in existence for twenty-five years and had been accepted as the gospel by abolitionists, refugee slaves, slavery men, politicians, newspapermen, and even historians. Francis, Trezvant, Waller, Turner, Gray. If Phipps and Will were to be believed, then *The Confessions of Nat Turner* was a lie. If they were to be believed, then Waller lied . . . and he lied for Nathaniel Francis.

Harriet removed the anonymous letter from the envelope, rereading the first two hand-copied entries:

On Saturday the 12th and the Monday following and also on Wednesday, the sun shown [sic] quite blue, fully as blue as indigo.

The indigo sun—it was the same blue sun Harriet and her brother Henry had witnessed twenty-five years ago, in 1831.

Twenty-third day—This will be a very noted day in Virginia. At daylight this morning the Mayor of the City put into my hands a notice to the public, written by James Trezvant of Southampton County, stating that an insurrection of the slaves in that county had taken place, that several families had been massacred and that it would take a considerable military force to put them down.

More than a quarter of a century ago, Harriet and Henry were young people living in Boston, the place where she had first heard the name "Nat Turner."

She rubbed a finger over the writing and stared at the mysterious letter in her hands. She would share them with Calvin. The professor would help her decide what she must do.

Chapter 3

Harriet poured tea for Calvin and smiled at him, really at the top of his head, his nose buried in his books. She placed jam and butter on the table, rearranged the purple crocuses in the small centerpiece, and then sat down at the table with him. Calmness and morning sunlight crowned the top of his head. She nodded; she could have been born into a different life.

Captivity was not as she had imagined. Though she had looked into the face of slavery in Cincinnati—speaking with and befriending fugitive slaves, attending a Kentucky slave auction—and heard many stories, she had still held on to a gentrified notion of slavery. A slavery of large, flourishing, romantic plantations, gallant men sauntering among the fields, and of women dancing the reel in great ballroom gowns. The slavery in her mind, despite what she had seen, was one of well-meaning slave masters, friends to their slaves, a benevolent though misguided aristocratic institution led by elderly well-mannered gentlemen with charming Southern accents. In her mind, though she knew slavery was wrong, she saw Kentucky bluegrass, mint juleps, and grace-filled slaves, faithful despite their occasional mistreatment.

The stories that the refugee slave William and the poor farmer from Southampton County Benjamin Phipps had shared with her forced her to confront a viler, more brutal kind of slavery. Now what filled her head instead of lace and the mellow aroma of cured tobacco smoke was the foul stink of slave ships, the screams of people chained onboard, the cries of women being raped at sea. Now, instead of kindly, elderly slave masters, she saw cruel men, boys really, given too much power—absolute power and with no respect for life. Now she saw starving people, poor people holding others captive to have status and power.

It made her ashamed that her people, white people, were the captors. Sometimes she thought it best to cover her people's shame rather than continue to write about it, to drag it out into the open. Then she reminded herself of history: Whites were not the only slave masters, the only ones tempted to think themselves superior—each race had wallowed in the wickedness. That truth did not excuse what was happening in her own time, in her own country, but it did make it easier to stare it in the face. It made it easier to believe that, like intemperance, it was a weakness that could be overcome. *There hath no temptation taken you but such as is common to man: but God is faithful, who will not suffer you to be tempted above that ye are able; but will with the temptation also make a way to escape, that ye may be able to bear it.*

No wrong could be righted that was hidden and unacknowledged. Without light, it would grow—a creeping, hidden, moldy thing that dragged its shadow with it.

Now Harriet saw the United States, the nation she loved, lend the force of law—judicial rulings against Dred Scott, congressional passage of the Fugitive Slave Acts signed into law by Presidents Washington and Fillmore, and wording in the nation's Constitution—to legitimize one brother's horror against another. A horror where people were stolen and others murdered all for the sake of profit, where families around the world were decimated. A horror that the purveyors said was justified by God's law, a horror that flipped His law end over end.

The Constitution asserted: *"No Person held to Service or Labour in one State, under the Laws thereof, escaping into another, shall, in Consequence of any Law or Regulation therein, be discharged from such Service or Labour, but shall be delivered up on Claim of the Party to whom such Service or Labour may be due."*

God's law commanded: *"For the LORD thy GOD walketh in the midst of thy camp, to deliver thee, and to give up thine enemies before thee; therefore shall thy camp be holy: that he see no unclean thing in thee, and turn away from thee. Thou shalt not deliver unto his master the servant which is escaped from his master unto thee: He shall dwell with thee, even among you, in that place which he shall choose in one of thy gates, where it liketh him best: thou shalt not oppress him."*

The horror kept creeping, drawing all manner of people, so that even the elect, the best and the brightest, surrendered and gave their efforts to aiding it. Neither education nor intellect offered any inoculation against infection. The words of the Fugitive Slave Act of 1793 were further proof. The horror leered over the shoulder of noble President George Washington, the defender of freedom and owner of hundreds of slaves, as he signed the act into law.

> *And be it also enacted, That when a person held to labor in any of the United States, or in either of the Territories on the Northwest or South of the river Ohio, under the laws thereof, shall escape into any other part of the said States or Territory, the person to whom such labor or service may be due, his agent or attorney, is hereby empowered to seize or arrest such fugitive from labor, and to take him or her before any Judge of the Circuit or District Courts of the United States, residing or being within the State, or before any magistrate of a county, city, or town corporate, wherein such seizure or arrest shall be made, and upon proof to the satisfaction of such Judge or magistrate, either by oral testimony or affidavit taken before and certified by a magistrate of any such State or Territory.*

She did not seek out public debate; she did not want to be pointed out as one of "those people"; and she tried to conduct herself as a proper woman, but left to shadow and silence, the horror grew bolder and greedier. Heroes were not immune; neither was clergy. Neither status, nor title, nor wealth protected one from greed, from selfishness, from the temptation to consider oneself above others. Instead, privilege seemed to exacerbate the temptation.

> *And be it further enacted, That it shall be the duty of all marshals and deputy marshals to obey and execute all warrants and precepts issued under the provisions of this act, when to them directed; and should any marshal or deputy marshal refuse to receive such warrant, or other process, when tendered, or to use all proper means diligently to execute the same, he shall, on conviction thereof, be fined in the sum of one thousand dollars.*

It grew stronger, forcing others to comply at threat of jail, poverty, or worse. It muted innocents so they could speak no words in their own defense.

> *In no trial or hearing under this act shall the testimony of such alleged fugitive be admitted in evidence; and the certificates in this and the first [fourth] section mentioned, shall be conclusive of the right of the person or persons in whose favor granted, to remove such fugitive to the State or Territory from which he escaped, and shall prevent all molestation of such person or persons by any process issued by any court, judge, magistrate, or other person whomsoever.*

The horror grew stronger, hobbling those who might speak against it, those who might not believe—forcing itself on them.

> *§7. And be it further enacted, That any person who shall knowingly and willingly obstruct, hinder, or prevent such claimant, his agent or attorney, or any person or persons lawfully assisting him, her, or them, from arresting such a fugitive from service or labor, either with or without process as aforesaid, or shall rescue, or attempt to rescue, such fugitive from service or labor, from the*

*custody of such claimant, his or her agent or attorney, or other
person or persons lawfully assisting as aforesaid, when so arrested,
pursuant to the authority herein given and declared; or shall aid,
abet, or assist such person so owing service or labor as aforesaid,
directly or indirectly, to escape from such claimant, his agent or
attorney, or other person or persons legally authorized as aforesaid; or shall harbor or conceal such fugitive, so as to prevent the
discovery and arrest of such person, after notice or knowledge of
the fact that such person was a fugitive from service or labor as
aforesaid, shall, for either of said offences, be subject to a fine not
exceeding one thousand dollars, and imprisonment not exceeding
six months, by indictment and conviction.*

Harriet sat at the table and looked at her husband, his nose
still buried in his books, research notes scattered about.

She might have been born into a different life. She might have
been born into the captive race, forbidden to dream, forbidden to
write. She might have been born into a different family, a family
that forbade her to speak her mind or think her own thoughts, a
family that thought women inferior. She might have married a
man threatened by her hopes, one who suppressed and discouraged her gifts. None of her good fortune was coincidental. It would
be ingratitude not to acknowledge it all, not to be and do the
things set before her.

Harriet cleared her throat. "Professor, I have been reading over
the letter—the excerpts from the Virginia governor's diary." She
placed a piece of toast on her plate, waited for her husband to
swim up from the text he was studying, to surface and acknowledge her. She buttered the bread and added a spoon of ruby-
colored jam.

Calvin looked over the page before him, inserted a bookmark,
and then looked at her. "Yes." He reached for a piece of toast.

"It seems to me that the governor had some doubts about the
trials."

He raised an eyebrow. "Do you have the letter?" Of course he knew she had the letter. She had been carrying it around with her for days. He smiled. "I don't want to impose, but might you read from it to me?"

She pretended to ignore his teasing and removed the letter from her pocket.

"Read to me," Calvin said, biting his toast.

Chapter 4

Harriet bit into her toast; she did not want to appear too eager to share—though, of course, she *was* eager. She chewed slowly. Calvin lifted his brows. She used her napkin to brush crumbs from her mouth, doing her best to look nonchalant.

"Please, Mrs. Stowe, I am keen to hear what might make you believe the governor was not in full agreement with Southampton County's handling of the rebellion and trials."

"Professor, I know you are busy. I do not want to trouble you."

"If you doubted my interest that would trouble me more."

Harriet cleared her throat, laid her napkin on the table, then began reading from the diary excerpts. "Governor Floyd begins writing on August 23rd, and it is obvious that he is most concerned.

"'I began to consider how to prepare for the crisis. To call out the militia and equip a military force for that service. But according to the forms of this wretched and abominable Constitution, I must first require advice of council, and then disregard it, if I please. On this occasion there was not one councillor in the city. I went on, made all the arrangements for suppressing the insurrection, having all my orders ready for men, arms, ammunition, etc., and when by this time, one of the council came to town, and that vain and foolish ceremony was gone through. In a few hours the troops marched, Captain Randolph with a fine troop of cavalry and Captain John B. Richardson with Light Artillery both from this city and two companies of Infantry from Norfolk and Portsmouth. The Light Artillery had under their care one thousand stand of arms for Southampton and Sussex, with a good supply of ammunition. All these things were dispatched in a few hours.'"

She looked up from her reading to meet her husband's eyes. "You recall, Professor, that Congressman James Trezvant had sent notice to the public that an army of two hundred or more runaway slaves from the Great Dismal Swamp had attacked Southampton."

Calvin nodded. "Go on."

"On the twenty-fourth: 'This day was spent in distributing arms to the various counties below this where it was supposed it would be wanted.'"

Harriet turned the page. "But on the twenty-fifth the governor receives word from the general in command: 'I received dispatches from Brigadier Richard Eppes, stating that with local militia those I sent him were more than enough to suppress the insurrection.'

"The next day the governor continues to receive requests for arms from other counties like Brunswick, Nansemond, Surry, and towns, including Greenville.

"On the third of September, he mentions trials and names I have heard before—Moses, Daniel, Andrew, and Jack. He seems to find the distance they were purported to cover astounding. 'The insurgents progressed twenty miles before they were checked, yet all this horrid work was accomplished in two days.'"

Harriet sighed and forced herself to take a sip of tea. "Governor Floyd finds the twenty miles incredible. What must he have thought when by the end of things the rebels were said to have covered fifty miles in two days?" She began to search the pages. "Over the days, he received records of scores of slaves condemned to hang in Southampton and other counties. Then on September 17th, I begin to sense some doubt.

"'Received an express from Amelia today, asking arms as families have been murdered in Dinwiddie near the Nottoway line. Colonel Davidson of the 39th Regiment Petersburgh states the same by report. I do not exactly believe the report.'

"The governor was so sympathetic when he first heard of the rebellion, or the insurrection, as he called it. But on the nineteenth Floyd writes, 'News from the Colonel of the 39th says the whole is false as it relates to the massacre of Mrs. Cousins and family in Dinwiddie. The slaves are quiet and evince no disposition to rebel.' The next day he writes: 'The alarm of the country is great in the counties between this and the Blue Ridge Mountains. I am daily sending them a portion of arms though I know there is no danger as the slaves were never more humbled and subdued.'

"On September 23rd, he mentions two trials in particular that troubled him: 'I received the record of the trial of Lucy and Joe of Southampton. They were of the insurgents.'"

Calvin leaned forward in his chair, his fingers steepled, his elbows on the table.

"Do you remember me telling you of them, Professor? Lucy and Joe belonged to the widow Mary Barrow and to John Clarke Turner, respectively. I remember when I was told of the trials that my heart was filled with doubt. The governor appears to have been doubtful also. He wrote, 'What can be done, I yet know not, as I am obliged by the Constitution first to require the advice of the council, then to do as I please. This endangers the lives of these negroes, though I am disposed to reprieve for transportation I cannot do it until I first require advice of council and there are no councillors now in Richmond, nor will there be unless Daniel comes to town in time enough.'"

Harriet pushed her toast away. She had no appetite. People died for no reason. She continued, forcing her way through the reading, "Then on September 27th, 'I have received record of the trial of three slaves for treason in Southampton. Am recommended to mercy, which I would grant ... but in this case I cannot do so, because there is not one member of the Council of State in Richmond. Wherefore, the poor wretches must lose their lives by absence of the councillors from their official duties.'"

Harriet refolded the letter and stuffed it back in its envelope. It was appalling how little care men had for their brothers. "All this is making me ill."

"And indignant, my dear Harriet."

"But it was so long ago, Professor. What good does it do to dig it all up now? It is twenty-five years hence and as the governor stated, the poor wretches have already lost their lives. I cannot bring them back."

"Perhaps, my wife. But the truth is still a precious gem that does not lose value with age. Truth might at least ease the suffering of loved ones left behind."

The two of them discussed the diary entries. "They are too detailed for me to doubt them." When they were finished it was decided. She could not travel to the South to investigate; there was a bounty on her head. Instead, Harriet would travel to New York to share the letter with Frederick Douglass and her brother Henry.

Nat Turner

Chapter 5

Cross Keys Area, outside Jerusalem, Virginia
Christmas 1830

Inside the stove warmed the small cabin that was packed with twenty to thirty people—survival made all of them heroes.

Nat Turner made his way around the room, greeting them: Sam, Hark, and the freemen. He leaned to kiss his mother on the cheek. In the corner the children played and he walked to join them. On Sundays, after church, he taught them to read. But before he could begin a lesson this day, his wife, Cherry, came to him.

"It is Christmas, husband, let them play." She led him to a chair. He looked down at his feet. They felt nothing now, but soon he knew he would feel spiky pain as they thawed.

Nat Turner looked around the small, crowded living space at the people gathered there. It had been a hard winter—hard for slave owners, brutal for slaves—no longer people but black-draped skeletons. Few of the captors had enough to eat and were hard-pressed to find heart to share the little that kept them alive with captives.

The warm air in the cabin carried the bittersweet smell of the hardworking people and mixed it with aromas from the kitchen.

God had sent him back for them.

Eyes shifted from the stove to conversations and back again. Nat Turner smelled the warm fragrance of baking sweet potatoes from the hosts' garden. A brine of vinegar and salt water steamed from a kettle on the iron stove. As people entered the cabin, shivering from the cold, they made their way to Thomas Hathcock's wife, freewoman and hostess, stationed near the pots. One would come with a few precious potatoes, a single squash, or a cup of dried beans. All of it swirled into the kettle. Each one brought a metal cup or pan, and when the food was finished they would share.

Mrs. Hathcock had a reputation. Though she was known for her preserves, she could make anything delicious. She did wonders with everything she touched.

Next to the kettle was a large pot of mixed greens—mustard and collards that her husband had rescued from the weather—already tender and kept warming. One of the women brought a small but prized piece of salt pork. Mrs. Hathcock added a tiny, precious portion to the greens to season them. She added lard and a bit of the salt pork to a cast-iron skillet and began to steam-fry a head of cabbage and bits more of it to some of the other dishes to season them.

Daniel came through the door with his mother, both of them Peter Edwards's slaves. It was rare, but their master kept them together as mother and son. In her hands was a bundle tied like treasure in a rag. She beamed.

"My master butchered last week and gave me these." Two pig ears, a snout, a tail, and four hooves, frozen from the cold. "There's chitlins, too—I cleaned them real good." She looked around at the people. "You don't have to worry."

The people's eyes followed the porcine jewels; their mouths salivated. Smiling, Mrs. Hathcock dropped them into the steaming pot of vinegary water.

Daniel helped his mother to a chair. She smiled. "Master Edwards let me have them instead of feeding them to the dogs." It was a Christmas treat; for most of them it was the only meat they would taste all year. Nat Turner heard the empty stomachs grumbling. He saw anticipation in their eyes and smiles.

Another woman came and set a lidded jar on the table. "This is something, right here!" From the jar she pulled three pig feet and one ear. She had boiled them and pickled them in brine. Nat Turner smiled back at her. He knew what a sacrifice she had made. She had gone to bed hungry many nights, knowing she had the pork, but saved this Christmas portion to share.

She got a knife and cut the treat, passing tiny pieces around. Children's eyes rounded and glowed as they sucked on the bones—gnawing on the bones, sucking on the marrow.

Smiling and gracious, his mother gave her portion away to Mother Easter, the old woman who sat beside her. Though his mother had been away from Africa more than thirty years, like a good Ethiopian Christian, she still did not eat pork. Cherry gave hers to their son, and Nat Turner gave his to her.

People huddled together, laughing and talking, gathered from the scattered farms they lived on. Communion was the gift they shared. There was no wine or unleavened bread for them. There were no hats, cloaks, mittens, or presents. There was nothing for them except the hardscrabble meal they had scraped together. Captivity had taken its toll—so many without coats and shelter froze to death during the night. So each one celebrated that he had awakened that morning, clothed and in his right mind. Survival was the gift they shared. All of them heroes.

This was not like the Christmases Nat Turner had seen and sometimes shared at his father's house.

At his father's house there had been evergreens. Nat Turner remembered the smell of pine. There was holly with red berries to decorate the room. There was glazed ham and a holiday goose then. The spicy, sugary aroma of apple preserves and brandied peaches filled the room. There was hominy baked with cheese. He could not eat with the others in his father's house, but his father would bring a plate to him and to his mother with bits of succulent things to taste.

He recalled holding in his hands candy and a book—sometimes a coat new to him, a hand-me-down—given as presents.

He remembered inside his father's church, where he and the

other black people were allowed to sit on the back pew when his father was alive. Inside, at Christmas, the church was filled with holly and mistletoe. He recalled the scents of dried lavender, rosemary, and rose petals.

The people gathered in this cabin had none of what Nat Turner remembered. God had sent him back from the wilderness for them.

Twenty-eight people crowded into the small cabin. The Artis brothers, part Cheroenhaka Nottoway Indian, sat talking to Hark, Sam, Dred, and some of the other men. "They have taken our land, saying we are not Indians because our mothers wed black men. Now we must pay rent to white men for our own land." Frown lines were worn into his cheeks. "Indians that marry white men keep their land," Exum Artis said.

"For now," his brother, Arnold, added. "But they want us to leave. They want all the freemen to leave because we remember. We remember that they were poor and they once worked as slaves—indentured men. They were treated like us. There were no lies that God made them special." All the freemen—black and Nottoway—and even white Berry Newsom nodded.

"They want us to leave, but we are just farmers. Where would we go?"

"We remember, so they want us gone. Our forefathers rode together, poor men—white, black, and red—beside each other against oppression in Bacon's Rebellion. We were all God's men then, before the powerful and wealthy found a way to separate and trick us. We all stood as men on the same even ground then. We remember, so they want us gone." The recollections smoldered in Thomas Hathcock's eyes.

"Good and bad, free and slave, was not based on color. A man of color could be a man of wealth and property," Exum Artis agreed.

"All that changed after Bacon's Rebellion. Suddenly the white man—good or bad—was given a halo and wings," Arnold said.

"Freemen? This is not freedom! They tell us where we can live and what we can grow. Nathaniel Francis rents to us, rent we cannot afford, all the while scheming to take what little we still have, or to take us as slaves for debts we owe. At the end of the season, they take most of our crops and tell us we still owe them more."

"We have had to sell land for medicine, for seed, and soon all we have will be gone." Thomas Hathcock shook his head.

"The doctors won't touch us. They look at us. Afraid the color will rub off."

"But we remember."

Nat Turner had heard the stories before. He carried the stories, breathed the stories.

"We know they were not kings and princes. We know they were just men, like us. We know, we were here, and we saw them. They struggled to live on the land, like us. We were here then when there were black and white and Nottoway landowners. There was no word from God, from the Great Father, that only white men were men. We know they are flesh like we are. We were here when it all began."

Nat Turner and the others knew that there was a plan afoot, a law, to send the freemen to other places, to wipe away the memory. The white men didn't want to remember themselves as slaves or as prisoners who came to America in chains. They didn't want to remember themselves as poor people with few choices. They didn't want to remember that, when they were starving and had nothing, they gave themselves permission to steal—land and people—until they had enough. They wanted to forget and so they had bought, stolen, and taken by force, the power to forget what they'd done—the power to rewrite history.

They bought horses and people and pigs, new clothes and new names. They made themselves titles and positions. They bought carriages, hoop skirts, built houses with windows and stairs, and then went about erasing and evicting those who dared remember their past.

When Thomas Hathcock's wife passed by, he stopped her. "But now our lives have changed. We have seen free people forced into chains. We had the good of God's land, but it has been stolen from us.

"See my wife's hands? She scalds them making preserves to earn a little money. Do you think they will let her sell her goods at the market? Years ago we could, but now she cannot sell there to white men. We cannot sell among ourselves; no one has money to buy." His wife sighed and then returned to the stove.

Thomas gestured around the small room. "But what they will not buy, they come to the house and demand. All the power is in their hands. If they steal it from her, who can we go to? There is no court for black men. There is no sheriff for men with dark skin. No black man can charge a white man with a crime."

"They tell us where to live, on land that belonged to us long before those we remember walked this earth. Almost every day there is a threat that someone will have us shipped out of this state away from the land that holds our fathers' bones. Shipped overseas to some land we've never heard of." Arnold Artis lowered his voice. "And they say we are free, but they treat our wives as their property. They take them when they want to, and there is nothing we can do . . . not if we want to live. How can this be called freedom?"

Nat Turner knew their shame. He lived their shame. It was his. The shame knotted his stomach, his fists, and tightened his chest.

Thomas Hathcock pointed toward the window. "Years from now, people who pass will forget who built the houses these white men live in and who cleared this land. Maybe some of us will still have families left alive to carry our names. But who will remember how hard we worked? 'Why didn't your parents make something of themselves?' others will say to them.

"What will our children or their children have to show for all our labor? They will be left poor."

He leaned forward in his chair. "How much more are we expected to stomach?"

Dred pounded one fist into the other hand. "They treat us

like animals!" His voice thundered in the small cabin. The women turned to look.

Arnold Artis's voice and body trembled with frustration. "It has been too long, decades, and it is all these little ones know." A hush came over the children. They stared, wide-eyed. One small boy began to cry.

Thomas Hathcock's voice raised, "I cannot stand it much longer!"

Nat Turner, listening to the men, felt for the gunpowder in his pocket. It would not be long. He looked at the people around him. It could not be long.

Thomas Hathcock's wife, stirring in the pot before her, called to interrupt her husband, a practiced calm in her voice. "What you say is true, Thomas. It will still be true when this day is past. But let us celebrate and enjoy this day with our friends."

Trembling, Thomas looked at his wife, staring deeply into her eyes until the trembling ceased. He exhaled. "You are right." He smiled at her and nodded. He clapped his hands. "Come, let the children sing."

The children looked at their mothers, waiting for nods of reassurance. Then two smaller children giggled tentatively, and then they began to sing.

> Joy to the world, the Lord is come!
> Let earth receive her King;
> Let every heart prepare Him room.

Other children joined in.

> And Heaven and nature sing,
> And Heaven and nature sing,
> And Heaven, and Heaven, and nature sing.

Nat Turner looked around the room at the people he loved. This Christmas Day the room was full of the living. What each of them had was not enough, but together it was a feast. He smiled, listening to his own son sing with the others. It seemed not long ago that he was as small.

Nat Turner looked at his son, Riddick, singing. God sent him back for him.

Harriet

Chapter 6

Brooklyn, New York
1856

To most of America, her brother Henry was the most famous preacher in the States, perhaps the Western world, but he was still Harriet's baby brother. Though she had heard him preach many times, she was no less amazed each time to hear him and to see him enthrall the congregation before him—hundreds of people, thousands, crowded into the sanctuary. It was the same across the country and overseas. He was paid handsomely to speak. Men, as well as women, wept when he preached, though in seconds his humor and antics had them laughing again.

When Harriet visited Plymouth Church, she sometimes sat on the back pew hoping to not be noticed. But today she sat in the front row so she would have a clear view of the notables who visited her brother's church. The poet Walt Whitman visited, as did the author and abolitionist Henry David Thoreau. Newspapermen attended, copying every word of Henry's sermons and publishing them in their papers. Politicians made their way to Plymouth, like the young Illinois lawyer Abraham Lincoln, who had ambitions to be senator. John Brown, Harriet Tubman, Sojourner Truth, William Wells Brown, and Henry Bibb had all been welcomed in the pews and sometimes in the pulpit at her brother's Brooklyn church.

Outside was Orange Street and beyond that, New York. Manhattan, Staten Island, Brooklyn, with Brooklyn's population swelling each day since the opening of the Fulton Ferry.

Each time she visited there were fewer trees—there was no

room for them or for undeveloped plots. Every inch was needed for more dwellings, more businesses for the people who crowded into the city. Immigrants and refugees, English, Dutch, Chinese, Germans, Jews, Catholics, Protestants. Printers, nannies, shopkeepers, seamstresses, clerks, poets, painters, singers, bakers, bankers, factory workers, professors, and chimney sweeps. Hundreds of thousands of them huddled in town houses and tenements, finding hope in the crush and anonymity. Wedged together in flats and apartments, the rich and poor, foreign and domestic. Bustling down avenues to department stores, public schools, police stations, to galleries, to synagogues, churches, town halls, storefronts, and cathedrals wearing forced shields of privacy.

There were tensions between the groups jostling for elbow room. But they needed one another. Mind-your-own-business people who learned the necessity of interdependence. The restaurateur, with no room to grow his own, needed the peddler for produce and needed the shopgirl to buy.

Carriages, trains, boats, and millions of footsteps. Novelists, newspapermen, butlers, stevedores, waiters, Central Park, and the Erie Canal. Home to the Sons of Liberty, the Battle of Long Island, the place of President Washington's inauguration, the first Congress, the first Supreme Court, Fort Hamilton, and Federal Hall. Home to the hopeful and the suffering.

Irish Catholics swelled the populous, swept across the sea by famine, hunger, joblessness, hopelessness, lynchings, floggings—and laws that forbade their education, voting, possession of arms, and property ownership. Refugee slaves, most swept North by starvation, joblessness—and laws that forbade their education, voting, possession of arms, and property ownership—and the hope of freedom, willing to leave whatever relations they had. Both risked all that was familiar. But disguised by hue and tongue, they did not recognize their brotherhood.

Most runaway slaves, fleeing the South, hitched a ride on the Underground. But some of the Negroes were former New York slaves.

Until 1827, New York City had almost as many slaves as Charleston, South Carolina. The city was home to slave ships and investors in slaving—lending money for land, looms, seed, and in Southern cotton. Many of the Northern slaves were purchased in Newport, Rhode Island. Beautiful, beautiful Newport with its Atlantic beaches, lobsters, sailboats, and slaves in chains sold on the wharfs. And beyond Newport were the islands of Cape Verde and islands like Haiti, where captured Africans were broken and transformed into slaves. Beautiful Newport, where schoolmarms and shopkeepers invested their pennies in the trade, hoping to reap shiny dimes.

There were no plantations in New York; the skilled slaves built roads, docks, churches, and Wall Street's wall. After 1827, the New York slaves were freed, but there were still scars and resentful former owners.

Into the slave city, into the darkness, drawn to the void, were the abolitionists, abolitionists more radical than their New England brothers and sisters. New York was home to the Radical Abolitionists Convention, abolitionists who argued that the United States Constitution forbade slavery . . . nor shall any state deprive a person of life, liberty, or property without due process.

Gotham was home to the Tappan brothers and the Grimke sisters, to William Wells Brown, Susan B. Anthony, Elizabeth Cady Stanton—abolitionists who argued that slavery was wrong legally and morally. Radical abolitionists argued that slavery was a demon that plagued America, who argued that all good men and women were legally and morally bound to help free the slaves. Slavery was as unlawful as murder, arson, or theft. Some even argued that slaves and their defenders had a duty to take up arms.

Many were not pleased with the abolitionists' growing presence in New York State—there had been antiblack and antiabolitionist attacks that continued to worsen.

Inside Plymouth Church, Harriet leaned forward, and across the room she saw Frederick Douglass's prematurely graying mane nodding as Henry spoke.

"Without love our faith is meaningless; it has no power. Without love our greatest philanthropy is less than a mere token."

Henry's voice shook the rafters in Plymouth Church—a sanctuary built more like an auditorium than a church—caused the air to vibrate, swelled, and then dropped to a whisper. Words came alive in Henry, or, better still, as Walt Whitman wrote, Henry's words were substantial and delicious. When Henry spoke he became the words, and though he was human and given to human weaknesses, he tried to live the words he spoke. "Without love, intelligence and knowledge have no value."

He not only preached freedom for the captives, he also used his church as a station on the Underground Railroad. He raised money to buy freedom for captive slaves. Henry purchased rifles—rifles that bore the nickname "Beecher's Bibles." At Henry's direction, Sharps rifles were shipped to Kansas along with Bibles to help antislavery men defend themselves against the strangling westward aggression of slavery, slavery discontent to remain within Kentucky's borders.

While some churches struggled to gain and hold any members, most that survived brimmed with women. But Plymouth overflowed with men. Henry offered messages of love to those who had been taught that their very being displeased God, just as her family had taught Henry and her. They were tainted by original sin and despised by God.

But Henry preached love, and they flocked to him like parched men to fresh water. His voice thundered, swept through the room, and then eased to a whisper. "Without love—not only for the greatest, but also for the least among us—all that we do is pointless."

From the front of Plymouth, Henry whispered to the congregation, "The only bondage in God's creation that is tolerable and desirable is the bondage of love."

Again, Frederick Douglass nodded his head.

Chapter 7

Mr. Douglass's hair was more silver than when she last saw him. Harriet lifted a hand to her own hair. Hers was changing, too.

He bore a heavy burden. He had escaped from slavery in Maryland and made his home in the North for many years now. If he remained silent, there was a good chance he might remain free. But he was not free, he said, until all were free—slaves and black freemen. He risked his life and freedom to bring attention to the plight of others, even fighting for women, including white women, to have the right to vote.

But it was not just others, not just those who were apathetic or slaveholders, whom he challenged. Frederick challenged her. Each time she conversed with him, she was surprised at how brilliant he was—surprised and ashamed that she was surprised. Her cheeks burned, even now, with the private embarrassment, embarrassment at her epiphany that she had expected less of him simply because of the color of his skin.

She knew he was a human being, a man created and loved by God. But somehow she bore diminished expectations. She did not expect him to reason so well, to speak so well, or to write so well—he had edited the Rochester Ladies' Anti-Slavery Society's collection *Autographs for Freedom*, which contained William Lloyd Garrison's work, Henry's work, and hers. She was too ashamed of her thoughts to share them with anyone, even Calvin. But they were there just the same.

If she had not conversed with him, she would never have known how exceptional he was, nor would she have recognized her own shortcomings. He had proven to be a thoughtful, capable man full of insight. In addition to author, respected orator, and editor, Douglass also was now a newspaper publisher.

He was a man of his own opinion and provided sound reason and argument. He was independent of thought, so much so that it appeared he might be parting ways with his friend William Lloyd Garrison. William now espoused abandoning both the Constitution and the Church; both, he felt, had been bloodied and rendered useless by slavery. Douglass believed both could be redeemed.

In the pulpit, Henry clutched his heart. "No man knows true happiness till he has learned how to love." The crowd cheered, and Frederick Douglass tapped his cane on the floor.

Without Frederick Douglass, she might never have met fugitive slaves like Henry Bibb, Harriet Tubman, and Sojourner Truth. Without him and others, she might never have heard the stories—and each story made her life richer.

Without Douglass's association, she might never have read the works written by the hands of black authors like William Wells Brown or Douglass himself. Why should she read them? What could their broken phrases and buffoonery, their clumsiness with language, have to offer her? Harriet was surprised at what she discovered.

It seemed impossible to her now, but there was a time when they and their thoughts were strangers to her, except for caricatures in her mind. Without Mr. Douglass, she might never have known that God had given the gift of elegant thought and word to His black children. She might never have read their beautiful prose and poetry and acknowledged that it was inspired by God. Their words were cousins to her own, sometimes offering lance and balm to places she had not known were tender.

Without Mr. Douglass's influence, she might never have shared a meal with a Negro—not as servant but as equally welcomed guests at the table. Certainly they would not have been welcomed at her father's house. As she observed them reading and taking part in debates, Harriet wondered who the refugees might have become but for slavery.

Challenged by Mr. Douglass, Sojourner Truth, and others, Harriet had come to realize that even she, with her good intentions and moral upbringing, had been poisoned by slavery's lies. Slavery denied that it was the cause of the slaves' condition—their poverty, their illiteracy. But by associating with fugitive slaves, she was learning to view them as people no different from she or her brother.

Perhaps the worst sin of slavery was the stunting of so many lives, seeds unable to blossom into what they might have been.

In the not too distant past, she had viewed the enslaved Negroes paternally: She must speak for them and protect them as creatures inherently incapable of certain higher thoughts and feelings—people entitled to freedom, but childlike, in need of care and unable to determine what was best for themselves.

As the music from the Plymouth Church organ swelled, she looked around the sanctuary, at Henry, and then back at Frederick Douglass. Before him, she had lived her life smelling only rare lilies and white roses.

Knowing him, and the other refugees, had turned the granite under her feet to sand; she often found herself tilting from side to side and even pitching forward.

She had not expected to find them as she. She had seen herself and her brother as champions of the lowly.

When the Negroes refused her thoughts, her gifts, or her offerings, she was at first angered by their hubris and then embarrassed by her own. There were times, she realized, when she felt betrayed and jealous that the hand of Providence might have blessed them with some insight He did not originally bestow upon her. She had devoted her life to God, and her face warmed with the thought that He might have given them some favor He had not given her. Then she was ashamed of her emotions. She was surprised to find pride hidden in her bosom.

She was ashamed to acknowledge that she had thought herself at least a little better. She was prepared to teach, not to be taught. She was prepared to lead, not to be led. Harriet had been prepared to give, not receive. She thought she needed nothing from them. But perhaps it was she who most needed the gifts that they in their poverty offered to her. She had never suspected that she was the needy one and they the ones chosen to give. How could she have lived so long and so near people all her life and known so little about them? How could she have known so little about herself?

Through association with Frederick Douglass and the other refugees, Henry's and her lives had been enriched. Through their efforts for the cause of enslaved Negroes, they had been transformed from an impoverished preacher's children—he into the most famous man in America and she from a poor theologian's wife into a celebrated author of means welcomed at royal tables. But the greatest changes had been wrought inside: Their challenges had taught her to love.

Frederick and the others had become her teachers. They had challenged and improved her writing. They had helped improve her heart.

She tried to imagine the faces of slaves she had passed on the street and to imagine what she might have missed. She imagined what treasure might have been hidden there.

Harriet had had a great deal of schooling. She had taught; she was well read and an esteemed author. Yet Douglass reminded her that she had much to learn about others . . . and about herself. *"Study to shew thyself approved."* Harriet was willing to learn.

Frederick Douglass leaned forward in his seat, his eyes intent on her brother.

Henry stepped toward the front of the pulpit. "To gain true happiness, man must learn how to love. How to love, not a little, but a great deal; how to love, not occasionally, but so that he is tied up by it; he is in bondage to it, it rules him."

He turned and walked toward them. Now Henry stood among the people. "For the only slave on God's earth that needs no compassion and pity is the slave of love."

Nat Turner

Chapter 8

Cross Keys Area, outside Jerusalem, Virginia
Christmas 1830

Nat Turner's feet were thawing and had begun to ache. He looked down at them, at the fissures—the bleeding cracks in his flesh, wide as a small child's finger. He looked around the room at all the suffering feet. Shoes, even old worn ones, would have been a gift of love.

The children had moved on to another Christmas song.

Jesus, Jesus!
Oh, what a wonderful child!
Jesus, Jesus!
So holy, meek, and mild!
New life, new hope to all He brings.

God had sent him back for them.

Listen to the angels sing,
Glory! Glory! Glory!
To the newborn King!

The aroma from the iron kettle, the sweetness of the corn bread, and the salty, vinegary smell of the pigs' feet filled the room.

Dred, one of Nathaniel Francis's slaves, spoke now. "More could be with us, but they are drunk, drinking the whiskey given to them to keep them drunk during the holidays. Christmas whiskey nothing but wet chains."

Nat Turner answered, "Maybe they drink to save their lives."

"Funny words from someone whose lips have never touched liquor." Nat's friend Hark laughed.

"These are hard times with no good choices. I don't think drinking is best, but perhaps they do what they have to not to explode—to dull the pain, to stay alive."

Whiskey for Christmas was what the white people gave them. A turkey and a full stomach would have been a better Christmas gift—a book to read, or even a coat to wear.

Three of the boys went outside for more wood to keep the fire burning. Joshing, coatless, and shoeless, they piled out the door.

Nat Turner, looking through a crack in the boards that covered the window opening, was reminded of himself and Hark. He remembered when the two of them were as young as the boys outside, boys stealing a moment's rest on Cabin Pond. He remembered. Hark always smiled, but he was truly the practical one, speaking back then about what he knew and what he had seen.

It was the debate they had been engaged in for years.

We are slaves and we are always gonna be slaves. That's how it has always been and that's how it is always gonna be.

But that's not how it always was. We were kings on this earth. There are places where we are still kings.

There you go again, Nat Turner, talking crazy about Africa. Why can't you leave it alone?

We are more than this. More than this! We are smart. Brave. Why can't we be colonel? Why always the slave?

Let them be colonel. Let them be president if that will make them happy. I don't want colonel. Colonel will get me killed.

Do you think God put us here just to be nothing? To tote, lift, and hold up walls?

God sees how things are down here. I don't see Him coming down here to stop it. He is a white God. He puts white people first. His people, white people, win.

He is our God, too. We are smart as John Clarke, smarter than Salathiel and Whitehead.

Don't let somebody hear you say that. Your mama will be holding a dead son.

Why should I lie? You see them. Why shouldn't we be more? Why shouldn't we dream?

Dream? What I'm trying to do is survive.

I don't believe God put us here just to do nothing, be nothing. Long ago, there were great kings of Ethiopia with names like Menelik, and a great king of Assyria named Xerxes, and they were black like us and—

And that was long ago, if it ever was. I never saw any of it. What I can see with my eyes is that somebody owns me and if I don't want to get beat, don't want to hang, I better not tell him he's wrong.

He is wrong!

Nat, one of these days you are going to get you and me both killed.

Just think about it . . . living in a big house, a mansion, commanding armies, and leading the nation!

Hark laughed. Giving speeches with flags waving over your head!

Why shouldn't we? Why shouldn't we dream?

I'm telling you, boy. Nat Turner, you gone get us killed.

The children were still singing, the women stirring in the pots. Nat Turner looked out the window again at the boys. They were at a dangerous age; physical signs of adulthood were about to betray them: It was dangerous for a black boy to show that he was a man.

They could be cute little black boy babies, but even at five things changed and mothers were already worried for their black sons, worried that they would not live. At eleven, twelve, thirteen even more danger. There was a change in the way people treated them; threatened by their maturity.

Cold air blew through the crack in the window board, and he looked out again at the boys tussling in the snow. They were growing into the bodies of men. They would need men's minds if they were to survive.

At twelve or thirteen, white boys began to grow the beginnings of what would be whiskers, then titles, deeds, stars on their shoulders, and dreams that dangled from their chests. White boys grew to be men while black boys grew to be stooped, gray-haired boys fighting to stay alive.

Most of the boys were no longer living with their mothers. Those mothers who still had their sons loved them, but wore worry on their faces. It was the look he had seen on his own mother's face. They worried if they could hold them, if they could guide them, if they could help the seed inside them to survive. Mothers with unlined faces and prematurely gray hair worried, mothers who were afraid for their sons to dream, feared their sons would not survive. One grabbed her son by the ear. "Little nigger, I will skin you alive." Thirsty, with no other liquids offered to her, she had drunk in violent words. They were the only words she knew, so she poured them out on her son to protect him, to show him he was loved.

Nat Turner noticed the boy Davy, the one Nathaniel Francis called Two Feet, standing off from the other boys, watching as he leaned on his stick.

Watching them, Nat Turner remembered that it was not long ago that he was the same.

THOMAS GRAY, A boy with peach fuzz around his lips and in his armpits, lay back in the grass. "My father is going to apprentice me to a lawyer so I can be an attorney like him or maybe a judge like my grandfather." He pulled a dandelion and blew it. "I think sometimes I would rather be a writer instead."

The boys laughed, most of them twelve years old or so. They were from scattered farms but sometimes got together to play, as they'd done since they were smaller children.

John Clarke Turner shook his head at Thomas Gray's words. "A writer?"

Richard Whitehead ran his hands over his hair to smooth his cowlick into place. "I'm going to be a preacher."

Young Salathiel chewed a blade of grass. He laughed. "Ha! You? A preacher?"

"I am going to be a farmer, too. Maybe I'll try my hand at cotton. But my mother, Caty, says that I would make a fine preacher."

Salathiel laughed again. "You have what it takes—full of gas and hot air." Whitehead punched him in the shoulder. Salathiel shook it off. "I'm going to be a landowner. The land as far as I can see is going to be mine." He turned to John Clarke Turner. "What about you?"

"A tobacco planter or cotton. I'll own a great plantation. I will be a wealthy man, smoke cigars, and have a beautiful wife and lots of children."

Salathiel laughed. "And make lots of slaves." He raised and lowered his eyebrows. "Make lots of money." The boys laughed, punching one another.

They looked at Benjamin Phipps. He shrugged. There was silence and then Thomas Gray, looking at the other free boys, spoke up. "Maybe our children will marry one another."

"Maybe." John Clarke Turner laughed.

Nat Turner and Hark stood off to the side, listening. The other boys weren't looking at them; the two of them weren't included in the conversation. He spoke up anyway. "I have been thinking that I would like to be a general, like Washington, and Hark could be my colonel."

Hark, who was a young slave on the Moore farm, struck a jester's pose. "That's me! Colonel!" The other boys laughed. Hark's eyes pleaded with Nat to stop.

"My mother wants me to be a preacher. She says God has smiled on me and that I am a prophet." Nat Turner looked at Salathiel and Richard Whitehead. "But maybe I'll also be a farmer or a plantation owner with a farm next to yours."

It was a joke to them that he, a slave, might have dreams. The free boys laughed again.

"One day I will be a freeman, like the great Bishop Allen from Philadelphia. I will pay the price for my mother's freedom. My mother will dress in fine clothes, wear a warm coat, and sit on the pew next to yours."

Salathiel stood, strode over to Nat Turner, and hit him in the mouth. "You will take care how you speak about my mother."

Nat Turner tasted salty blood on his lips. He would not let them kick him aside. He would not let them make him less.

THROUGH THE CABIN window, Nat Turner watched the boys tramping back inside from the snow. Davy trailed behind them.

"Kick the snow off your feet," one of the women warned them. "Act like you got good sense. Act like you got home training or you'ah be sorry." Better her threats than a hangman's noose; angry words spoken out of love.

Nat Turner looked at the mothers and the sons, then across the room at his own mother. This would be his last Christmas. The God Who Provides for All had told him to watch for a sign in the heavens.

Hathcock and the Artis brothers had resumed talking. "We are just farmers. We only want peace. They force our hands."

The dreams that the captors had for the captive farmers were not enough. What they wanted for him was not enough. What they dreamed for the boys and girls was not enough—there were no dreams.

God sent him back to ransom their dreams.

Cherry, his wife, rubbed a warm hand on the side of his face and he turned to her. He kissed her hand. "Dinner soon." He had been focused on the boys and the men and had not heard her slip up behind him. In her eyes he saw she loved him. In her eyes he saw she worried. It was always worry mixed with love—strawberries and rhubarb, bitter turnips mixed with sweet greens—between black men and women.

She knelt before him and rubbed her warm hands gently over his feet. Nat Turner looked at the people sitting around him. He smelled the Christmas dinner cooking.

"Don't worry," she said. Brown eyes framed with black eyelashes, the love between them was unfair to her. Without him, there was less danger for her. He should let her go. Then Cherry would smile and he melted to her. "No worries now, Nathan." She smiled. "At least for today." When she was sure no one was watching, she leaned over and shyly kissed his palm.

He had never intended to marry.

Chapter 9

Even when they were boys, each direction Hark's head turned, he saw a girl or a woman he desired. But Nat Turner's plan, even as a boy, had been to never have a wife. Most of the priests in Ethiopia were married men with families, his mother had told him. There were just a few who kept themselves apart, and he thought he would be like the few. Marriage would keep him bound.

Nat Turner did not want to wait for freedom. If he never had a wife, he could escape. If the others were too afraid, let them stay behind. If they were content, let them live the way they wanted. Unencumbered, he would be free.

He would escape one day to the Dismal Swamp, then to Norfolk, the Chesapeake, then the ocean, and finally make his way to Ethiopia. Then to the Nile. A wife was just a part of the Master's plan to hold him down.

Since the age of twelve, when his father died, his mind had been fixed on running away. His mother was the only thing that held him, but his plan was to free himself and then come back for her.

Five springs came and went after his twelfth, the year he was turned out to the fields as a slave. When the sixth came, there was more hard work behind the plow.

But even for slaves there were flowers everywhere. And that spring all Hark talked of—when they were not working, and even when they were—was girls. Yellow ones, black ones, thin ones, fat ones—he was like a bee drawn to all kinds of flowers.

The night before, there had been a storm. Though the air was clear now and the sky blue, the ground was wet. A dead tree had fallen across the road with no name, and the two of them had been sent to clear it away.

As they chopped the tree in pieces so they could haul it away in the wagon, Nat told his friend about his plan.

Girls would only get in the way. "You think it is passion, but it is strategy—women for men and men for women to keep us pacified and chained so we won't leave. But they breed lust in us, not love, so we won't make war to free the ones we bed, so we won't be attached to our children and make war to free them. It is all calculated."

The two of them hacked at the dead tree. "They teach us new customs so we will forget our homeland and never leave. The captors rape our mothers, then deny their paternity. They hide their relationship to us, but then use it against us so we will feel allegiance to them, so we will long for them to acknowledge us, so we won't make war—like the Babylonians and Romans among the Jews. So we won't kill what is part of us. So we will never ever leave.

"Whiskey at Christmas, the only time we have to rest and clear our minds. So they give us whiskey to pacify us and stupefy us. Women and whiskey to give us pleasure—to dull the ache—to keep us bound." Nat swung his axe, then grabbed three firewood-size pieces and threw them in back of the wagon near them.

Hark was the calm one, the one easy to laugh. He survived because he took it all as it came. Hark nudged him and winked. "I can turn down the whiskey, brother, but not women. If that's the plot, then they have me. I have no food, no clothes, but keep feeding me women and I won't ever leave!" Hark chuckled. He grabbed six large sections and with no effort tossed them on the wagon pile.

"Is that all we are? Breeders?" Nat Turner wanted to convince his friend. Each baby born was one more slave—like they were.

And it was easier to keep his vow if he was not alone. "We are just animals to them that breed more livestock that they can sell or use in the field. Is that what we will allow them to make us? Just studs who leave our children like calves scattered here and there? No thought for them or their lives and futures? That is not who we are." Nat Turner raked his arm across his sweaty forehead. Lifting the wood was not easy for him.

"We could be like Shadrach, Meshach, and Abednego. We could be like Daniel and refuse to get drunk on what our captors offer us. We could fast from pleasant things—temporary pleasures that kill us and our people while they grow rich. We can fast from pleasant things that keep us slaves."

Hark leaned on his axe, laughing out loud. "Fast from pleasant things? You expect me to give up the one thing that makes my life tolerable?" His face sobered. "I didn't make this world or this life I suffer. Am I not entitled to some comfort? I couldn't live without women. You wouldn't want to know me if I lived without women." He lifted his axe and began to chop again. "Maybe being alone is why you brood too much. It's not safe for a black man to think too much."

Nat wiped his face with his arm again. "Well, I will do it alone then. I would rather die a man with honor, alone, than to live as a beast they use. I will take the vow to live alone."

"No women?" Hark threw more wood on the wagon. "I am not as strong-willed as you, my friend. Not for the rest of my life"— Hark chuckled—"not until next week even. I am just doing what I have to do to stay alive." Smiling, he shook his head and threw more wood on the pile.

Nat Turner looked at his friend, his brother. Hark had grown to look like a warrior, as Nat imagined St. Moses the warrior saint, like a giant statue carved from onyx.

"You are my friend, Nat Turner, and I believe you have good intentions. I believe you are a holy man if ever I saw one. But I think you should have made your vow in winter." Hark looked at the sky, the grass, and the wildflowers around them. "Let's see what spring has to say about your plans."

They finished their task in silence. Nat felt safe telling most of his thoughts to Hark. But there were some things kept private. A man's mind was a secret place.

There was truth that people held to themselves about the people they lived with—secret thoughts that mothers held about daughters, sons about their fathers, and husbands about their wives. There were thoughts kept behind a veil, thoughts that even lovers did not share.

In his life, at the end of his life, he wanted his mother's secret, sacred thoughts of him to be that he was a good man. He did not want her to see him become a breeder, he did not want her to see him grow into a man with no self-control, but he also did not want to risk his heart.

He did not believe he could know a woman's mind—not enough to trust his heart and thoughts, his insecurities to her. He did not believe he could share all he was, and all he was not, with her. He had seen too many women who frowned when their men weren't looking, too many sisters who grimaced when their brothers' backs were turned. He didn't want to live his life with a wife who secretly hated him, or bed with a woman whose sacred thoughts of him were that he was a weakling or a coward. Marriage between slaves was not really marriage—the masters could separate them or rape the women when they chose. What woman could respect a man who could not protect her and her children?

But then, there was something even more.

Hark said that Nat was strong-willed, but they really were not so different. Like his friend, Nat found women—all women—fascinating. Their singing, their dancing, their washing, their kneeling—there was no end to what intrigued him. And so that he would not be a glutton, he decided he would have none.

"I won't make it easy for the captors, Hark. I won't make it comfortable for them to keep me in captivity, to pretend that I am not who I am. I won't get drunk on their whiskey. I won't sing songs to entertain them when I work in the fields. But most of all, I won't let them use women against me. I won't marry."

Hark tossed the last piece of wood on the wagon and laughed. "We'll see what spring says." He pointed at the sun and the flowers. "Let spring have the last word."

Not more than two weeks later they heard girls' voices, voices like birds singing or water dancing over smooth stones. The sounds drifted to them from the pond, not far from their secret place.

Chapter 10

Hark ran first, Nat Turner followed. The two of them ran as though they were being called, like the work bell was calling. Peeking through branches around the pond, they saw the girls floating in the water, giggling, washing away winter's skin layers.

He and Hark watched them through the leaves. Nat Turner staggered, intoxicated. He and Hark tried not to giggle.

They had seen girls before: worked with them in the fields, and there was no privacy for slaves, neither in the fields nor in the barns. But they had not seen them this way, not in spring, not without rags, not with their hair undone floating in the water . . . not with the sun kissing their brown skin.

He and Hark knew the girls, had seen them all before. Teased them, jostled with them—at least Hark had while Nat Turner watched. But this way—with birds singing while they floated on the water, among the sweet perfume of spring flowers—was something more.

Cherry dived into the water, her head first, then hips, and finally her feet. He had known her since she was a little girl. The water closed around her, and Nat realized that he had forgotten to breathe. Beautiful, he thought, and finally understood the word. When her head gently parted the water and she reappeared, the first thing he noticed were her full, dark lips.

Hark's hand grabbed Nat Turner's shirt and pulled him back before he stepped out of the cover of the trees. He had not realized that he was walking toward the pond.

After that day he could not stop saying her name. Cherry. He found excuses to say it. Cherry. Every breeze, raindrop, even the sunshine reminded him of her.

When he saw her again, Nat Turner made his intentions known to her. She took his hand as though she had been waiting all the time. Cherry kissed him. His lips and then his neck, and he forgot all the promises and vows he had made. He forgot what would happen to him and to his children. With a kiss it all melted away.

Hope was the nectar on her lips, and each one of her fingers touching his face told him that things would be better. Hark helped him to laugh, but Cherry helped him to forget. When she smiled, the burden lifted. There was sweet life in Cherry.

Chapter 11

After years as a bothersome little girl, Cherry finally stole his heart away.

Then, just as suddenly, she seemed to change. All her life Cherry had been following him. Now she ignored him. She made it hard for him, walking away when she saw him.

He did not want to marry anyway, Nat Turner told himself. It was too much trouble, too hard. But he could not get Cherry out of his mind.

Then he remembered what his mother had told him. "It is the nature of men to only value what is hard to come by. We Ethiopian women know it is true. Anything worth having is worth working for."

But it made no sense to him. Always Cherry had been there, always waiting for him.

"A woman who gives herself easily to you will give herself easily to another," his mother said.

It made no sense to him. Why should things be so complicated?

"In Ethiopia," his mother told him, "your father would search for the perfect wife for you, a woman of great value. As her intended, you would offer gifts—gifts for her and her family. Our two families would meet to be sure you were both suitable and to discuss the bride-price. You would court your bride—an honorable woman wants to know that she is important to you, that you value her. The very best maidens come with a very high price, a price that cannot be paid by just anyone."

Nat Turner had no father to find a bride for him. He had no expensive gifts to give to Cherry. He took her a sunflower. She smiled and then walked away. He caught a butterfly and carried it to her. She kissed his cheek and walked away.

She knew he had nothing. What did she expect from him?

He sneaked and gathered apples for her, apples for which he might have been beaten if he was caught—sweet, red apples with no blemishes—and left them on a trail for her. He left them at special places for her—on a stone, in a tree hollow, beneath a mulberry bush. Cherry hugged him when she found them all, and then walked away.

He found a honeycomb hidden in a tree and sneaked her wild honey. He scooped some with a finger and she allowed him to drizzle it on her tongue. She smiled at him, kissed him, and then walked away.

It was too hard. What did she want from him? It was too much work, this courting. But he could not forget her or the taste of hope on her lips.

He saw her walking on a path one night; the moon followed her. He walked beside her, half-hidden among the trees. "You are black and comely. 'Behold, thou art fair, my love; behold, thou art fair; thou hast doves' eyes.'"

Cherry stopped to listen to him.

"'As the lily among thorns, so is my love among the daughters.'" She smiled, turning her head, arching her neck to see him. He whispered the words. "'The flowers appear on the earth; the time of the singing of birds is come, and the voice of the turtle is heard in our land; the fig tree putteth forth her green figs, and the vines with the tender grape give a good smell. Arise, my love, my fair one, and come away.'"

Cherry beckoned to him, and Nat Turner stepped into the moonlight. "Sing to me," she said.

He shook his head—he never sang. He spoke again. "'Behold, thou art fair, my love; behold, thou art fair; thou hast doves' eyes within thy locks: thy hair is as a flock of goats that appear from mount Gilead.'"

Cherry kissed his cheek.

"'Thy teeth are like a flock of sheep that are even shorn, which came up from the washing; whereof every one bear twins, and none is barren among them. Thy lips are like a thread of scarlet, and thy speech is comely: thy temples are like a piece of a pomegranate within thy locks.'"

Cherry wrapped her arms around him.

"'Thy two breasts are like two young roes that are twins, which feed among the lilies. Until the day break, and the shadows flee away, I will get me to the mountain of myrrh, and to the hill of frankincense.'"

She touched his face with her hand.

He breathed her in. "Marry me," he said.

Cherry stayed.

Chapter 12

In Ethiopia weddings lasted seven days. There were feasts and prayers, and priests playing timbrels, dancing, and beating on drums. Nat Turner imagined that he and Cherry were marrying in his mother's way. In Ethiopia, he would not have been able to marry her if she was his cousin within seven relations. He would not have been able to marry her if he could not pay the bride-price. How would he have ever hoped to pay for and marry such a woman?

Her eyes were hope's promise, and when she smiled and said his name, he knew that God loved him. Nathan Turner knew, when he breathed in Cherry, that God knew his name. When she, his wife, snuggled onto his lap, he knew that everything his mother had told him about Ethiopia was true.

The skin on her legs was hairless, smooth, and cool, but the tips of his fingers felt fire. She wrapped around him like brown ribbon. Her kinky hair was his pillow. She made him more of who he was than when he was alone.

At night she entwined one leg with his and slid her fingers into the curls at the nape of his neck. In the dark, he saw fireflies. When they were alone, Cherry sang him made-up songs. "My love is prince of Ethiopia," and Nat Turner, Negasi, forgot where he was.

When he was with her, they were clouded in silks and there was gold on their fingers. There were roses and orchids, spices and sunsets. In the distance he watched elephants and giraffes promenade, and zebras, leopards, and antelope lope by. When he was with Cherry, he left Virginia far behind.

Ethiopia was a paradise, and her colors kissed the sky. Her

mountains bore the sweetest fruit, and all her valleys were myrrh. Stars crowned her head, and flowers kissed her feet; she lived in the midst of a rainbow. Solomon bowed at her beauty, and the Nile was the cradle and the birthplace of all life. Cherry was a garden, and Africa lived in her hair.

WHEN TEN FULL moons passed, Cherry bore their first son, Riddick.

In the woods, far away from the barn and underneath the moonlight and the boughs of trees loaded with spring blossoms, Cherry moaned as Riddick fought his way into the world.

Not far away, but as though she were in Ethiopia, his mother prayed ancient prayers in Amharic and sang songs her mother had taught her. She lifted prayers to protect and comfort Cherry, to welcome the baby into the world.

Nat Turner held his baby in his arms, his son, his tiny son. Tiny perfect fingers curled around one of his own. Brown eyes full of wonder looked into his—eyes that believed him, that trusted him, that thought he was a king.

He kissed his son's forehead and kissed his hand. "Things will be different for you," he whispered to Riddick. He kissed his precious son and then slowly lifted Riddick to present him to the village, to his ancestors far away, and to God.

Beside Nat Turner, his mother spoke words and sang songs to honor her grandson, Amharic words forbidden in America. *Born today is the son of nine generations of warriors! Born today is the son of eleven generations of prophets! Born today is the son of eight generations of wise women! The son of ancient fathers who walked with Abba Selama! Behold their aspects bloom in him!*

Nat Turner lowered his son to his shoulder. "I promise. Things will be different for you." He enfolded Riddick in his arms. "On my own life, I promise you a better one. On my own life, I promise you a better way."

Cherry was a quiet wife, and he hoped no one would notice

her with the scarf around her head and her rags on. He did not talk about her to others because he wanted to keep her for his own. Riddick was a quiet baby, and Nat Turner kept him close. He was quiet with his family; he did not want others to notice them.

But he knew. They had already taught him. A slave could not have anything.

NAT TURNER LOOKED across the room at Cherry and, though it was winter, he smelled apple blossoms. She bent over the stove in the kitchen, helping with Christmas dinner. Watching her, her brown hands and sweet brown face, still did the same things to him. When she combed her hair, when she smiled, when she touched his hand, she still took his breath away. As he was to his mother, she was his shame and his glory.

He came back to do the will of God. But in truth, he also came back for Cherry. He came back to never leave her, to be a man who would never abandon her, no matter the cost.

His presence was his sonnet to her. She read it; he could see it in her eyes. He came back for her and for his son.

Harriet

Harriet

Chapter 13

Plymouth Church, Brooklyn Heights
1856

The service over and all the visitors and congregants greeted, Harriet retired to the pastor's study with Henry and Frederick Douglass. Henry, still full of life, bounded through the door and onto his favorite sitting place, the sofa, in his favorite position—on his knees, curled almost into position like a Cheshire cat. "Hattie, do take off that atrocious bonnet, you look like a country schoolmarm."

She glanced at Mr. Douglass to see how he was receiving her brother's foolishness. "Henry, please!"

"Oh, Hattie, settle your feathers. You are both at home here and we are all family." Smiling, he reached for a nearby plate. It appeared to have once been full of cookies, but now there were only two left. "Here, a peace offering."

"No thank you, brother. We have business to attend to."

Henry half pouted, half smiled. "Don't be cross with me." He turned to Frederick Douglass. "You see, a prophet is without honor in his own family." He turned in the seat like a five-year-old, not like a world-famous pastor. "Please have one. They are delicious ginger cookies. See the crumbs? But I saved these last just for the two of you. I knew you would be famished. Take one, and then pour tea so that you will be refreshed." He beamed at the two of them, his blue-gray eyes sparkling. "I thought of everything." He pouted again. "Please, Hattie."

When they each had tea, Harriet and Frederick accepted the last two cookies. Frederick nodded at Harriet. "Please, ladies first."

Harriet sipped her tea and then bit into the cookie.

Henry leaned forward, one eyebrow raised. "Delicious?"

Harriet frowned and then, without thinking, she spit crumbs onto the floor.

Henry clapped his hands, lifting partway from his seat. "Perfect!"

She gulped tea to wash the taste from her mouth. "Henry, the cookies are horrible!"

"I know." He giggled. "One of the good church ladies baked them for me." He looked back and forth between Harriet and Frederick. "The sweet woman's eyesight is not what it once was. I believe she reached for the salt when she thought she had the sugar." He laughed out loud. "I threw most of them away, but I wanted to share my good fortune with friends."

Frederick Douglass attempted to cover his laugh with his napkin.

Her younger brother had always been a prankster, and age had not cured him. "I should have known better." She looked at Frederick. "Did you know about this, Mr. Douglass?"

Frederick shrugged, trying not to smile. "This is a family matter. I never step between brother and sister."

"You are both children. I am here on a serious matter, and you both waste time with silly games."

The two men laughed aloud. Henry bounced on the sofa like a child, sputtering, "'A m-m-merry heart doeth good like a m-m-medicine.'"

Frederick wiped tears from his eyes as he chuckled. "'The joy of the LORD is our strength.'"

"How can the two of you laugh when there are such heavy matters before us?"

Henry and Frederick began to outdo each other, quoting Bible passages.

"'They that sow in tears shall reap in joy!'"

"'Make a joyful noise unto the LORD, all the earth: make a loud noise, and rejoice, and sing praise.'"

They paid no attention to her. "Henry, behave!" With each

round of quotes, the two got louder and louder. "Hush, you two, anyone about will think you have gone mad." They ignored her and continued.

"'But let all those that put their trust in thee rejoice: let them ever shout for joy!'"

"'Be glad in the LORD, and rejoice, ye righteous: and shout for joy!'"

It was unseemly. The two of them were shouting now. "What kind of example are you two gentlemen—if I may call you that—setting?" Her protests were futile. "You are infants! I have come all this way to discuss the letter I have with me, and the two of you are playing whirligig and rolling the hoop."

Frederick Douglass stood and bowed. "'Rejoice in the LORD, O ye righteous: for praise is comely!'"

"Henry, you have had a terrible influence on Mr. Douglass. You have turned a perfectly intelligent gentleman into a jokester, like yourself."

Not to be outdone, Henry stood this time and sang his quote in a booming baritone. "'Hitherto have ye asked nothing in my name: ask, and ye shall receive, that your joy may be full.'"

"What would Father say, Henry?"

Mr. Douglass joined Henry in song. The two linked arms, raising one toward the ceiling. "'Rejoice in the LORD always: and again I say, Rejoice!'"

Harriet tried to hold back the smile creeping onto her face. "A couple of blasphemers is what you two are. If only the newspapers could get wind of this." A giggle leaked out. "I think I shall tell them myself." She let go and laughed.

No matter the circumstances, Henry had always been the child in the family to brighten events by making everyone laugh. She had been so worried, had cried so many tears. Laughter was medicine. Harriet pressed her napkin to her face and allowed herself to laugh and weep.

Chapter 14

The three of them divided the pages of the letter containing excerpts from Governor Floyd's diary. Each one shook his head as they read—Henry perched on his sofa, Frederick Douglass behind Henry's desk, and Harriet in the great chair—pausing at times to read out loud. Next to Frederick's pages was a copy of *The Confessions of Nat Turner*.

She had read the entire letter over and over again; it still made her flinch. Deep in thought, Frederick rubbed his fingers over his beard, sometimes pulling at it. He looked up and spoke. "Twenty-five years have passed since Nat Turner's hanging, but these excerpts make it all seem contemporary." He tapped the pages in his hand. "Even at that time, during the confusion surrounding them, the governor had doubts about the trials."

He began to read excerpts from the governor's diary. "'This day the record of the trial of Mischek, a negro in Greensville for conspiracy was brought. The evidence was too feeble and therefore I have reprieved him for sale and transportation.'"

Frederick Douglass shifted forward in his chair. "We hardly hear about the others who were hanged, or slated to be hanged, and this poor fellow was not even from Southampton County."

Henry nodded. "I imagine that in addition to rampant fear, lucre tempted them. The average family in the area might expect to make little more than one hundred fifty dollars in a year's time. My wife, Eunice, and I sometimes reminisce about when I was hired to pastor, making twice that amount and still we would have starved had it not been for donations of food and such.

"With such easy convictions and Virginia paying for each convicted slave, the temptation to sacrifice slave lives for money must have been overwhelming. Their consciences were already dulled." The smile was gone from Henry's face, his cheeks reddened, and Harriet thought she saw tears in his eyes. He was a prankster, and a man's man, but her brother was so compassionate that he was easily brought to tears.

Henry read the entry for October 30, 1831. "'Received news that the dead body of the negro which was supposed to be Nat had been taken up and examined by General Smith of Kanawha.'" He paused, looking over the top of his pages. "Kanawha? The county is more than three hundred miles away from Jerusalem, in western Virginia. It makes me wonder how many other slaves died at the hands of men seeking the bounty on Nat Turner's head. And the poor fellow who lost his life means nothing to them."

Harriet began reading. "'Twenty-seventh day, September, 1831—I have received record of the trial of three slaves, for treason in Southampton. Am recommended to mercy, in this case I cannot do so, because there is not one member of the Council of State in Richmond.'" She lifted her eyes to look at the others, swallowed, and then continued. "'Wherefore the poor wretch must lose his life.'" She coughed nervously and then pressed on. "'I have received this day another number of the "Liberator," a newspaper printed in Boston, with the express intention of inciting the slaves and free negroes in this and the other states to rebellion and to murder the men, women, and children of those states. Yet we are gravely told there is no law to punish such an offence. The amount of it then is this, a man in our States may plot treason in one state against another without fear of punishment, whilst the suffering state has no right to resist—'" Harriet choked in indignation and stopped reading.

"Treason? Treason?" She realized she was yelling and lowered her voice, though she felt her heart thumping and blood rushing in her ears. "Inciting slaves and free negroes to rebellion and murder! Because we oppose slavery, because we insist that this country must live up to its promise of liberty for all, then we are described as disloyal. And it is ridiculous to accuse Garrison of inciting slaves and free Negroes to murder—he is a devout pacifist, for goodness' sakes." She fanned herself with the pages. "Plotting treason . . . and rebellion? Slaves have every right; in fact it's their duty, to stand up against the tyranny imposed upon them. But Governor Floyd describes us as the villains."

"Garrison speaks the truth." Harriet was surprised to hear Frederick Douglass speak in support of the man who had openly criticized him. "He shines light into the gray, swirling storm of slavery. Why, even Governor Floyd is double-minded. He argues against abolitionists, seeking to have them prosecuted. He lays the blame for the rebellion not on man's desire to be free, but on Negro preachers, saying, 'The whole of that massacre in Southampton is the work of these preachers as daily intelligence informs me.'" Douglass thumped the pages. "The governor does not once consider that the intelligence might be false. Or, at least, not before it is too late.

"Yet, in the next breath, he seeks to save the slaves from the noose and declares, 'Before I leave this government, I will have contrived to have a law passed gradually abolishing slavery in this state.'

"Governor Floyd did not seem to recognize that his thoughts, if not brothers to Garrison's, were at least cousins."

"Gradual emancipation? He is indeed double-minded. He speaks of emancipation but thunders against efforts by Garrison and the others, efforts to ensure liberty and peace." She continued, "Floyd says, 'If this is not checked it must lead to a separation of these states.'"

Frederick lowered the pages he held. "Garrison's *Liberator* and the words of abolitionists are thorns in the sides of Floyd and his compatriots. They cannot deny the truth of what Garrison says, but they don't want to hear it, so they accuse him of plotting murder and rebellion."

Harriet pressed on, reading from Floyd's diary. "'If the forms of law will not punish, the law of nature will not permit men to have their families butchered before their eyes by their slaves and not seek by force.'"

She looked up from her reading. "It is senseless to me. One man insists he has a right to defend his family while he insists that another, who seeks to do the same, is a criminal. There is such venom in Floyd's words when he writes of Negro preachers and abolitionists.

"If we do not conform to his way—if we do not conform to the ways of slavery men—then we are the worst kind of villains and traitors, not worthy of citizenship. What is it that we say that is wrong? It is the teaching and the prayer of Christ that we all be one."

Henry nodded. Her thoughts were mirrored in the sadness she saw in his eyes. He began to speak softly. "'Blessed are ye, when men shall hate you, and when they shall separate you from their company, and shall reproach you, and cast out your name as evil, for the Son of man's sake. Rejoice ye in that day, and leap for joy: for, behold, your reward is great in heaven: for in the like manner did their fathers unto the prophets.'"

Harriet sighed, looking at the two men who shared the study with her. She turned back to her pages. "Here Governor Floyd continues, 'An anonymous writer from Philadelphia gives me to understand that the Northern fanatics are in that city plotting treason and insurrection in this State and planning the massacre of the white people of the Southern States by the blacks.'"

Harriet paused. "I do believe he is referring to the Philadelphia Convention." She blushed. "You see? The governor refers to people we know, describing these lovely patriots as though they are the worst sort. Listen. 'Allen, a negro of Philadelphia and two white men of Boston, and some of New York'—most likely the Tappans—'besides a numerous band of white men and negroes in their train.'

"To think of him describing Bishop Allen in this manner, Garrison, the Tappans—these are some of America's great patriots and God's great servants." It was disconcerting to hear them described as though they were criminals to be hunted. It was strange to hear them described as though they meant harm when their intent was to deliver others from harm. "I read it and I am ashamed, infuriated, and confused all at once. It is all very odd to me. He does not speak of strangers, but people we know. He speaks of us."

Harriet touched her face. She was a preacher's daughter, the famous Puritan Lyman Beecher's daughter. She wrote Sunday school lessons and Bible tracts. She sewed flags and sang "Yankee Doodle" at Fourth of July outings. Her brother was a pastor who preached love, a husband and a father who would give all he had to help a soul in need. And Frederick Douglass was as charitable, as intelligent, and as deserving of freedom as Floyd or any other man. How did standing up for another's freedom make one a turncoat or a criminal?

Henry shrugged. "We call what they do sin and it offends them. We propose taking away their stolen treasure and they do not want to relinquish it."

Harriet looked at her brother. "I read it over and over; I try to understand the logic of it, but to no avail."

Henry laid his pages on the couch beside him. "The devil's work most often makes no sense. Still we are deluded and go gaily skipping behind him."

Frederick Douglass went straight to the point. "Has this letter convinced you to retell the story of Nat Turner?"

She was prepared, even excited, to share the anonymous letter. But, foolishly, she had not prepared to answer the issue they had been pressing her about for months. "What is here, in these excerpts, does match the stories told me by Phipps and William."

Henry nodded. "You must begin writing at once, then."

Harriet reached out for the papers she had shared with her brother. She had made only trouble for herself by sharing them. "I think I need more."

Henry's gaze was unrelenting. "More? Why?"

Because she wasn't sure. Because for so long, like everyone else, she had thought of him as a baby-killer and a ruthless, indiscriminate murderer. Because . . . she was not comfortable. "I want to be certain."

"What would make you more certain?"

She turned at the sound of Frederick's deep, authoritative voice. "Everything I thought I knew has turned out to be a hoax. I have no idea who Nat Turner was. What kind of slave, what kind of man must he have been to have these men, men who had all power in their hands, bother to concoct such an elaborate lie?"

Henry picked up his pages from the couch. "Governor Floyd says of President Andrew Jackson, 'Jackson with all his unworthy officers, men not gentlemen, who lie, mutilate records, alter dates.' Maybe the men in Southampton were infected by the behaviors of the reigning administration."

Truthfully, Harriet felt pressure from all sides now. At first, the pressure had come from without—from her brother and Frederick Douglass, who wanted her to write the story. Now she felt pressure from within—as though her heart was wrestling with her mind. "Perhaps if I could speak with someone who knew him I might be more reassured."

Frederick Douglass's gaze was sympathetic. He seemed to understand her struggle, but still he pressed her—as though he were saying that what needed to be done was bigger than her insecurities. "You have spoken with Will. Would you speak with him again?"

"No!" The word popped from her mouth, too soon for her comfort. She breathed then went on speaking. "No. His anger, his passion distress me."

Henry was her brother, and he was not so gentle with her. "Be reasonable, Hattie. How would you expect someone who has suffered as he has to behave?"

Harriet looked back at the pages she held, wanting to change the subject. She did not want to see William again. She did not want to speak with him. He frightened her. She worked to regain her composure and slow her breathing.

She began to read again, taking a lighter tone. "Governor Floyd calls us a 'club of villains.' A club of villains 'maturing plans of treason and rebellion and insurrection in Virginia and the Southern States.' He speaks of withdrawing from the Union." She looked up from her reading. "South Carolina and the others have threatened secession each time something did not suit them. Do you believe the South really might secede?"

Henry nodded. "They might try."

"And if they do?"

"Then there will be war."

There had already been bloody skirmishes, like the gory massacre and firing of Lawrence, Kansas, by slavery men. And John Brown had used rifles, like Henry's Beecher's Bibles, against proslavery men. She did not want to think of the nation at war. Each of them had sons. She did not want to think of their sons marching off to war. "I do not want disunion. I do not want war."

"Perhaps, if you will consent to write the story," Henry said pointedly. "*Uncle Tom's Cabin* has already done so much good. If the nation knew the truth about Nat Turner, more might be persuaded to stand against slavery. It might die without bloodshed, like in England."

Harriet tried to laugh away her anxiety and pressure about the Nat Turner story. What did it all have to do with her? "I'm a Yankee, you know. We're mind-your-own-business kind of people. I'm not sure this is my business."

Henry would not let up. "You believed *Uncle Tom's Cabin* was your business. How is this different?"

"This mishmash with Nat Turner is the South's business, isn't it? Let men like Governor Floyd work it out. Who am I to interfere?"

Frederick Douglass looked down at the pages in his hand. "But men like Floyd, fence straddlers, haven't been able to work it out. His attempt at gradual abolition failed, these notes say, because the slave-holding portion of his state threatened to secede from Virginia if pressed about slavery."

Still perched on the couch, irritation lacing his voice, Henry frowned. "Are we not our brother's keeper, Hattie? You sound like our older sister, Catherine. Do you really believe this is the South's private affair?"

"Maybe she is right."

"You know better, Hattie! It is fear I hear speaking, not my courageous sister."

"Maybe Governor Floyd was right. We are staunch abolitionists. But, perhaps, how the South resolves the issue of slavery is their affair—like what happens behind a family's closed door. Maybe we should mind our own business." Harriet was surprised by her own words and thoughts.

"Nat Turner was the thud against the wall." Frederick Douglass's voice cut through her efforts to reassure herself, to make room to step away from it all.

"I don't understand."

"Even with neighbors, who respect one another's privacy, there is a time to step in." Frederick Douglass rubbed his beard again. "Nat Turner was the black eye, the scream from the apartment next door." He lifted *The Confessions of Nat Turner*. "This lie and his death say we cannot sit back and do nothing. Because of Nat Turner, we can no longer pretend not to know what is happening right next door to us. Can we turn our backs and pretend we don't hear or see? We cannot leave them to suffer. We must do what we can, even if we must invade their privacy, to end the suffering. Even if it means risking our reputations, or even our own lives."

The three of them were silent. Harriet heard the clock on the study mantel ticking. "Do you think there will be war?"

Frederick's voice was no more than a whisper. "Though my heart is heavy, I think it is inevitable." The clock sounded even louder in the silence. "We must do what we can to prevent it."

Henry stood then and came and knelt before Harriet. He took her hand. "We must summon the courage to speak up, to say clearly who we are and what we believe. We must have the fortitude to confront lies with truth. We must do all we can, with all that has been given us, to set the captives free. Courage today or there will surely be carnage tomorrow."

A tear stung her cheek. She looked deeply into the eyes she had trusted all her life. Harriet squeezed Henry's hand.

"When would you like to meet with William again?"

She turned toward Frederick. "I do want to find the real Nat Turner." If she was going to commit to truth, she might as well begin now. "But William makes me uncomfortable. He alarms me."

Frederick nodded. "If we would seek after truth and love, the path will lead us through dangerous places, past strangers who frighten us. But if we find the courage to persevere, we will find what we seek."

Harriet nodded and agreed that Mr. Douglass should arrange a second meeting as soon as possible.

Nat Turner

Chapter 15

Cross Keys Area, outside Jerusalem, Virginia
Christmas 1830

Nat Turner bowed his head to pray with the others over their Christmas dinner—beans, corn bread, greens, and cabbage flavored with pigs' feet and tails. He dipped his spoon into the food and tasted. He nodded his compliments to Mrs. Hathcock.

Some had criticized him years ago, after his return from the Great Dismal Swamp, telling him they would not return to slavery for anything or for anyone. He looked at the men, women, and children around him—at his wife and at his mother.

Some understood now why he had returned. Others might never understand. He had come back in obedience to God. He had come back for his people.

Nat Turner looked at Cherry, who sat beside him. No matter what, he would never leave her again.

She was Giles Reese's captive now. When she bore children they belonged to Reese to do with as he pleased. Nat Turner turned his head away. He would not think of it. Still, when he was with her now, there was ache in his delight. There was a wound in his side, and life leaked from it.

But he loved her. Only death could force him to leave her. Even the humiliation could not drive him away, even if he could see her only now and then, he would not leave.

He looked around the room at all the people gathered in the small cabin for Christmas dinner. He would remember every face, every movement, every smile, and every tear.

He looked at the cracked feet and imagined the broken hearts he could not see. His son, Riddick, came to him then. Nat Turner wrapped an arm around the boy, rubbed a hand through his hair, and then they shared food from his plate. God had sent him back for his son.

Nat Turner tilted Riddick's head back and kissed his forehead. He smiled at Cherry and then, together, he and his son ate the last of the cabbage on his tin plate. It would be his last Christmas.

When the early night of winter came and they were all full from the holiday dinner, or what passed for full, Nat Turner led the people out. He had been planning for months. Cherry walked beside him. He felt in his pocket for the gunpowder, then took Riddick's hand. He held a piece of burning wood aloft as a torch to lead the way. The people followed behind him, silent with anticipation.

Light from the torch made a golden circular pool against the darkness that bobbled, sometimes lighting the trunks of the dark trees. His feet had thawed in the warm cabin, but they were rapidly numbing again. He looked back at the old people and children who followed, and nodded to encourage them. Nat Turner smiled at Cherry and squeezed Riddick's hand.

Young and old, men and women, they followed Nat Turner along a hidden trail that led to a quiet clearing he knew of deep in the woods. He heard bare feet, hard frozen like clubs, crunching in the snow. Occasionally a child giggled, a woman laughed. He motioned for them to be quiet.

If they were lucky, there would be a patch free of snow beneath the tree branches that arched high above the clearing.

When they reached the spot, there was a bare place as he'd hoped. Nat Turner directed them to form a circle around him, older ones—to honor them—and little ones—so they could see—in the front. He didn't have much of the powder, none to spare.

He dumped it out on the ground and formed it into a mound. He stood then and looked around at them. God had sent him back for them. "For God who loved us enough to send His son! For freedom!" He touched the torch to the powder and leapt back. There was an explosion and a white flash!

The people stood in awe, their mouths open, their eyes wide. Christmas. Their Fourth of July! One woman raised her hands. Then they shouted and stomped. The children jumped in the air. All the people clapped their hands.

God had spoken. Now Nat Turner waited for the sign.

Harriet

Chapter 16

Harriet looked around William's Boston shop. She was struck again by the peacefulness of the place. But outside the shop, in Kansas, in the halls of Congress, and even in the streets of Boston, bloody skirmishes continued about slavery and particularly about the 1850 Fugitive Slave Act.

Her brother Henry and Frederick Douglass insisted she meet with William again. *But there is no one else to do it. People are suffering and you can help them; you have the attention of the world.*

During their last meeting at Plymouth Church, they had discussed Governor Floyd being double-minded. But her mind also was divided. Harriet did not want war, and she was committed to working to end slavery. She was willing to write—she had proven that with *Uncle Tom*—and she was willing to accept the ridicule of those who disagreed with her stance. But she was not certain about Nat Turner. She no longer knew what to believe.

For years she, like the rest of America, had believed what she read in *The Confessions*. The document was signed by six judges and the Southampton County clerk. How could it not be true? And if it was a lie, what kind of man was the real Nat Turner?

Harriet was unsure. She only committed to listening.

There had been riots in Boston, Philadelphia, and even in small towns like York, Pennsylvania, when slave catchers had come North trying to reclaim slaves. People like William, a slave refugee from Virginia, and even Frederick Douglass, were at risk—they could be sent back South in chains. But the people in cities and towns, risking their own freedom, were rebelling against the Fugitive Slave Act and hiding, or even rescuing, the refugees by force. They were so brave, but all she felt was a nagging fear.

"I have not agreed to write his story." She paused, sizing up William, the man who sat across from her—a coconspirator in Nat Turner's uprising. "They tell me you know more about him than any man alive." Harriet looked down at her notes. "But you said, before, you did not like him."

William nodded. "But in the end, he was my friend. He gave me the gift few people would choose to give another. He gave me my life. He gave me hope."

"Hope?" How could anyone who had been a slave, who had been through what the slaves had been through, speak of hope? She would not have known where to go or where to begin looking. "I cannot imagine."

"I found my sister still in bonds, the light stolen from her heart and beaten out of her eyes." William lowered his voice, his shoulders tensed. "I must decline, for the safety of others, to tell you where I found her or the exact circumstances of my spiriting her away." He seemed to relax again. "She was the first missing part of me that I found." The light flickered out in his eyes. "I still have not found my wife. Though I still sometimes muster the strength to hope, there is no sign of her." His hands clenched and then unclenched.

Silent, Harriet looked around the shop and then back at William.

He cleared his throat. "God gave me back part of my life. He gave me back my sister and, with her, a niece. He gave me a voice." William lifted his teacup, smiled briefly at Harriet, and then set it back on the saucer. "There is hope for bloodthirsty men." He briefly flashed another smile.

Moved, she knew she mustn't be so sympathetic that she failed to ask him the difficult questions. Harriet looked toward the other room where her brother and Frederick Douglass were waiting. *The Confessions* described Will as an executioner. How would he react to her questions? "What about all the lives you took?"

Surprisingly, William seemed nonplussed. "How many slave cheeks do you suppose were turned and lives taken? How many knees were bowed and pleas made? But it seems that violent people only understand violence. What remedy would you recommend to God for those who murder His children, or even your own?" The muscles at his temple throbbed. "They justify what they did to us by twisting the Old Testament. How long did they expect to continue before God unleashed Old Testament vengeance?

"Do you think God actually stood back without care and watched as His children were slaughtered?" William straightened his collar.

Though he was silent for a moment, his nostrils flared. "I believe that He wept. I believe from the beginning He planned to deliver us."

Then William's face was suddenly surprisingly emotionless. "They pretend to be God-lovers, but they are man-haters, and God will not be mocked. How can you torture your brother and say you love him? You cannot imprison others and say you love freedom. You cannot breathe war and say you are a peacemaker.

"It was God's command. War. Judgment. But it was their choice—they could have chosen to repent; they could have chosen mercy for themselves." His demeanor was placid as he delivered the words. "They held money, property, and power more valuable than men's souls. It was their choice."

"You seem to doubt that they were or are Christians."

His eyes bore into hers. "I am no judge, but in the wake of a Christian's footsteps, there ought to be love."

It was strange to hear William talk about love, to speak words that seemed kin to Henry's. Before her sat a murderer speaking of love; she looked for some sign of insincerity.

"Slavery men are angry and discontent; they do not see themselves. They leave a trail of bitterness and sorrow behind them. They try to make their lives full with more houses, more servants, more lace, more money. They cannot even say they are wrong and repent to God. They cannot humble themselves and apologize." A slight smile, an ironic one, played at the corner of William's lips. "I know what it is to be angry, to choose judgment rather than mercy."

His expression sobered. "I was bound, I was a slave, but the worst bondage was what I suffered inside. The worst was what I had to admit and confess before I could speak again, before I could love again."

"Love? But you killed so many people." Harriet looked for something in his eyes, some sign of deceit.

"It was a war for freedom. Nat Turner, the others, and I were sent to do battle with the giant, to warn him that he would fall. They gave no mercy, so received none."

"What about the baby?"

William looked confused, as though he did not know how to respond.

"The baby. The one you went back and killed. Are you saying God directed you to kill the baby?"

William lifted his shoulders and shook his head as though he didn't understand. Then his eyes widened and sarcasm crept into his voice. "Some folly from *The Confessions?*"

Harriet pressed him. "Did you find satisfaction in . . . in war . . . in killing all those people?"

William was matter-of-fact. He did not turn away. "At first. For a moment I was ecstatic—but the pleasure of lust is temporary satisfaction. When I was empty, bloodlust was the only thing that seemed to fill me. But not for long. In time, I repented, as any soldier repents; but I did what had to be done. It only satisfied me when I was not filled with love."

Harriet looked for signs of insanity, some sign that William would lunge at her. "Love? But you still speak harsh things."

He leaned back from the table. "The truth is a great weapon. You know that. You are a wordsmith. Words of truth are a double-edged sword. It cuts, but I always speak out of hope and out of love. I didn't speak at all before."

His eyes fixed on hers. "I fight with words now. I am still ready to die for what I believe." He paused as though he wanted the truth of his words to sink in. Harriet felt chilled but fought to keep her composure, hoping William would not see.

He seemed to calm and, though he still held her gaze, he spoke more softly. "But I hope for life. Before, I was quiet but there was murder in my heart. Now I speak words like swords, but in my heart there is love. In my heart is the prayer that someone will hear me and turn." He nodded at Harriet. "Love does not always appear as we think.

"I found my sister, I found forgiveness, I found the God of my fathers who was lost to me. Nat Turner led me there. Then I found my name—Love."

"You speak so much about love. Other men think it is a weakness."

He smiled and then shook his head. "Nat Turner told me it is not the weak but only the courageous who love. The ones who cannot love are the cowards. Only courageous men love. Only the bravest men, ferocious men, love their enemies." He spoke loving words, but between the sentences his countenance was sometimes painted with anger.

A murdering slave who changed his name to Love? His visage was gray clouds and sunshine, and Harriet wasn't certain what she believed. William was not the man she'd thought he would be. "When all this is over, will you be able to let it go, to move on with your life and forget it all?"

She was surprised by the sudden look of sympathy in his eyes. "Have you and I been able to forget the loss of our children?"

She had not been able to pray away, to think away, or even to write away the death of her infant son. She still had a full life, and love, and joy. But she could not forget him. Harriet stared at William—she would not, or could not, answer.

She did not want to think about baby Samuel. "You said you hated him ... Nat Turner."

"At first. But I learned. He shared his life with me. You might say that in the end, he was my confessor and I his."

"Then, please, tell me what you know." Harriet settled in to listen to his story.

Nathan "Nat" Turner/Negasi

"Rebellion to tyrants is obedience to God."

—Thomas Jefferson

Chapter 17

Cross Keys, Virginia
February 1831

Christmas was past, and left behind a hard, cold winter that looked as though it would never end. But rather than despise it, Nat Turner reminded himself to cherish the wonder of each day. He made himself feel it and marveled at the snow.

It was a wonder how the weather changed each day. He took note that sometimes the clouds shifted in layers, and he took inspiration that the sun had courage to do battle with the night in order to rise each day.

He would never see another February.

In the barn, Nat Turner looked out at the barren trees. Hark stood beside him helping ready the wagon. Their lives might have been different.

There had been a time when Nat Turner hoped for more, when he hoped to be a boy like other boys—a time when he, Hark, and even Thomas Gray, though they were from isolated farms, joined together to play childhood games.

THE AFTERNOON SUMMER sun made their shadows long on the ground. The boys tromped through the woods on the way to the clearing where they would do battle.

The sun filtered through the boughs on the trees that towered over them, but the leaves worked together to keep them cool.

A little girl with chocolate skin, large round eyes, and lips like berries trailed behind them. Barefoot, in nothing but a tattered

shirt, she kept her eyes on Nat. "Get away, Cherry." The little girl
had been following him about since she first learned to walk, and
he supposed he had not discouraged her affection, often pinching
her cheek and lifting her in the air. But at times like this, her devotion was embarrassing. This was no time or place for girls.

She stopped, but when he turned back toward the other boys,
she inched along behind them. Nat turned around to scold her. "I
told you go back, Cherry. This is no place for you. There's nothing
but boys here."

Cherry didn't say a word, just stared up into his eyes.

"Go on now, girl!" Nat raised a hand as though he was going to
swat her. "You get away from here." He tromped on behind the
other boys and looked back to see her standing where he had left
her, the hem of her shirt bunched in her hands, staring at him and
biting her bottom lip.

Salathiel Francis led the trek. He carried his baby brother,
Nathaniel, on his shoulders. John Clarke Turner and Richard
Whitehead marched behind Salathiel. Behind them walked the
smaller-framed Thomas Gray. Nat Turner and Hark, walking side
by side, followed Thomas, while Benjamin Phipps, wiping from his
nose the evidence of his perpetual cold, made up the rear.

When they came to the clearing, each of the boys scrambled to
find the perfect weapon, the stick that would magically transform
into a sword. After each one had selected his saber, Salathiel announced the battle. "We will fight a sea battle." He pointed at
Thomas Gray. "You lead the other side." For his own army, Salathiel
chose his younger brother, Nathaniel, John Clarke Turner, and Richard Whitehead. "We will be the Virginians. You will be the British."

Thomas Gray objected. "Why must I be British?"

"Look at you. Look at your family. Aristocrats is what you are.
Wealthy just like the Crown."

"But I don't want to."

Salathiel used his superior size—he was a head taller than the
other boys—to make his point. He stepped close enough that his

chin almost pressed the top of Gray's head. "You are the British," he insisted. "You can be the colonel," he conceded.

Nat and Hark had played the game long enough that they both already knew that they had no say so in the matter. They would be what they were told to be.

Benjamin Phipps, using his torn shirtsleeve to wipe his nose, only succeeded in spreading the sage-colored mucus farther across his face. "I want to be an American. I want to be a Virginian."

Little Richard Whitehead laughed. "We don't want you on our side, you weakling." He waved his sword. "Don't get too close. You'll give us consumption!"

Not much bigger than Whitehead, Nat Turner stepped in front of Phipps. He lifted his sword. "Don't worry, boys! Let's give them hell!" He leapt upon a log, an imaginary gangplank. The clearing was transformed to a great British warship; the Virginians were privateers seeking to steal the Crown's wealth. Nat's clothes transformed from tatters to a turban and robes. He was an Ethiopian prince, African royalty engaged to assist his friend the British sea captain Gray. He raised his sword to do battle with Richard Whitehead. Their swords clacked together and they inched back and forth, balancing with arms in the air so they would not plunge to their deaths from the shifting plank to the depths of the briny sea beneath them.

Hark, even at ten, was like a black Adonis, some great black warrior. Sometimes Nat Turner imagined Hark and himself as brother leopards—Hark the black panther and he the spotted leopard—climbing the mountains of Ethiopia. Wearing a turban and jeweled belt, Hark jabbed with his sword at John Clarke Turner and soon had outmaneuvered the other boy. Hark knocked the sword from his opponent's hand and then tripped him to the floor of the ship. "Surrender!" he yelled. "Or be run through!"

Nat jumped from the gangplank and ran to begin climbing the highest mast, the white sails billowing around him. Whitehead followed and balanced; there they clashed, fighting for life and for honor.

Neither Benjamin Phipps nor Thomas Gray was any match for the much stronger Salathiel. Though he was not graceful, being hampered by an eye patch and peg leg, Salathiel jerked Benjamin's sword from his hand, pushed him to the deck, and then turned to do battle with Colonel Gray while Benjamin crawled behind a leafy bulwark.

Nat Turner was still at battle with Richard Whitehead. The small boy, his cowlick atop his head like a feather, was proving a worthy opponent. He was not quick, but he was tenacious. Whitehead slipped, almost plummeting to his death, but flailed with his arm to recover his balance. Nat Turner advanced, hoping to force Richard off the mast and into the sea. He called to his friend Hark. "Help him! Help Colonel Gray!"

Salathiel was getting the better of the smaller boy. He attempted to jerk Gray's sword from his hand, but the British sea captain would not surrender. Instead, he held his weapon fast, a hand gripping either end. But the wily Salathiel was determined. He grabbed Gray's weapon in the center and used it to toss the smaller boy about while his younger brother, Nathaniel, really too young to play, waved his small blade in the air and chased behind his brother.

It was glorious! Nat Turner looked up at the sun and breathed in the salty sea air. Swelling white clouds drifted overhead while seagulls circled in the air. The sails billowed about them. The men yelled and cursed, as men do in battle. Nat Turner jabbed at Whitehead with his sword.

Hark rushed to Gray's aid, stabbing Salathiel in the side with his saber. Salathiel, stomping about on his peg leg, laughed. "I will take the two of you at one time!" Holding fast to Gray's sword, he used it to swing Gray about, using the small boy to batter Hark, knocking the Ethiopian swashbuckler off balance and onto the ground. Salathiel raised his sword and then quickly plunged it into the two fallen men.

Nat looked at his fallen comrades and quickly whacked

Whitehead on the leg, causing him to flounder and sending his arms flailing. The Ethiopian prince made short work of the privateer, and then jumped from the high mast to the deck to face Salathiel.

Salathiel grinned, baring all his teeth and glaring with his one good eye. "Prepare to die!"

He towered over Nat. He was stronger, but wit was on the Ethiopian prince's side. "You will not prevail today, sir," he said while brandishing his weapon.

"You talk too much!" the pirate captain bellowed.

"And you think too little!" Nat Turner threw his sword in the air and as Salathiel, surprised, stopped to gape as it turned end over end and glinted like gold, Turner tackled him to the ground. He sat atop the bigger boy. "You have been vanquished, sir! The British, with the help of the brave Ethiopians, have prevailed!"

February 1831

NAT TURNER LED the horse from the barn, tying the red mare to a post. He rubbed her muzzle to reassure her and then returned to the barn for the tack. With the harness and rigging in hand, he stroked her head and mane and then started the work of harnessing her.

"Quiet, girl." He took the collar in his hands. He wasn't sure it would see another season; it had been repaired so many times. Nat Turner slid the collar over her ears and into place against her breast. "Steady, now."

It had been more than twenty years since they had played the swashbuckling games as boys. But he could still smell the grass, mixed with wild onions, and feel the warmth of the sun on his face.

"GET OFF MY brother!" Little Nathaniel Francis swiped at Nat Turner with his tiny sword. "Get off my brother!"

Nat Turner laughed. "Surrender, you Virginians! You are defeated!"

"Get off my brother!"

"The British have won!"

Salathiel pushed him off, and Nat Turner fell to the deck, laughing. "The British have won!"

Salathiel was no longer smiling. "The British can't win." He stood to his feet—one good foot and a peg leg.

"We already won!" Nat danced about, waving his sword in the air. He reached for Gray's hand and Hark's hand and pulled them to their feet.

"I said," Salathiel said pointedly, "the British cannot win."

Nat Turner held on to the game, held on to the ship, the sea, and the blue sky. He was not going to see this game end like all the other games. The British had won, and he would not give up the victory. Nat Turner stepped forward so he was only inches away from Salathiel's chest.

Off to the side, Richard Whitehead began to whoop, waving his sword in the air. "We won! We have to win. It is history!"

John Clarke Turner waved his sword. "You were defeated before we started." The mast crumpled and the sail disappeared. The deck vaporized under their feet.

"But we won!" Nat Turner would not back down. He looked to the sky for the seagulls. He breathed, hoping for more free salt air.

This was the point he always hated in the games, the point to which things always came—the point where the rules changed so that he could not win. "We won," Nat insisted. "We bested you, and fair is fair."

"You cannot win. We always win."

They were in the clearing again. Virginia had returned and, again, they were in Southampton. Nat drew back his fist.

Thomas Gray caught it. "You win," he said to Salathiel, then he looked at Nat to remind him. "It was a good battle. Good sport. What difference does it make? It's just a game."

Nat Turner looked at Gray's hand on his arm and then at

both his friends. He and Hark were shoeless, dressed in rags again. Their sticks were lying on the ground. He was tired of backing down, tired of playing games whose end he could see from the beginning.

"It was an excellent battle," Gray said to placate the other boys. He stuck out his hand to Salathiel.

The taller boy stared between Gray's hand and Nat Turner. The patch was gone from his eye. He frowned at Nat and then, reluctantly, shook Gray's hand. A smile crept across his face, the same smile as before. His game continued. He looked at his younger brother. "Corporal, arrest the prisoners."

"The battle is over." Gray nodded. "Let's head back."

"The battle is not over yet; there are always the spoils." Salathiel pointed at Gray and Phipps, who had finally come from behind his tree. "You two can go free, but these two," he pointed at Nat and Hark, "will be slaves."

Nat Turner clenched his jaw and gritted his teeth. He lunged at Salathiel, but Hark and Gray held his arms. It wasn't fair. It wasn't fair not to even let him make believe.

Salathiel taunted him. "Let him go. Let him try it. I'll break every bone in his body. Then we will strip the skin right off of what's left."

Nat struggled against his friends. He was willing to lose to Salathiel in a fair fight; it would be worth it. But just once he needed the game to conclude without them twisting the end.

"It's not worth it, Nat," Hark whispered in his ear. "Let it go."

Salathiel looked at Gray and Phipps. "You two may join us." He stepped around Nat Turner and raised his sword. He tapped his blade on Phipps's and Gray's shoulders. "You, sirs, are now Virginians." He nodded at his little brother and then at Gray and Phipps. "Help the corporal take the prisoners." He turned from them and slapped Nat.

The slap stung his face and brought water to his eyes, but he would not cry. Salathiel slapped him again. Blood trickled from

Nat's nose. He knew what Salathiel was saying. He was reminding him who he was, that he was a slave and not a boy. Salathiel was reminding him that even in play, he was a slave. He was reminding him that the rules to the game had been written before both of them were born, and that even at play, he was superior. Only Salathiel could call the end and the finish to the game.

Games were never games; they were always teaching lessons. Watch what you say, watch what you do, and don't try to win—because you could be beaten, taken away to some torture, some cruelty you could not imagine. Winning, they were teaching him, would bring him only trouble; when he was about to win, they wanted him to be afraid and surrender the victory.

They were teaching him. He had learned that white was a frightening color. In the middle of the night, some large, rough white hand might cover his mouth and drag him from his mother. He could imagine the hand that would take him and the sadness in her eyes. She had lost her country, her culture, her esteem among them, had lost her family, and a daughter she could not bear to mention. It would kill her if she lost him. One wrong word to their whiteness—not their boyishness, but their whiteness—and he might cause his mother to die.

One wrong word, one wrong move, and his mother—the one who held him, who kissed him, who told him stories—might be dragged away screaming, bound in chains. They were teaching him to live each day worrying that his only family might be spirited away. Then he would be like the others with ghost eyes saying he had seen her no more in this lifetime—their only hope of reunion would be resurrection after death.

They were teaching him to never think or speak or act without thinking two, three, four times. They were teaching him when he saw whiteness to censor and measure every word. They were teaching him that no game was a game; his life always hung in the balance, and they could take away everything based on one movement or word.

John Clarke Turner was teaching him that though they shared a father, they were not brothers. Along with the others, he was teaching him that their whiteness, their loyalty to their tribe, transcended any friendship or relation. John Clarke was the son to go to picnics and to be held up in the sun. John Clarke was the white one who had freedom of speech. John Clarke was the son bequeathed liberty.

John Clarke was teaching Nat Turner that—despite what their father promised—he would grow up to be his brother's slave. When they would become men he would whip him; the law would help and put him in chains.

John Clarke was teaching him, showing him in front of the others, that he was the one who mattered. All his father's dreams were for John Clarke Turner. There were no dreams of what Nat Turner would become. Even if their father at night brought Nat Turner sweets, publicly he would deny his paternity. Nat Turner's whiteness brought him nothing—mixed with even a drop of blackness, his whiteness did not exist.

They were teaching him that their forefathers across the ocean were worth more than his. Their ancestors were treasure and they took them out to show off and to play with. They made crests and held parades. But his black ancestors were stinking refuse and he should hide them away. His forefathers swung from trees, cannibals, heathen. They were teaching him to resent the black—his hair, his skin, his eyes, his heart, his spirit—within him. It was the cursed blackness that kept him from winning.

They were all learning. They were learning to choose sides. They were learning to choose tribes. No game was just a game. They were teaching him the lessons all black children silently learned in the "land of the free."

Salathiel nodded at Gray. "Secure the prisoners."

On the way back, Nat Turner and Hark walked ahead, their arms behind them as though they were bound. Little Nathaniel Francis walked behind, prodding them and flailing them with his switch. He walked next to Gray, who pretended to hold their chains. When they stepped out of the forest, Cherry was still there waiting, her tattered shirttail in her hand.

February 1831

IT WAS A clear but cold February day and frost blew from Nat Turner's nose and the mare's. He attached the hames while Hark offered the animal a handful of oats.

"Awful quiet today, Nat. Even for you."

Nat Turner nodded to his friend, uncertain how to respond.

In the midst of his certainty, he was unsure. It had been ten years since his return from the Dismal Swamp and he still waited for a sign. It had been so long that sometimes he doubted his memories. Maybe it was all in his imagination.

Things still went on the same. People were beaten and still heartbroken. Summer and winter still came and went. There had been years of corn in the fields, but Nat Turner had seen no battles—the sun had not darkened and the moon still gave her light.

Perhaps, like a merciful father, God had changed His mind. After all, the captors were also His children and He also loved them. What torment it must be for a parent to have to destroy one child to rescue another.

The truth was Nat Turner loved those he was preparing to kill. There seemed to be no choice: to save one brother he would have to pass judgment on another. So he prayed for mercy on them in the same breath he prayed for their destruction.

But when he awakened this morning, he had seen an eagle circling overhead. Nat Turner remembered an old circuit rider telling him it was an omen, a symbol of resurrection.

Though he still smiled and joked, Hark had seemed more thoughtful since Nat Turner's return from the Great Dismal. It was as though his friend sensed something. "Why you suppose

God put us here? If God loves us so much, why are we treated like animals? If Africa is where we are from, why didn't He leave us in Africa?"

Even after the vision in the Great Dismal Swamp, even after returning, Nat Turner had not wanted to believe that this was his fate. He had not wanted to believe that God's judgment began with the families he knew, with the church that bore his father's name. But it was no accident, then, that his mother had been brought to Southampton County against her will. It was no accident that his father named him Nathan, after a prophet of old. It was no accident that he was born just beyond a town called Bethlehem that was on the road to Jerusalem, Virginia.

Nat Turner nodded. He stroked the horse's mane. Soon he would not see the creature again. "Wherever there are greedy men, they will find the ones others think are least to misuse for their profit.

"But what men see as worthless, God sees as treasure. And who knows but that our suffering is a sign of God's favor." Nat Turner stroked the horse again.

"But why is it that the black man is chosen to suffer?"

"We are not alone. Look at our Nottoway brothers. Maybe we are here to teach. The Bible is born of Eastern men—of our forefathers around the Red Sea and the Mediterranean—those who were first part of the Great Church—and it is full of Oriental thought. We know He is a living God, a God of power, a God of miracles, and we know He hears us."

Hark scoffed. "Oriental thought? I was born and raised in Virginia."

"We have been gone from our homeland for generations, but the thoughts and ways of our forefathers still live within us—share with your brother, honor your elders, sacrifice this life for a better life after. The truth is in our hearts, the fire burns in our bones. It seems to me the captors read the Bible with frozen hearts."

Hark listened, but he did not answer.

"Even if I lose my life in this world, eternally it is for my good. This life is just the beginning and we are promised something greater—that is what my ancestors taught. We are willing to be last because we believe the promise that one day we will be first.

"We are willing to suffer in this world in hope of a better after-life. That is the lesson taught us by our fathers, by our ancestors, a thought buried in the Eastern heart. Our troubles have made us forget who we are.

"Sometimes I believe God sent us on this journey. He knew it would be an arduous voyage, a life-or-death struggle—most would not survive—so God only sent the strongest, those He knew could endure. He sent us, the best of us, as part of the First Great Church. Perhaps He sent us here to teach what was taught to us by those who came before us—to teach of caring for one's brothers more than for one's self. He knew He was sending us into the hands of a great enemy, but perhaps we are here to teach about love."

He had known and trusted Hark almost all his life and he wanted to tell him about the vision in the Great Dismal Swamp. He wanted to tell Hark about the mission ahead of him. But it was not time yet. Nat Turner waited for the sign.

Chapter 18

Hark was Nat Turner's friend, his best friend. Hark and the others were his people, God's people, and he had come back for them.

When he was a boy of ten, his father had promised Nat Turner his freedom and promised to make him a trustee in the church his father donated land for, the church he planned to build: Turner's Meeting Place. "You are the smart one, Nathan. You have the gift for numbers. You are a boy, but I would trust you to manage the books for this farm even now," his father told him. "You are the devout one and I think it is only fair."

His father did not say explicitly that his freedom and the trusteeship were payment for his silence, but Nat always felt they were. His sisters never guessed—they did not want to know—but John Clarke resented Nat Turner's paternity and their shared fraternity. He resented the relationship. He resented that their father intended to free Nat. He resented that Nat Turner's name—Nathan Turner—was added to the Turner's Meeting Place deed.

But Nat Turner dreamed that one day he would replace the small wooden church his father planned with a cathedral like the ones his mother had told him were spread throughout the ancient Ethiopian city of Lalibela.

Nat Turner had never owned anything of his own except his Bible. There was nothing for him to leave behind. But in the deed, the church and the land were given to the trustees and their heirs forever. The trusteeship was something he could hand down to his children.

It had been something of a scandal when Old Benjamin listed

Nat Turner's name first, as trustee. It was irreverent and illegal, some said, to list his name at all.

The Southampton County clerk, along with witnesses, had come to the farm and insisted on speaking with Elizabeth, Old Benjamin's wife, alone before they would witness the document.

Persimmon-faced over her husband's humiliating indiscretion, Elizabeth told the visitors she grudgingly approved—she would not go against her husband—but hoped to die before the shame came to pass. Some people said it was the disgrace of it that eventually killed her.

Old Benjamin had thought he would live to see not only the land cleared and the church built but also to see Nat Turner grow to manhood. Benjamin Turner had thought he would live to see Nat Turner manumitted, quietly, so the state could not interfere. Perhaps it was Old Benjamin's way of atoning eternally for the shame he had caused Nancie, Nat Turner's mother. Old Benjamin thought he might live to see Nat Turner become a Methodist bishop like Richard Allen.

Old Benjamin lived to see the church built and saw to it that Nat received what his father called "proper Methodist instruction." He saw to it that his son was referred to as Nat Turner, as a human being and not an animal.

Benjamin Turner lived to see the building dedicated by a circuit-riding Methodist preacher.

Nat Turner listened to the teachings of the circuit riders. He studied the Discipline, the Twenty-Five Articles of Religion, and the tenets of Methodism. He learned the Methodist history of Francis Asbury and Thomas Coke. He studied the writings of John Wesley and memorized the words, the words to John Wesley's prayer.

O thou God of love, thou who art loving to every man, and whose mercy is over all thy works; thou who art the Father of the spirits of all flesh, and who art rich in mercy unto all; thou who hast mingled of one blood all the nations upon earth; have compassion upon these outcasts of men, who are trodden down as dung upon the earth! Arise, and help these that have no helper, whose blood is spilt upon the ground like water! Are not these also the work of thine own hands, the purchase of thy Son's blood? Stir them up to cry unto thee in the land of their captivity; and let their complaint come up before thee; let it enter into thy ears! Make even those that lead them away captive to pity them, and turn their captivity as the rivers in the south. O burst thou all their chains in sunder; more especially the chains of their sins! Thou Saviour of all, make them free, that they may be free indeed!

He prayed the prayers himself. "Oh Lord, turn our captivity and make us free indeed! Do great things among us so that even the heathen will see. Send us, Lord, a deliverer!"

When his father had told him about the church, about Turner's Meeting Place, he had believed that all things were possible. His father had dreamed that it would be like Nimmo United Methodist Church in Virginia Beach, where Negroes would be allowed to worship inside, along with the white people.

His father promised him that one day he might be a leader in Turner's Meeting Place and reminded Nat again that he might even be a black man leading white men, a great man like Richard Allen.

Bishop Richard Allen had been a slave and he had studied the Bible. His master had allowed him to attend the local Methodist church. Allen was so bright, it was said, that he soon became a leader—a slave sometimes teaching among black and white people.

Allen bought his own freedom. When some whites later objected to Negroes sitting with them in church and wanted to segregate, Allen led the black people out of the church. Ordained by Bishop Francis Asbury, Allen started the African Methodist Episcopal Church and became the first black bishop.

A circuit rider told Nat that Bishop Allen lived in Philadelphia, and Nat Turner hoped to be like him. He dreamed of traveling to meet him.

A black leader? A black church? It had seemed impossible and Nat Turner had wondered if the circuit rider was joshing him.

But, as proof, his father had driven him one Sunday past Emanuel African Methodist Episcopal Church in Portsmouth. "Don't ever tell the others I brought you here, Nathan. My children, my family, they would object. It would only cause needless confusion. You know."

Nat Turner had been stunned. Negroes, black people like him, milled around the church. It was true. There was really a Richard Allen. And he could be like him. He could be a trustee in his father's church.

His father showed him the deed and pointed out his name. "This is yours, Nathan. And, should you have children, it will pass from generation to generation. No one can take it from you. And if I don't survive, your eldest brother, Samuel, has promised to free you when it is safest, when you are twenty-one."

Nat Turner's father lived to see the small church full of people, black and white, though the blacks—slave and free—had to sit on the back pews or stand in the back of the tiny sanctuary. Nat Turner rode in the back of the wagon following the family carriage when Old Benjamin and the rest of his family went to visit the Nimmo United Methodist Church in Virginia Beach. He still remembered the whitewashed walls and the high-backed wooden pews. He had sat in the balcony there with the other blacks and looked down on his father, brothers, and sisters below.

Benjamin thought he would live, but no man can be certain of the day of his demise. Despite his plans, Old Benjamin passed away while Nat Turner was still a boy.

Perhaps Elizabeth had extracted a secret promise from her first son, Samuel, and his wife, also named Elizabeth, to never let the wicked offense come to pass. As executor of his father's will, Samuel announced, "I promised my mother. None of it will ever come to pass!"

OLD BENJAMIN THOUGHT he would live to see it all. The afternoon of his burial, the people in the church—Nat Turner's brother Samuel, and the others named on the deed, his father's friends—made a pact.

Nat Turner had stood outside the window that afternoon when he was twelve years old. His older brother Samuel and Samuel's wife, Elizabeth, were in their twenties. The other trustees and their wives, who advised Samuel, were closer to their father's age.

Samuel Turner led the meeting. The other trustees—Samuel Francis, John Whitehead, and Turner Newsom—and their wives gathered in the church to agree that Nat Turner would never have what legally belonged to him.

"He was an old man," Samuel Turner said of his father.

"Feeble," John Whitehead, sitting in the church on the first pew, added. Since Old Benjamin had died, no black people had been allowed in the church. They were not even welcomed any longer to stand behind the back row.

"In his right mind, Old Benjamin would never want to bring this kind of shame upon his family . . . not for a slave," Turner Newsom added.

"It doesn't just shame his wife and family; it shames our church and the whole community! Who ever heard of such a thing, making a slave, a darkie, a trustee?" Brown-haired Caty Whitehead fanned herself.

Samuel's wife, Elizabeth Turner, shook her head. "It shames you, my husband, as well as your dear mother. I always thought it was a shame Old Benjamin let the darkies sit inside the church with us anyway. It gave them the wrong notion.

"Whatever was your father thinking? And he listed that wretch's name first—even before yours!"

Samuel Francis turned the screw as he did with his own sons, Salathiel and Nathaniel. "Nat Turner is not only a darkie, but he is a child! Why would Old Benjamin put him first? Was he saying that Nat was smarter than his own, John Clarke, and even you, Samuel? If Old Benjamin wanted to name a boy trustee, why not John Clarke Turner? Poor John's name does not even appear on the deed!"

Samuel Francis's wife sniffled. "Did Old Benjamin really think so little of us?"

"God could never have wanted this." Samuel Francis tapped a finger on the deed.

His wife began to cry. "How could Old Benjamin even think to sit us under a son of Ham?"

Samuel Turner looked pained, humiliated by his father's actions. Turner Newsom's eyes were full of empathy. "How could he have thought that white men and white women would sit under the direction of a jig?"

John Whitehead's face reddened. "Do you think he really believed it, really intended it? It's as ridiculous as thinking a white man would sit under a black preacher."

Mrs. Whitehead nodded. "That would be a devilish thing." She fanned herself again. "We shouldn't even have to have this dreadful conversation. Can you imagine a darkie trustee advising a white preacher? It would be appalling!" She sputtered and huffed.

Almost more to herself than to the others, she added, "I had always imagined my young son, Richard, a preacher. Who would give such authority to a slave?"

Mrs. Francis began to cry harder. "How could I let my children—Wiley, Salathiel, Sallie, and Nathaniel—attend here?" Her face clouded. "That darkie Nancie, do you think she might have used some sort of black magic she brought here from Africa?"

Samuel Turner, boyish and shamefaced, looked at the older woman.

Nat Turner ducked beneath the window that afternoon so

they would not see him. He had known these people all his life.
They had patted his head. They had said he was too smart to be a
slave, and they had acted as though they cared for him. They had
said he knew the Bible better than anyone. Now, in God's house,
they were stealing what was his.

When his father was alive, they had told his father that Nat
Turner was so intelligent that he was a mystery to them. Now they
were stealing his birthright.

He was the one who had studied the Bible. He was the one
who knew chapter and verse. *Turn again our captivity, O LORD, as
the streams in the south. They that sow in tears shall reap in joy. He
that goeth forth and weepeth, bearing precious seed, shall doubtless
come again with rejoicing, bringing his sheaves with him.*

THEY HATED TO go against Old Benjamin's wishes, but it was
best for everyone. Benjamin was tenderhearted and deluded. Now
things would change.

Negroes were banned completely from Turner's Meeting Place.
And Nat Turner? It was best for the community, and even best for
Nat Turner, to correct things now.

It was against God's laws, wasn't it, for a slave to manage a
church's money and land? What did a slave know about such things?

Twelve years old. There was no point in setting him to a task at
which he could never succeed. How could a black man lead white
men? If they left him to it, he would probably destroy himself as
well as the church. Better to correct matters now so that by the
time he reached twenty-one, he would be acclimated.

They decided that afternoon: Nat Turner would be neither
free nor trustee. Better to set him, then and there, to his rightful
place—a place where he would be happy and content with his life.
Samuel Turner agreed. Nat Turner would be turned out into the
fields.

"What must we do to correct the deed? I suppose we must
take the matter to the county clerk."

Turner Newsom had shaken his head. "Nothing needs be done. No court would hear his claim."

Samuel Turner assured them Nat would never protest. That afternoon Samuel began to call Nat Turner "slave." "The slave's only defense would be to call reputations into question. He would not do that to my departed father. He would not do that to my sisters or my brothers."

Samuel Turner was right in how he judged his younger brother. That afternoon and forward, Nat Turner participated in the lie. He participated with his silence. It shamed him—every day it shamed him more. But they were his sisters and they were his brothers. It was his duty to protect them, to protect the image of his father, even if he caused injury to himself.

They were his father's white sons and daughters, all claimed, but not he. He could not help but wonder what other things his father had not shared with him. What could his father not tell him because he could not face who Nathan Turner was?

It did not matter to his father how he felt; it was Nat Turner's duty to bear it. He was slave even to his father. He was a thing. He did not need to be included.

In short order, his brother sent him, at twelve years old, to the fields as his slave.

Still, Nat Turner prayed and hoped his older brother would keep his promise and free him. Years passed and every day he worked, every day he planned to leave.

Then Cherry happened. He settled in and they married. They had a son, Riddick. Nat Turner gave up thoughts of leaving; it would be enough to be a freeman.

On his twenty-first birthday, Nat Turner confronted his brother.

Chapter 19

It was impudent, Samuel Turner said, for a slave to demand to be free, to demand inheritance.

"I am a free man, Samuel! Give me my papers and my copy of the deed! You promised our father when he died!"

His older brother Samuel struck him. "Liar!"

Nat Turner was never supposed to speak the words. He was supposed to keep up pretenses, to keep his father's secret. No one was to know—except poor Samuel, who was to bear the eldest son's burden. Except for Elizabeth and John Clarke . . . all of them pretending not to know.

Nat was to deny who he was before his father's wife, before his sisters Nancy and Susanna, his brother John Clarke, and his baby brother, Benjamin. "I beg you to repent and give me my freedom, my trusteeship. Please . . . brother." Samuel struck him again.

Two more years passed. When his eldest brother lay dying, Nat Turner was certain that Samuel would repent and free him. Called to his sickbed, Samuel whispered in Nat Turner's ear, "Your mother, your family is free. You were never my property. You were always a free man."

Samuel's will bore no mention of Nathan, Cherry, or his mother, Nancie, as property. His family was free! He was a free man!

Chapter 20

But Samuel's wife, the second Elizabeth, had other plans.

Still in widow's weeds, Elizabeth Turner stopped Nat Turner on his way to the fields. "They treated you too kindly, like a family member and not as the slave you are," she snarled. "But now your fate is in my hands." She motioned to the man beside her. "I have sold you this day to this fine gentleman, Thomas Moore." She pointed and sneered behind her veil.

Nat Turner opened his mouth to protest. But disbelief left him stunned, mute.

He was a freeman. How could this be happening? His brother's widow had no right to sell him. She had not been bequeathed Cherry, his mother, Nancie, or him and his son.

She snarled at him. "Not one word! Not one, Nat!"

"Nat Turner," he insisted.

"I said, 'Nat'! And if you make things difficult, if you run, I will sell your mother away." She waved the handkerchief in her hand. Elizabeth had sold him to a man without scruples. "And you needn't worry about your wife, Cherry. I've made arrangements for her also. She and your son will become the property of Giles Reese.

"It was hardly worth the bother. Less than one hundred dollars for both of them."

Nat Turner pleaded with Thomas Moore to purchase his wife also. He would live as a slave. Nat Turner and Cherry would both be his slaves, if they could be together.

Thomas Moore shrugged. "The arrangements have already been made."

One hundred dollars. Even old people and children brought more than one hundred dollars. Elizabeth Turner could have given Cherry to Moore for nothing or sold her to him as a breeder.

But Elizabeth Turner was making a point about who was master and who was property. She despised Nat Turner—who he was, who God had made him. She hated him because Old Benjamin had dared to list him first—Nathan Turner before Samuel Turner, before her husband—on the church-house deed.

The order lessened her, along with her husband, and their standing in the community. Through the sale Elizabeth Turner was simply correcting things. "Stay in your place," she told him.

She was sending the white men of Southampton a message: There were rules that even white men had to obey. There was a certain divine order. Slavery and life favored white men and there were certain indignities white women had to bear. But no white woman would stand for such public shame and humiliation. There was an order and everyone had to play his or her part. No white man, no matter how bewitched he was, had better put a black bastard before any of his lawful white children. Elizabeth Turner simply set things to right.

She was sending Nat Turner's mother a message. Old Benjamin was gone now and Nancie had no voodoo magic, no womanly magic, that could control Elizabeth Turner. The entire Turner family had been shamed long enough—all because of Nancie's darkie bastard.

Elizabeth Turner would sell Nat Turner away—out of sight, out of mind, almost as though he never existed. But not too far— she wanted to enjoy his pain. She would sell him to a man who held him in no special esteem—who was not enthralled with his reading, his writing, or his gift for language. Then, to seal it, she would sell his wife to a man who wanted to breed her.

Nat Turner was strong-willed and he would find a way to make peace with being sold. But losing Cherry would bring him to his knees. Alone, each day he slaved he would be reminded of his place in civilized society.

Elizabeth wanted him to obey the rules. She wanted him to be who she thought him to be. She needed to affirm that she was naturally better and more powerful.

Nat Turner was not a man; he was property. He was not a trustee. He had no right to a church—he was forbidden to even enter. He had no right to a wife or to a marriage. She needed him to know—he would never be anything but a slave. Cherry's sale would teach him.

Elizabeth Turner was right. It was not the plow or the rod that broke him. It was losing Cherry and his son.

Chapter 21

Nat Turner pleaded with the people he knew. There was no other choice; there was no refuge in the courts for him—no court would hear a black man's case against a white woman or man. No court would listen to his protests that he and his family were free people forced into slavery.

He would have been able to endure if Elizabeth Turner had only enslaved him, but she had also stolen Cherry. How could she sell free people, people she couldn't even pretend to own? He pled his case to each of the Turner's Meeting Place trustees individually—the Whiteheads, the Newsoms, the Francises.

He pleaded when he saw them on the roads. He walked to their farms. He called to them as they rushed into church. He was free, and they and their families all knew it. They knew his father's plans. But they turned their heads the other way.

Losing his wife was the worst of it.

Nat Turner had hoped that no one would notice Cherry, would not notice their love and take her away.

But Elizabeth Turner had told Giles Reese about her. She had planted Cherry in his head. Giles Reese saw all he needed to see; he saw that Cherry could bear children and that Elizabeth Turner was almost giving her away.

When he came to fetch her and saw Nat Turner, Giles Reese saw more. He saw what only Nat Turner before then had seen. He saw that Cherry was a river; life was on her shores. He saw that Cherry was Nat Turner's wings and spirit, and that by taking her, Reese and the others could break Nat's heart and bring Nat Turner back to earth.

Giles Reese bought her—though he knew she was free and not for sale—and Nat Turner's son was thrown into the bargain. Giles Reese didn't need her. She was a nice-to-have. Then Giles Reese, when he was closer to her, recognized that she was beautiful and he wanted her. There was life in Cherry and Giles Reese wanted to live.

Nat Turner watched them being taken away. He had no gun. He had no law and no sheriff to call. There was no army. He balled his hands into fists. His nails lanced his palms, causing them to bleed.

He had promised his son things would be different. But he had lied. He was one man against an army, a government. How could he make things different?

Giles Reese loaded them on the wagon. There were tears in Cherry's eyes. She looked away. Nat Turner's son reached back for him. He struggled on his mother's lap. Riddick kept reaching for him—small hands, pleading brown eyes.

"Daddy?" First a question. Then as they pulled farther down the road, the word became a shriek. "Daddy! Daddy!"

He had made Riddick a promise to protect him, to give him a better life. How could he hold his head up in front of his son? How could any captive man hold up his head?

Chapter 22

Cross Keys, Virginia
February 1831

Nat Turner stroked the horse's mane before placing the bit in its mouth. When the horse was bridled and hitched and the wagon was readied, Nat Turner helped Sallie Francis Moore Travis aboard. She was on her way to a Valentine's Day party at the Whiteheads'.

They traveled down the road with no name and past Giles Reese's farm, where Cherry lived now. Anxiously, she prattled behind him, speaking more to herself than to him.

At night sometimes he dreamed of rescuing his wife and son. He dreamed of his hands wrapped around Giles Reese's throat.

If any man had touched his wife, Reese would have gone insane. Other white men would have thought Reese justified for shooting someone who tried to steal his wife. They would have joined Reese in gutting the thief, hanging him, castrating him, and worse. So sometimes at night Nat Turner dreamed the same dreams and woke with broken straw gripped tight in his fists.

He looked toward the Giles Reese farm and would not allow himself to turn away. He made himself feel it—the shame, the rage, the anger, the betrayal—so he would be one with every other man who suffered, every black man who for generations had had his wife, his family stolen away. He would not allow himself to hide from the suffering. In the past, he had been carving peace for himself by not feeling, but now he opened his heart and mind to it. He forced himself to feel it now and to remember.

Chapter 23

Cross Keys
1821

Every ominous thought, everything he could imagine crowded in on Nat Turner. Losing his family hurt as badly as he imagined it would in the days when he vowed to stay alone. It tormented him to think of his family held captive, of his wife lawfully raped by another man.

After Cherry was gone, Nat Turner was obsessed with her.

In the darkness, he crept to Giles Reese's farm, where he watched outside Cherry's window. Sometimes he stole nearer and gazed at her lying on her bed. He told himself he must stay away.

He was sad, he was angry, and then he felt betrayed—betrayed by Cherry because she stayed with Giles Reese. Nat Turner knew there was nothing she could do, no place she could go. He knew she did not love the man but had no choice. He knew Giles Reese did not love her, and that compounded the damage done.

How could it be that a man who did not love her could tell him, her husband, *when* he could see Cherry or *if* he could see her at all? It tore at his insides that men who would kill a man for looking at their wives or daughters were now laughing about Giles Reese's association with Cherry. Now Nat Turner had to ask their permission.

Nat Turner was tormented thinking of it. Reese had discussions with Moore over whether the two of them would be generous enough to allow Nat Turner to visit his wife and son. The two of them—Reese and Moore—would laugh about what Reese now knew about her—"she has a spider on her back"—and then give permission.

Reese would not even lower himself to speak to Nat Turner man-to-man. Instead, Moore would pass the word to Nat Turner second- or thirdhand. "On Sundays you may see her, if Reese doesn't have her otherwise busy." Because he was not a man, in their eyes, they took his wife and son so he would know it, too.

It was not Cherry's fault, but he could not help but feel betrayed. She was the weapon they used against him. Betrayed by her. Betrayed by God.

God had put Cherry before him, had made him love her, only to allow Giles Reese to steal her away. He had not asked God for her. He had wanted to be alone. He had not wanted a wife or a child. He had not wanted to be in love. He had taken a vow. He had resisted it. But he had heard God whispering to him to open, to love her.

Nat Turner ran into the woods deep enough that only the trees could hear him. Even there he would not allow himself to cry or scream. He plowed his fist into a large cypress to dull the pain.

He did not ask for this life for himself, but he had not complained. He had managed the life and the burden, the debt that he'd been given. But now the pain was unbearable.

Now the grief of who he was and where he was, of his condition, pushed him to rage. He rolled in the dirt, in the marshy, decayed leaves of old winters that lay on the ground. His anguish was wild and heavy in his bosom, a feral beast that rent his guts.

How could he look at her, his eyes saying to hers that he could not save her? He could not visit his son in shame. He could not settle for this. He could not visit them pretending to be contented. He was useless to them, dead to them. He could not bear for his wife and his son to see his humiliation, to see that this was the kind of man—one in form but not in spirit—that white men had made him.

Where was God?

Nat Turner ran until he came to the pond and he dived in, still wearing his clothes. He didn't want to feel anymore. He didn't want to live.

His head parted the water.

Before his feet submerged, Nat Turner had a plan.

Chapter 24

He would leave. There was no way he could see his wife sold and made to be another man's concubine and call himself a man. Nat Turner didn't want to be the kind of man who gave up his manhood just to survive. He didn't want Cherry to become the kind of wife who smiled when he was looking but frowned when he turned away. He would leave Southampton County; he had no choice.

The captors said there was no such thing as black love—husbands did not love wives, fathers did not love children, and brothers did not love sisters. Blacks were no more than dogs, or rooting pigs.

He had no choice but to leave. He had gone along with the charade long enough—too long. He had given up freedom to stay with his family. But no longer—he would simply walk away. No one could come after him. No one could produce ownership papers that said he or she owned him.

Before he left Cross Keys, Nat Turner wrote himself a pass so if anyone stopped him as a slave, he would have written permission to travel. Though whoever stopped him would most likely not be literate, a written pass looked official enough that he would not be challenged as a runaway.

Nat Turner dressed in a pair of worn pants, a shirt, a pair of his father's shoes that he had hidden away. He never wore them in public, fearing they would be taken from him. But now he wore them and dressed in a coat and hat that had been his father's and made his way on foot south and east forty miles to the Great Dismal Swamp.

Nat Turner did not say good-bye. He pulled his collar up around his ears and lowered his head, slinging his small bundle over his shoulder, his axe stuck through it.

Presidents had already visited the swampland—Washington and Monroe—but the Great Dismal had defied them. President George Washington had thought to earn money from the area by controlling the planned waterway, harvesting trees, and exploiting other resources there. They had used slaves to do the dirty work. But his efforts brought little success.

The Great Dismal was a mysterious place and everyone around had heard the rumors. The swamp was filled with escaped slaves who could not be tracked or found in the tropical forest.

Animals and insects were there that civilized men had never seen before. It was said that the trees talked and at night the water whispered. White men died of diseases there—all nature seemed to conspire against them.

People told stories of whole families of black people who had escaped and found a way to be free in the Great Dismal Swamp. The slaves who holed up there, it was said, were desperate, angry, ready to die—ruthless avengers who would kill a white man sooner than look him in the eye. Some lived there permanently, but for others it was a temporary refuge. Nat Turner knew that if he made it there, no white man from Southampton County would enter the swamp to search for him.

He wanted to hide where he could be swallowed into darkness, into a place of great sadness.

When he traveled previously—when it was winter, so there was little farmwork, and he was hired out to repair mills—Nat Turner always carried his Bible, the one his father had given him. Who knew when God would give him a word for the people? He had preached all over the area, like a Methodist circuit rider, even as far away as Norfolk. But this time he left the book behind.

He pulled his hat snug on his head so no one would notice

the curls in his hair. Head down, he walked quickly, like a man who had business to attend to. But not so quickly he would attract attention.

He was fair enough that, at a distance, passersby might think he was a white man. He would have even more chance of not being discovered if he traveled by night.

As Nat Turner walked, he heard Sister Easter—a captive on Nathaniel Francis's farm. He heard her voice singing to him.

> In the word of God
> I got a hiding place.

He needed a hiding place. Nat Turner was desperate for a place where he could hide from his troubles, from his thoughts.

> In the word of God
> I got a hiding place.
> Throw me overboard
> I got a hiding place.

The Great Dismal Swamp would be his place of escape—his Hebron, his city of refuge. It would swallow him and he would hide forever.

Chapter 25

Nat Turner shook the reins and clicked his tongue at the red mare. As they rode past, he forced himself to look at Giles Reese's farm, at the place where Cherry was held captive.

There was an old oak tree not far from Giles Reese's farm, only noticeable in the winter. In the spring, the leaves from the other trees camouflaged it. But in the winter it stood alone. Its girth was more than six men around and its roots must have reached to the center of the earth.

Nat Turner looked at the tree and wondered at all it had seen—the native people, the white man's coming, skirmishes for the land, and the enslavement of God's people. Before he had noticed only the oak's bark, its shedding of leaves—the physical suffering. But now he saw underneath, he saw the flesh, the heartbreak.

He saw spirits that panted, barely alive.

He thought then of Hark, of Mother Easter, of his mother and the others. The worst chains weren't on their bodies—those chains could only make them bleed or finally kill them. The most horrible chains were on their hearts and minds, chains they passed to their children.

He felt their doubt, saw their doubt of God's love. He saw the hurt. He felt it twisting their insides and his own. Each feeling was his teacher.

In the wagon behind Nat Turner, Sallie Francis Moore Travis chattered nervously. She was on her way to the Whiteheads to sit among the other white women as they celebrated Valentine's Day. She felt rejected and unwelcome, he knew, but she went anyway. She had been convinced by the others that her clothes and shoes made her a woman. His wife, Cherry, had no fine clothes or shoes. There was no one to braid her hair; she had no ornaments or jewels, but she outshone them all.

But still, Sallie was like the others. The children of scullery maids and porters, the offspring of peasants and serfs, had come to America and reinvented themselves as lords and ladies. They threw lavish parties, bought petticoats and shirts with stiff collars. They built houses and purchased slaves they could not afford: Now they were masters and mistresses. They forced their servants to bow and curtsy to them, to honor them with "yes, ma'am" and "no, sir." Reading and writing were fashionable, but slave ownership not only offered status, it also reassured them. Every insult they or their parents had received, they returned tenfold. They lorded it over those they forced to serve them.

He knew Sallie in the way a captive, the way a pet knows the people with whom it lives. Because those things were considered inferior, the owner's guard was down, and Nat Turner—like the other slaves—had seen it all.

Sallie was a lonely woman. Her brothers and mother treated her as though she were retarded and infirm. In return, to protect herself from their criticism, she sacrificed those who loved her most to the god of her family.

She had once been close friends with Jacob Williams's wife; the two of them visited each other regularly. But when her family was around and Mrs. Williams was not, Sallie offered them parts of her friend. "She is not the best housekeeper." She would giggle. "If you ask me, she drinks too much."

So when Sallie's family saw Mrs. Williams again, they talked down to her and turned their heads away from her. She wasn't good enough for their Sallie—their Sallie was an incompetent idiot, but she belonged to them, and Mrs. Williams wasn't good enough for their Sallie. Soon enough, Mrs. Williams stopped trying.

Sallie wept. She took no responsibility for the death of her friendship; it was just another case of others not loving her enough. She seemed not to understand why things had gone awry.

Now Sallie offered her husband. Her brothers and her mother picked at his bones.

She sat an arm's length from Nat Turner, but Sallie was a world away. She did not see him or the other captives. She did not understand. She could not see the suffering and the despair—she was color-blind.

Nat Turner could not afford the luxury of turning away. He was one of them. He was a captive. They were one.

The captives wondered if there would be anyone to lift up a shield for them. They wondered if God would send someone to lift their heads. Where was God?

Chapter 26

The Great Dismal Swamp
1821

He would never return to Southampton County. Nat Turner walked past great trees—oaks, Virginia pines, cypresses, walnuts, and magnolias—past roads he had never seen before. He could not bear to live in Cross Keys without Cherry and Riddick. The Great Dismal Swamp was days away.

Nat Turner was a hopeless man.

He had never had a complete family. Except for his mother, his African family was lost to him. His American ancestors were never known to him—he was never invited to meet his grandfather, never included in family outings. There were secrets and things given to his white brothers that would never be given to him.

His dreams of education—his labor had paid for a wasted education for his brother John Clarke—of a career, of a farm had been stolen away. To comfort himself, he had buried himself in the leaves and the pages of the Bible. He could not serve in an Ethiopian cathedral or monastery, but he had been promised a place, by his father, in the little country church.

Then that dream had been stolen.

But he had wanted peace, and he had set about making compromises with life. If he could not be a trustee or sit in the church, then he would be a circuit preacher, preaching throughout the countryside to the rejected and despised. He would be like the patriarch Jacob and satisfy himself with the speckled, spotted, and brown sheep. Maybe one day he would travel far enough to Philadelphia to meet Bishop Allen.

He had told himself, before Cherry was stolen, that he would be satisfied with the gift of her love and the gift of his small family. Maybe this was all there was, maybe slavery was God's will for him; some men had cruel fates. Nat Turner would bear up under his. The love of his wife, Cherry, and of his son was God's gift to him and made his existence bearable. Perhaps his dreams were only dreams and God planned no more for him than bondage— with his family as his consolation.

Nat Turner loved his Father. It was not lavish gifts that God said He wanted as proof of His children's love. What God wanted was unyielding obedience. So Nathan Turner had been a most obedient son.

He had obeyed his mother, and to honor God, he had obeyed the earthly masters put over him. He had obeyed the earthly laws—he did not steal, he did not curse, he did not drink. Nathan Turner had obeyed not only the letter but also the heart of God's law—he had loved God with all his heart, soul, and mind. He had loved his neighbors and his brothers—those of all nations and tongues—as he loved himself. He had even given the most difficult obedience: He had loved his enemies. As a son of peace, he had learned to turn the other cheek.

He was God's obedient servant, even if it cost him his dignity. He had obeyed God in laying down his own will and allowing himself to love Cherry. He had laid down his own desires—to own a farm, to be a scientist, to be a bishop, to be treated as an equal. To be a man. He compromised his own desires all for the Father he loved.

In return, God made a promise: *Eye hath not seen, nor ear heard, neither have entered into the heart of man, the things which God hath prepared for them that love Him.*

Nathan Turner had obeyed by love and faith even when it did not seem reasonable to other men. In return for his love and obedience, God had made him a promise.

*Then shall thy light break forth as the morning, and thine health
shall spring forth speedily: and thy righteousness shall go before
thee; the glory of the* Lord *shall be thy reward. Then shalt thou
call, and the* Lord *shall answer; thou shalt cry, and He shall say,
Here I am.*

*If thou take away from the midst of thee the yoke, the put-
ting forth of the finger, and speaking vanity; And if thou draw
out thy soul to the hungry, and satisfy the afflicted soul; then shall
thy light rise in obscurity, and thy darkness be as the noon day:
And the* Lord *shall guide thee continually, and satisfy thy soul in
drought, and make fat thy bones: and thou shalt be like a watered
garden, and like a spring of water, whose waters fail not.*

*And they that shall be of thee shall build the old waste places:
thou shalt raise up the foundations of many generations; and
thou shalt be called, The repairer of the breach, The restorer of
paths to dwell in.*

Now Cherry and Riddick were gone.

Where was God now? Instead of the promises, Nat Turner
had received only sadness and more humiliation. What he got in
return for his love and obedience was the pain of watching his
heavenly Father chase after those who did not love Him. What he
got in return for his obedience was God giving His favor to those
who disobeyed Him, to ones who called themselves master. Nat
Turner could see with his own eyes that God favored the sons who
mocked Him.

No matter how hard he prayed and studied, no matter how
temperate he was, no matter how he turned the other cheek and
forgave others, God did not love him enough to spare him or to
spare his family.

He was alone in the world.

Maybe he had not heard God at all. Maybe all along he had
been deceiving himself. Maybe the One he had loved most in the
world had never loved him.

Abandoned. Betrayed. God had vanished into thin air.

God had been his comfort: There was no big house, no wealth that he could look to for reassurance. All that he had was God, and Nat Turner had given his life to Him. God had been the only Father he could whisper to, the only Father to wrap an arm around his shoulders. God's spirit and His Word had raised him. But now he was alone.

Nat Turner kept from the road and walked among the trees. The shoes were good protection, though he missed the feel of grass beneath his feet.

Maybe he had not heard God at all.

Maybe all along he had been deceiving himself. Doubt. God did not love him—denied by even his heavenly Father. The only Father he had been able to trust, the only Father he could openly claim, had turned His back on him.

Nat Turner had stood up for God and for righteousness because he loved Him. He had spoken the words that God had put in his mouth, and for them he had been beaten and ridiculed. He had stood up for God, but God had not stood up for him.

He was disconsolate. He was forsaken while those who did not love God, who mocked God and disobeyed His Words, prospered. Nat Turner continued walking, head down.

> *Righteous art thou, O* Lord, *when I plead with thee: yet let me talk with thee of thy judgments: Wherefore doth the way of the wicked prosper? Wherefore are all they happy that deal very treacherously?*

Nat Turner paid little attention to the sky or the birds singing around him. Instead, he thought of those he had known all his life, the men and women of Cross Keys—the Francises, the Whiteheads, the Turners. He thought of the ones he had overheard plotting against him in his father's church.

Thou hast planted them, yea, they have taken root: they grow, yea, they bring forth fruit: thou art near in their mouth, and far from their reins.

He thought of the farms they had and the houses they'd built. He thought of the Whiteheads' foolish son, a false prophet, in the pulpit. He thought of the power in Elizabeth Turner's hands—soft hands that had never suffered. She had everything.

The wicked men and women had families and land and no one sold them away, hanged them, or bound them in chains. A wicked man stood in God's pulpit and God did nothing. The wicked ones had murdered their brothers and sisters, sold them into slavery, and even murdered the land with their dreams of cotton's wealth. Those who called themselves masters had committed adultery, raping slaves, and sold their own children away, and still the Lord said nothing.

Nat Turner thought of his mother, Nancie, of Hark, of Easter, of Will, of Berry Newsom, of the Artis brothers, and of all the others who had suffered. It did not seem fair that the ones who believed had nothing to show for their love and their labor. It did not seem just that those who made only a show of God were benefiting while the ones who turned their cheeks suffered. When would God send someone to vindicate them?

All over America, and throughout the world, the false prophets spread hatred. A precious gift of adoration, words of love smeared by power-lust, greed, and bigotry that oozed out of teachers' mouths, dripped from pages as messages of hate. They blamed their wickedness on God. The stink of their lies spread like smoke from a wildfire.

God had turned His back on His darker children. The lighter ones said the proof was in their hands—they owned and controlled everything, including other men. The darker children of the world suffered, crying out, stretching their hands toward heaven.

The wicked ones, the plunderers, beat and murdered and stole and raped in His Name! Where was God? How long would He be silent?

How could anything change without God's intervention? If God didn't move, then faith was for nothing.

> But thou, O LORD, knowest me: thou hast seen me, and tried mine heart toward thee: pull them out like sheep for the slaughter, and prepare them for the day of slaughter. How long shall the land mourn, and the herbs of every field wither, for the wickedness of them that dwell therein?

Then Nat Turner stopped himself. He looked briefly at the sky. God did not hear him. God did not know him. God did not love him; He preferred to prosper the wicked. He preferred to be the God of only white men.

If God turned His back, then Nat Turner would turn his.

He was finished with compromise. He would not pray anymore. He did not want to hear from God. He would find his own way to survive. He would make a life of his own and sail away.

The roads were mostly deserted. No one stopped him.

It took Nat Turner three days to reach the Great Dismal.

I got a hiding place.
Throw me overboard.
I got a hiding place.

He stepped into the forest, and darkness swallowed him.

Chapter 27

It was like the forest he had known all his life. Why would anyone be afraid to set foot there? They were all woodsmen and knew how to wield an axe. Perhaps the stories of the Great Dismal were lies, like all the other lies he had been told.

But as he walked farther in, the trees began to thicken so that there was less light. Tangled, he tripped over roots and had to stop until his eyes adjusted to the darkness.

As he moved even farther in, the trunks of the trees were wider, the leaves denser. The grass and the weeds from the ground seemed to mesh with the tree branches and leaves, almost like a net.

Deeper still, the vines, leaves, and boughs became a wall, and Nat Turner had to hack his way through. The softness of the light that did filter through changed the color of things—so that the trees, the leaves, and the grass darkened in hue. The ground beneath his feet softened, turning to wet sponge, and sucked at his shoes.

The trees engulfed him and gave him refuge. He was more than twenty-one and now, at last, his first taste of freedom. No landmarks. Alone with his thoughts, he walked among the trees, a primordial cathedral.

He smelled green plants, he smelled musk, and then suddenly sweetness. He heard sounds he recognized—the screech of an owl, the scampering of a squirrel up a tree. But he also heard animal calls that he had never heard before—far away—and then just over his head. He heard rustling on the ground beside him and thought he heard wings flapping. Nat Turner gripped his axe tightly.

The trees engulfed him. Nat Turner looked around for a bent

tree or a branch that would orient him, but this was not the forest he knew. There was no way to know left from right, and for all he knew, he was walking in circles. He moved forward, only stopping from time to time so that his eyes could adjust.

He had to hack his way through now, to fight for every inch, had to fight to untangle his feet. The leaves rubbed his face and his hands. He wanted to stop to examine them, to wipe off the moisture and whatever else clung to him. But Nat Turner knew he must keep moving and he knew why white men were afraid.

The Great Dismal Swamp was a dark, wild place, an untamed place, maybe as it was in the Garden of Eden. There was little difference between day and night. He saw plants and shapes he did not recognize. The Dismal was magnificent and menacing.

The swamp seemed to breathe, the air felt as though it was expanding and contracting around him. It was alive, beautiful, but it was dangerous. The trees whispered to one another, and the animals had no fear of man. It was lush and exotic. And he was certain that serpents watched, crawling near each footstep that landed.

He made his way over marshy ground, into deeper greenness that was blackness, until he was in the belly of the swamp. He found comfort in the darkness away from all other men he had known. He found healing in the green, the brown, and the blackness.

In the belly of Hebron he found a clearing. From high overhead, gentle light filtered through the tree boughs and leaves. There were fallen trees waiting for him and he made himself a lean-to shelter. There was a narrow bubbling stream of brown water. The birds sang to him in the morning and frogs croaked and crooned to him at night. There were salt-marsh mallow flowers and morning glories growing wild around him. He had expected to find it all blackness, but he soon adjusted and found that he could see. He used his axe to cut wood and used a flint that he had brought with him and sticks he found to make a fire.

He would follow the old ways, as in Ethiopia. He would fast some days and he would eat no pork.

Nat Turner learned to see.

It was a strange place, but there was comfort for him in the darkness, away from all the others he knew. Healing in the green, the brown, the blackness.

The Great Dismal Swamp was a place of refuge, his Hebron, his hiding place. Nat Turner did not ask God any questions and he ignored the answers that drifted down from the sky, sifting through the leaves and riding to him on the breezes.

At first Nat Turner saw no one else, but in a few days, his eyes and ears acclimated. Again, he learned to see.

Chapter 28

February 1831

When they arrived at the Whitehead farm, Nat Turner looked out at the fields. It was cold, but the captives were still at work—Richard Whitehead's make-work: moving stones and logs. They sang the mournful songs of suffering people, the praise of the brokenhearted.

Just as the sun fought to rise each day, Nat Turner saw the courage of those who worked in the fields. Each morning they rose to bend their backs at work. They prayed to endure and for their suffering to end. Each day they found the courage to find some reason to hope and endure in spite of their circumstances.

Nat Turner pulled the wagon into an open space beside a leafless tree, away from the fancy carriages. "Don't you get into any trouble, now, Nat Turner. You hear me?" Sallie said it loudly to show off to the other white women, so that they could see she had a slave she controlled.

"Yes, ma'am." He helped Sallie from the wagon and then spoke to some of the other captive men gathered at the Whitehead farm, men who had driven the wagons and carriages for their captors.

He saw Yellow Nelson, Hubbard, and Tom. The farms they worked on were far apart and weeks might pass, especially in the winter and during harvest, before they saw one another.

Nat Turner nodded at Mother Easter when he saw her arrive with Lavinia Francis. Another broken heart. He looked at her captor, Lavinia. Two.

But his gaze was drawn back to the fields. The captives sang, but beneath the words and the melody he heard sorrow—and an inexplicable enduring hope. No one sang the story of God's love more than someone despised, grateful for the tiniest sign of God's love. It seemed as though he had seen the same people in the Great Dismal Swamp.

Chapter 29

The Great Dismal Swamp
1821

The runaways, the Maroons in the swamp, were invisible to him at first. Then he began to see other black people—individuals, families, groups—walking by, keeping the silence of the Great Dismal Swamp.

Nat Turner understood as he watched the swamp people moving without sound, without disturbance; they had finally allowed him to see them.

There was a gray-haired man among them who kept his face hidden. The man seldom spoke, only nodded or pointed. He directed Nat Turner to places along the stream where fish waited, ready to be taken. He showed him places to catch small animals for his supper.

The gray-haired man led him through the swamp and showed him the slaves who worked there, chained so they would not escape. There were slaves working even at the edge of the Dismal Swamp and some slavers who made their places there. The man showed him that others, the refugees, the escapees, worked and earned money, no questions asked.

He could use his axe to cut and collect shingles and sell them for a price. The money Nat Turner earned would be his own to use as he pleased.

Soon Nat Turner learned of flatboats that traveled the shallow canal waters carrying goods up and down the Chesapeake. In a short time he talked a boat owner into hiring him. The owner didn't care and didn't want to know whether Nat Turner was a runaway slave. The owner did not even want to know his name.

There was joy for him on the water that splashed his face and wet his feet. He learned quickly, and other boatmen taught him that the Chesapeake Bay flowed into the Atlantic Ocean. Freedom called to him from the water.

The canal water was brown, darker brown than the water that flowed at the stream near where he slept. As he moved along he saw fish leaping from the water, sometimes felt something in the water nudge his boat. Overhead the trees—reaching high into the sky—arched from each shore, joining hands to make a green lace canopy above him.

The flatboat, rising and falling, felt like a living thing beneath his feet. Each journey he took by flatboat, carrying supplies to different places along the Dismal Swamp Canal, Nat Turner poled his way a little farther, a little closer to the bay. Making deliveries along the canal, along the way that led to the bay, he met men who told him how he could go about being hired onto a ship at the bay or in Norfolk. It seemed that the great ships, like the ones he'd dreamed of as a boy, were always looking for hands.

Each day Nat Turner rode the canal was revelation. Each night he fell asleep quickly and refused to listen or pray to God.

IN JUST SHY of a month's time came the opportunity he hoped for, a load that was to be ferried all the way to the bay. Nat Turner forced himself to be calm, so that anyone standing on the shore wouldn't know—wouldn't know that each time he plunged the pole into the water, each time the tip of the pole touched down, each time he pushed against pressure points underneath the currents, he was moving forward and away. He didn't want any casual observers—slavers, slaves, or Maroons—to know that he was inching closer to his dream, to freedom, to Ethiopia.

He wanted observers to look at him and believe it was just another run. It was not an escape, only a delivery. It was a dream he did not want stolen away.

He trembled at his first sight of the Chesapeake Bay. The great expanse opened before him, inviting him to sail away. The water stretched out before him—water that could not be held in place by two shores. The sky arched above him, stretching until it met the water at a distant horizon. He saw them, the great ships, first appearing as dots. Nat Turner had trouble distinguishing them from the land or the water. But as he drew closer, he recognized them.

Chapter 30

The vessels were just as people along the canal had told him. The wharf was crowded with great ships—greater than the ones he had imagined as a boy—with enormous masts like great trees that reached up toward the sky. As large as the ships were, they bobbed in the endless water like leaves on a pond. Sailing to and fro were ships bigger than any house he had ever seen, bigger than five houses. Ships big enough to sail to Philadelphia. Big enough to sail around the world.

Ships big enough to carry him home.

There were ropes and riggings he had not imagined. There were sails that caught the sunlight. Like Southampton breezes fluttering wildflowers, great invisible bay winds effortlessly rippled the immense stretches of canvas. There was a snapping sound like fresh, wet linens hung out to dry, wet sheets snapping in the wind.

Birds cried overhead. He saw black men among white men, brown men, and yellow men, clambering on the ships. He would blend in; others would take no special notice of him.

He paused to listen to the sailors singing.

O Shenandoah! I hear you calling!
Away, you rolling river!
Yes, far away I hear you calling,
Ha, ha! I'm bound away, across the wide Missouri.

My girl, she's gone far from the river,
Away, you rolling river!

An' I ain't goin' to see her never.
Ha, ha! I'm bound away, across the wide Missouri.

Nat Turner breathed in the song. It was a song of freedom. He was bound away.

O Shenandoah! I hear you calling!
Away, you rolling river!
Yes, far away I hear you calling,
Ha, ha! I'm bound away, across the wide Missouri.

He inhaled the air. Sea air. Free air. Nat Turner filled his lungs again and then laughed out loud. Dreaming. His heart pounded. He steadied himself so that in his excitement he would not lose his pole, or his cargo, or his head.

He drew nearer. The men boarding the boats carried few belongings—unencumbered by what had or had not been. Nat Turner promised himself he would join them.

He pulled his flatboat, still loaded with supplies, aground. The Chesapeake waters foamed like gray chargers racing into the shore. Clam and crab shells mixed with rocky gray sand. He pulled off his shoes so that his feet touched the water—ebbing and retreating, baptizing his feet. He inhaled, smelling distant shores. He would sail away to those distant places and forget everything that was behind.

He saw terrapins swimming near the shore. He would sail away. He would not look back.

He inhaled the smell of crab-filled waters and then remembered a promise he had made as a boy to his mother. *"When you make it to great waters, you must speak to your grandmother across the sea in Ethiopia. She was a doting mother and I know she still waits for me. I know she is still by Tis Isat Falls searching for me."*

The waters called to him, the ancestors' call, and though he had promised that he would not, Nat Turner raised his arms to pray the ancient prayers his mother had taught him—the prayers that his people had prayed for more than a thousand years. "Our Father in heaven, Your name is Holy and Righteous. You are the Living God, Father of us all."

> *Our Father Who art in heaven, hallowed be thy name. Thy kingdom come, thy will be done, on earth as it is in heaven. Give us this day our daily bread and forgive us our debts as we forgive our debtors, and lead us lest we wander into temptation, but deliver us from the evil one, for Thine is the kingdom and the power and glory unto ages of ages. Amen.*

He prayed the prayer to honor Maryam, the Kidane Mehret, "the Covenant of God's Mercy" with Africa, as his mother had taught him.

> *As Gabriel greeted you, Hail, Mary, full of grace, the Lord is with you though virgin in conscience as well as body. Blessed are you among women and blessed is the fruit of your womb. Holy Mary, the God-bearer, pray that your beloved son, Jesus Christ, may forgive us our sin. Amen.*

Nat Turner spoke across the water to the grandmother and grandfather he had never known. He introduced himself to them. He used his Ethiopian name. "I am Negasi." He knew that his grandmother was a worrier, and he knew that he must not upset her. He could not add to his grandmother's burden, to her broken heart, so he told his grandmother that her daughter, his mother, was fine. "I will board a ship and I will come to Ethiopia, and one day she will also return."

The sky overhead was blue and rose, the sun golden. He spoke to his sister. It was the first time he had spoken her name. "I greet you, my sister, Ribka."

And then he spoke across the water to all those like him and like his mother, children of the captivity, and he prayed for them.

"Awaken!" He prayed that they would raise their heads, stretch out their arms, and make their way to freedom. He prayed that they would find great ships to carry them home.

Fell's Point, Baltimore, Maryland

FREDERICK BAILEY, A boy of less than ten, stood on the opposite shore of the Chesapeake. He lived in Baltimore as a slave on loan to the Auld family. It was his duty to care for the family's young son, Tommy.

Whenever he could, Frederick looked out at the waters that lapped at the shores of Fell's Point. He was hypnotized by the bobbing rhythm of the water. Before him were ships whose sails caught the sunlight and birds that flew overhead to wherever they pleased.

When he looked out over the water, he spoke to the ships, "You are loosed from your moorings, and free. I am fast in my chains, and am a slave! You move merrily before the gentle gale, and I sadly before the bloody whip."

Each time he looked out over the water, he spoke to the birds, "You are freedom's swift-winged angels, that fly around the world; I am confined in bonds of iron. O, that I were free! O, that I were on one of your gallant decks, and under your protecting wing! Alas! Could I but swim! If I could fly! O, why was I born a man, of whom to make a brute! The glad ship is gone: She hides in the dim distance. I am left in the hell of unending slavery. O God, save me! God, deliver me! Let me be free!—Is there any God? Why am I a slave?" Each time he spoke, there was no answer.

On the banks of the Chesapeake, young Frederick stopped this time, as though a voice called to him. He turned from the poor white boys he paid wages of bread to teach him to read. He stared out over the water. He had gazed out at the water many times before. He had prayed the same prayers many times before. But this day something seemed different. Escape was no more probable or possible than it had been the day before, but this day he felt a quickening. It was as though he heard a voice across the water calling to him.

He watched the ships cut through the water, saw the wind catch their sails, and heard the birds cry above. Frederick pledged to himself and to God that day that he would be free. "I will run away. I will not stand it. Get caught or get clear, I'll try it. I had as well die with ague as with fever. I have only one life to lose. I had as well be killed running as die standing. Only think of it: one hundred miles north, and I am free! Try it? Yes! God helping me, I will. It cannot be that I shall live and die a slave. I will take to the water. This very bay shall yet bear me into freedom."

It was as though the hand of God touched Frederick and he knew—if he had to fight, or starve, or risk his life, he would be free. "Let but the first opportunity offer, and come what will, I am off. I am but a boy yet, and all boys are bound out to someone. It may be that my misery in slavery will only increase my happiness when I get free. There is a better day coming."

Chesapeake
1821

NAT TURNER STOOD on the shores of the Chesapeake staring at the ships. Men of all hues boarded, none of them in chains. They were all men sailing into their futures. He would be one of them.

He walked the wharf marveling at the most insignificant things—wooden planks under his feet, seagulls in flight. He stopped a sailor and asked him how a man might go about finding a job. The man pointed at a line of men and told Nat Turner the ship was still hiring.

He stood in line watching the birds fly overhead. He breathed deeply, intoxicated by free air.

When he reached the hiring man, Nat Turner told the man he

would do anything. He was handy and smart, and he was willing to learn. He knew farming and hard work. He had worked as a millwright.

The man did not ask for his pass. He did not ask where Nat Turner had come from. Nat Turner was hired aboard the ship. They would set sail in three days.

AFTER HIS DELIVERY was made, Nat Turner steered the flatboat back down the Dismal Swamp Canal. It would be his last time. He would sail away on the boat harbored now on the Chesapeake and never see Southampton again.

Chapter 31

Outside the Whiteheads' farmhouse, Nat Turner and the other men stomped from foot to foot, moving in an attempt to stay warm. As they passed, they greeted one another, occasionally gathering in brief clusters.

"Brother Nelson." Dred nodded to the other man.

"Good day to you, brother," Yellow Nelson, the preacher, responded.

"A cold day," Sam answered.

Preacher Nelson rubbed his hands over his arms, sometimes clapping hands, to stay warm. "Yes, but we're still alive. One more day in our right minds."

Nat joined them. "Another chance." He nodded to Nelson. "Is there a word today, preacher?"

Yellow Nelson laughed softly. "Oh, there's always a word from the Lord, Prophet Nat!"

Smiling, Dred shook his head. "Don't get him started, Prophet Nat. You know how you preachers are. We'll be out here in this cold until Kingdom Come. And it's too cold to be out here."

"That's the truth," Sam added.

"Too cold," Nelson echoed.

"Too cold," Dred repeated, the tone of the conversation changing rapidly. He nodded toward the slaves working in the Whiteheads' fields. "No kind of way to treat people, out in this cold." He nodded toward the house. "Just so they can be inside at a tea party." He nodded, like the others, so that the whites wouldn't notice them pointing.

Nelson nodded. "Dickie has them out there in the fields keeping them busy. He should be out there bending his back."

Sam stomped his feet. "He's the one who needs to be kept busy. He's a trifling little preacher."

Nat Turner and Yellow Nelson answered at once. "He's no preacher."

"A title and a collar don't make you holy," Nat Turner added. "A tree is known by its fruit."

"Out here freezing. But they don't care," Dred insisted.

Nelson shook his head. "They don't see . . . unless there are too many of us gathered together at one time."

Without a signal, the captive men began to separate. Slaves were invisible and unimportant unless they moved too suddenly or too quickly—a running slave was sure to gain the captors' attention, attention that might cost the slave his life. They had learned not to laugh or speak too loudly, not to frown, point, or shout. White men might gather, shout, laugh, or yell. But the captives had learned that such behavior was risky. So the captives dispersed quietly, no sudden movements.

Nat Turner moved away. He rubbed his hands together to keep them warm.

The captors said they believed the captives were content in servitude. But they knew better. Their whips, their dogs, their overseers, the guns on their hips said they knew better. Their fear of three or more black men gathered together said they knew better.

Nat Turner felt the captive men's anger and their humiliation that they were treated as accessories and not as humans. Their anger and humiliation were his own. They burned in his belly.

The men moved about separately, and then when each felt it was safe, they moved slowly back together.

Yellow Nelson nodded toward the Whiteheads' carriage. "Look at that foolishness." The men looked at the top-heavy box perched on large, spindly-spoked wheels. He chuckled, but not too loudly. "What good is that thing in the country? Always stuck in a rut, Caty Whitehead flapping around like a hen. The Whiteheads have to keep boys with them all the time to lift or pull that thing out of the mud."

Sam nodded toward Mary Barrow's coach. "That one is even crazier." His shoulders shook, but his laugh was almost silent. "Did you see the cape she had on, all those feathers? I'm expecting an angry bird to swoop down here any minute, come to get his feathers back."

Nat Turner smiled. They joshed to release the steam pent up inside them.

Yellow Nelson grinned, his back to the house. "Did you see old Hubbard when he greeted her at the door?" He widened his eyes, mimicking the Whiteheads' elderly Negro doorman. "I thought his eyes were going to pop out of his head."

Nat Turner chuckled, imagining Hubbard.

Nelson went on with his story. "Hubbard says, 'Mistress Barrow, that is a coat you got on there, if I do have to say so myself!' Oh, she lit up like the Fourth of July, the vain thing."

The men chuckled, but not loudly enough to attract attention. Owners of nothing, they had become masters of words. Mary Barrow didn't recognize the subtle insult hidden in Hubbard's words, words that said the coat was not a beautiful one but one that woefully defied description.

The temporary ease provided by the laughter didn't last long and they fell into silence.

"Too cold to be out here." Dred looked toward the Whiteheads' fields again. "No way to treat people. No way to treat a man." A grumbling sound echoed from his throat. "As if we don't have any other dream but to wait on them."

His back toward the house, Yellow Nelson was free to frown. "A day is going to come."

They all understood. They agonized over those in the fields, over their wives and children, over their mothers and fathers, and over themselves. Their hope and sanity rested on their faith that one day things would change.

"A day is going to come," Sam repeated.

"Someday," Nat Turner added. "Judgment comes and that right soon."

Each man lost in his thoughts, they separated again. Nat Turner looked up at the sky, blue and cloudless. A day was going to come. God had told him so in the Great Dismal Swamp.

Chapter 32

As he sailed back down the Great Dismal Swamp Canal, Nat Turner committed to memory the ebb and flow of the canal's curative brown waters. He stared at the trees so he would not forget them and the way the treetops seemed to join hands above the canal. He would remember the exotic birds he saw in the swamp—birds of orange and blue, large birds of prey with pink and purple among their feathers. Together, his recollections would be his memorial painting of the Great Dismal Swamp, of Hebron, his refuge. He was leaving the swamp. He was leaving Virginia. He was setting sail.

He would work aboard the ship and that vessel would carry him to Baltimore and then on to Philadelphia, where he would search for Bishop Richard Allen. He would work, save money, and buy his mother's freedom and passage, and then the two of them would sail away, back to Ethiopia.

Nat Turner looked toward the canal shore, where he saw several white men. He looked away from them and back at the brown water. In three days' time he would be free of the slavers. In three days' time his new life would begin. In three days' time he would no longer have to worry about hiding out or being discovered. In three days' time he would sail away.

He looked back at the white men onshore. Two of them held the arms of a naked black woman. Her stomach was swollen with child. In awkward jerks she pulled against the hands that held her, trying to free herself. The two men forced her to the ground.

He knew what it meant, what they were going to do. But in three days' time he would be free. In three days' time he would have what he had dreamed of all his life; he would have what his mother had prayed for him. He could not save the world.

Nat Turner continued to pole the flatboat down the canal. It skimmed, as though it were floating above the water. His jaw muscles tightened. This was his Hebron, his refuge. He had not seen anyone beaten since leaving Southampton County. He had pretended to himself that what happened there happened nowhere else. He had convinced himself that things were better here. It only happened in Cross Keys. Cruelty did not exist in the swamp or beyond.

The woman screamed now for help. Nat Turner looked back over his shoulder at the woman and her tormentors, his pole still pushing him downstream, away from them. The men tied the woman's ankles and wrists to stakes in the ground. Then, laughing, their voices drifting over the water, out in the open, they began to beat her. Her screams followed their laughter, echoing across the canal.

Long after he turned his head, long after Nat Turner had passed the spot where the men beat her, he still heard the woman's shrieks.

Chapter 33

Nat Turner made his way to his clearing, to his stream, but the torment in the woman's voice was still with him. In three days he would be leaving. He would not think of her. He would leave it all behind. He would not be burdened, carrying thoughts of Miss Easter, of Cherry, or even of his mother.

He was only one man and he could not change the world. He was no god. There was no help for the people of Cross Keys, no help for any of the captives. If God ignored the people He created, Nat Turner thought, then why shouldn't he?

There was a new life waiting for him. It would be a life with clear skies, calm seas, and there would be no one to make him bow down. He would have a life of travel and adventure where he was treated like all other men. He would forget about the naked woman on the shore. Who was he to her? Who was she to him?

He would prepare himself to leave. Three days. But first he would eat and get himself a good night's sleep. Soon this would all be over and he would be far away.

He made a fire but Nat Turner saw the woman in the flames. He heard her screams and saw her struggling. His stomach churned so that after preparing food, he could not eat. If he could not eat, then he would sleep.

He settled into his sleeping place. He was young and strong, his whole life open before him like the bay, like the sky. He would sail to Ethiopia, where he would become a priest. Or maybe he would marry an Ethiopian woman, a wife no other man could steal. He would forget about the woman on the shore, about Cherry, and about all the others.

Sometime that night, in the twilight of dreaming, Nat Turner heard the voice of God.

Chapter 34

The voice of God.

Nat Turner was paralyzed, but he felt what seemed like lightning running through him. His eyes were closed, but he saw the swamp clearing lit around him. In the place where he lay, he felt God's glory and it filled the Great Dismal Swamp.

He struggled to move, wanting to free himself from what held him. He wanted to run, to see, but he could not move and could not open his eyes. He was dreaming. But he could not wake himself.

Who will go for us? Who will defend my people?

The trees bowed and trembled at the sound of His voice. Amber flashes of light and smoke filled the dark clearing, though Nat Turner smelled nothing burning. He struggled, trying to resist Him. Nat Turner wanted to cry out, but even his mouth was frozen.

He had felt God come alive, moving in him, when he prayed or read scripture or when the people sang. He had heard God in the thunder or talking through the leaves blowing in the trees. He had seen God in people's eyes or heard Him in things people said. Sometimes when he closed his eyes, he could imagine glory. What he experienced now, Nat Turner had only heard of in stories.

Come back to Me. I have loved you with an everlasting love. With loving kindness have I drawn you.

Nat Turner struggled against what held him. He could not speak, but thoughts filled his head. How could this be called love? Your people have been beaten, hanged, and scattered all over the world. Simply because of the color of our skin, we have been taken in chains and held captive, doomed for generations. How could a God who loves treat His people this way?

I told you the ones I loved would fall by the edge of the sword. I told you the ones I loved would be led away captive into all nations. I told you they would lay hands on you and persecute you. I told you the Gentiles would trample on Jerusalem until the times of the Gentiles be fulfilled.

But they stole the women and raped them. They stole the children and murdered them . . . and the babies. You watched it all and did nothing!

I told you the day was coming when people would say blessed are the barren—the wombs that never bear, and the paps that never give suck.

They murdered us. Skinned us alive. Hanged us from trees, castrated us! My own brothers betrayed me. My own father held me captive. My brother's wife sold me and my family into captivity. Why? What have we done to deserve this?

I came and walked among you to warn you so that you would not lose heart. I told you that in Jerusalem, because of your suffering, you would say to the mountains, "fall on us" and to the hills "cover us." I told you they would be crueler in the dry season after I was gone. I told you you would be betrayed by parents, brothers, relatives, and friends, and they would even put some of you to death. I told you men would hate you because of Me.

I warned you so that you would not lose heart.

Nat Turner heard thunder. His eyes still closed, he saw lightning arc across the black sky. But I was obedient. I loved You. Even with nothing in this life, I loved You. You abandoned me, rejected me. I only had one thing, the one thing you gave me, and You watched while they stole her, You let them steal her.

I suffered. I suffer. Are you greater than I? My love for you is everlasting. Being My son is not only power and prayers and singing. It is bearing and being nailed to the cross.

But she was the only thing I had. My only love. Why would you give her to me only to take her away? The ground shook beneath him. The air vibrated around him.

Nat Turner fought against it. He did not want to hear the

answers. He did not want to ask the questions. This had been his Hebron, his place to hide. This place had been his sanctuary from Southampton . . . and from God. Was there no place for him to run?

Fear slipped away and anger replaced it. Nat Turner could not open his mouth to form words, but his thoughts spoke for him. You abandoned me! Everything taken from me!

Will you only love Me if I give you what you want? Will you only obey Me for an expected prize? Will you only love Me if you never suffer?

Nat Turner had prayed for years for deliverance for him and his people. He had prayed for years for simple mercy. All his hope had been for nothing. But I didn't ask for them. You gave her to me, gave me a son, and then took them away!

Others have suffered without receiving. Why not you? Was it acceptable for them—for Jeremiah, for Elisha, for Isaiah, for Moses, for Hosea, for My son, Jesus, and not you?

All his hope had been for nothing. Now he could not move, his limbs frozen as though he were bound in steel. Those who were disobedient, who were selfish, who misused others got the best. Why were he and the others who prayed like him always suffering?

I told you many prophets, and wise men, and scribes would be killed and crucified. I told you some of them would be persecuted from city to city.

How can a servant have compassion for My people if he or she has not known their sorrow? Are you not willing to suffer if it means their redemption? Will you not suffer, even if it means a better life, a better hereafter, a resurrection for them? My first begotten endured shame and sorrow for you. Are you too good to follow His footsteps? You have obeyed your earthly masters; now you must obey Me.

Obey? All his life he had been obeying, with nothing to show. He had a chance now for a new life. He had a chance now to sail away.

There are not many who are strong enough to go through life and endure the agony . . . only a few are chosen . . . only a few are worthy—wise enough, loving enough, obedient enough—strong enough to endure the suffering to liberate others. If you love Me, if you love Him, you must pick up His yoke.

Yoke? He had been bound long enough. He had been born in chains. What he wanted were waters that never ended and sky that reached to forever.

I sent you as a sheep among wolves. Did you think you would never suffer? You rage against abandonment; would you abandon the others who need you now? Would you leave your son to die? Would you leave your wife? Your mother? Would you turn your back to the moaning woman? If not you, then who will go for us?

You have obeyed your earthly masters; now you must obey Me. If you love Me, if you love Christ, pick up His yoke.

Nat Turner stopped struggling against what held him. He had been struggling only against himself.

Cry aloud and spare not and show My people their transgressions.

No one had listened to him before. Why would they listen now? No white man wanted to hear him say the man was wrong. No white man wanted to hear him preach.

They would make excuses. They wanted to be first. They wanted the dream to be only for themselves. They were never going to give mercy.

Nat Turner felt the bands tightening again. Did God mean to offer forgiveness to the captors, to the ones who had shown no mercy?

My mercy is from everlasting to everlasting. It is available to all men, if they choose it. Men may choose justice for themselves, but I offer mercy that is eternal. It is their free choice. This mercy you offer to those who have harmed you is greater than any sacrifice you have made.

In binding others they have bound themselves. In weighing down others they have burdened themselves. They have betrayed you and sold you into slavery, so they betray and doom themselves. As their brother, will you offer them the choice—justice or mercy? You have obeyed your earthly masters; now will you obey Me?

Is not this the fast that I have chosen? to loose the bands of wickedness, to undo the heavy burdens, and to let the oppressed go free, and that ye break every yoke? Is it not to deal thy bread to the hungry, and that thou bring the poor that are cast out to thy house? when thou seest the naked, that thou cover him; and that thou hide not thyself from thine own flesh? They appear clothed and fat, but who is more naked and bereft, more bound, than they?

It was the very reason why he had come to the Dismal Swamp: to hide away, to hide from those he loved—those who loved him and those who would not. He had already poured out. He had given enough. He had no more left inside him. How could he help others when his own heart was broken?

Surely God could not ask him to lift the burden of the oppressors? They had everything in the world and it was still not enough for them. Surely God could not expect him to offer them absolution? Surely God could not expect him, after all he'd suffered at their hands, to offer mercy?

I am the Father of all; I am the Many Breasted One. They are My children, too, and I have no desire that any would be lost. They have disobeyed Me, but they are also My children. They have betrayed you, but still, they are your brothers.

Obey Me and I will make a promise to you. Obey Me and then shall thy light break forth as the morning, and thine health shall spring forth speedily: and thy righteousness shall go before thee; the glory of the LORD *shall be thy reward.*

First, you must give them a choice; you must offer them mercy. You must offer them forgiveness.

Then shalt thou call, and the LORD *shall answer; thou shalt cry, and He shall say, Here I am. If thou take away from the midst of thee the yoke, the putting forth of the finger, and speaking vanity; and if thou draw out thy soul to the hungry, and satisfy the afflicted soul; then shall thy light rise in obscurity, and thy darkness be as the noon day.*

Relieve the burdens of the wicked captors? Why offer them mercy? When would the suffering of the oppressed end and the captivity be turned?

Did you not hear Me when I promised your redemption? I am your Redeemer! But you must obey Me. No judgment comes without warning; I am Love and I am Mercy. Mercy or justice: each man must make his choice.

They must be warned. No judgment comes without warning. You must plead for the deliverance of the downtrodden; you must beg the captors to set the oppressed free—if they give mercy, they will receive mercy.

But I tell you this, the captors' hearts will be hardened, their necks stiff, and they will not listen. They will not be like Nineveh; instead, they will mock you, unaware that they mock Me. They will refuse the mercy; they will not listen. They will be like Egypt.

Will you give up this temporal freedom before you and follow after Me?

Nat Turner heard the scripture he had memorized as a boy carried on the breezes that reached his ears. *And whosoever shall not receive you, nor hear your words, when ye depart out of that house or city, shake off the dust of your feet. Verily I say unto you, It shall be more tolerable for the land of Sodom and Gomorrha in the day of judgment, than for that city.*

Behold, I send you forth as sheep in the midst of wolves.

Lightning flashed. *They have lived Old Covenant lives—the men of Cross Keys, of Jerusalem, of Virginia—every man doing that which is right in his own eyes. They extend no grace or mercy. They exact the letter of the law on others without mercy, truth, or love—whitewashed walls, all form with no substance. So they will receive as they have given. Judgment will begin at*

My house in the center of Cross Keys. If they will not hear Me, you will take up arms against them. If they will not hear, the root must be destroyed.

You will be My messenger. Wake up the mighty men, let all the men of war draw near; let them come up. Tell them, Beat your plowshares into swords and your pruninghooks into spears: Let the weak say, I am strong.

For the time is come that judgment must begin at the house of God: and if it first begin at us, what shall the end be of them that obey not the gospel of God?

Nat Turner had seen the ships. The chance he had hoped for was open before him. One more trip up the canal, then aboard the ship, and he would leave the cruel life he'd known far behind.

What good was it to fight the captors? All power was in their hands. We have no army. We have no weapons. We have no government on our side.

Rise to your feet!

Nat Turner felt himself being lifted, as though great hands held him underneath his arms. He was lifted until the feet of his wilted body dragged the ground while his heart lifted up toward heaven. The clearing glowed about him; small lights flittered past like butterflies. He smelled jasmine, lavender, and then frankincense and myrrh.

Some trust in chariots, and some in horses; put your trust in Me. Beat your plowshares into swords. . . . Judgment will begin at the house of God; you will slay those who mock Me and persecute My children, even as they are called by My name. Under My strength, you will carry out My judgment.

He was just an ordinary man, a slave. This was a dream. It would never come to pass.

You will know when the time comes. You will see signs in the heavens. The sun will be turned to darkness and the moon to blood before the coming of the great and dreadful day of the LORD.

Why me? Why now? Why call me back when I have just

seen, just tasted freedom? Why call me back to Southampton when I am pledged to the sea?

The cries and moans of My people have risen to My ears. Their prayers for mercy are ever before Me. I have bottled all your tears—yours, your wife's, your son's and mother's, the tears of your people. Will you give up your freedom for them and obey Me?

Go and smite those from your earthly father's church, and spare not; but slay both man and woman, infant and suckling—all those who have without mercy disobeyed Me and held slaves. Do not leave an heir alive. The law is not for the righteous, but for those who are lawless and disobedient—the whoremongers, the liars, the murderers, the manslayers and the menstealers.

Judgment? At Turner's Meeting Place?

You are My precious sons and daughters! And they have cast lots for My people; and have given a boy for a harlot, and sold a girl for wine, that they might drink.

And he that stealeth a man, and selleth him, or if he be found in his hand, he shall surely be put to death. If a man be found stealing any of his brethren of the children of Israel, and maketh merchandise of him, or selleth him; then that thief shall die; and thou shalt put evil away from among you. It is the law: Death is the judgment.

He was an ordinary man, even smaller than most.

The captors will be stunned by the loss of their children and loved ones, just as it was in Egypt long ago. Rage will fill them.

They will bear you in chains to Jerusalem. They will hang you from a tree. But even then they will not be satisfied.

Nat Turner saw a vision of himself being beaten. He was bloody, bound in chains, and being dragged to Jerusalem. He saw himself standing before ten judges. Why would ten judges hear the case of a slave?

As Nat Turner was lowered again to his resting place, the breezes of the Great Dismal Swamp whispered to him. *And ye shall be brought before governors and kings for My sake, for a testimony against them and the Gentiles.*

They will hate you for doing what I have commanded. They will hate you because you have heard My words.

They will mourn at the lost families and say they will promise to set My people free. They will say your blood is enough. They will make promises to free the captives. But then their hearts will harden. They are a stiff-necked people. Like Egypt, they will make things worse for My children. In the end, they will not free the captives until the nation's blood has been shed, until their own blood has watered the earth. The war has already been loosed in heaven.

Then the voice of God spoke to him of a more distant future.

I will raise up an army to fight for you; they will take up arms against themselves. And the brother shall deliver up the brother to death, and the father the child: and the children shall rise up against their parents, and cause them to be put to death. And ye shall be hated of all men for My name's sake: but he that endureth to the end shall be saved.

Nat Turner saw men wading through fields, carrying weapons. He saw white men fighting other white men, saw their blood sprinkled on the corn. Then he saw black men fighting with white.

My children will be free in name, but it will not be over. Those who hold them captive will remain prideful and arrogant. They will put themselves first while they ignore the suffering of others. They will demand for themselves the best homes, the best food, the best of everything, while others around them suffer.

But despite them, freedom will come. They will see before their eyes the valleys being exalted and the hills being leveled. They will see the crooked places being made straight, just as I promised. They will see before their eyes Ethiopia being exalted. Princes shall come out of Egypt; Ethiopia shall soon stretch out her hands unto God. They will see the end coming and the threat of their own captivity, but they will still be hard-hearted and refuse to repent and turn. They will rail and set themselves against what I do.

He had already sacrificed so much, too much. Everything Nat

Turner dreamed of had been taken away from him. He had lost his dreams and the only family he had ever had. Why did he have to give more? Why give his life?

I have called you from beyond the rivers of Ethiopia, My son. You will not live to see freedom. You will fall for My sake; the yoke of Jesus will be upon you. It is a hard thing to hear; but the first resurrection will be your reward.

Behold, at that time I will undo all that afflict thee: and I will save her that halteth, and gather her that was driven out; and I will get them praise and fame in every land where they have been put to shame.

At that time will I bring you again, even in the time that I gather you: for I will make you a name and a praise among all people of the earth, when I turn back your captivity before your eyes.

But we have waited too long. We have cried ourselves dry. We have fainted, and we have died.

Will you take up My yoke?

I am not Jonah or the Prophet Nathan. I am not a prince or a prophet. Just a slave.

You are who I say you are.

Whereas thou has been forsaken and hated . . . I will make thee an eternal excellency, a joy of many generations. Thou shalt know that I the LORD am thy Savior and thy Redeemer, the mighty One of Jacob. Violence shall no more be heard in thy land, wasting nor destruction within thy borders; but thou shalt call thy walls Salvation, and thy gates Praise. The sun shall be no more thy light by day; neither for brightness shall the moon give light unto thee: but the LORD shall be unto thee an everlasting light, and thy God thy glory. Thy sun shall no more go down; neither shall thy moon withdraw itself: for the LORD shall be thine everlasting light, and the days of thy mourning shall be ended.

Thy people also shall be all righteous: They shall inherit the land forever, the branch of My planting, the work of My hands, that I may be glorified.

When strength came back to him, Nat Turner opened his eyes.

Still lying on the ground, he thought of the woman he had seen tethered by the canal. He thought of Cherry and his mother, he thought of Hark, and Nat Turner thought of his son. He thought of poor Mother Easter, and the girl Charlotte. What peace and joy would he have knowing that they were left behind and suffering? He thought of the babies and the old ones abandoned by the road.

He sat up, bowed his head, and prayed. He prayed for forgiveness. He prayed for strength, courage, and wisdom to obey all God had commanded. And because he knew the wrath of God, Nat Turner prayed for his enemies.

He saw Sallie and young Putnam; he saw the Whiteheads and John Clarke Turner. The people whom God had called to judgment were people he had known all his life. He had lived among them. Nat Turner prayed that, like Xerxes and all of Nineveh, the people of Turner's Meeting Place would turn, repent, give mercy, and beg for their own.

He rose and bathed himself in the brown, healing water of the stream that ran beside him. He ate enough to fortify himself. Then he fell asleep humming an old Methodist hymn he had been taught as a boy.

Equip me for the war,
And teach my hands to fight,
My simple, upright heart prepare,
And guide my words aright;
Control my every thought,
My whole of sin remove;
Let all my works in thee be wrought,
Let all be wrought in love.

It was a tune he had not thought of in years.

O arm me with the mind,
Meek Lamb! which was in thee,

And let my knowing zeal be joined
With perfect charity;
With calm and tempered zeal
Let me enforce thy call,
And vindicate thy gracious will
Which offers life to all.

He slept, deeper than he had slept in years, and then rose at daybreak. Nat Turner left Hebron, peace, and freedom behind him—he made his way back through the forest. He made his way back to Cross Keys.

Chapter 35

He left the covering of the trees, the healing stream, and made his way back into the world of white men. After a month in the spongy marsh, the ground outside was hard and dusty under his feet, and Nat Turner saw the roads and the farms differently. The world outside, with its houses and farms, had seemed natural to him before his time in the Great Dismal. Now, as he traveled back, it seemed to him that the trees had been taken captive and that much of the land had been starved, raped, and finally murdered.

All his life, his mother reminded him that they were captives and not slaves. As Nat Turner walked, he began to understand. There was hopelessness and resignation in the word "slave." But there was hope for captives—captivity could be turned. Those held captive were stolen, and manstealing was a sin, a sin punishable by death.

On the third night after leaving the Great Dismal Swamp, Nat Turner had reached Southampton County and Cross Keys. He stood at the edge of Giles Reese's farm. The house was dark except for dim candlelight shining from the window of the room where Cherry slept.

By now the ship that hired him had set sail. By now he could have been on board in free waters. Instead he was in Southampton about to give himself back into the hands of his captors. But he wanted to see his wife first. He wanted to, for once in his life, and maybe the only time, stand in front of her as a free man.

He hooted to her like an owl, hoping she would awaken and recognize his call. He hid himself behind a tree where he would be able to see her if she came to the back door. He called three times before he saw someone stirring inside. When she came to the door, Nat Turner stepped out of the shadows to reveal himself.

Cherry ran to him and wrapped him in her arms. He felt her warm tears on his face. He didn't know what to say, so he said nothing. He ran with her to the great oak.

She whispered into his ear, "You could have gotten away. You could have hidden someplace where no one knew your name. I imagined you in Philadelphia or on board a ship sailing to Ethiopia. Why would you come back here?"

Nat Turner felt the warmth of his wife's body pressed against his own. No man could separate them, no law. He might not see her, they might be miles apart, but they would always be one. "How could I leave the one who is my life? I will never leave you. I will never leave my family again." They held each other and swayed underneath the moon and stars as if there was music playing. "I will never leave you."

He was humbled by her love, by her beauty. She had been scarred and shamed, she had been abandoned, but she found the courage to still love him. "I will never leave you again," Nat Turner promised.

Chapter 36

Cross Keys
February 1831

Ten years had passed since Nat Turner's return from the Great Dismal Swamp. Now he waited for a sign. Standing next to Yellow Nelson, he looked over the Whitehead farm, then back toward the fields, toward the singing. No one told the love story like a prostitute, a leper, a slave. There was nothing like God loving you when everyone and everything said He should not, including the law.

He had learned to give thanks for them—for the singing captives and their troubles—just as he did for the cold and the frost on the ground.

They believed each day might be the day when God would turn their captivity. It was strange that no one seemed to believe God's promises more than those who had already paid with their blood.

Since his return, Nat Turner had continued his prayers—for the captives and for the captors. He prayed that he would be ready for war at the same time that he prayed for change, hoping there would be no need to be ready. He prayed that the captors would turn, and each day, with the miracle of each new sun, he prayed for the miracle of new hearts. He prayed for mercy. He prayed for vengeance, that the captors would receive their just reward.

How long, Lord? The men were tired and angry. The women were heartbroken. The children had never learned hope.

Nat Turner carried a burden—a burden from his mother and from Christ's yoke—he hoped he would never have to lay on his people's shoulders. Every day he prayed for mercy for his enemies—his brothers. Every day he prayed that the call he'd been given would not have to be fulfilled, that they would choose mercy and not judgment.

God had given him the gift of His holy confession, but it was a weighty gift. It was a God-sized burden resting on his too-human shoulders.

Every day he prayed it would not happen. Every day part of him tried to convince himself that he had hallucinated. But when he looked around him, at the suffering of the people, Nat Turner knew it was true and he waited for a sign.

He preached to those who would listen to the warning that God had given. Most of them laughed and called him crazy. No white man would listen to a word from a black man, not even a word sent from God. But there was the case of the cruel overseer Ethelred Brantley.

Brantley was known and admired about Cross Keys, in Jerusalem, and throughout Southampton County as a violent and sadistic man. There was nothing he would not do to torment a captive. He had been known to hack limbs off those he had charge over for missing quotas. He smiled as he beat them, even killed them—man, woman, or child.

But there was a time when, covered with boils, Brantley sought out Nat Turner. Brantley had heard there was healing in Nat Turner's hands. He preached to Brantley God's warning. Nat Turner expected the man to beat him, to be like Pharaoh, but instead Brantley fell to his knees and begged forgiveness. He became a follower of the way and begged to be baptized.

Many of the slaves had grumbled at the thought of Brantley being forgiven. They had nodded agreement—though for different reasons—when Richard Whitehead, the pastor of Turner's Meeting Place, refused to baptize him.

"How dare you approach me, you savage? You might be pampered and fawned over by others, but I know who you are. I've known who you were since we were boys. You are a soulless demon using your tongue and your wit to fool innocent people. But I know who you are!" Richard Whitehead spit at him.

"You may think you are more than the others, but you are nothing. I would no more baptize you, no more baptize you with Jesus' sweet name than I would a dog!"

Whitehead pointed a shotgun at the two of them. "You have seduced this fool Brantley, Nat Turner, but you will not fool me. You are a cunning one, aren't you. What is your plan, to be baptized and then petition the court for your freedom? You heathen!

"You think you will be a preacher or a trustee? You think your mother will sit on a pew next to mine? All you will ever be is a nigger!" He spit at Brantley. "And you are a nigger-lover!" Whitehead yelled after the two of them. "Get away from here, you devils!" Whitehead ran him and Brantley off his farm.

Nat Turner had chafed under the people's criticism when he baptized Brantley at Pierson Mill Pond, was saddened that some still did not understand his return to slavery from the freedom of the Great Dismal Swamp.

There had been white people who mocked him and Brantley as they arose from the water. But it was the mocking of those he was risking his life for—the condemnation of the other captives—that hurt Nat Turner the most. He understood their suffering and their anger; he was a partaker, too.

But he reminded himself that he had not been sent back to please them; he came back to obey and please God. He had not come back for their praise; he had returned for their deliverance.

The morning passed quietly into the afternoon. His stomach rumbled. It was winter and there were no bruised apples lying on the ground. He smelled the aroma of good things being baked in the Whiteheads' kitchen.

A cock crowed.

Nat Turner looked up then.

The sky darkened.

The sign.

Chapter 37

The moon eclipsed the sun; in Southampton County the sky darkened. It was as though God Himself had turned away—as though the Lord's mother, Maryam, the Kidane Mehret, had turned away—and Nat Turner knew the time for mercy was finished. Nat Turner saw the darkness and it was good.

> The sun shall be turned to darkness and the moon into blood before the great and terrible day of the LORD come.

The singing in the fields ceased. There were no birds in the air and no breezes. The horses were skittish. He had prayed that God would give him the courage, that God would give him flintlike resolve. Now the day was here. Judgment would begin at the house of God. Nat Turner recalled God's pronouncements to him in the Great Dismal Swamp.

Loose the bands of wickedness, undo the heavy burdens, let the oppressed go free, and break every yoke . . .

They would strike down the pastor, Richard Whitehead, the trustees, and their heirs. The members of Turner's Meeting Place who professed God but whose hearts were full of cruelty and wickedness, who gave no mercy, would see this world no more.

He and the other warriors, God's soldiers, would do their business in secret, by the light of the sickle moon. There would be others, those who didn't have the courage to fight, who would bury the dead. When the survivors awakened it would be a great mystery to them, like Jamestown.

Nat Turner's tongue was loosened then and he began to share

the revelation of the Dismal Swamp and of the Lord's coming judgment. "*Beat your plowshares into swords . . .*"

They had no voices. Their actions would speak for them. So they would steal no money, damage no property, and rape no women. They would not dishonor God. They would plan carefully, every detail. It was not murder; it was a war for freedom. It was the only language left to them.

Nat Turner saw the visions again. He saw the battle—white men fighting their brothers, then black men fighting white men in heaven. He saw the blood on the corn and knew the time would be in summer. He shared God's message with a few trusted men— Nelson, right then. Yellow Nelson said the Lord had already confirmed the plan with him.

Later he shared with Hark, Dred, Sam, Tom, and a few trusted others. Hark said he was ready. They planned their strike for Independence Day, July 4th, 1831.

When they were alone, Nat Turner spoke to his friend, his brother Hark. "Are you certain? You are not compelled to come."

Hark laughed at first. "You have been trying to get me killed for years." Then his face sobered. "How can I not come? I see, I feel. Even women have not been able to blind me." It was the most serious Nat Turner had seen his friend. "I believe God and I have never known you to lie—even when it would have been best for you. You are God's prophet.

"If you are caught they will say I was with you anyway." Hark laid a heavy hand on Nat Turner's shoulder. "You are my brother. How could I not go with you?" Hark stared at him quietly for a while and then laughed again. He plucked Nat Turner's right biceps. "Scrawny. You need me. God would never let me rest in peace if I didn't go with you!"

War was the price of hope. It was the price of the coming generations' freedom. It was the price for his wife, for all the innocent brides who were defiled. July 4th. "Strengthen our arms, Lord."

God had given His sign.

Chapter 38

Spring had come again. It had been a dreadful winter, but a flower here, a robin there, were the harbingers of renewal. The sky had darkened in February, but now it was spring and they planted the season's corn and planned the July 4th harvest. The visions from the Great Dismal Swamp—blood on the corn—were always before Nat Turner.

He walked through the woods on the emerald carpet to the hidden place where he would meet Thomas Gray. They had been friends since boyhood. But since they had come of age—long past the time when boys played with sticks that magically turned to swords—it could be dangerous for the two of them to be seen together. It was illegal. Nat Turner shifted the package he carried to his other hand. He kept them covered so that if someone came across him, they would not see that he carried books.

Nat Turner passed the twin oaks and paused. They were wrapped with wisteria vines that climbed five times a man's height. The lightweight clumps of purple flowers that hung heavy from the vines like bunches of sweet grapes were heartbreakingly beautiful. He had torn some vines away from apple trees earlier that morning.

It was a shame to have to choose—the beautiful purple flowers or the apple blossoms. Nat Turner was tempted when he saw the vines scaling the trees to let them grow. He would prefer to allow both to live—the apples were sweet, fragrant, and might fill his stomach; the wisteria's flowers were beautiful to behold.

But the wisteria vines with their lovely flowers were deceptively strong. Veiled by the flowers, the vines would grow lush, full, and unyielding with no respect for the value and beauty of the host tree it squeezed. If he left them, without destroying the root of the wisteria, the vines would grow to the circumference of a man's arms and choke the apple tree—eventually, despite the vine's beauty, there would be no apple trees or apples left.

The wisteria grew unyielding, uncaring, unaware, as though it were the only plant worthy of life. It would kill a sapling before it grew to maturity and squeeze the life out of an elder tree. Nat Turner looked at the hanging lavender-colored flowers and breathed in the sweet smell. Eventually the vines would overpower even the ancient twin oaks.

He continued on his way to their meeting spot, past trees thick with leaves. Birds flitted from limb to limb. He pushed the branches out of his way. He and Thomas always met in the same small clearing—a place with a boulder in the center, a good place to sit and rest. The two of them would be cloaked by nature so that no one would see them.

Everyone knew that Nat Turner could read and write, but it was still forbidden by law. Thomas Gray had made it a habit to lend him books to read, sometimes newspapers. Thomas had even once shown him the Declaration of Independence reprinted in a Fourth of July newspaper. Then the two of them would meet to discuss, every two months or when the weather would allow it, what Thomas had shared. Nat Turner would return the loaned items and usually Thomas Gray would have something new for him.

Sometimes Nat Turner shared his experiments—like trying to make wallpaper or trying to make gunpowder and small fireworks. He told no one else about them; it was dangerous for a slave to dream beyond what others planned for him. He showed Thomas Gray plants he had discovered and rocks that he had collected.

They discussed history and war heroes, like Nathan Hale and Crispus Attucks. Thomas Gray fancied himself a literary critic and thought he could, if he wanted, be a great writer. So, often, they debated novels. In past times there had been tales like *The Ingenious Gentleman Don Quixote of La Mancha* by Miguel de Cervantes. This time there had been two plays: one written by Shakespeare, a story of family jealousy and betrayal; and the other a translation of a play authored by a French playwright, Alexandre Dumas.

There was no doubt that Thomas would find something wrong with *Hamlet* and the new play *Charles VII at the Homes of His Great Vassals*. He was critical of every story—every story except Voltaire's *Candide*.

Though he was grateful when his friend brought him books, Nat Turner often felt that the cost was Thomas Gray's lording it over him. Gray always had to assert himself as better; he always had to know more, to be more. But Thomas Gray was still Nat Turner's friend. Gray was jealous of those he loved. Gray was not perfect, but now that there was so little time left, Nat Turner valued what he had.

Since the sun had darkened, he had traveled throughout the area preaching to the captives—preaching against the lies about God and Africa. When they would listen, he even preached to the captors, warning them and hoping they would turn.

He could no longer count the number of people he had preached to throughout the coasts of Virginia and North Carolina. He never held back; he didn't mince words. He told them what God told him to tell them. He had seen the sign in the heavens and he knew the end was near. It was worth their tears or offense if he could help protect their immortal souls.

But it was much easier preaching to strangers. It was hard to speak the truth to friends and loved ones, especially a friend whom he could see dying before him.

Nat Turner knew his friend Thomas Gray did not believe that God would ever punish him. Wrong and sin had been assigned to others, to scapegoats, and bypassed him. Thomas Gray was absolved, and so he didn't worry about God or what God wanted. He considered hell, and all he considered superstitious, fit only for poor folk and slaves.

The two of them had remained friends since childhood, though now they kept their discussions to books and weather; at least Nat Turner did. Thomas Gray could discuss anything; he was a free white man. But Nat Turner didn't know if their friendship could survive what he might say if his tongue were freed.

Thomas Gray wasted too much time with people who despised him. He drank too much. He was throwing away his life. Nat Turner wondered if he would have told his friend the truth if they were just friends and not a slave speaking to a master, not a captive speaking to a captor.

But he knew in God's eyes they were brothers, not slave and master. He would not be forgiven because he bowed down and did not speak the truth as a slave; he would be held accountable for failing to act out of brotherly love.

In truth, he and Thomas were friends closer than his own brothers. The two of them shared thoughts and feelings that Nat Turner never would have been free to share with Samuel—and especially not with John Clarke, whose heart was too full of envy to have room for friendship or love.

Nat Turner swept past the trees and through the brush lush with leaves. He looked up at the sky. He reminded himself to remember this day and not to waste any opportunity. Brotherly love. He had so much to tell his friend. There was so much to say, so much he did not want to say.

You are wasting the gifts God has given you because you are afraid to even try. You are afraid of life. God will hold you accountable for keeping men and women in chains. There was so much to say, but Nat Turner did not want to say it. Hypocrite. Sot. Wastrel. Adulterer. Mansteeler. They were all names he could use, but he did not want to hurt his friend, his brother. It was easy to be a prophet among strangers but more difficult among those who were your own.

Better to risk their friendship in this world than to doom their brotherhood eternally. Nat Turner did not want to lose his friend even though it was, he admitted to himself, a shallow friendship. They stayed in shallow relationship because it was safer and there was less likelihood of drowning.

Nat Turner looked forward to their talks about the books. For a few moments, when they met secretly, they could exist in a world without skin color, without class, without rules, and without slavery. Both of them could drop their struggles with who they were and with whom they wanted to be. But there was so little time—the sky had darkened and the corn would soon be bearing, and there was so much left to say.

When Nat Turner saw Thomas Gray, he extended his hand. There had been many years since their imaginary sword fights. Their lives were different in ways Nat Turner had not wanted to imagine then. They both were married—though his own marriage was considered counterfeit—and they both had children. Thomas Gray had a daughter whom he adored.

But Thomas had become a practicing lawyer, though a discontented one, while Nat Turner had become a slave. July 4th was fast approaching. This might be his last opportunity to see his friend, to warn him. "Thank you for sharing these with me." Nat Turner handed the books to Thomas Gray.

"So, how did you enjoy Mr. Shakespeare, Nat?" In the forest alone there were no titles; they were Thomas and Nat. They were friends . . . almost.

"Very much so. He might have been writing about Cross Keys as well as Denmark."

"I thought his writing might agree with you, but then you find something good in most writers." Nat Turner's friend shook his head. "If I wrote, I would never write like that. It's all too much drivel and just a waste of time. Tell me the story, don't preach to me." Thomas Gray tied his horse to a nearby tree. "For my money, I prefer the swashbuckler. There is too much romance in Shakespeare, but I did enjoy Romeo's swordplay."

Nat Turner rested on the boulder.

"So much fighting, you would have thought they could get along." Thomas Gray smiled and gave him a baiting look. "It rather reminds me of the fighting among your people in Africa."

Nat Turner did not want to argue. He wanted his last memory of his friend to be a pleasant one.

"Why do you people always fight one another?"

Nat Turner laughed to hold back the bile. "Why do *you* people always fight one another?"

"You mock me."

"No, I answer you."

"We do not fight. White men live in peace with each other as civilized men. We have laws and courts to decide our disputes."

"In Ethiopia, we have elders, wise men, who settle our disputes."

"But you are still always fighting. Black men are always fighting one another."

Nat Turner laughed again. "*You* are always fighting one another. White men, the British, came here in 1812 to fight you, other white men. And you are still afraid; you worry at night thinking they will invade again."

"But they are British. We are Americans."

"Like you, we are Montagues and Capulets. We are Ethiopians and they are Sudanese or Moroccans."

"But you are all black—fighting each other."

"You are all white. The kings and queens of Europe who fight each other, they are all white and all related, aren't they? They play and fight with each other on soil that does not belong to them and play with other people like rag dolls. They put meal sacks and white gloves on farmers so they can play their make-believe games."

Thomas's face reddened. "It is not the same. You people brutalize each other, beating one another with clubs and stabbing one another with spears."

"A spear, a club, a cannon—it is exactly the same. Is it more civilized, more humane, for one man to kill another eye to eye or for one man to stand at a distance and kill hundreds or thousands who never see his face? Anger, greed, power lust have no color. Everyone who looks like you does not mean the best for you." Hutu and Tutsi. Poles and Russians. Serbs and Croatians.

Nat Turner looked at the rifle in Thomas Gray's saddlebag and the whip next to it. "Tell me who wants to kill others." He looked back at his friend Thomas. "Why create weapons if you do not dream of violence? The evidence is against you."

Thomas Gray did what he always did when the water got deep: He paddled for the shore. "I think Hamlet feels sorry for himself. If he doesn't like what his mother and uncle are doing, he should leave Denmark and move on."

His friend could be casual about family relations because his family had never been threatened. He could be casual about leaving because he had never been stolen away; he was free to go where he pleased. There was no pass required for him to leave; Thomas Gray had to find only the courage. "I find Mr. Shakespeare's writing too laborious, moralistic, and romantic. Too melodramatic for my taste."

Thomas Gray could criticize Shakespeare because he avoided criticism by never writing a word. "Why don't you try your hand at writing, Thomas?"

"Someday. Perhaps, when I'm less busy."

Thomas noticed a scar on Nat Turner's temple. "A recent gift from our young friend Nathaniel Francis? Why do you taunt them, Nat? Why do you make your own life hard?"

"I didn't make my life hard. I didn't make myself a slave."

Thomas sighed, shook his hands with exasperation. "Why do you fight against it, Nat? We have the lives that are given to us. Did you ever consider that this might be the best life for you and the others? Maybe you are happier this way as slaves. Sometimes I think I would be happier being a slave—no responsibility, no expectations."

"No one wants to be a slave, Thomas."

"All right then, a simple farmer with a pretty wife on a small farm tucked away in a place no one could find us—that might be a better life for me. My wife and I, we would have six children, fat babies with no shoes, and I would be a writer. It's true; I might be happier with that life. But that is not the life that has been given to me. I must make the best of the life I have."

"But the life you have doesn't make you a beast to be beaten, to be lashed, to be raped or stolen. The life you have does not manacle your children. The life you have doesn't force you to work a lifetime with nothing to show for it."

Thomas shrugged. "It might have."

"But it doesn't. Is slavery the life you would choose for your daughter? Would you make your sister a slave? Would you stand by and say 'be patient' if it were your daughter being raped? We have hearts and blood like you. We have feelings like you. We are all Abraham's children."

Thomas Gray looked away. "But why do you taunt them, those like Nathaniel Francis? Why can't you be more like Red Nelson?"

Nat Turner knew Gray's thinking. Like the other captors, thoughts that he knew better and was better were unconscious. Like a man living on a dung heap, he had lost the ability to smell his own arrogance.

The thinking had gone on so long no one remembered when it started. No one even noticed it; it—thinking he *knew* better and *was* better—seemed the right and natural thing. Only standing against the thinking caused a sensation. Feeling superior must be seductive as well as insidious. Nat Turner knew his friend would not want to give up what he had inherited.

"How can you tell me who I should be like, Thomas? Perhaps I think you should be like Ethelred Brantley or Benjamin Phipps."

Thomas Gray did not answer; instead, he began a new conversation. He rose to stick the packet of books in his saddlebag. On the way he paused and shook the books. "I could do better than this. At least I could do no worse. Maybe I should have gone into writing after all. Who knows? I might write a great work of fiction."

"Why did you choose the law?"

"The law chose me. Really, my family chose it for me."

"Your family?"

"All of us are lawyers. It was a family expectation. It's what my father wanted me to be. It's what my family counted on."

"As a free man, you couldn't say no?"

Thomas Gray bristled, turning to face him. "I could have said no."

"You couldn't leave this place? Do you think slave catchers would come after you?" There was more cynicism in Nat's voice than he intended.

"I do not like the way you are talking. There is no need to be snide."

"You have choices and freedom and you are telling me that you allow fear to steal them from you? You are a free man, and it is good enough for you to just make do?"

Thomas sighed. "What is the point? Law just does not suit me." He flopped down beside Nat Turner on the stone. He gestured with his hands as he explained. "The law is not about helping people; it is about helping those who *have* to get *more*. It is rules and regulations and manipulation of those rules and regulations by people who already have power. If I were to write, I could say what I pleased. I could write and maybe change the world, or at least please myself. Writers have freedom. My pen would be my own."

Nat turned to him. "You think if you wrote there would be no price or struggle? There is a price for freedom no matter what profession or circumstances—writer or slave. There is a price whether you are in a courtroom, writing at a desk, or walking behind a plow."

"You don't understand, Nat. Be grateful. You talk about a world you will never know. They put pressure on me to get the verdict, not to do what is right, but to do what they want done."

Grateful? Thomas's skin color, his gender, his family name with its connections, entitled him to a certain position and station in life. He did not work for what was handed to him. He did not question it. It was nothing great; it was only fair. It was natural, comfortable, and right to him. Since he was comfortable, he could not, did not want to, understand anyone else's discomfort. Nat wondered how many times he had underestimated someone else's burden.

Thomas did not know, did not *have* to know, did not *want* to know about the other side of life. The same ones who made Thomas's life easy told Nat he wanted something for nothing. They were the same ones who took everything he hoped to own. He was a thief and a troublemaker to them. Nat Turner's dreams labeled him a menace. "Freedom requires courage, Thomas, and the willingness to fight—perhaps to shed your blood."

"You don't understand. You are a slave. You have no responsibilities, and choice has been taken from you. You don't know it, but you are better off."

No responsibilities? Thomas wanted Nat's life to be what he imagined—a carefree life singing songs, playing banjos, and eating watermelon. He had never worked in a field, so Thomas didn't know what it meant; it was nothing to him. He didn't have to worry about how his family would eat or if they would live. Thomas had no idea what it meant to be a black preacher, a circuit rider. It was dangerous and there was no earthly reward—Negro preachers were mocked and given no respect. But it was not Thomas's life, so he did not understand. He didn't need to understand.

"I don't understand why you make things so difficult for yourself, Nat Turner. You imagine trouble and mistreatment everywhere. You are as melodramatic as Shakespeare."

Nat looked at his friend, trying to see the person he remembered, the person who was on his side. It was not so long ago that they were all boys playing together.

Chapter 39

1831

The four of them—Thomas, Hark, Benjamin Phipps, and Nat—took over the ship's deck, waving their swords. They sailed the seven seas searching for pirates' treasure. Ahoy! They sailed in search of newfound lands.

But they were no longer boys. They were men now struggling with the things of men. Thomas Gray wasted the freedom for which so many others prayed.

Nat Turner imagined that if he were free, he would choose and read whatever books he liked. He would read until his eyes were dimmed.

He would be an inventor and he and his family would travel the world. He would travel from church to church reminding people that their freedom was a gift from God they should not waste. He would use each opportunity that freedom afforded; he would wring life until it was dry. He would not waste it.

If she were free, he imagined that his mother would fly back to her beloved Ethiopia and find the family left behind. If Mother Easter were free, she would not scrub any more floors and maybe she would learn to read and open a dress shop. He could imagine Hark and even Will becoming gentlemen farmers or maybe shop owners. "I think it is a sin to waste your life, Thomas."

"What do you know of my life, Nat?"

"I know that white men only listen to other white men."

Thomas rose and stood in front of him. "I am your friend, Nat Turner, and it is cruel of you to accuse me. Though I would be disowned and beaten myself if others saw me, a white man, speaking to you this way, sharing books with you, I come here to listen to you as a friend. It wounds me that you think of me with so little care." Thomas Gray pulled at the vest he wore. "We are talking about you and me, Nat. I try to speak with you as an equal, as no other white man would, but you mock me. I think you take me for granted."

"You hear but you don't listen. We only listen to those we love and respect."

Thomas's forehead reddened when he was angry, just as it had when he was a boy. "We are lifelong friends; of course I care for you. I risk my reputation for you!"

"When I speak my thoughts to you, Thomas, unless I agree with your thoughts, you tell me I am wrong. We do not reason together."

"What you say is outlandish. When I disagree, I am trying to help you, Nat. Is there no room for me to help you? Can I not correct you?"

"Do you honestly believe that only you know the truth? Do you honestly believe that God only speaks to you?"

"You make me sound arrogant, Nat." Thomas smirked. "Besides, I have never said that God speaks to me. That honor belongs to you, I think."

They had been friends a lifetime, but there seemed so wide a gulf between them. "When you tell me how it feels to be a white man, when you write or speak about how you feel, I listen. I say to myself, 'Ah, this is how my friend feels,' and I try to understand.

"When I tell you how it feels to be a black man or share something I have written with you, you tell me I am wrong—unless my thoughts match your own. You disagree unless I think what you believe I should."

"This is ridiculous. Do you wish to cause trouble between us? How can you say I don't respect you, Nat Turner? I have told you that you are one of the smartest natural men I've known . . . perhaps the smartest. But I don't understand you . . . or this anger I think I see."

Nat Turner tried to calm himself, to quiet his heart. He had not meant to show so much passion. But he had been pressed down so long, held in chains so long. "I have never been a scion, a plantation owner, or a slave owner. So I listen for you to describe it to me, to help me understand."

Thomas Gray's expression was both earnest and perturbed. He sat beside Nat Turner again.

"You have never been a slave, never beaten. You have never gone without enough in your stomach. You have never been bound so that you could not set your own course. When I tell you what it is like for me, you tell me I am wrong. To be right, I must see my world as you imagine it. Otherwise you call me misguided and impatient. You tell me it is not that bad, never having been lashed or spit on. You believe it's not bad because you have never had your wife and child stolen." He felt a burning in the pit of his stomach, felt his hands clenching.

"'We give you plenty to eat,' white men say as though they feel the emptiness in our stomachs. 'You people do not have hearts; you don't know love,' they tell us as they steal and sell our families away.

"I don't know what it is to be above, to be in front, to be the one whose favor everyone wants to court. But I do know what it is to be despised. As my friend, I want you to listen, to try to understand how I feel without telling me I am wrong."

Thomas was silent. He did not look at Nat. He looked past him. "I am only trying to encourage you. I am trying to help you not to be morose."

"I have every reason to be morose! If you want to help me not be miserable, then help free me! Don't tell me I am wrong—join with me to change my circumstances, loose my bonds."

Thomas Gray sighed. "What you ask of me is too hard for one man."

"You romanticize slavery because it serves you. If you are my friend, care enough to make my heartbreak your own. Be willing to be poor so I can be free. If you are my friend, raise your voice, raise your pen to set me free! You choose to not understand because it benefits you. You don't have to help me because you discount me because you think I am inferior to you—it is easier to believe God meant this life for me than to stand up and do something about it. We give our lives to make you rich; risk your life to set us free!"

"You wound me, Nat Turner. You push me too far."

"I know what I say is not safe, my friend. The safe thing is to tell you what you want to hear, to be Red Nelson. But that is not the honest thing. That is not the truth. And is that what you really want, for me to be a buffoon like Red Nelson?

"If a nail goes in my foot and it hurts, you understand; we have this pain in common. But you seem not to want to understand that a burden too heavy for your back is also too heavy for mine. My heart hopes like yours. My heart breaks when you steal my son as yours would if your daughter were stolen."

Thomas rose and turned away.

Chapter 40

There was no way for Thomas Gray to know that this was Nat Turner's last summer. There was no need to tell him; he wouldn't believe.

Thomas Gray had romantic notions of slavery. He thought life would be easier as a slave, a slave with no responsibilities, a slave with no choices. He thought that if he were a slave, though he was bound, it would mean freedom for him. No one would care what he did.

Summer was coming, harvesttime, and this might be the last time he would see his friend. He did not want to part with angry words. "We are not so different. Each one of us must choose and fight to be free. In the end, we are all slaves if we don't have courage."

Thomas turned back to him. "I've been thinking of your dilemma and I think I have a solution."

Nat Turner turned to face his friend. "My dilemma?"

"You should never have been a slave; it was never meant for you. But I'm sure you will agree, those Negroes that drink, and brawl, and steal should be slaves. What else are we to do with them?"

"You treat me differently, think of me differently, because you know me. If we were not friends, you would count me as one of the nameless, faceless ones you think are only worthy of slavery. Slavery was never meant for anyone."

"There are white men, I think, who deserve no more than to be slaves."

"We are not judged by how we treat those we love, but by our treatment of those we despise."

"It is always religion with you, Nat Turner. Why the allegiance to a God who has no allegiance to you? If it were not for God, notions of God, there would be no slavery. If I were in your position, I don't think I would believe. How can you sniff after the white man's God? All it brings you is trouble."

The words brought Nat Turner to his feet. He grabbed Thomas by his vest, almost lifting him from the ground. "You have stolen my homeland, my wife and family! Now you wish to steal away the God of my fathers!" Nat shook Thomas. How much more was he supposed to bear? How much more could be stolen from him?

Thomas tried to pry his hands away.

"My fathers knew Him long before you. He was never the white man's God. Any man who says so is a liar and does not know Him. He is the God of all nations!"

Thomas struggled to loose himself from Nat's grip. "What is wrong with you, Nat Turner?"

Nat Turner hit him then. A red mark appeared near Thomas's mouth. Even as boys he had never raised his hand to Thomas.

Thomas jerked himself free. "Are you mad? How dare you!" He bent forward, collecting himself.

Nat Turner looked at his hands. The rush of anger had surprised him. He had been hit by others but had never struck anyone himself. His hands seemed to have a will of their own.

He had seen fear in Thomas's eyes. It was a new sensation. The power felt good, but the feeling startled Nat.

Thomas straightened his clothes. He swiped at his mouth, checking for blood. "How dare you hit me? If we were not friends . . ." They circled each other in the clearing like two wolves ready to attack.

Thomas snarled at him. "I happen to think your life might be more pleasant without your brooding over a god who may or may not exist. It seems all the cruelty in the world is somehow connected with your religion." Thomas Gray was goading him now, trying to get under his skin.

"Don't try to take God from me! What is my belief to you? Atheists rape, steal, murder, start wars. Look what you do for the sake of wealth—enslaving people, stealing from them—and you don't believe."

"Must everything with you be about slavery? Slavery and religion? Oh, my little Candide, you are so innocent and trusting. Someday you will see that all this belief that you set such store by is for nothing. It only torments you. You'll likely hang for it!"

"Take my life then! Everything else has been stolen from me." Nat was tired of being threatened. He'd lived his life under threats. "If I allow you to steal this one thing I have left from me, what will you give me in return? If I don't believe, do you mean to tell me that white men suddenly free me?" He lifted his shirt, showing his back. "Will these scars magically leave my body? Will you return my mother to Ethiopia? Will you return my wife to me?"

Nat Turner stopped himself so that he would not pound his friend, who stood now in the place of all other captors. "If I give up God, what do you, a mere man, have to offer me?" What could Thomas Gray give him? His fear? His doubt? His discontent?

Thomas Gray waved his hand dismissing the argument. "Whatever the case, you are a slave. That is your lot. Make peace with it; it will not change!"

The game always ended the same.

Chapter 41

"We won," Nat insisted. "We bested you and fair is fair."
"You cannot win. We always win."

They were in the clearing again. Virginia had returned and, again, they were in Southampton, boys holding sticks instead of swords. Nat drew back his fist.

The slap stung his face and brought water to his eyes, but he would not cry.

Nat looked about the clearing. Make peace with slavery? How could he make peace with it? How could he make peace with something so unnatural? It was Thomas Gray who had brought Nat Turner the Declaration of Independence to read. How could he be content without the rights given to him by God? How could he make peace with allowing another man to usurp rights that could not even be given away? How could Thomas Gray consider something so ridiculous?

"I am no man's slave. I am a captive held against my will."

"You are always quibbling over words, Nat." Maybe it was no surprise that Thomas didn't understand; years ago, when they were children, Thomas had been learning, too.

Nat didn't want to argue about slavery. He wanted to sit with his friend. He wanted to talk about the books. It might be their last meeting.

Thomas walked to his horse, preparing to leave, and then he turned. "I could purchase you." From the expression on Thomas Gray's face, Nat Turner could see that he was sincere. "I would pay more than you're worth; poor Sallie would be grateful for the money. Her husband and she are poor as church mice."

"More than I'm worth? I will not be bought by you or any man again."

"Why do you fight against it? Why does my offer to help offend you? Is there nothing I can say that does not anger you? Do you wish to die?"

"Your plan of rescue, at best, only rescues *me*. What about my family? What about the others? How could I have peace with my family in chains? How could I have peace with you in chains?"

Thomas laughed. "Me? In chains? You know if you continue to speak this way, I really will believe you are crazy. Even worse, if others hear you, you will end up dead." Thomas Gray did not recognize how the life he had accepted kept him bound. He thought like others that it was all to his advantage.

"I do not want to die, Thomas—I want freedom, I want hope. But if a sacrifice must be made, better me than my child. There are worse things than death."

He slapped Nat Turner on the back. "I think my offer is a fine one, and I still don't understand why it offends you."

"I am offended, my friend, because you ask me to be satisfied with what is wrong. You ask me to depend on you for my peace and happiness. You know me better; you know this could not satisfy me. If you owned me, how could I ever cross you or disagree? Some business or illness could change my fortune. It would make you my god, and only God is my master.

"If God only desired my freedom, I never would have returned. I would have boarded the ship I was hired on and sailed far away." He had returned to deliver his people. July 4th would come soon. "You have many gifts, Thomas."

"So have you—you are not formally educated, but you are probably the most intelligent man I know."

"You could change things, Thomas. You could do so much good if you had the courage."

"The courage?"

"You are intelligent, you can write, and you can tell a story. You might change the whole country if you used your gifts for good."

Thomas Gray's smile was tinged with bitterness. "You speak as though I had so many choices."

"You do. You are a free man."

"Free is relative, my friend." Thomas forced a laugh. "This has been a fine afternoon—a spirited talk about religion and books, and even a round of fisticuffs." He leapt to the saddle. "Your principles will be your undoing, my friend."

It was a strange way to say good-bye. Nat Turner had imagined they would part with kind words. He had imagined they might embrace as friends. He walked nearer to the horse, took the bridle in hand.

Chapter 42

There was no way his friend could imagine his struggles, nor could he imagine his. "You're right, Thomas. All of us have some darkness we must fight, even if it is only ourselves." The worse thing Thomas Gray could imagine was death. "If it is God's will for me to live, then I will live. If the price for speaking the truth is death, then I am willing to pay the price."

Nat Turner needed to convince himself of the truth of what he spoke. He needed to let go of life in this world. "I will die anyway. But there is no doubt that nothing will change if no one tries to stand against it. If no one stands, hundreds of years from now, things will still be the same. Greedy, selfish men and the wicked spirits that fuel them will not give up what they have stolen without a fight."

Thomas Gray's horse bowed its head to nibble at the grass, and Nat stroked its mane. "You are my friend, Nat. Perhaps the only friend I have who understands me, the only friend I can tell that I am dissatisfied with my life, the only friend who says, listen to your heart. Maybe I am as selfish as the others who would keep you a slave. I would rather have you alive as a slave than to see you martyred to some romantic notion."

"Cruelty is not romantic. It is a blow to the body, the heart, the mind, the spirit. There is nothing romantic about that."

"Maybe you are who they say you are—a fanatic—and I am a fanatic for listening to you."

Thomas's smile reminded Nat Turner of their boyhood summers. "If I am a fanatic, is it any wonder?

"I see possibility in everything around me. It is who I am. God made me. If He intended me to be nothing more, why would He have me to see flowers and wonder what can be made from them? I hear the wind and see it blow the trees and I wonder what can be done with this wind. Can I harness it to draw the plow through the fields? Can I press leaves or skins to make parchment? Can I use black powder to make fireworks? What if? What if? I cannot stop dreaming." Nat felt the anger draining from him. They were boys again.

"This life that men have decided for me means that I cannot dream. I am punished for dreaming, for having a mind, for using the mind that God has given me. I see white men do things and I think, I know a better way. But if I want to stay alive, I must pretend to be a brute.

"Then, if stealing my hope was not enough, my family is stolen. What man can exist without family? What man is not crazy without love?

"Why would God set up such a world? If I know to do good and I do not do it, that is sin. This system forces me to sin, to pretend I do not know what I know. It forces me to do less and be less than I can be. That is sin."

"You drive yourself crazy, Nat. I tell you, Candide, that your religion, your mythical god, is at the heart of all this."

"You don't believe that, Thomas. Scientists do harm, artists do harm, even lovers do harm, but you do not speak against them. The miracle, the proof of God, is that I still exist after all that the captors have done to me. The miracle is that I still love and still hope. The miracle is that I somehow still call you friend. You would not like who I would be or what I would do without God in my life." He heard the bitterness in his voice. This was not the conversation he had planned.

"You speak of all white men as if we are one, as though each of us is responsible for one man's foul doings. I am no Nathaniel Francis, I am not like John Clarke." Thomas Gray's face flushed.

"You stand with him as one. You are a slavery man."

"Why do you rail at me, Nat? You have known me since we

were children. It is not I who beats slaves. I am good to those I own. They are better off with me than if they were free in this world, unprotected. Why trouble me?"

"You are my friend and it is true that you do a little good, but it does not erase the wrong.

"Perhaps you are better, wiser, and more talented than Nathaniel Francis and all the rest of us, Thomas."

"What are you talking about, Nat? You are one of the most brilliant men I know."

"But you believe you are better. Be honest; part of what you cherish about our friendship is the difference in our stations. No matter how smart I might be, you are smarter. No matter how many books I have read, you have read more. No matter how great my vocabulary, yours is greater."

"You think wrong of me, Nat Turner."

"Don't hear in what I say that I do not love you, my friend. I have enjoyed being in the presence of your sharp mind and even sharper tongue, to hear you expound on things that would otherwise be hidden from me.

"But let us just suppose for a moment that I am correct—that you think yourself greater—better, wiser, and more articulate. Even more, let us assume that you are right in your thinking.

"What good is it, my friend, to be smarter, wiser, and more talented than everyone around you if you do nothing with your talents? What good are your superior gifts if you bury them or drown them in alcohol?

"What good is it if you use your knowledge and words to harm others? What good is it if you only use your many words to break others' hearts and weigh them down?"

Thomas Gray was frowning. He picked at the leather strap he held in his hands.

"It is better to be poor."

"I could have your head for speaking to me this way."

"You could."

"You play upon my friendship, my affection for you. Sometimes I think others are right. You have the devil in you, Nat Turner. I have done nothing to harm anyone."

Nat Turner was tired; tired of explaining and reasoning, tired of trying to help people understand what seemed so simple. He was weary of being hated because he wanted to do good while those who did wrong were rewarded. No one called them devil. Society celebrated men like Nathaniel Francis, gave awards to men like those he had seen beating the pregnant woman on the banks of the Great Dismal Swamp, called them heroes. "What is it that I have done wrong that I am called devil?"

"This is craziness you speak."

"It would be no wonder if I were crazy, if I lunged at every white face I saw. Enough has been done to leave me crazy. Giles Reese buys my wife, misuses her so that his children are born between her thighs. Then he calls both his children and mine slaves; the law supports him. The church agrees with him, participates with him, in the name of God. I am the one who is crazy? The miracle is that I still hope. It would be more rational to poison my wife, tie my baby in a weighted sack, and throw him in the river to die. That would be rational."

"Nat, you are being melodramatic again. If the truth is told, slavery benefits both of us. If you were not a slave, you'd be in some godforsaken jungle. I think you are choosing to see only the bad. You have food, you have clothing, and a roof over your head. You have a pretty wife and a family. Those who complain about beatings and punishments bring it on themselves. I do not see what is so bad."

"You have no idea what has been stolen from me." Before him, Nat Turner saw the rolling, green hills of Ethiopia. He felt sea breezes blowing on his face.

"You have no idea how I suffer. We are friends. We are brothers, but your joy in the midst of my despair is proof that our friendship is shallow. I am bound in chains, but you do not try to free me."

"Nat, you sound as though you are ready to say the word, claim it as your own."

"What word? Freedom? Abolition? I am ready to *be* the word!"

"If you say *abolition* in the South, Nat, you might as well say *traitor* or rebellion. White men will have your head."

"What is better? If I satisfy myself with the life slavery men want for me, I am as good as dead. I stand against the very will of God."

Thomas raised an eyebrow. "And how would you know God's will, Nat?"

"He speaks to me."

"He speaks to you?"

Harriet

Chapter 43

Harriet stood by a window in William's Boston shop. She looked over the notes of her earlier conversations with Benjamin Phipps and with William. The story was a puzzle and she worked to put the pieces together.

She wondered if the meeting between Thomas Gray and Nat Turner might have been the one that Nathaniel Francis had witnessed from his hiding place in the woods. Harriet read from her notes about Nathaniel Francis—notes of Nathaniel's conversation with Thomas Gray at Waller's still—a conversation about seeing Thomas Gray with Nat Turner.

"This past spring, near Cabin Pond. I saw the two of you. Had him in the site of my rifle. You handed him a package. You were speaking to each other earnestly. Not like slave and master, but like friends."

Harriet tried to imagine what it must have been like for Nat Turner and Thomas Gray to have been friends in 1831. She imagined how difficult things must have been for Thomas Gray after Nat Turner's rebellion.

A quarter of a century later, there were still people who criticized her brother and her for associating with Negroes, for inviting them to their homes. There were people who were furious with Henry and had vandalized his Brooklyn home because of his work as an abolitionist and because he welcomed Negro visitors to his church and his pulpit.

It was extraordinary to think of the two men, separated by law, custom, and culture, still struggling to be friends, to understand each other.

"Excuse me. I thought you might like this." William returned with two cups of tea and biscuits.

Harriet returned to the small table where they had been working. She sat and then sipped at the tea, but her thirst overcame her. Her cup was soon drained dry. Her face warming, she looked across the table at William. "Please forgive me. I am mortified."

"Please forgive me for being such a poor host." He called to his sister to bring more tea and offered Harriet one of the biscuits. "It was thoughtless of me. I should have noticed that you were famished."

She touched his hand. "You owe me no apology, Mr. Love." Harriet quickly removed her hand. They were strangers, almost, but they were sharing the intimacies of so many lives. She looked down at her notes again. "So Thomas Gray and Nat Turner were indeed friends?"

William nodded. "Though they were born to different circumstances, they were born the same year in the same area."

But for slavery, the two of them might have been even greater friends, almost brothers.

"The story is still told in Southampton County that not only Thomas Gray but also Sallie Moore Travis were Nat Turner's friends."

Harriet looked across the table at William. It was unacceptable and unheard of, even in Massachusetts, for a white woman to touch a Negro man's hand. What did it mean for Sallie and Nat to be considered friends? Was cooking for him, in a time when no mistress cooked for her slaves, enough to have made them friends?

The story of Nat Turner being revealed to her was one she could never have imagined.

William's sister returned with a pot of tea. "Thank you." Harriet smiled to her. When his sister was gone, Harriet nodded to him. "Thank you, Mr. Love."

She adjusted the napkin on her lap, then lifted her pen and pressed it to the paper in front of her. "Let us resume."

Nat Turner

Chapter 44

Cross Keys
1831

Nat Turner had never shared his intimacies with God with Thomas Gray. It was deeper water than they had ever trod. He held his breath waiting for the onslaught of his friend's disapproval. "He has shown me things and given me visions. I saw a battle unleashed in heaven—black men struggling with white men. I saw a great battle loosed here on earth and blood spattered on the corn. God said to take the yoke of Jesus upon me."

"You? King of kings? A slave king? Who's the man with grandiose dreams now? If you were a drinking man, I would say that you are intoxicated."

It was too late to regret telling Thomas about the vision. They had already argued over so many things they had never touched on before.

"It is preposterous to say that God, if He does exist, speaks to you . . . a mere man . . . a mere nobody . . . a mere . . ."

"A mere what? Slave? You believe God speaks even to Richard Whitehead, but not to me? Because of the color of my skin?"

Thomas Gray grimaced. He rose in the saddle, then sat, rose, then sat, as though he were undecided. The horse beneath him sidestepped restlessly.

"Perhaps, because of what I say and believe—in freedom, emancipation, and equality—you will turn away from me."

"I am your friend, Nat. I do not see color."

"If you did not see color, you would not speak to me as you do. You would not own slaves."

"You don't know all that I risk to be with you. Can you imagine what others would say if they saw me? If they heard our conversation or saw me sharing these books with you, they would run me out of town like your Ethelred Brantley. But I am your friend and I will always, no matter what, be your friend, Nat Turner."

"Don't say 'always'; the price might be too high one day."

"I will be your friend forever, no matter what the cost."

They parted as friends and shook hands, as was their custom. "Until we meet again."

Nat Turner wound his way on foot back through the woods, down the traces he knew. He passed by the twin oaks. Then a thought stopped him.

This might be the last time. He might never see his friend again. The day of God's judgment was coming.

A bird called. A butterfly drifted by.

Then Nat turned. He ran.

Chapter 45

He would not have blood on his hands. Nat Turner plunged through the thicket, leaves and branches smashing against his face. He crashed through the bushes, scratching his arms. Time was running out. He had to give Thomas the warning.

Nat Turner stumbled as he ran, crashing downward, but then regained his balance. He yelled when he caught sight of his friend. Still picking his way through the woods, Thomas Gray reined in his horse before he entered the road.

The clearing was quiet; even the birds seemed to have stopped singing. "Hypocrite!" Nat Turner was surprised to hear the word leap from his mouth. The only sound, other than his voice, was the irregular clomping of the anxious horse's hooves. "You are my friend, but you are a coward! You lie to yourself! You are too afraid to stand apart from Nathaniel Francis and the others.

"You mock writers like Shakespeare, while you are afraid to risk doing anything yourself." Thomas's life and soul were at stake. This was no time to mince words.

"You lie to yourself, Thomas! The difference between you and Nathaniel Francis is not much more than appearance. You exchange the false friendship of drunkards like Nathaniel for transforming the world. What good are your gifts if you do nothing with them? What good are the blessings you have if you waste them on wickedness instead of using them to do good?"

Thomas looked beyond the trees to the road as though he wanted to bolt away.

Winded, Nat Turner grabbed the reins of Thomas's horse. His

lungs burned, his chest heaved. "Repent now! As your friend and brother I beg you. God's judgment is coming!"

"Nat, quiet yourself, you fool! Someone will hear!"

"Perhaps you will escape the first death because you don't believe. But trouble will find you where you stand in the middle, Thomas."

"You sound like a crazy man!"

"You judge yourself lightly but for others you use a heavier measure! You tell yourself you have no problem, you are just a little drunk. Ask those who are sober if you are a drunkard!

"You and the others like you try to judge for yourselves if you are bigoted, patting yourselves. Ask slaves and free black men if you are fair, if you are without stain! If you want to know if you have a problem, ask the ones you have harmed. Better still, if you truly have courage, ask your enemies!"

Nat Turner loosed the reins and stepped back from Thomas's horse. He stretched out his arm and pointed his finger at his friend. Then, his heart pounding, he gave the pronouncement he had given many times to others.

"God has sent me to the oppressors, to the captors, to plead with you to turn. The cries and moans of my people have risen to God's ears. I warn you, even now He is preparing the death angel.

"God has seen your sins and the hardness of your hearts. Turn before it is too late, before brother rises against brother and nation against nation, before plowshares are turned to swords!"

Nat Turner planted his feet. "Woe to you because you demand justice and turn away from mercy!

"Woe to you because you want the best for yourselves and ignore your brothers in need!

"Woe to you because you withhold justice from the alien, the fatherless, and the widows!

"Woe to you because you point out sin in other men and ignore your own!

"Woe to you because you deny your own children, abandoning them to slavery, and selling them for concubines."

Thomas Gray stood in his stirrups. "You are a crazy man, Nat Turner. A religious fanatic! You will be sorry for the words you have spoken to me this day!"

Nat Turner could not stop. The pronouncements controlled his mouth, controlled his words. He did not want Thomas Gray's eternal blood on his hands. He wanted his friend to awaken. He wanted his friend to live. "Woe to you because you put wealth and titles above brotherly love!

"Woe to you because you set yourself in high places and look down on those who are not like you!

"Woe to you because you leave a curse on your generations to come!

"Woe to you because the blood of God's children is on your hands!

"Judgment will begin with the house of God! I am sent to warn you and pray that you will turn. If you refuse, at the Final Judgment Ethiopia the Queen of the South and Nineveh will stand to give testimony against you; for even they heard the word of slaves and turned! Choose ye this day and turn!"

When Nat Turner was finished, he fled and disappeared into the woods.

Chapter 46

July 17, 1831

It was Sunday, and Nat Turner, Hark, Mother Easter, and the others made their way to Turner's Meeting Place.

Sallie had forbidden him, since late spring, to preach there. She had forbidden him to speak the name of the Lord anywhere. Her brother, the young bully Nathaniel Francis, had seen his last meeting with Thomas Gray and accused Nat Turner of stirring up trouble.

All the captives were warned against gathering at Turner's Meeting Place, but still they walked the road with no name—even Davy, the boy Nathaniel Francis called Two Feet, walked with them, leaning on his stick.

Despite Sallie's command, Nat Turner could not abandon his people. They could not be expected to show courage if their leader shrank from serving the Lord out of fear of man.

July 4th had come and gone. Instead of waging war, Nat Turner had spent the day writhing on the barn floor. Sickness and pain had gripped his stomach, and a headache blinded him. Hark spread the word to delay the battle.

When illness had overtaken him on Independence Day, Nat Turner thought it might be a sign from God. Maybe God had repented of His judgment against the captors. Maybe during the night, with Independence Day dawning, the white slave owners of Southampton had seen their hypocrisy and turned. Perhaps, instead of reveling, they had put on sackcloth and ashes on the Fourth of July. Perhaps instead of drinking and gorging, they had humbled themselves like Nineveh.

He had wanted to believe it, and all day as he groaned he had prayed. But when he recovered, Nat Turner found nothing had changed.

It was not over. So, after he recovered, Nat Turner found a place, a quiet sacred place in the woods, and visited it each day waiting to hear from God.

That is when they began to visit him. They came to him, at first one by one. They came, at first only by day, but then even in his dreams.

The martyrs came, the battered, the prophets, the captives. The old ones hobbled along. The women came—some moaning, some staggering, and some with babies crawling beside them. One of them, he was certain, was Misha—his mother's cousin who died on the passage to America.

The martyred men came—some of them weeping, some bowed low, and some shaking their fists. Among them were the crucified, the beheaded, those who had died in passage, or refused the bonds of slavery. Among them were the rejected, the despised, the spotted, and the forgiven abominable.

They sang dirges to him. The martyrs told him of their suffering and they told him how they had tried to love and walk in peace. They came to him from all ages, from all nations; they spoke with different tongues. The martyrs were the witnesses and he heard their testimonies. Before him were all the souls who had walked God's path only to be slaughtered.

He had no choice, they told him; he was born to avenge them. They demanded audience. The time for judgment had come. "Slavery is the wine that fills the cup of the whore of Babylon," they told him.

"It is time for harvest; thrust in your sickle," they said. They promised Nat Turner that, though he would die in service to God's kingdom, he would be with them. "It is a hard thing," they told him, "but you will be a part of the first resurrection."

They encircled him in the holy place and whispered to him. "'Blessed and holy is he that hath part in the first resurrection: on such the second death hath no power, but they shall be priests of God and of Christ, and shall reign with him a thousand years.'" Their voices were as many choruses, folding end over end. "'Blessed are the dead which die in the Lord from henceforth.' Rest. Your works will follow you."

They told him it was God's nature to choose a man of peace to make war. "'Thrust in thy sickle, and reap: for the time is come for thee to reap; for the harvest of the earth is ripe.'"

The time was short—before summer's end. He had no choice, they whispered. The time of mercy was over; the captors must die. "'He that leadeth into captivity shall go into captivity: he that killeth with the sword must be killed with the sword. Here is the patience and the faith of the saints.'"

Nat Turner prayed. *Make me ready, Lord! Give me the heart I need to do battle!*

The witnesses spun in the air, just above the grass, whirlwinds at their feet. Now dressed in white, the witnesses whispered to him. "'Lift up your heads, O ye gates; and be ye lift up, ye everlasting doors; and the King of glory shall come in. Who is this King of glory? The LORD strong and mighty, the LORD mighty in battle.'"

Nat Turner felt himself getting stronger. "'Lift up your heads, O ye gates; even lift them up, ye everlasting doors; and the King of glory shall come in.'"

The witnesses, the martyrs stopped the dirges and began singing songs of glory.

> *Him that overcometh will I make a pillar in the temple of my God,*
> *and he shall go no more out: and I will write upon him the name of my God,*
> *and the name of the city of my God, which is new Jerusalem,*
> *which cometh down out of heaven from my God:*
> *and I will write upon him my new name . . .*

Some danced and played instruments like the saints in Ethiopia. The elders encircled him and laid their hands on him. "'And God shall wipe away all tears from their eyes; and there shall be no more death, neither sorrow, nor crying, neither shall there be any more pain: for the former things are passed away. And he that sat upon the throne said, Behold, I make all things new. . . . He that overcometh shall inherit all things; and I will be his God, and he shall be my son.'"

Nat Turner had the promise of the first resurrection, the promise that he would be God's son, a Father who would never forsake him or leave. He was promised everlasting love, a Father who would wipe away all his tears and heartbreak.

Nat Turner could not walk in fear now that he had received the words of the martyrs. Two weeks had passed since Independence Day, since the night of his sickness. But the words of the martyrs reminded him that his life was not his own. He must stand with his people. He must serve those who suffered now and the witnesses.

Despite Sallie's command, he must first honor the Master's word. Nat Turner could not deny the Father he had prayed to for so long. So, despite Sallie's command, he made his way along with the others to his Father's church. He would not walk in fear. He would lead his people with courage. They would walk as men made free by God.

He raised his voice to lead the captives, the living martyrs, in song. Nat Turner spoke the words clearly; the others sang, repeating his words.

> Am I a soldier of the cross,
> A follower of the Lamb,
> And shall I fear to own his cause,
> Or blush to speak his name?

They weren't true, the stories people told about courage. Most of what passed as bravery was only brutality or craziness. He looked around at the captive people, the living witnesses, who traveled with him—his mother, Cherry, Hark, Nelson the preacher, Sam, and the others. They had no weapons and no army. Every stand they took, even a small one, risked their lives. But they persisted, risking their lives for what was right. They came despite their fear.

Nat Turner saw the church ahead of them. Cypress trees lined the road they walked. They could stop in a grove along the way. There was no need to face what they knew lay ahead. Nat Turner continued to lead the song and the others followed.

Must I be carried to the skies
On flowery beds of ease,
While others fought to win the prize,
And sailed through bloody seas?

Courage was what he saw on the people's faces. Courage was standing to do what was needed, even afraid. Nat Turner's Meeting Place was their church home, too. God was their Father, too. They wouldn't deny Him, no matter the consequences.

Are there no foes for me to face?
Must I not stem the flood?

No matter how afraid his body was, he was warrior in his heart, and he knew his cause righteous. Nat Turner looked at the faces of the suffering around him. Indignation and courage swelled in him.

Captive hands had built this church. Driving teams of horses and mules, they cut the road. Beneath the hot sun they cleared the land. Their axes felled the trees. They cut the boards.

Nat Turner stepped to the building and rubbed his hand over three nails. Standing next to his father long ago, he had pounded them into place.

Captive sweat and blood stained the floor inside. Nat Turner stepped away from Turner's Meeting Place and turned back toward the other captives.

Sure I must fight, if I would reign;
Increase my courage, Lord.
I'll bear the toil, endure the pain.

They stepped onto the grass of the churchyard, walking toward the building. Nat Turner put one foot in front of the other.

Courage was summoning the strength to keep living. He looked at his mother's face. He could only imagine the horrors she had already endured. Yet she still fought. Courage, despite the odds, to keep fighting. They knew what awaited them.

Thy saints in all this glorious war,
Shall conquer though they die.

They held hands, except for young Davy, Two Feet, who stood on the church steps, rejoicing, waving his stick in the air.

They view the triumph from afar,
And seize it with their eye.

Before Nat Turner and the others finished the song, Sallie Francis Moore Travis, Nathaniel Francis, Richard Whitehead, and the others charged from inside the church, out the doors, trampling Davy—who was invisible to them—on the steps.

Chapter 47

Nathaniel Francis, Salathiel, and Richard Whitehead did not notice the boy Davy; their anger was focused on Nat Turner.

His memory was jumbled now, trying to recall it; they beat him so badly.

He remembered pleading with them for their own salvation. "The mercy you extend to others is the mercy you shall receive." Nat Turner was not certain that they heard the words; they were garbled by the blows. They growled at him, their teeth like sabers. They would not listen.

The mob drew closer. Weapons and whips and threats. As he spoke, Nat Turner steeled himself for the first blow. "This is the word of God to you. 'I will also gather all nations, and will bring them down into the valley of Jehoshaphat, and will plead with them there for my people . . . whom they have scattered among the nations, and parted my land. And they have cast lots for my people . . . a boy for an harlot . . . a girl for wine.'"

They were drawing closer and closer. He felt the heat from their bodies and their anger, the meanness from their spirits. "God has warned you. I warn you again. The Lord has commanded: Love your neighbor." Nat Turner swept his arm toward the black people behind him. Couldn't the others see that they were also children of God? Couldn't they see how much God loved them? "Love your neighbor as yourself." He pointed toward the sky. "God is watching; we know and He knows what you have done. You have stolen freedom, you have stolen property, and you have stolen and sold God's people. You keep His people from the Lord's salvation. You steal their dreams.

"'And he that stealeth a man, and selleth him, or if he be found in his hand, he shall surely be put to death.'

"As Jonah pleaded with Nineveh, so I beg you: Turn!"

Nathaniel Francis shook his fist. "You are forbidden to be here! My sister gave you an order. Who are you, you crazy man, you nigger, to try to preach to us? You think you can speak to me this way? You think you talk this way to all of us? You forget that we are your masters."

They transformed in front of him, no longer the people he knew. Instead he saw the twisted faces of the spirits inside them, the curses and demons that tormented them. Nat Turner knew that he was still speaking, but the words came from his belly and not his mind. The crowd was shouting around him and he could no longer hear. He fought to speak the truth to them before God's judgment; he did not want blood on his hands. Nat Turner heard a final statement come from his mouth, "'Prepare war, wake up the mighty men, let all the men of war draw near; let them come up: Beat your plowshares into swords and your pruninghooks into spears: Let the weak say, I am strong.'"

Then they fell on him—men, women, and children. Fists and threats. Being righteous did not lessen the pain; it was no physical protection; it did not stop his blood from flowing. With whips, they took turns beating him—even Sallie.

Chapter 48

Nat Turner drifted in and out of consciousness. The witnesses, dressed in white, floating, drifting in and out, visited him in the barn. "You shall not die, but live," unseen by others, the martyrs whispered to him.

> They compassed you about like bees
> They thrust at you with swords
> But the Lord is your strength and song
> The Lord is your salvation.

They fed Nat Turner with hymns and spiritual songs.

> The right hand of the Lord is exalted
> You shall not die but live and declare
> The works of the Lord!

His people came to him by night when no one could see them. They—his mother; Cherry; and Charlotte, the sad-eyed girl held captive by Nathaniel Francis—came with broth and bits of corn bread and mashed greens soaked in pot liquor. They kneeled beside him on a bed of hay in the Travis barn. "Don't leave us. We need you, Prophet Nat. You must live!"

The men visited him—Hark, Sam, Yellow Nelson, and Dred. "We will pick a new date. You'll see. Vengeance will come."

Slowly, Nat Turner felt himself returning to life. He began to distinguish, again, night from day. The witnesses came back to him and told him he should await a sign in the heavens.

He spoke to the men who secretly visited him, "My body is mending." Then he told them about the sign the witnesses said they should look for in the sky. He could not describe it, but they would recognize it when it appeared, he told them. It would not be an eclipse. It would not be an ordinary thing. "When it appears, we will gather at Cabin Pond."

Chapter 49

August 1831

S weat trickled down Nat Turner's neck as he stood in the field among the corn. It had been unbearably hot and there was no breeze to cool him. The wounds on his back and on his legs still ached, sometimes itched, but he was able to work, and he watched for the sign.

He hacked at the corn with the scythe in his hands. Back and forth, gliding, and the stalks fell before him. Back and forth, back and forth. He lost himself in the rhythmic motion.

Like the scythe, Nat Turner's mind swung back and forth. Weeks had passed. He had watched people all his life in an effort to figure it out. What was it that made some people comfortable exploiting other people? What made them believe that others existed only to serve their needs? Nat Turner used his arm to wipe the sweat dripping from his forehead. If he could find the one thing, then he could fix it. If he could find the one thing, then he might better reason with the ones who took advantage.

Though he knew it was senseless, he still hoped it would all end. Back and forth. Back and forth. Yet it seemed the captivity would never turn.

Since his illness on the Fourth of July, since the beating two weeks later, nothing about the captors had changed. If anything, they seemed to consider his beating a victory.

Was it white skin that made them aggressive and unfeeling? The white people around him had built institutions with racial superiority as their foundation. The exploitation they created was based on color. It would have been easy to follow the path they created and believe it was whiteness that made them ruthless.

Back and forth. Back and forth.

But not all white men were ogres. Some, like Phipps, refused to play along, even at their own peril. There were some, like white abolitionists he'd heard of, who openly took a stand against slavery. While others, like Gray, had troubled consciences but not the courage to take a stand.

In truth, there were cruel black men who exploited fellow slaves to make their own lives easier. And his mother had told him stories of the slavers on the ships—men of all tongues and colors.

And in his Ethiopian homeland there were many who made slaves of their own kin. His mother had been *chewa* once, master over her cousin Misha. She had not beat Misha; she had not physically bound her in chains. But Nat Turner knew. He knew firsthand the heartbreak of hopelessness, the shame of misuse, and the despair of rejection— pain greater and longer-lasting than whips or chains. Because of slavery in his own Ethiopian family, there was a family debt he owed.

Thomas Gray said it was religion that made men cruel, that made men believe that others were created simply for their profit and pleasure. There were cruel preachers who were manstealers, fornicators, murderers, and rapists like Richard Whitehead. But religion also made some men better men, better versions of themselves, called to noble visions and to serve.

Back and forth. Back and forth.

Indifference. Some men thought it was their right to lord it over others. Though sometimes it seemed that the lords thought others were lording it over them. They used any excuse to get their way and to convince others to follow them. Men and women, like children, gave themselves permission to be bombastic, to be cruel, to be bullies, or even to be kind.

Back and forth. Back and forth.

Finally, it was just a choice, free will. And some used their will to steal the will and gifts of others.

Back and forth. Hunger burned his stomach. Sweat dripped in his eyes.

Lurking behind it all was fear. Fear and something more—insecurity, doubt. Behind the captors' behaviors were baseless thoughts of not being good enough. The solution was to force someone else to be less, to be the scapegoat.

Nat Turner reached for the thought, hoping to capture it, to understand. The twisted solution of bullies, of those who felt unloved, was to force others to be less, to dim their light in hope that the bullies' own would shine brighter. The irrational solution seemed to be to box others in, to chain them.

Though the captors felt less, they would be pharaohs; they would force themselves into the place of best and force others to serve them. Every bright light had to be dimmed or extinguished. Everyone capable of exposing the lie of their superiority had to be captured, chained, and hidden away.

Nat Turner wiped his arm across his forehead. Back and forth.

The unloved, the captors, secretly believed, behind their pretense of superiority, that God despised them—their bodies, their thoughts, their spirits. He could not bear to look upon them. The captors believed that instead of mercy, the invisible God waited, numbering their sins, waited with glee until He could punish them. They believed in a loveless God who saw them as monsters, a God who lorded His superiority over them, forcing them into servanthood.

Though they felt unloved and despised, they believed they were created in His image. To earn His approval, they must be like Him and treat others as mercilessly as their merciless God treated them.

The solution was hate. The solution was oppression—oppression hidden behind color, academics, religion, economics, and theories of power. The captors would treat others as their God treated them. They would hate others and make them their despised servants.

It was an irrational solution that required the oppressed to be at peace with and desire the solution: The only good slave was the quiet, obedient slave—one who mindlessly submitted to captivity, even craving it and demeaning himself. The bad slave was one who desired his freedom, to be more, to be a light in the world. The solution required boundless attention and energy, constant vigilance to keep the oppressed, the captured, in place beneath them. Steely control was required. More hate. Violence. Each act of oppression took both the captor and the captive further from what they both desired.

Back and forth. Back and forth.

The solution was no solution. It was impossible to keep control—a flower, a son, a thought might break out anywhere. God-given, by the One True God, whose name is Love, there was no way to contain them.

The solution was no solution, no medicine real medicine for their disease, because the only true antidote for the problem of insecurity and fear was love.

Back and forth. A drop of sweat dripped from his nose and made a dark dot in the dust where it landed. How long? He saw discouragement on the faces of his people and didn't know how much longer the captives would have faith to believe. They all had been waiting for what seemed like forever.

He heard the mournful prayers and songs. He saw the anger building. He saw them on bended knee. He saw the hopelessness.

Nat Turner preached to them, when they gathered, to be patient. "Be patient, brothers and sisters. The day of the Lord's harvest is coming. Only He knows when the yield is ripe. We must wait for His sign." Only those who knew of the coming revolution understood the true interpretation of his words. "The Lord is full of mercy, even for our captors, but He has promised the harvest will come. 'Be ye also patient; stablish your hearts: for the coming of the Lord draweth nigh.'"

But the captive people he spoke to had not been to the Great Dismal Swamp. They had not heard the voice of God. It was August, most of the corn harvest was over, and still nothing had been seen in the heavens. They were losing patience. They were losing hope. They were losing faith.

Nat Turner prayed as he worked culling the weeds from among the corn that remained, prayed as he had so many times. This time he prayed without words.

Back and forth. Back and forth. The suffering seemed forever, endless. Nat Turner hoped and waited for God.

THOUSANDS OF MILES away, in Ethiopia—in Lalibela, in Aksum, in Gondar—the old ones prayed, prayers that shook mountains and made clouds weep.

A small storm began in the highlands there. It continued to grow. The old men and women—toothless, ancient, gnarled, and wrinkled—said it was God blowing; the storm had a special mission. As in the time of Moses, God had heard the captives' cries, they said.

The storm left Ethiopia and traveled over the Sahara, picking up warmth. Weeks after the tiny storm began, gaining strength as it traveled, it spread its enormous fury out over the Atlantic Ocean, expanding into a great hurricane.

ON AUGUST 12, 1831, waters off the Caribbean coast, blown by the Ethiopian winds, battered the slave-holding state of Barbados. Back and forth. St. John's Church and Bridgetown Synagogue were swiftly turned to rubble. People, before the water and wind swept them away, pointed at the blue sun in the sky.

Sailors pointed at blue sails before their ships tumbled end over end in the ocean. The wind shook slave shackles in Puerto Rico and Cuba, including Guantánamo Bay. The hurricane, led by the smoldering indigo sun, killed people in the American slave states of Mississippi, Alabama, Florida, and Louisiana and battered the shores with hail and water. Men, horses, houses, and ships crumpled, tumbling like dried leaves. Back and forth. The waters of Lake Pontchartrain flooded the slave port of New Orleans. The auction blocks were swept to sea. The Great Barbados Hurricane, the hurricane of the blue sun, left more than twenty-five hundred people dead.

BACK AND FORTH. The corn fell before his scythe.

Nat Turner had read all the scriptures, had sung all the songs to himself, and whispered a lifetime of prayers. Just once, this once, he begged to see a prayer answered. He needed it before he died. He thought of all the people he had preached to in Southampton and beyond. He saw their faces, their scars, their broken hearts, and the tears in their eyes. He breathed the scriptures instead of speaking them.

> *Righteous art thou, O Lord, when I plead with thee: yet let me talk with thee of thy judgments: Wherefore doth the way of the wicked prosper? wherefore are all they happy that deal very treacherously?*

Nat Turner held the scythe at his side, closed his eyes, and prayed to his Father. He wiped the sweat from his face again. "Abba, help us."

Back and forth.

There was eeriness in the air in Southampton. In the still, in the heat, Nat Turner thought he smelled death. He raised his head from where he had bowed it. A small, cool breeze kissed the back of his neck and he opened his eyes. His arm stilled.

The sun, as he stared, turned from yellow to green to blue—bluish-gray, the color of death, and then to an ominous indigo.

God had been forced to choose and He had chosen. It was August 12, 1831, the year and day of the Lord's judgment. Gripping his scythe, Nat Turner left the field where he worked.

Running, he headed for Cabin Pond.

Chapter 50

He could not turn around. He would not turn around. Nat Turner waded through the corn headed for the woods. He took no thought of overseers. This was the moment. God had sent him back for His people, for the children, for their dreams. He would blind the overseers and stop their ears.

Again, as he ran, Nat Turner heard the voice of God.

Fear not: for I am with thee: I will bring thy seed from the east, and gather thee from the west; I will say to the north, Give up; and to the south, Keep not back: bring My sons from far, and My daughters from the ends of the earth; Even every one that is called by My name: for I have created him for My glory, I have formed him; yea, I have made him.

As he ran, God's words filled his ears and encouraged his heart for battle.

Yea, before the day was I am He; and there is none that can deliver out of My hand: I will work, and who shall let it? For your sake I have brought down all their nobles, whose cry is in the ships.

Nat Turner's bare feet pounded the ground. What was before him seemed like a dream.

I am the LORD, your King, which maketh a way in the sea, and a path in the mighty waters; which bringeth forth the chariot and horse, the army and the power—they shall lie down together, they shall not rise: they are extinct, they are quenched as tow.

Remember ye not the former things, neither consider the things of old. Behold, I will do a new thing; now it shall spring forth; shall ye not know it? I will even make a way in the wilderness, and rivers in the desert to give drink to My people, My chosen.

Though he charged ahead, Nat Turner felt slowed, as if he ran through some thick substance like honey. It must have been the same for Washington, Nathan Hale, and Crispus Attucks. Each step forward brought him closer to the beginning. Each step forward brought him closer to the end. Nat Turner's feet touched familiar grass, took him past trees he had grown with since a boy. Branches he had touched a lifetime ago reached out to touch him.

Going to Cabin Pond meant people, people he knew, people he was raised with, people he loved, were going to die. It was the price of freedom, revolution, and war.

Would any of the captives have the courage to meet him at the pond? Would they recognize the sign?

But there was no doubting the sign. The indigo sun was the sign of God's judgment. God had made His choice and the time of mercy had ended.

The captives had talked—they were ready to be God's army, they were ready to die for freedom. But they had had lifetimes of being afraid, of obeying tyranny just for survival. Now that it was time, would they have the courage to join him? They were farmers, not warriors—the descendants of generations of farmers stolen from Africa. They were peaceful people who wanted only to grow things from the soil. Who could expect them to do battle?

Nat Turner ran on, stopping at moments to use the scythe to hack his way through the brush. It would be a miracle if any of them came. His people had been frightened and tortured for so many years; it would be a miracle if someone had not already betrayed him. After waiting so long, there might be a hangman's party waiting for him rather than an army.

The harvest had come. People would be killed—the roots of Turner's Meeting Place—the pastor, the trustees, and their heirs. He had known the names all his life—the Whiteheads, the Francises, the Turners, the Newsoms. They would be the first among the deaths of the church's members—all those who used God's name in vain, pretending to be holy and pretending to love.

But it was not only family names; the names also belonged to faces. Like Sallie. Nat had known her since they were children. Nathaniel and Salathiel. Richard Whitehead. Nat Turner thought of all the faces. All of them were captors, but they were also his childhood friends and brothers. Brother to both captors and captives, he should not have to choose.

His own brothers would have no part in it—Samuel was already dead and John Clarke had no place in the Turner's Meeting Place deed.

The blue sun was hot on his neck and shoulders. It changed the color of everything around him. The grass beneath his feet was dark gray, no longer green. The wind that blew about him lifted the leaves and the branches. Each step brought him closer to the end.

Chapter 51

He thought of the people who would be lost, the ones who cried, "Lord! Lord!" Pretending to be holy, pretending to love God, but breaking God's greatest commandments.

Nat Turner forced his feet to keep moving. This would be his last harvest. No turning back. He was the instrument of God's judgment. It was not his will—he was no more than an axe in the hands of God. He had surrendered his choice. *"And that servant, which knew his lord's will, and prepared not himself, neither did according to His will, shall be beaten with many stripes."* The yoke of Jesus was upon him. He had surrendered ten years ago.

No turning back. It was the sure and righteous judgment of the Lord. He moved faster now. No birds, no dogs barking, only the steady sound of Nat Turner's breathing and of his feet pounding the earth. Conviction grew with each step.

The witnesses, dressed in white, came to him then as he ran. They sang to him, swirling around him. "Remember Mother Easter." He saw her gray hair and her eyes reddened with tears. So many tears. So many broken hearts. The witnesses sang laments about Cherry, about Charlotte, and about his mother. They reminded him of the children who had been violated and stolen. The murdered ones. They showed him the bleeding, cracked young feet and the calloused, tormented hands and feet of the elders—hands that had scrubbed and plowed too much, feet that had seen too many fields. So many tears. So many broken hearts. They sang him requiems of those who had been betrayed, like him, their hopes slaughtered.

"What is the price of a man's dignity?" they sang, whispering in his ears. "What is the cost to generations that follow?" They showed him black people—ivory, pecan, ebony—weeping and praying. Most he did not know. Then they showed him Mother Easter again, this time asleep on the floor. He felt her bones aching and heard her heart weeping. He could hear her murmuring prayers as she slept, begging for rescue. Other voices were added to hers, so many he could not decipher the words, but he understood their meaning.

They reminded Nat Turner that he was God's son chosen to do this special work. They reminded him of the reward promised him. *Blessed and holy is he that hath part in the first resurrection: on such the second death hath no power, but they shall be priests of God and of Christ, and shall reign with Him a thousand years.*

Thrust in thy sickle, and reap: for the time is come for thee to reap; for the harvest of the earth is ripe. The witnesses sang a sad hymn of summer harvest.

> *For afore the harvest, when the bud is perfect,*
> *and the sour grape is ripening in the flower,*
> *he shall both cut off the sprigs with pruning hooks,*
> *and take away and cut down the branches.*
> *They shall be left together unto the fowls of the mountains,*
> *and to the beasts of the earth: and the fowls shall summer upon them,*
> *and all the beasts of the earth shall winter upon them.*

He was breathless now and looked up at the unmoving indigo sun. Then Nat Turner clawed through the bushes in front of him and stepped out onto the edge of the waters of Cabin Pond.

The sad-eyed girl, Charlotte, was waiting there for him.

Chapter 52

Sad-eyed Charlotte—she was tiny, not much more than a girl. "I know where they meet. I know where they go—Nathaniel Francis and his friends. You can find them at the still on Sunday nights, drinking at Waller's." She pleaded with him. "Let me help. Let me go with you." She had overheard Sam and Dred speak of the revolt; she always kept her ears open. She knew the meeting place. "I've been waiting for the sign."

"This is no battle for women. We will all most likely die."

"I am already dead, Prophet Nat. Don't women want to be free? Don't women suffer enough to fight?" Charlotte cried as she confessed to him the things that had been done to her.

"We will come back to the Francis place for the rest of his heirs. It is the judgment of the Lord; no heirs are to be left alive."

"I can help you," she told him. "I can make your way clear. And Mother Easter and I can make provision for you."

He patted her head. She bore too much burden for such a small girl. But her eyes said she had already seen too much, been hurt too much. Her dress poked out in front of her. Charlotte lifted her head in defiance. "No child of mine will die a slave. Please. Let me help."

He walked with her to the clearing where others were waiting. So many betrayals. So much heartbreak. "Judgment will begin with the house of the Lord," he told them. "No heirs can be left alive. We must destroy the root." Nat Turner knew the faces and he knew their stories—their suffering was his—they were one. Too many beatings and too many brinings. He looked at sad-eyed Charlotte. Too many rapes and violations. He looked around at all the men. Too much cruelty—whippings, amputations for missing quotas—and too many deaths.

"We are not murderers! We are innocent men! We are men of peace forced to take up arms against our brothers to save our lives. They have forced our hands."

A man in rags, his head bowed, spoke up. "Is there no other way?"

For years Nat Turner had pleaded the same thing himself. He looked at the speaker and then at the other men. "What haven't we tried? Haven't we prayed? Haven't we begged? How many times have we asked them, begged them to turn? What else could we do to reconcile?

"How many times have we prayed for a deliverer? God has heard our prayers. Look at the sign." He pointed at the indigo sun. "We are to be our own deliverers! We are God's hands here on earth." Nat Turner looked back at the man. "We cannot turn back now. No matter what happens, we are victors.

"God has decreed that the time for mercy is over. If we do nothing, they will continue to kill us. They kill us daily, wrapping themselves around us like vines—choking our wives, our sons, and our daughters, our dreams, our faith, and our land.

"Like them, we are all children of God. They are our brothers, but they have asked our Father to deny us. They show us no respect. They say we are mindless, heartless." Nat Turner looked at Hark and Yellow Nelson, the preacher. "They say we are animals who deserve nothing. Animals." He looked at Will, Sam, and Dred. "But God is our Father and we are His sons. We are men of honor, and where He leads we will follow—even if He leads us to death. It is a reasonable sacrifice for our freedom, for our children, for our seed who will follow."

Then Will stepped into the clearing. Nat Turner looked at Sam and Dred, also captives of Nathaniel Francis. They shook their heads; neither of them had told Will.

Nat Turner had seen Will when he preached on Sundays. He was a silent, solitary man, but Nat Turner had heard his story—

the loss of his family, of his wife and little daughter. He had seen the war on Will's face—the war between anger and hurt. He knew that Will, like many others, was looking for a way out, for deliverance, a way to make the pain go away—even death—his own death or the death of others. "Why are you here?"

"I am as willing to die," Will said, "as anyone." Nat Turner looked into the eyes of the Death Angel. It was settled then. Will's presence was the last sure sign of the judgment of the Lord.

Nat Turner looked into the other men's faces. "God has remembered the covenant He made with our forefathers—with Abraham, Isaac, and Jacob. His spirit is among us to rescue us from our enemies." When Nat Turner looked away from Will, Charlotte was gone. "We are the army of the Lord, come to ransom His people.

"We are his obedient servants—judgment will begin at the house of God." They worked through the details. They would do their work at night. When the morning came, what happened would be a mystery to the captors who survived. "We will not kill those who have no part in this battle unless we have no choice. If we are discovered, it is kill or be killed—we have no way to hold prisoners."

He planted his feet. "We will rape no women. We will destroy and steal no property. We will not return the evil done to us. We will behave with honor; we are soldiers of the Lord.

"But to our enemies, we will give no mercy; they have shown none. The Lord has said to kill all those whose feet walk upon the ground, those who say they are His children but mock the truth and love of God."

The men were quiet, their eyes focused. "The darkness will cover us. We will not falter. Even the night will be light around us." Most of them would die—captives and freemen. The Artis brothers, both Cheroenhaka Nottoway, Hathcock, and even white Berry Newsom had come to join them. "We must be in our places. We must hold our tongues. We must follow the plan; each man's life—

your brother's life—depends on it. We are comrades. We are patriot brothers and servants of the Most High God." They would divide into squads. Each would have its responsibilities.

His scythe in his hand, Nat Turner swept his arm in front of them. "In ten days, the night of the sickle moon, when it gives its least light, we will begin." During the ten days' time, they would make preparations. "May God bless the solemn work of our hands, and may He have mercy on each one of our souls."

They made plans. There were too many places and too much distance; they could not all go together. The leaders would meet at the first location to commence together. They agreed on the farms they would target. They made plans for the captors they would take at Waller's still.

As he looked at the men around him, Nat Turner saw some men weeping. On their faces he saw joy and sorrow, fear and courage. Other men's faces were set like stone. This was the beginning, the end. "No turning back!" Nat Turner told them. "We have the sign. The time for mercy is over. Take axe to the root!

"Wake up, men! Awake from the living death. Come forth from the tombs where you have been buried. Feel the muscle and sinew come alive on the bones. Feel your hearts beginning to beat again." He lifted his arms in the air. "Your strength is come, the blood begins to flow. Your minds awaken. 'Lift up your heads, O ye gates; and be ye lift up, ye everlasting doors; and the King of glory shall come in.'" The men in front of him began to stir. "Your hearts are pounding now! Feel the hope, feel your heads begin to rise!

"You are men now, lively men—mighty men, mighty warriors of the Most High God! Feel the strength in your legs—your ankles, your knees, your loins! Come forth! Come out of your tombs! Come out of your prisons! Shake off the grave clothes! Feel the power in your arms! Feel the courage, the power, the Spirit of God surging through you! 'Who is this King of glory? The LORD strong and mighty, the LORD mighty in battle.' Lift up your heads!"

Nat Turner saw the men before him gaining strength, gaining courage. "In their lifetimes our white brothers received good things while we received trouble, but now God says it is our turn and we will have our promised portion. They have made pledges of freedom for all men to God; they must keep their vows!" Some of the men were cheering. Some of them were shaking their fists.

Nat Turner quieted them. "Be sure of what you are doing. It is dangerous business. We are forced to take arms against our brothers. They are well armed; we will suffer. It is a hard thing, but most of us will bleed. Most of us will die.

"Some others will have the courage to join us along the way—warn them. More will stay behind to clean up and minister to the dead. But don't doubt: Most of us will die, and if we survive the revolt, we will most likely hang." The men were quiet now, some of them shifting foot to foot. "It is a hard thing to hear, but what choice do we have? What do we have to lose? I can promise you no reward here, but for your service to the Lord, I promise you that you will join me in the first resurrection."

When they were sobered, Nat Turner lifted them again. "Lift your heads, men, mighty men of God! Rise to defend our families! Rise to defend our humanity! Rise to defend our dreams!

"We rise to fulfill God's judgment! We rise in service to the King of kings! We are the great and powerful army of the Lord!"

There would be no Ethiopia for him. This was his final homeland now. "Rise as men of spirit! This is our native soil. We have paid the price for it! This is the land where we have toiled. This is the land where we have spilled our blood. We will have what has been promised us. Arise, men, to arms!"

Chapter 53

The captive warriors had farm instruments—swords made from scythes, like Nat Turner's, and axes—clubs made from fence posts, hammers, and tree limbs. They met at Cabin Pond to baptize one another and pray—victory prayers and prayers of absolution—except for Will, who stood apart from the rest of them.

When the night was black, ten days after the day of the indigo sun, beneath the sickle moon they made their way to the Travis farm. Nat Turner touched the passes he had written for any who might escape after the revolt, so they could travel—no black man could be on the road without a white man's written permission. He had wrapped the passes in a rag and tied them tightly around his waist.

Nat Turner stood outside of Sallie Francis Moore Travis's house with Will and the others. This was the beginning of the revolt, of the resurrection of his people; he would cast the first blow. The dogs were silent, as though the animals conspired with them.

Nat Turner secured the ladder against the side of the house so that he could enter the second-floor window and then open the front door to the others. He began to climb. He could not think about Sallie or her family; they had not cared about the suffering of others. There was no doubt: God had given two signs—the eclipse and the blue sun. The witnesses sang to Nat Turner as he climbed. *"Lift up your heads . . . and the King of glory shall come in."*

"Who is this King of glory?" The moon was barely a sliver against

the black sky. Silently, Nat Turner stepped through the lace curtains, through the window. "*The* LORD *strong and mighty, the* LORD *mighty in battle.*" He was no longer a man; he was an instrument in His Father's hands. Nat Turner stole down the steps and opened the front door. He was a servant bound to do his Master's will.

Will and the others, silent as coming winter, crept in and went to their work. Nat Turner reclimbed the stairs with Will. They made their way down the dark hallway to the bedroom. "*Who is this King of glory? The* LORD *of hosts, he is the King of glory.*"

Nat Turner and Will stood on either side of the bed over Sallie and Joseph Travis. Nat Turner had known her all his life. He put thoughts of her as a child out of his mind. Instead he saw her at the church house with the whip in her hands. He saw her teaching her son to be an oppressor.

She did not own him. She had held him and his people captive long enough. He was no man's property. He was a warrior priest sent to ransom his people. He belonged to God.

No turning back; it was kill or be killed. Nat Turner raised his sword, his scythe, to do the will of the Sovereign Lord, to strike the first blow for freedom. "You have given no mercy and so you shall have none: This is the Lord's judgment." Sallie opened her eyes. She recognized him. Then Will. Her husband awakened. Nat Turner raised his sword higher. " 'He that stealeth a man, and selleth him, or if he be found in his hand, he shall surely be put to death.' This is the judgment of the Sovereign Lord!"

His sword cut through the soft flesh of her neck and severed her head from her body. The warm blood sprayed and covered his hands. Will lowered his axe and made short work of Travis. A grim smile on his face, Will raised and lowered his axe over and over again, as though he was no longer thinking—like a wheel turning on a mill, a grim smile on his face. Will stepped in close so he was baptized in the blood.

On the floors beneath them, the others took care of Sallie's son, Putnam Francis Moore, and her nephew, Joel Westbrook. Nat

Turner was no longer a man; he was an instrument in the hands of God. He was a patriot, a warrior now, a comrade to his brothers. He closed himself to what he had seen and done and kept his mind on moving forward.

They left the Travis farm. Nat Turner could not think. If he did, he would go mad. He was not a farmer or a preacher now; he was a soldier. They were Knights Templar executing a plan of battle.

Nat and the other captives made their way in the dark on foot, over the paths and traces they knew. They waded through the cornfields and skirted among the trees.

They smelled the blood, all of them. They saw the death, all of them. They felt the power of men with blood and life and death on their hands. They were at once exhilarated and exhausted. But they must stay true to the work ahead of them; they could not let down the others.

They passed the Widow Harris's place and Will, raising his axe, turned to go in. Nat Turner touched Will's arm and shook his head, no. "We are God's army," he whispered. "We must stick with God's plan. Only His judgment. The Lord's will be done." They made their way to the home of Salathiel Francis.

Chapter 54

They listened for every sound, every snap. Any creak in the darkness might be a group of captors who had discovered them. Every rustle in the brush might mean they had been betrayed. "Be with us, Lord," Nat Turner whispered. Maybe he had told too many people. Maybe there was a spy among them. An owl screeched. Wings flapped. Nat Turner stopped. Was it really a creature, or a man with a gun?

They ran again, straining to hear; their nerves on edge. Nat Turner glanced up at the stars. He might never see them again. A cloud passed over the sliver of moon, and then they were in perfect blackness.

When they reached Salathiel Francis's, as they'd planned, one man pounded on the door. The others waited among the corn that grew from the fields up to Salathiel's small ramshackle cabin, covering the window, the walls of the shack, everything except the front door. Red Nelson answered.

When the matter was put to him, he joined them. He awakened Salathiel. The man was a giant. When he stumbled outside, half-asleep, it took several men to hold him.

Nat Turner raised his sword. "'He that stealeth a man, and selleth him, or if he be found in his hand, he shall surely be put to death.' This is the judgment of the Sovereign Lord!" They dispatched Salathiel Francis quickly.

They divided then—the leaders left to join their squads and render judgment on the others, as they had agreed. Nat Turner had Will now, and he needed to keep the man with him. Yellow Nelson needed someone strong, and they had decided Hark would be the one.

The two of them, Nat Turner and Hark, embraced as brothers. Nat touched his hand to his waistband. "I could give you a pass now," he whispered to Hark. "You could get away. Head for the Dismal Swamp, get on a boat. Women from all over the world." Nat Turner hoped his friend would take the pass. He hoped one of them would get away. "You could be gone before anyone discovers us."

Hark shook his head. "I understand now. You came back for me, brother. Why would I leave you now?" They shook hands.

Hark looked over his shoulder. "Don't look after me sad-eyed." Hark smiled. "You will see me again."

"We will meet at the great oak."

"Or at the first resurrection." Hark nodded, still smiling, though his eyes were sorrowful. "If I don't see you again, know this—women are my delight, but you are my brother—you made me a better man."

Words never failed Nat Turner, but he was bereft. "Keep your eyes open," he whispered. "And your head down."

Hark was still smiling when he turned, calling over his shoulder. "Why be careful now? You've been trying to get me hanged since the day we met."

Nat turned with his team and began to make their way to his sister-in-law's, Elizabeth Turner's farm.

Harriet

Chapter 55

Boston
1856

Harriet jumped to her feet, pressing her napkin to her mouth. This was the portion she did not want to hear. She did not want to hear about blood and deaths. She looked at William; he rose to his feet.

There was no anger on his face; instead he seemed troubled by her alarm. "Would you like to stop now? We don't have to go on."

Harriet could not speak. Her chest heaving, she worked to hold back the tears. She did not like to think of bloodshed or war, not even for a worthy cause.

She looked at William. She did not like to think of the man that she was conversing with as a murderer. She did not want to think of him covered in blood.

Harriet turned and walked toward the window. So many had already lost their lives—she did not want to believe that the only path to liberty was a crimson-stained one.

England had managed to abolish slavery without bloodshed. Something must be done here. Someone, someone must be found who might turn the country from the bloody path down which it seemed headed.

Behind her, distress in his voice, William spoke. "I mean you no harm. We can stop now." His concern sounded sincere.

Harriet Tubman, Henry Bibb, Frederick Douglass, Sojourner Truth, and so many nameless, faceless others—they had all faced so much more and there was no turning away for them. She didn't have to live it; she had only to hear the story.

Harriet dabbed her face and then, taking a deep breath, she turned and began walking back to the small table. "Courage today or carnage tomorrow," she said.

Nat Turner

Chapter 56

Cross Keys
1831

I**n his ears, Nat Turner's own breathing was too loud. His footsteps were too heavy. His heart pounded, his nerves jumped. Every shadow was a trap, a hand reaching out to catch him and the others.

It was late—the sun would rise in only a few hours—but still hot. His ragged, burlap shirt was plastered to him and drenched with sweat. Black dark. They felt their way through familiar places, moving through air like blackstrap molasses. His feet knew the grass, the moss, the furrowed ground. His soles felt the gnarled bumps of the roots of ancient trees. His hands touched the bark, the damp moss, and waxy leaves that he had known all his life. Still, in the familiarity there was danger. Every limb heavy with leaves held a waiting net. Every vine was a rope waiting to trip him and hang him and the others. Nat Turner steeled himself.

He was not like Will. He did not have anger to fuel him or a desire for revenge—he could not afford those emotions; they would have driven him off course. He was not like Hark—it was not brotherhood or loyalty that led him. For loyalty's sake he might have continued to pursue a different way.

It was justice that sent him through the night. It was obedience to God's service. An obedient son. Nat Turner repeated the phrase to himself as he ran. An obedient soldier.

He could not stop. There was a family debt he owed.

Keep me as the apple of the eye, hide me under the shadow of thy wings, from the wicked that oppress me, from my deadly enemies, who compass me about. They are inclosed in their own fat: with their mouth they speak proudly.

They passed by the home of Nathaniel Francis. They would confront him at Waller's still.

There was no choice now. There was no turning back. It was war. Kill or be killed. He would not turn back. There was a family debt he owed.

Chapter 57

Elizabeth Turner stared at him with red-rimmed, wild eyes. They dragged her and her visiting neighbor, the widow Newsom, and her overseer, Hartwell Peebles, from their beds. It was Nat Turner's older brother's house. There were traces of Samuel, ghosts of him—an old pipe, an old coat, and a picture of him hanging on the wall.

"Where is the deed? Where is the deed to Turner's Meeting Place?" Nat Turner yelled and the other captive men watched as he searched the drawers and cabinets. "You know I am not a slave! Where is the deed?"

Elizabeth Turner hissed at him, "There are no papers for you. You will never find them! I'm Samuel's heir. You are a nigger slave and you will die a slave!"

He stepped closer to the sofa so he could see them. There was only one candle lighting their faces in the pitch-black room. "You know I am not a slave. You had no right to sell me, to sell my family!" He wanted to choke the life from the old hag.

Her eyes narrowed as she looked around at Nat Turner and the others. "I will see all you niggers hanged!" Elizabeth spat at Nat Turner. The widow Newsom cowered, clinging to her. Elizabeth looked around again. "I've got all your names. I know you! Don't try to hide there in the dark. I see you! They will skin you, gut each one of you, and feed you to the dogs." Elizabeth cackled. "And I'll be there to watch!" The widow Newsom sat white-faced, mumbling to herself. The overseer sat with them on the sofa. The burly man's face looked confused, as though he thought he might be dreaming.

Nat Turner turned from them and went to search another drawer. "Where are the papers, Elizabeth? You have stolen property. You have stolen lives!"

"Elizabeth? You dare call me Elizabeth?" An icy snicker accompanied her words. "My, you are a prince with your band of thieves. But not for long! I'm not your weak, sniveling father! You will hang! You'll be skinned alive!" Elizabeth snarled. "There is no such thing as a nigger with property. I would rather die than see you with an inch of this land—even a church!" She scowled at Nat Turner, a cruel, defiant upturn to her lips. "No such thing as a nigger trustee. The only good nigger is a slave, and the best nigger is a hanged one!"

Nat Turner stopped searching then. His hands balled into fists. He had never hit a woman. But she was not a woman. She was a thing, filled with the spirit that kept slavery alive. He blew out the candle and by moonlight he saw a wisp of smoke curl in the air.

He would never find the papers. It wouldn't matter; no court would listen to him. It wouldn't matter; he bore the yoke of Christ, and they would kill him in the end.

There was just enough moonlight now to see the shapes of the people sitting on the sofa. The widow Newsom began to scream.

He had a job to do. He could not be distracted from his task—not by anger or vengeance, or even mercy. He could not fail the others who were doing their work in Cross Keys this night. It was kill or be killed.

Nat Turner looked at the men who had come with him. He was there to serve the Lord's judgment. He was an obedient soldier, an obedient son. He could not fail his Father.

He pronounced judgment on the offending heirs of the Newsom and Turner families—those who belonged to Turner's Meeting Place. When the three were dead, Nat Turner and his men moved on—it was war. Kill or be killed.

Chapter 58

For the lives of my wife and child!" Nat Turner imagined that on the other farms the warriors were uttering similar cries. Time was running out. It would be daylight soon. The darkness that held them, that protected them, would be gone. In what was left of the night his group made their way to the Whiteheads' farm.

They could not sing to encourage themselves. They could beat no drums. There was no fife, no fireworks, no standard-bearer, and no flag. Each man spoke to God for himself. Each man had to be convinced and strengthened within himself. *Arise, O Lord, in thine anger, lift up thyself because of the rage of mine enemies: and awake for me to the judgment that thou has commanded.*

It was grim business. They were doing what had to be done—poor men, farmers, captives transformed into the army of the Lord. *It is God that girdeth me with strength, and maketh my way perfect. He maketh my feet like hinds' feet, and setteth me upon my high places. He teacheth my hands to war, so that a bow of steel is broken by mine arms. Thou hast also given me the shield of thy salvation: and thy right hand hath holden me up, and thy gentleness hath made me great.*

He, Hark, Dred, Sam, Will, and the others were God's soldiers. Nat Turner forced himself to breathe slowly. Soon it would be over. *I have pursued mine enemies, and overtaken them: neither did I turn again till they were consumed. I have wounded them that they were not able to rise: they are fallen under my feet. For thou hast girded me with strength unto the battle: thou hast subdued under me those that rose up against me.*

He thought of his mother and Mother Easter. He would never see them again. He could see the eyes of sad-eyed Charlotte, and Nat Turner felt Cherry's hand in his hair.

Thou hast also given me the necks of mine enemies; that I might destroy them that hate me. They cried, but there was none to save them: even unto the LORD, but he answered them not.

They had no voices. There were no epic poems to celebrate their battle. Nat Turner wondered if people would remember them, if they would write songs for those who died in battle. He wondered if they would be remembered, if their names would be recalled as revolutionaries. Would later generations remember the story of what happened in Cross Keys, in Southampton County?

They were only the beginning. They fought so that their people, their children, a remnant, could survive. They sacrificed themselves for those who came after. They raised their hands to do God's judgment—taking axe to the root. The song from the Great Dismal played in his head.

Equip me for the war,
And teach my hands to fight,
Let all be wrought in love.

He remembered the witnesses. He thought of all the people he had preached to, all the brokenhearted and betrayed. He thought of his family—his mother, his wife, and his son. He could not turn back; he had promised God.

He and the others tramped solemnly over the traces for miles, avoiding the roads so they would not be detected on their way to the Whiteheads'.

Chapter 59

Outside the gate of the Whiteheads' farm, the captive warriors called in to Reverend Richard Whitehead, pastor of Turner's Meeting Place. "Come out, Dick!" they mocked him. They knew who he was. They all knew what he had done and that he had hidden it behind his collar, behind his mother's skirts.

Nat Turner sent men in to get the preacher and the Whitehead women. They brought Richard Whitehead out first. Still in his nightshirt, he jerked and flopped in the darkness like a handkerchief pulled by a string. Will and the others held him, forced him to his knees, and Nat Turner stood over him. "'Woe be unto the pastors that destroy and scatter the sheep of my pasture! saith the LORD.'"

Richard was haughty at first. "You black heathen! Don't you shout scriptures at me! I will see you hanged, you black devil!" He looked at his faithful servant Hubbard. "Get them off of me, Hubbard! Run, Hubbard, get the boys from their houses! We will roust these niggers!"

Nat Turner looked at the Whitehead captives who were gathering, carrying torches. Not one of the captives—Hubbard, Venus, or the others—lifted a hand to help the preacher. Not one took off running to alert authorities, to rescue the family.

Nat Turner looked at the faces, lit by the fire, and spoke to them. "'My people hath been lost sheep: their shepherds have caused them to go astray, they have turned them away on the mountains: they have gone from mountain to hill, they have forgotten their resting place.'" Men, women, and children gathered;

some Nat Turner had seen only from a distance in the fields. So many broken hearts. There were tears shining in the darkness. One small girl ran forward and spit on Richard Whitehead. So many people covered in shame. "'All that found them have devoured them: and their adversaries said, We offend not, because they have sinned against the LORD, the habitation of justice, even the LORD, the hope of their fathers.'"

Richard Whitehead looked at the captives surrounding him. Some of them had begun to yell, cursing him. He looked at Nat Turner and the captive warriors with him with scythes, posts, hammers, and axes in their hands. He sobbed for mercy. Nat Turner thought of Ethelred Brantley, of the captives in the fields, of so many broken hearts. "You have given no mercy and it is the judgment of the Lord that you will receive none."

Richard Whitehead was wailing now. "Hubbard! Hubbard, help me! You've known me since I was a boy!" He called for his mother.

"'And he that stealeth a man, and selleth him, or if he be found in his hand, he shall surely be put to death.' This is the judgment of the Lord!" Will stepped in close, the grim smile still on his face, and swung his axe. Will's shirt was blood-soaked, his face a bloody mask.

When Richard Whitehead was dead, the men brought out the other heirs of the Whitehead family. One of the girls escaped. Hubbard promised to find her before morning.

Nat Turner wanted to look away. He did not want to spill blood, but he was a soldier. He was the leader. He steadied himself. Kill or be killed. Destroy the root or die. He smelled the blood. He saw the death. Will swung his axe.

Nat Turner felt himself floating above it all. He saw the captors' bodies on the ground. He saw the captives gathered around, watching, holding torches. He saw himself wield his sword and then a wooden post.

He drifted on the healing brown waters of the Dismal

Swamp. "No more slave songs. No more bowing," he heard Hubbard say below him.

When his band departed, some of the captives from the Whitehead farm joined Nat Turner. Hubbard stayed behind to lead those who would minister to the dead.

Still drifting above them, Nat Turner watched as he and the others made their way to Waller's still.

Chapter 60

Nathaniel Francis would be at Waller's still. Sad-eyed Charlotte had told Nat Turner that he would be there with Jacob Williams, Thomas Gray, and John Clarke Turner. They would be gathered there with others in the hours before dawn, drinking corn liquor—made from corn stolen from starving people's mouths—at Waller's still.

He prayed that his friend Thomas Gray would not be there. Thomas was not a member of Turner's Meeting Place, but if he was present, there would be no choice. Kill or be killed.

Nat Turner prayed that his brother John Clarke would not be at Waller's still. He imagined the face of his brother and wanted to spare him. But he was called to do no less than the others. God's judgment required the lives of cousins, sisters, and fathers as well as brothers.

He knew the captors, even under threat of death, would deny their relationships. The captors felt no brotherhood; they sold their relations, beat them, sold them for prostitutes in New Orleans, and even hanged them. He must deny friends and relatives just as he and the others had been denied. It was a battle for freedom. It was God's justice. Kill or be killed.

Nat Turner signaled the men to take care as they approached the still. Lamps were burning inside the building but there was no sound. It might be a trap.

Nat Turner hunkered in the grass. His muscles screamed. His head throbbed. Overhead and in the woods, owls called warnings from the trees. Waller, Gray, Francis, and the other captors might be waiting, guns sited on the captives.

If the captives were discovered, the captors would shoot at them from a distance; they would not fight them hand to hand. The captives' axes and clubs would be nothing against shotguns, rifles, and handguns loaded with lead.

Nat Turner and the others crawled on the ground toward the still, listening for sounds, cautious of the slightest movement from within. But there were no shadows or noises. They inched toward the cabin.

Chapter 61

Deserted. Only flickering lamplight inhabited Waller's still.

When they reached the small cabin, it was deserted. Nat Turner was certain now—Nathaniel Francis, Levi Waller, and the others had been alerted. He felt a sinking feeling. Nat Turner and the other captives whispered urgently among themselves. They were betrayed.

The root must be destroyed. He had wasted precious time searching for the deeds and papers at Elizabeth Turner's, time that might cost others their lives. The militia might be gathering, might already be searching for them. But there was no turning back now. Kill or be killed. They had to finish what they had begun. Dawn was almost upon them.

All the men agreed that before they left the Waller farm, they would have to search his house. Levi Waller, Nathaniel Francis, and the others might have gathered there, thinking to arm themselves, thinking to defend Levi's family. There were horses tethered at Waller's still, but Levi or one of the others might have gone on foot to alert the militia. There was no choice—kill or be killed.

Nat Turner and the other captives made their way to Waller's home, their eyes scrutinizing every branch, every leaf that moved. They approached the house expecting to be fired upon. It would be their last stand.

But there was no gunfire. As the first light of dawn appeared, Nat Turner entered the house with no resistance. Neither Nathaniel Francis nor Levi Waller was there, only Levi Waller's family and the schoolteacher.

All inside were asleep. Nat Turner and the others had crept inside the large, one-room shack quietly; they could leave the family undisturbed with none the wiser. He signaled the men. They would back out the door—it was Nathaniel Francis they were after.

But Will froze in place. He shook his head.

The others backed out the door. Nat Turner motioned to Will again, but still he would not move. He stood as though he were frozen.

Then, as pale light came through the window, there was a shriek.

Chapter 62

They had agreed that if they were discovered, they could leave no witnesses alive—no witnesses to alert the militia.

Nat Turner looked at the screaming family. Seconds seemed like years.

He and the others would simply leave the family alive—their conspiracy had already been uncovered. The militia was probably already searching for them.

He did not want to kill them. Waller's family had not been part of the plan.

Nat Turner looked at his men. There was sorrow on their faces. But Will was still frozen in place, his axe ready.

Nat Turner looked at the panicking woman and her children. How could he choose one life over another? How could he choose to end their lives to save his wife and son?

But there was no choice. *You must destroy the root.* The time for mercy was over. He was a soldier. He had to obey. Nat Turner raised his sword.

Eyes wide open, tears burned his face. But then he saw and heard the witnesses, the martyrs. Nat Turner saw the pregnant slave woman on the shores of the Great Dismal Canal. *You must destroy the root.* He saw Misha, with her baby still tied to her, floating in the water. He heard the screams of the women and children on board the slave ships. Millions.

Kill or be killed. It was war. Uproot the vine to save the tender saplings.

Will raised his axe. Nat Turner raised his sword. They made short work of it. Kill or be killed. Daylight was upon them now and, as they had planned, the men dispersed.

The early morning sun chased Nat Turner to his hiding place. Some would return to their captors' farms. Others would hide away in the woods. When night returned they would assemble again at the great oak. But, no matter what, he would have to go back for Nathaniel Francis. *The root must be destroyed.*

How could he sleep? He didn't want to sleep; he didn't want to dream. Not until he met with the men again that night. Each had his own hiding place, unknown to the others. It was safer that way. Only Hark and Will knew this place.

Nat Turner had dug himself a cave, a pit, at the base of the great oak tree. He pulled branches and fallen logs in behind him. From underneath, he covered the opening with the logs, branches, and leaves. It was light outside but dark in the cave.

Nat Turner smelled the rich, loamy smell of the earth. He sat propped against the damp, musky wall. He did not want to sleep. He did not want to dream. He was afraid to dream. He did not want to think; imagining the worst would do no good. They were all in God's hands.

There was no food, though he was not sure that he could have eaten. Exhausted, Nat Turner leaned back against the wall and prayed for night to come. He prayed for his men. He prayed for news of their safety.

Against his will, the dark and mossy smell lulled him to sleep. Mercifully, he dreamed of Cherry. He dreamed of his mother. He dream of Ethiopia.

He startled awake. He was still exhausted, panting, though night had come again. Holding his breath, Nat Turner listened. There were three shrill calls, mockingbirds' cries. It was the signal he and Hark had agreed on. It was his friend, his brother. Safe.

Nat Turner waited until he saw a shadow and heard footsteps above him. He reached his hand through the branches to make an opening. He made out the shape of one of his men.

It was not Hark. It was the death angel: It was Will.

Chapter 63

Will had not kept to the plan. Instead of hiding, he had joined Yellow Nelson and Hark's band. He had met up with them at Benjamin Blunt's farm.

"Blunt was already alerted, his men on guard."

Nat Turner was certain of it now. Someone had given them away.

Will was panting. "Handguns and shotguns. They were barricaded in the house. They shot at us. We could not get close to them."

Even in the dark, Nat Turner saw that Will was covered with blood. He smelled the saltiness. But where was Hark? Nelson? "But the plan was if we were discovered we would scatter. Where are the others?"

Will did not seem to be listening. He was lost in his thoughts. "The men were still on foot."

"But without ammunition and guns, there was no way you could fight—"

"We decided then and there to take a stand. It might be our last chance. We would die fighting."

It was not the plan. It was not as they had agreed.

"It was a slaughter. We had clubs and axes against shotguns and rifles. We could not get close enough. Most got away. A few are dead." Will paused, breathing heavily. "They captured Hark."

The wind was knocked out of Nat Turner. He slumped back against the wall.

Chapter 64

Nat Turner and Will planned in the darkness. They would find the others. They would try to gather those still alive. Nat Turner would rescue his brother Hark.

Will's breathing was ragged. "Hark made himself a target so the others could get away." As Will described the encounter, Nat Turner realized it was the first time he had heard the man's voice. "Hark was like a bear! Like a bull!"

They would wait for darkness and then they would find the others. They would attempt to rescue Hark.

When darkness came again, they left the cave to search. They flagged down one of the Cheroenhaka Nottoway freemen, one of the Artis brothers riding on the road. "It's not safe for a black man to be out," he told them. "Not even for a freeman." But he promised to gather the others he could find—Berry Newsom, the Hathcock brothers. He told them to wait until the next night and then they would meet.

Nat and Will scrounged for berries and wild corn on their way back to the cave. It was hard waiting, both of them tormented with worry for the others. Nat fought imagining what the captors might do to Hark. He did not want to sleep; he might dream of Hark suffering, or of Sallie and the others. But sleep captured him and he dreamed of Cherry in the moonlight.

When they were not sleeping, Nat and Will sat in silence, occasionally whispering. They would meet with the Artis brothers and the others. They would get horses from the freemen and this time they would have weapons.

But when darkness came, the roads were already thick with

whites carrying torches and rifles. From their hiding place, Nat and Will saw the flickering lights of passing torches and heard the crack of firing guns.

They heard the faraway screams of captive men, women, and children. It was over. The revolt was over.

Chapter 65

They sat together in silence.

Both of them could not die. Someone had to get away, to tell the story. Nat Turner could not leave: It was his fate. But Will could get away. Nat Turner stared in the other man's direction. "Did the blood take the pain away?"

For a while, Will did not respond. Then he said, "I am not afraid to die." Will's voice was full of venom. "I won't be finished until I see them all dead."

"Has it made you better?"

"You question me? You started this whole thing, *Prophet*. We are both here together in the same hole. Are you better?"

"You are here because you wanted revenge. I am here because I want to see men live."

Will's arm pounded against the earthen walls of the cave. "What difference does it make?"

"You could live."

"Live? I am a dead man. I been dead a long time. How can I live when I have lost everyone I love?" Then, as though a scab had been torn away, Will told Nat Turner the story of his family, the land they lost, and how they came to be slaves. He told him of the loss of his father, his mother, his sister, his wife, and his little girl. "They killed me when they took my wife and child." Nat Turner thought he heard him sob.

Will told Nat Turner about the things Nathaniel Francis and his friends had done. "I been watching, biding my time." He told Nat Turner of the things he had seen done to Charlotte, and about Two Feet, Easter, and the others. "I will not be satisfied until I see all of them—all white people—dead. I waited for years for this day to come, for my revenge. When I die, I'll take as many of them as I can with me. I will bathe in their blood."

"You don't have to die, Will. You get away. This death is not for you."

"I am as willing to die as anyone."

"This death is not yours. Someone must live to tell the story. This death is mine. I will stay here, here with my family. You go. Go and find yours."

"Find them how? Like a needle in a haystack. I will never see them in this life again."

"You will find them."

"How? The patrollers will catch me on the road. Even if I slip past them, where would I begin to find my family?"

"None of us is here by happenstance. Let Providence guide you."

"Providence?" Will's laugh was bitter. "God abandoned me long ago."

Nat Turner felt the rag still at his waist, the rag that held the passes. "You will travel by night. I will tell you the way to go and give you a pass."

"They will catch me. They will kill me."

"What is the difference if you are already a dead man?"

Will was silent.

"While others have died, you still live, Will. It is for a reason."

"You still live, Nat Turner. Why don't you go instead?"

"My place is here, near my family. My place is here: It is God's will. When my time comes, they will deliver me up. My brothers will deliver me to death, but not before the truth is known. I bear the yoke of Christ, but it is not for you." Nat Turner swallowed. "There is a family debt I owe." He coughed to clear away the stone in his throat. "You can live again. Let yourself hope again. Go and find your family.

"The road will be long, but you will find your way. Don't be afraid."

"I'm not afraid. I'm willing to die!"

"Dying is easy, Will. You have been bathed in their blood. Has it taken the ache away? Are you satisfied? Is your heart full? Is your loneliness gone? Has any of it brought back your daughter?" The questions hung in the darkness. "Has their blood brought you new life?"

"How can you question me, Nat Turner? You are the one who began this battle. You started this."

"You have done your part. Those who have been captured will die. I will die. But you will live. You think your life is over, but there is new life for you in Christ."

"Christ? Where was He when I needed Him, when I begged Him not to let them take my family? What does the white god care about black men's burdens?"

"You need to be alone with Him. If you ask Him He will give you the answers—if you really want them."

"Why should I live? You are the preacher. You have a family. I am a slave with no family. I am no one."

"If you don't live, there will be no witness. Our voices will die. They will bring false witnesses against me. But you will live and carry the truth with you of what was done to God's people and what happened here. The day will come when you will be called to be a witness. But first you must find life again. You must find love again. You must go and find your name."

"But why me?"

Nat Turner sighed in the darkness. "I would like long life. But that is not God's plan for me. I am His servant. I will do His will. Our people will get to the Promised Land—I have my part to play in it and you have yours. I have been the hand of God's judgment. Now you must be His witness.

"Though I have had loss and suffering in this life, the Lord has given me some small joy. It was at my time of greatest suffering, buried in it, that I discovered my true joy." He thought of his time in the Great Dismal Swamp. Nat Turner thought of his mother, his wife, and his family. He thought of his friendships with Hark and Thomas Gray. He thought of his experiments, the books he'd read, and preaching as a circuit rider. "That time is over now. This grief and sorrow is for me to bear until the end.

"For the Lord's sake, and for the sake of His people, I have put on righteousness as a breastplate and salvation as a helmet. I put on vengeance for clothing and zeal as a cloak. I have meted out the Lord's judgment. According to their deeds, accordingly they have been repaid. I have carried out judgment and I will receive my reward." Nat Turner thought of all the times he had seen Will at church. Always alone. He had never seen Will smile. "I have loved, I have lived, and I will live again.

"But you are a lonely man—no family, no friends, no wife, no daughter."

There was silence again, only the wind rustling the leaves of the tree above their cave. "The Lord has looked past your anger. He sees it is just a mask you wear." In the silence, in the dark, Nat Turner saw and heard Will's broken heart. "He has seen that you have lost your way. He has seen your broken heart. He is a God of mercy. Make your way to the place of refuge. Make your way to Hebron; you will find healing there. Freedom. He will give you new life. He will lead you home."

"I have seen enough of the white man's freedom." Will told Nat Turner the story of his father-in-law's death, of finding his moldering, unburied body. "What has God to do with me? He killed me long ago when He took my wife and my daughter. I am a dead man," Will repeated. "I have had enough of the white man's god."

"Not the white man's freedom. Not the white man's god. I speak of the One True God, who is God of all men, God of all nations, God of heaven and earth."

"If God loves black men, how can He forgive white men?"

"Because He is Father to all; He is Father to those who offend and to those who have been offended. He is the Father and we are all brothers. God takes no pleasure in the death of His children, not even wicked ones.

"I have lost my family, too. But we must not confuse God with the power that pretends to be Him. He is love. He is the God of our forefathers."

Nat Turner told Will the history that his mother had told him—of Sheba and Solomon. He told him of the great stone churches of Lalibela, and the Nile. "Lift up your head.

"God chose us to be here in Southampton, to be His mighty army. He could have chosen other men, greater men, but He chose us. We are His chosen—the foolish things, the weak things, the despised—sent to confound those who think they are favored above all others.

"He came to restore the lost and mend the brokenhearted. Why not us? Why not you? He is the God of judgment and also the God of love. Let Him bind your broken heart. Let Him free you.

"The blood of a thousand men could not make up for what has been done to you. Go find the One who can give you peace. Find the One True God, the God who smiles on Africa. Let Him be your Father, your friend. Find hope."

In the darkness, Nat Turner told Will of King Xerxes' wicked reign and his repentance before God. He told him about Apollos the African from Alexandria, the great first-century orator and teacher who converted many to Christianity. He told him about St. Moses of Ethiopia, the warrior priest.

"He is Lord of all." Nat Turner told Will that the first pictures painted of Christ and His mother were in Ethiopia, pictures from the fourth century that showed them with African skin and features. He told Will of the great cities of Aksum and Gondar and of the African saints. "The Lord thought the people of Africa so precious that He gave us to His mother as a special gift to care for and intercede for—she is our Mother of Mercy.

"He loves you. You are His son.

"He came to restore the lost, heal the sick, raise the dead, and mend the brokenhearted. I believe He wants to restore your life. God is a God of judgment and righteousness, but He is first the

God of love, of comfort, and restoration. In the midst of this warfare, I believe He seeks you.

"Go and find the One True God who sent His son, the Christ, the Light of Ethiopia, the Light of Africa, the Light of the World, to die for all of us.

"There is peace, my brother. Go and find your name. You will find life again—you will find it somewhere chiseled in a stone, carved in a tree, or flowing through some stream. Go and find yourself again, find your family, and then be a witness—tell the whole world our story. Find a new life; find a new heart; find a new name."

"How will I find them, my family? I have been a man without words."

"Now you have a reason to speak. Now you have questions. Open your mouth now, my brother. When you are armed with words, aim to do good."

"I have blood on my hands."

Nat Turner sighed in the darkness. "In one way or another, we all have blood on our hands."

"But I am a dead man." There was silence, then he spoke again. "I am a bloody man. Why would He want me?"

"There is power to resurrect you, and it is available to you, to each one of us—no matter how wretched, no matter how heartbroken.

"There is only one thing that can wash the stain away. Make your way to the place of refuge, to Hebron, to the Great Dismal Swamp."

Nat Turner told Will the way to go and all that he remembered. "You will be tempted to do what you know, to use your axe to be a shingle-getter and to chop down trees. But seek to be a deliveryman, drive the flatboats down the waterway.

"Bide your time there in the swamp. When things are quiet—when the captors are no longer searching—make your way to Norfolk. Let your ears guide you. Souls in the swamp will help you make your way."

After Nat Turner had given Will a pass and pointed out the direction, he reminded Will to keep to the woods and travel by day. He must try not to be seen—but once he was outside Southampton County, he was less likely to be suspected of being a runaway traveling in daylight. At night, the patrollers would assume he was trying to escape. "Remember me, brother. There is hope. There is comfort in the swamp, there is healing in the darkness," Nat Turner told him.

Nat raised his head above the opening and watched Will walk away. The revolt was over for him. "Go to the place of refuge, be healed, find your voice, and then go tell our story."

Chapter 66

Without Will the days were silent. Autumn was coming—Nat Turner saw it in the moon and felt it in the air. Fall was coming in the way she came to Virginia, walking slowly to let everyone know she was in no hurry. The days were still warm, but the nights were cooler. The evenings came sooner and a few leaves had fallen. Autumn was adorning herself in bright colors—crimson, ginger, and gold—though most of the leaves were still green. Nat Turner smelled her perfume—smoke from hearth fires and the heady sweetness of fermented valley apples.

He wanted to make a fire—there were rabbits and squirrels to catch—but he knew he would be discovered. Instead, when he was out, he gathered more leaves and branches to warm himself.

Night had become his daytime. In the darkness, he gleaned in the abandoned fields. He found corn gone to seed, rotting potatoes, shriveled apples, whatever was left behind. He got bolder over time, creeping nearer the farmhouses so he was able to snatch a few eggs.

In the daylight he sheltered and waited in the darkness of the cave. From where he sat, he sometimes saw deer moving gracefully across the forest grounds or rabbits hopping by.

Nat Turner passed most of his daylight hours sleeping. In the beginning he had been afraid to sleep. He thought his dreams would be tormented by Sallie, by the Wallers, and the others. But God was merciful. Mostly he dreamed of Cherry and the last time he had seen her dancing near the oak in the moonlight in the early summer.

In his dreams he smelled her flowers. He heard her laugh. He smelled her hair. In his dreams he heard rhythms of a place he knew but had never been. He felt the cool tickle of the highland breezes on his neck.

Soon it would be winter, the days would be cold, the leaves would all fall, and his hiding place would be exposed. But for now, he was safe.

Two days had come and gone since Will left. The armed patrollers still guarded the roads at night on horseback, carrying torches. But one night, not long ago, he had risked letting Cherry know that he was alive and still near to her, and that he had kept his promise: He would never leave her again.

He had crept as close as he dared to Giles Reese's farmhouse. Remaining in the woods, but close enough that he could see the candlelight in the windows, he had used the bird call and hoped she would recognize him.

The next night when he had awakened he had found a piece of corn bread and two pieces of fried salt pork wrapped in an old cloth near the tree. Cherry did not dare come to him herself; the captors were watching her. But she sent others she trusted to the tree.

It was dangerous to come, so it was not unusual for weeks to pass before anyone came by. They threw him leftover bread, sometimes a tiny precious morsel of meat, and they dropped him tidbits of news. They never entered the cave and he never came out. His visitors risked speaking only a few whispered words. "Hearings have started. Old John Clarke Turner fingered you." He heard in the messenger's voice that even he felt the sting of a brother's betrayal.

More days and weeks would pass before anyone came again—days of wind, rain, more leaves falling, less food to be scrounged from the land. Then there was news of men being hamstrung—their tendons severed—and women being raped. There was word of men hanging from trees, their heads atop poles. Then weeks later, "All's quiet now."

To pass the time Nat Turner would try to imagine his visitors, to recognize the voices. Was it one of the freemen? One of the trusted captives who had recently visited Giles Reese's place?

"A reward out for you," he was told during his next visit. "Over one thousand dollars!" Almost seven times what a farmer could expect to earn in a year in Southampton County.

More weeks passed, weeks of prayer, prayers for the living and the dead, for captives and captors. Hark was gone. Sam was gone. Yellow Nelson and Dred gone. . . . *Holy Maryam, the God-bearer, pray that your beloved son, Jesus Christ, may forgive us.* His life was never going to be what he had hoped. He would never see Ethiopia. There was never going to be a family of brothers who welcomed him, who loved him. Like Canaan, it was his own family who condemned him to slavery. Like Joseph, it was his own brothers who beat him, though it was a brother's wife who sold him into slavery. It was his brother John Clarke who betrayed him.

Nat Turner prayed for the witnesses to come, to comfort him, to reassure him. But he was alone. Only the words he had memorized comforted him. *Blessed are the poor in spirit: for theirs is the kingdom of heaven. Blessed are they that mourn: for they shall be comforted.*

Then one day the news came he had dreaded. "More hangings." Nat Turner mourned them. *Blessed are the meek: for they shall inherit the earth. Blessed are they which do hunger and thirst after righteousness: for they shall be filled.* Another visitor passed. "More hangings." There were names among the deceased who were not part of the army. *Blessed are the merciful: for they shall obtain mercy. Blessed are the pure in heart: for they shall see God.*

But it did not end there. There was more suffering. "Nathan, Curtis, and Stephen." It was torment to hear the roll call of the dead. There were faithful soldiers among them. But the captors were also killing innocent men, women, and children—exchanging captive lives for money. *Blessed are the peacemakers: for they shall be called the children of God.* "Joe and Lucy gone to the gallows. Little Moses sold, sent Deep South. Beat him. Poor little fella lied to save himself, just like Hubbard and Venus." Lucy? A girl? And little Moses? Nat Turner wept over the names and the lives. He wept over the deaths of the innocents.

Nat Turner wrestled with himself. Perhaps, if he surrendered, the captors would free the others. But he knew, even as he prayed, that his death would bring peace to no one. It would cause heartbreak for his family, for his mother, and for Cherry. His surrendering now would do no good. He could not force his time to come. His hour and time were in the hands of God. *Blessed are they which are persecuted for righteousness' sake: for theirs is the kingdom of heaven.* "Jim and Isaac hanged." All the innocents sent to slaughter. *Blessed are ye, when men shall revile you, and persecute you, and shall say all manner of evil against you falsely, for my sake.*

There were more leaves now, and green had given way to orange and scarlet. There were still patrollers with torches on the roads, but not as frequent, and there were fewer gunshots. The sun was shorter and the moon longer. Weeks passed and then Nat Turner got the word he dreaded most, "They beat your Cherry! Beat her awful!"

Chapter 67

Nat Turner roared from his hiding place, tearing through the boughs and brush that hid him so that he frightened Berry Newsom and knocked him down. "They wanted Cherry to tell them where you were, Prophet Nat. Wanted all your papers. They got your papers and your Bible. But no matter how they beat her, she wouldn't tell!"

He grabbed hold of Berry. "Who was there?"

"Congressman Trezvant, Levi Waller, John Clarke, and the others. Even Thomas Gray." Nat Turner let go of Berry's collar. *Even Thomas Gray?*

"Nathaniel Francis led them. Cut out a plug of her hair before Giles Reese stopped them," Berry said.

Not his Cherry, not her beautiful black hair! Nat Turner moaned, pressing his hands to his head.

"Giles Reese finally pulled a pistol on them, but he was afraid, too!"

Nat Turner pushed past Berry, past the trees that hid him, making his way toward the road. He would kill them all!

He heard Berry panting to keep up with him. "The others were out of control, Nat! What could Giles do?"

Nat Turner knew the paths, the traces through the woods, but he was blinded. He tripped over jutting tree roots, stumbled over withering blackberry bushes; he charged through the woods. Berry Newsom chased behind him and tackled Nat Turner when he finally overtook him.

"Use your head, Nat! They want to roust you out of hiding! You'll get Cherry, me, and all the others killed!"

Covered in leaves, the two of them sat on the forest floor, panting. Berry was quiet for a moment. "You'll get us all killed," he repeated. "Not that my time is far off. They're sending me with the freemen to be prosecuted. They're getting rid of all the freemen, getting us out of the way—to shut us up and steal the land."

Nat Turner buried his head in his arms. He knew that Berry was right. But the thought of Cherry being beaten and savaged was more than he could bear. Berry seemed to read his mind.

"You'll only make it worse. She's all right, Nat." Berry picked up his hat and knocked the dried leaves off his clothes. "Who are you going to go after, anyway? Cherry might be stronger than all of us."

Berry was right. It was almost over. There was just one more thing that Nat Turner was required to do.

Chapter 68

In the black of night, Nat Turner crept closer and closer to the farmhouse. At the edge of the woods, he saw the dwelling across the clearing. He had been close many nights before, had taken food from the garden and eggs from the henhouse. A candle was always burning in the window. Nathaniel Francis sat in a chair, awake, facing the door. Young Nathaniel Francis never slept and there was always a rifle on his lap. *You must kill the root.*

Quietly, slowly, Nat Turner inched along, crawling on his belly. The clearing between the forest and the house was the most dangerous place; if he was discovered there was no place to hide. Nat Turner edged nearer, his eyes riveted on Nathaniel.

He had only this last chance. Winter was coming soon. He had seen the ducks flying overhead; he had heard the geese honking as they flew farther south. The great oak was shedding its leaves. Nat Turner's time was drawing near.

He crouched in the winter garden, closer now to the house. Nathaniel Francis had a glass of corn whiskey in his hand. The young man had still not looked up to see him.

Nat Turner crept across the yard, avoiding the light that came from the window. At the house, he pressed his back flat against the wall. An inch at a time, he eased closer to the shaft of light that marked the window. *You must destroy the root.*

Nat Turner gripped the worn wooden handle of his sword, once his scythe, in his hand. This was his last opportunity to do what must be done. He pressed his back closer against the wall. He tried to slow his heartbeat and quiet his breathing. This was his last chance.

Chapter 69

Nat Turner risked everything. Kill or be killed. Outside in the dark, he looked in through the window at Nathaniel Francis.

If there was such a thing, Nathaniel was the worst, the vilest. Not much more than a boy, he treated the people around him like cornshuck dolls, like disposable toys. He had made the lives of so many miserable, had destroyed lives—Mother Easter, Will, Sam, Charlotte, Davy. And when he was tired of them, he sold them to a hangman's noose for money to buy more things. How had Nathaniel grown from a boy to become this monster?

The younger man, a rifle across his lap, jumped at every sound or movement—a log shifting in the fire or the candle's flickering flame. Across the room, on the floor, Nat Turner saw poor Mother Easter. Without cover, without even leaves, she was curled into a ball lying on the cold, hard floor.

He stared inside, knowing that with the flame inside and the window's reflection Nathaniel Francis could not see him. Nat Turner gripped the scythe tighter in his hand, felt every notch and nick.

He had no gun so he would have to strike within arm's length. Nat Turner ducked under the window so there would be no shadow and then, squatting, inched his way closer to the door. Closer. Closer. *You must destroy the root.*

Closer.

One of Nathaniel Francis's dogs began barking. Nat Turner tried to quiet the dog, but it wanted to play. The dog continued to bark. Nat Turner held his breath.

Then a crash inside; Nathaniel Francis stumbled from his chair.

Nat Turner heard the younger man's hand jerking the door open. Nat Turner turned to run. Past the window, through the stream of light, he heard Nathaniel Francis shout, "You black devil!"

Before he stepped from the clearing into the darkness again, Nat Turner heard a blast, then heard and felt something whiz by his head—a pellet from the shotgun blast. Nat Turner's chances were over. Nathaniel Francis had seen him.

The captors would let no one rest until they found him.

WHEN HIS NEXT visitor came to the great oak, he brought bread and news. "Hunting you. They've gone after the freemen—the Artis brothers, the Hathcocks, and Berry Newsom—hoping to rout you."

Nat Turner sent for Benjamin Phipps.

Chapter 70

Nat Turner looked down at his feet instead of at the man standing in front of him. He knew Nathaniel Francis had seen him and that he and the other captors would not rest until Nat Turner was in chains. They would beat, lynch, and burn others until they had him swinging from a tree.

Nathaniel Francis was still alive. The captors had not turned. The war had just begun—he and the others were only the first ones. He would not see the end.

The trees were almost bare and he would not be able to hide. It was colder now and winter would come again soon. With winter would come snowfall and freezes. Outside in the cold with no fire, he would not survive. Even in the cave, unable to move about, he would soon freeze to death.

It was the end of October. His thirty-first birthday had passed. Nat Turner could no longer bear the solitude. Though he prayed for them to come, to speak to him and comfort him, not even the witnesses visited him. It was time.

Nat Turner knew his fate. They would drag him to Jerusalem on All Saints Day. But he would remember St. Moses of Ethiopia and St. Masqal-Kebra. He would think of his mother and of the Mother of Mercy; they would help him be strong.

He looked at the man standing before him, a man in clothes as ragged as his own. Benjamin Phipps was a poor man, a good man, and the reward would be a help to him and his family. The reward was being offered for Nat Turner's capture, dead or alive. And of the white men Nat Turner knew, Benjamin Phipps was most likely to get him to a place of safety alive.

"Are you sure you want to do this, Nat?" Nat Turner saw tears welling in Benjamin Phipps's eyes. "They've got dogs and hunters looking for you, but you've always been smart. You could still get away."

Benjamin Phipps and his family barely scraped by, but honor was priceless, and he had grown into a peaceful man willing to stand his ground. Nat Turner shook his head. "It's time."

"You know what it means?"

Nat Turner nodded his head.

The two of them agreed that they would make their way to Peter Edwards's home. "You tell them you found me here. You were out hunting, you held your rifle on me, and I did not resist. Be sure to keep the rifle trained on me when we reach Peter Edwards's farm."

"No one's going to believe that. No one's going to believe I turned you in; they know I'm not a slavery man. And Peter Edwards? They will question why I took you there."

"His farm is nearby." Nat Turner laid a hand on his childhood friend's shoulder. "They dislike you, but they hate me. They want me. They'll believe you, and Peter Edwards will help us convince them."

"There have been all kinds of rumors about what happened. First, there were reports that it was runaways from the Dismal Swamp. Then John Clarke Turner pointed the finger at you. What really happened, Nat?" Benjamin Phipps hung his head. "I hate to be the one. I remember when you defended me that day . . . that day in town when Nathaniel Francis shoved me."

"You would have done the same for me."

"I would like to think so." Benjamin looked away. "But I hate to be the one."

"Think of the reward. You are a poor man, like me. It will help your family."

"Blood money."

"No, not blood money; it is payment for helping me." He saw

anguish on Benjamin's reddened face. "Who else can I ask? There is no one I trust more."

Phipps's face was gray and his eyes teary. "I can't go with you all the way to Jerusalem. I can't bear to see it."

Nat Turner laid his hand on Benjamin Phipps's shoulder. "It is a good thing you do, my friend. I go to God now."

Chapter 71

They started out at sunrise. When they reached the Edwards place, Peter Edwards's eyes widened and his face blanched. Benjamin Phipps looked at his feet, mumbling the tale of how Nat was captured. Nat Turner nodded at Peter Edwards to confirm Benjamin Phipps's story.

Inside, there was a fire roaring in the fireplace. It had been months since he'd been inside, even in a barn, and as he warmed, Nat Turner realized that he had been shivering. There was a mural, probably of the English countryside, painted on one wall, and a chandelier hung overhead.

Peter Edwards led them to the living room, where wood burned in another ornate fireplace. The polished hardwood floors felt smooth, but still warm, under Nat Turner's bare feet. There were rugs here and there that felt like patches of soft spring grass. Sunlight poured through the windows bordered by heavy blue drapes.

At the center of the room was a large table surrounded by padded chairs. Peter Edwards motioned to him to sit down. Nat Turner, hesitating, shook his head. He was covered with mud and there had been no place for him to bathe.

Peter Edwards waved his hand. "Sit down. It's only a chair. New ones are easily purchased." Nat Turner sat on the wooden chair, the bottom padded and covered with tapestry. He slid his hands over the smooth fabric.

There was a wine decanter on a silver tray and a bowl of fruit in the center of the table atop a large lace doily. So this was comfort. Was it worth all the lives required to secure it?

Peter Edwards frowned. "You know they'll tear you apart

when they get their hands on you. I won't be able to help you. Trezvant and Nathaniel Francis continue to make trouble. None of this would have happened if not for Nathaniel Francis. . . . Now he dupes Levi Waller into lying for him while Nathaniel grows rich sending poor wretches to the gallows. All the while James Trezvant is in cahoots with Francis. Our good congressman sends stories to the newspaper and he has taken control of the court, intimidating the rightful judges. He runs back and forth to Richmond, using this tragedy to build himself a national reputation, with sights set on the Senate or governorship. When things begin to settle, the two of them stir things up again."

He paced back and forth. Peter Edwards continued to frown. "We had heard rumblings that some slaves were dissatisfied. But Nathaniel and his ilk are men with property rights. How could we interfere?" Peter Edwards resumed pacing, then stopped. "Enough have already been killed. I could put you in a wagon and get you away from here."

"I will not leave my wife and son."

"For goodness' sakes, man! We have all been through enough. Let it die down; let this whole rotten affair end. Get away! Your family can follow!"

He could sail to New Orleans and pretend to be Creole. He could sail to India or Armenia and hide among them. He could return to Ethiopia. Would his people recognize him as one of their own?

Nat Turner shook his head. He could not leave his wife; he had promised. He had promised his mother. "There is a family debt I owe." He could not leave, he could not turn back; there was a family debt he owed. The only acceptable payment was to set the captives free.

PETER EDWARDS WRUNG his hands. He opened his mouth as though about to argue and then sighed. "It won't be safe to take you into town alone, Nat, with just the two of us. We'll have to send for an armed guard." Peter Edwards raked his hands through his hair. "Why didn't you come to me before? It could have been taken care of peacefully. All of this could have been avoided."

"What could you have done?"

"We all knew the Cross Keys bunch were troublemakers, poor white trash! It was better when white men like them were still slaves!"

Edwards's face reddened when he looked at Phipps, remembering that he was present. "I didn't mean you, Mr. Phipps, I meant..."

Edwards turned to a well-dressed servant waiting nearby. "Get these men some food." Then Peter Edwards shoved his hands into his pockets. "A hundred Negroes, maybe more, have been killed right here in Southampton County—more around the state. Good people killed because of the color of their skin ... and money."

His eyes filled with tears. "My Sam . . . his mother is beside herself with grief... a month after the whole business was over.... John Clarke and some other ne'er-do-wells dragged poor Sam from her house ... beat ... hanged him ... liars!" Edwards pounded the table. He flopped into a nearby chair and buried his face in his hands. Edwards looked up. "You could have come to me, Nat!"

Nat Turner stared and then Edwards turned away. "You knew but you did nothing. What choice did we have but war?"

"War?" Edwards looked back at Nat Turner, startled, then perplexed. He rose from the table and hollered toward the kitchen. "Hurry with the food!"

A servant entered the room carrying food and drink for Nat Turner and Benjamin Phipps. There was roasted chicken; the skin was crisp and still warm from the oven, served on a white ceramic plate with blue trim along with a hunk of bread made from white flour, spread with warm butter.

Nat Turner lifted the blue earthenware cup set before him. In it was hot tea sweetened with sugar. He tried not to stuff the food in his mouth, but he had been hungry too long. His hands and mouth took control. Across from him at the table, Benjamin

Phipps was having no more luck being civil than he—the salty grease from the chicken smeared his face and dirty hands.

Peter Edwards sighed looking at Nat Turner. "This is probably the last decent meal you will eat."

He allowed them to finish the meal, and then Peter Edwards sent a rider for the sheriff. "Stop for no one else," he told the captive he sent. "Only speak to the sheriff. Tell no one else what was said or done here. Tell no one else that Nat Turner is here!"

The captive's eyes met Nat Turner's briefly and then looked away. The captive would remember. He would have a story to tell.

It was late morning, but the hutch and table shadowed the room. Nat Turner looked around at the heavy, dark, highly polished furniture that filled the room like great animals watching them.

Edwards's farm lay at the edge of Cross Keys and there was often discussion among the white captors about whether his farm was actually in Cross Keys or at the edge of Jerusalem—both groups wanted to claim the plantation was in their jurisdiction. When other farmers talked of how large they wanted their farms to be, how large they wanted their homes to be, how many windows, how big the front porch, how many slaves—Peter Edwards's place was always the standard. His home was the fantasy.

The portraits on the walls, the tiled floors, the crystal chandeliers, the stuffed velvet settees—how many captive people had died, how many lives had been stolen and ruined as others dreamed of having what Peter Edwards had?

Most likely, the elder Francises and the Whiteheads, and other Cross Keys families were once indentured to the Edwardses, the Parkers, and other wealthy landowners. But those memories were gone. White slaves had become captors, murdering and stealing to wipe the memory away.

There was a knock at the door. Congressman Trezvant, acting as senior judge, and acting judge James Parker had heard the news from the sheriff. They were first to arrive.

Chapter 72

The early afternoon sun framed their figures in the doorway. Trezvant looked down at Benjamin Phipps, gingerly tapping him on the shoulder as though he did not want something to crawl off Phipps onto him. "You have done a great thing for Cross Keys, for Jerusalem—why, for all of Southampton County—bringing this scoundrel to justice!"

Young James Parker shook Benjamin Phipps's hand, but Phipps kept his gaze on the floor.

Trezvant continued speaking. "I had my doubts about you, Mr. Phipps. You are not a slavery man and you did not ride with us to help us roust the blackguard. Who would have thought you'd be the one to turn him in? But we white men must stick together at times like this." Grinning, he clapped Phipps's back harder. Then, dramatically, his face sobered. "The fiend wanted to kill all the good white people of Southampton County. Why, I believe the little preacher thought he could march to Richmond and take over the state. But we showed him." He looked down his nose at Phipps. "Of course, there is the matter of the reward. Over a thousand dollars." He leaned to whisper to Benjamin Phipps. "If you need my assistance, my office is open to you."

The senior judge quickly dismissed Phipps and turned to Peter Edwards. "Where is the villain? Do you have him secured?"

"He has made no struggle or attempt to run."

"Lead me to him." Trezvant cleared his throat and then, as an afterthought, he acknowledged Parker. "Lead us to the bandit." As Trezvant followed behind Peter Edwards—from the foyer, down the hall to the living room—from where he sat, Nat Turner watched the congressman's face. Trezvant seemed to be taking inventory, making a list of things he needed to acquire to be in fashion. He seemed to be tallying desks, chairs, portraits, light fixtures. How many captives would have to be bred and sold or hanged, how many acres of corn would he have to beat out of the captives to attain what was required of a proper gentleman?

As they walked, Peter Edwards turned to speak to Trezvant and Parker. "Has he been assigned a lawyer? I'm not sure it's proper for you, as judges, to speak with Nat Turner before the hearing. Shouldn't the sheriff take him into custody and question him first?"

Trezvant was in control. "The sheriff is coming soon. He's gathering guards. But as officers of the court, I have decided that the two of us must interrogate the black rascal first."

Keen-eyed, Trezvant swept into the house, and Peter Edwards's living room became Trezvant's stage, Edwards's table his judicial bench. Tall and thin with sparse gray curls plastered about the sides of his head, age had not been his ally. He continued inventorying Peter Edwards's living room where they sat, as though he were looking to be sure there was nothing there that he didn't already have—still tallying crystal, frosted glass, a chandelier.

Nat Turner had seen the man and his brother, the general store owner and postmaster, before on occasions when he went to town. The congressman, lawyer, militia colonel, was now chief justice of the court called to oversee the rebellion trials—if they could be called trials. Whether he officially had the authority was no matter; the congressman had wrested control.

From his pocket, Trezvant withdrew glasses that he perched on the tip of his nose. He did not look through them but over them, like props, as though the glasses themselves made him a judge. Despite his thinness, all of who Trezvant was strained at the seams of his clothes, pushed at his buttons, puffed his face, and pooched his stomach. It reminded Nat Turner of something his mother had told him about Americans cinching themselves in clothes rather than wearing robes, as though they were afraid bits of themselves, or the best parts of them, might fly away.

At Trezvant's side was the much younger, and adequately insecure, James Parker. Nat Turner had heard that the thirty-year-old farmer and slave owner was the youngest judge sitting for the slave trials. Parker fidgeted, his eyes darting from place to place.

It was easy to figure why Trezvant and the others had chosen the young man to sit as judge. Parker was suitable because he did all the right things and bore the right name. He was the soft-spoken son of the outspoken Parker family, a family known for having the courage not to beat their slaves, a family that had the courage to feed their captives adequately, despite criticism that they were too generous. The Parker name appeared to lend balance to the court: A Parker was watching so there would be no mistreatment of the slaves.

But looking at the younger man, Nat Turner knew that he had the name but not the family courage or self-assurance. James Parker was ginger-haired, clean-shaven, and perpetually red-faced. He did not have the experience or the confidence to stand against the formidable will of Congressman Colonel Judge Trezvant.

Trezvant alone was Grand Inquisitor. He was Pontius Pilate, and it was clear, as he peered over his spectacles, from the lift of his brow and the wrinkling of his forehead, that he was certain Nat Turner was no match for him.

Trezvant looked around the room, settling his gaze on Peter Edwards's liquor cabinet. He stared at it until Edwards ordered that a glass of whiskey be brought to him. Then Trezvant began the questioning.

"You don't look like the big, black strapping sort of fellow who I would think the jigs would choose to lead their murdering, thieving enterprise. But then I understand you've been living in the woods, not far from here. Dining on wild nuts and berries? That might account for your thinness, though not your lack of height." Trezvant chortled and lifted one brow. "Thought you'd come in for a meal?"

His left hand moving like a snake's tongue, Trezvant slapped the servant who stood nearby and grabbed his arm, jerking him toward Nat Turner. "How dare you seat him on an upholstered chair. He stinks to high heaven! The chair will be ruined, you imbecile! Get him off the chair and fetch a wooden stool."

Peter Edwards looked away, dropped his head, faded into the curtains.

The stool the servant brought was rough and unpainted. Nat Turner sat on it, thanking the servant, who would not look at him. This captive, too, would be a witness: He would have a story to tell.

Trezvant stared over his glasses at Nat Turner and pursed his lips. "Comfortable?" The old man meant to rattle him. "So you're the general, the leader of a band of murderers! No tears? No remorse? You are a coldhearted fellow."

"I am guilty of nothing. I struck the first blow for freedom, but it was not murder. I am no guiltier than George Washington, Nathan Hale, or any other soldier. We were an army working together. Everything we did, we did in common. It is war, the Lord's judgment."

Trezvant shook his head and looked around the room at the other white men. "See how childish and simple the darkies are that they would allow themselves to be led by someone like this? They might have chosen someone to follow like Red Nelson. But they chose this . . . this thing." He gestured at Nat Turner. "Well, they all deserve what they got. They brought it on themselves. But, of course, we're the ones to suffer; look at all the lost property."

"Some slaves were loyal," Parker inserted.

"Indeed. But the filthy insurrectionists got just what they deserved. They are the cause of hundreds of their kind being killed all over the state—even in North Carolina." He pointed at Nat Turner. "Look at the culprit. His stench is unbearable."

All his life white people had been speaking of Nat Turner as though he wasn't there, as if they knew better than he what was best for his life.

Trezvant's expression and tone changed. He smiled at Nat Turner as though seconds ago he had not insulted him. "Your life held so much promise. Many white people were taken with you. You could have followed after someone like Red Nelson, someone more like you, and stayed in your place. Why did you choose to be with the others, to be with the darker . . . the common field hands?"

All his life, he had held his tongue; it was the only way to survive. Now God had removed the muzzle, and he would say whatever came to his mind and to his heart. "I didn't choose; you chose for me.

"But the truth is, if I have to choose between standing with captives or captors, I would always choose to stand with those in chains."

Trezvant looked over his glasses and smiled. This was a debate, a debate Trezvant was certain he would win: He was smarter; Nat Turner was inferior. Nat Turner would lose the contest and die.

Trezvant began to drill Nat Turner with questions. He took notes on sheets of paper spread in front of him. "I have heard that you are an intelligent creature, but your battle plan makes no sense. Did you think with no weapons, no training, and with your simple minds, that you'd be able to take over Jerusalem? Take over Virginia? This whole nation? Do you know how many white men there are? How many guns we have? Only a crazy person could think that unarmed and with so few men you could take over the county, let alone the state."

"Some trust in chariots, and some in horses, but we trust in our God.

"This was not a war against Jerusalem or Southampton County or Virginia or all white men. It was the righteous judgment of God; we beat our plowshares into swords, judgment began at the house of God."

"But you were not successful. Was it worth it? The odds were always against you. Do you regret what you did?"

"Does America regret its revolution? Some causes are worth fighting for, even if defeat seems sure." This was only the first battle. War would grip the nation. "History will judge if our small battle, our small beginning, helped win the war that is to come. This is only the start of God's harvest. I do His will."

"So now you are Moses or some other prophet." Trezvant stared at him as though he were insane. "So you killed Sallie and Joseph Travis?"

"I struck the first blow for freedom."

"Did you kill the Williamses?"

"We were an army moving as one."

Trezvant peered over his glasses and dipped his quill in the ink that Peter Edwards had provided him. "What about the White-heads? Were you there?"

"We were an army. We all worked in common."

Nat Turner thought then of Will. He would aid his escape. He would make it so they would hope to never find Will. They wouldn't want to speak of him. "But I will tell you that the fiercest warrior of us all was Will. He vowed to kill everything white that moved—man, woman, or child. He was executioner. Most of the kills were his. He was a fury, an angel of death wreaking vengeance."

Trezvant did not counter. Instead, he looked at his notes, returning to his questioning. "You killed more than fifty people—women and children among them—yet there are no tears, your head is not bowed." Trezvant narrowed his eyes. "What kind of creature are you?"

"You say I am a creature. If I am, why should I weep? Does the wolf weep after devouring its prey?"

Trezvant stopped scribbling and stared over his glasses at Nat Turner. "There is ice water in your veins, Preacher. It does not seem to faze you, all the blood and murdered bodies you've seen."

"As a slave, I have been well trained. I have seen a great deal of blood, many wounded and murdered bodies in my lifetime, and I have been taught that I should not react. The overseer says slave life is nothing—kick the body out of the way, then back to work. Peculiar that now someone seems to care."

Trezvant's face reddened with anger momentarily, then it was back to his interrogation. "Were you at the Whiteheads'? Were you at the Barrows'?"

"We were an army moving as one—you cannot separate me from my men; what one did we all did. Just as you are all guilty of hanging innocent men, even a woman. I hear that Virginia pays handsomely." Trezvant intended to win, but Nat Turner would exact a price. "There is innocent blood on your hands, and that blood will damn you." Nat Turner turned and looked at young James Parker. "There is blood on both your hands."

Trezvant did not speak again until he had regained his composure. He looked at Parker. "This is what comes with allowing niggers to read, treating them as equals, and allowing them to strut around and call themselves preachers." He muttered to himself. "Nigger preachers."

He turned back to Nat Turner, paused, took a deep breath, and reapplied his sheepish smile. "Nat, you don't have to put on airs for me. Speak naturally. Feel free to speak your own language."

"My own language?"

"You know, the way you people speak."

"Do you believe that it is the way I speak that makes me a Negro?"

"I mean you should be more like the others. Less formal. You know, nigger talk, gibberish. Speak like your people. You would have gotten less agitated if you had not tried to be a white man, if you had acted like the others. You would have been happier if you acted like old Hubbard or Red Nelson."

"Who are you to choose how I speak or whose lead I follow? Or is it that you want me to play the Zip Coon for you, to dance and shuffle my feet like Red Nelson does to entertain you white men?"

They still did not see who he was. They did not treat him as who he was, but as they thought they saw. They treated him as the role they created for him. When he did not play his part, they were angry. They wanted him to be less and accept less. He was their brother, but they were only satisfied if he played the role of inferior and slave.

They deceived themselves: He spoke one way but they heard another.

They said he was ignorant, so he must be ignorant. They said he was a frightening savage, and in their minds it was so. "It is all a lie. You don't see the truth in front of your eyes. You don't see goodness or intelligence cloaked in black. You don't recognize evil if it has white skin.

"None of us has any value to you except as your property—property you are willing to destroy for money. We have no value in your eyes unless you say so."

Nat Turner had held his tongue for so long. The words rushed from him like an unpent dam. "Who are you to tell me how to speak? You want me to play a part for you that justifies your not treating me as a man. I won't do it!"

Trezvant glared; the veins bulged in his neck. He stopped and seemed to stuff his anger back into his suit. Then he sighed as though Nat Turner were a willful child, shuffled his papers, and then resumed his questioning. "How much money did your banditti steal? Was it worth the lives of so many people?"

"We didn't steal money or property."

Trezvant chuckled, looking at Parker, and then turned back to Nat Turner. "Do you mean to convince me that you did this all for some noble cause?" Trezvant smirked and leaned back in his chair. "I'm a military man, myself—a colonel in the militia. Do you know what that is, a colonel?"

Nat Turner was silent.

"Do you mean to tell me that as the leader, as the general, as it were, of this little . . . band . . . this little group of niggers, that you expected no spoils or money? Perhaps ten dollars a week for you and five dollars for your captains? Here and there snatching a bank note or a gold coin as you romped through an old widow's home? No one would hold it against you for pocketing a few coins. Even white men are tempted."

"I have no interest in money. God provides—"

Trezvant interrupted, leaning forward again. "Then tell me why. Did you plan to rape the women, but they fought you off?"

"Why would I want to rape a woman? I married the woman I desired. And there has been enough rape among us, don't you think? My mother was raped.

"We are men of honor! We are godly men! We fight for freedom and for honor. We fight to do the Lord's will."

"Godly men? You are murderers and nigger fools!" Trezvant's face remained emotionless, though he was one of the culprits who attacked Cherry.

Nat Turner could not help thinking of his wife. Cherry, sweet Cherry with exotic Africa in her hair. He would never see her again, never feel the softness of her skin or her arms wrapped around him. None of the captors was worthy of her. "It is my wife and other captive women who need protection from the likes of you."

Suddenly angry, Trezvant pounded the table. "Don't you get smart with me, black devil! I hold your life in my hands!"

"You hold no power over me. I have already seen the worst.

"All this is in my Father's hands, hands greater than either yours or mine. I am in the hands of the Awesome Defender of the motherless, the poor, and the alien. All this is His doing. Does it not strike you as odd that I—a simple man, a captive, a mere slave—sit before you great men? You should not even notice me. But it is the will of God that I am here. God's judgment is upon you.

"I have learned to fear Him which is able to destroy both body and soul. You cannot harm me."

"Just as I have heard, you are insane! Only a crazy man would speak as you do." Trezvant shook his head and rustled his papers as he turned in Parker's direction. "We are talking to a crazy man, a nigger zealot."

Trezvant pushed the papers from in front of him, laid down his pen, and spoke again to Nat Turner. "All right then, holy man, tell me why, in your twisted thinking, you shed so much innocent blood?

"Even as insane as you are, you must admit that Travis was a good master. Nathaniel Francis tells me that Travis and your mistress, Sallie, doted on you. You know it is true; all the men in Southampton are known to be good masters. Slavery here is probably of more benefit to the slave than it is to the master." Trezvant nodded his head, looking about at Parker and Peter Edwards. "We Virginians are known for being kind to our slaves, unlike our heavy-handed brothers in the Deep South," Trezvant said as though to comfort them. He turned back to Nat Turner. "Though slaves like you make me believe our more Southern brothers may be correct in their judgment of how to treat you darkies."

"So, you take pride that you are kinder masters: moderately cruel, but not exceedingly cruel? Where is the line?"

Trezvant's mouth puckered and his eyes narrowed to slits, as though he needed to see better, to reassess his prey. He paused, tapping the paper in front of him, and then asked, "If you had complaints, why did you not come to us? Look at all the blood that has been shed, your own people's blood. Your masters were kindly."

"A kindly master? The first word comforts you but the second word tells the tale. You have never worn chains or felt a whip. How can you be the judge of kindness?

"Good master? Good or bad, kind or evil, he keeps the captives from freedom."

"You are a cold-blooded fellow, sitting here calmly while white people have died! You sit here without crying, with your head held high; don't you know you're going to hang for what you've done?

"They were good white people, all of them. I knew them. Yours was a heartless crime."

A sardonic smile tugged at Nat Turner's lips. "Good to you. If I am guilty of crime, then all soldiers are guilty."

"What?"

"I said, the people you speak of were good to you. Their kindness to you has nothing to do with how they treated their captives. Kind or not, they were mansteaIers. You cannot judge from where you sit how they treated us when you yourselves are guilty of the same crimes."

"Crimes? We've done nothing against the law." Trezvant's tone was defensive.

"Then I say the law itself is criminal and has no authority over me." Whose laws did they uphold? The captors created laws that justified and benefited them. "'Every way of a man is right in his own eyes, but the LORD pondereth the hearts.'

"The law you created as men gives you what you want. But if you judge by the law of God, then you are guilty of the worst crimes. You are liars, thieves, and murderers. You are manstealers and God Almighty finds you guilty. His is the highest law on earth!"

Nat Turner looked around the room at the heavy draperies, the carpets on the floors, the polished silverware in the cupboards. He looked at the fine clothes the men wore and the shoes with buckles. They surrounded themselves with nice things and told themselves that their wealth was proof of their righteousness. "We came to you in the past, begging for help. Like Pharaoh, you were cruel to those who complained. You choked the life from us just as you have choked others who got in your way.

"There is no respite or refuge in the courts. There is no sheriff or army to take back what has been stolen from us. What did you expect us to do?"

"You and the other slaves had plenty to eat, warm clothes, and roofs over your heads. Why?"

"We starve. We freeze. We bleed. We die. And you do not know why? You truly do not know why? You have not heard your brothers' cries of despair or our blood crying from the ground? You have not heard our stolen wages howling in the land?" Nat Turner was not afraid. Death was already promised to him. "If you do not know what you have done to thousands, millions, if you cannot see our suffering, then God help you: You are reprobate!"

Chapter 73

The midafternoon sun changed the shadows in the room. His mouth was dry. Trezvant had been questioning him for what felt like hours. But Peter Edwards could not offer him refreshments in front of Trezvant. Even the slightest courtesy would make Peter Edwards look like a sympathizer, a nigger-lover, and wealthy Edwards could not afford that.

Trezvant and Nat Turner seemed to be the only two people in the room. Parker and Peter Edwards had faded into the background. Even Benjamin Phipps seemed to have disappeared. But Nat Turner knew there were others watching. Normally stationed in the kitchen, at the front door as butler, or standing by as a boy to do the masters' bidding, the captives were watching and listening. They were silent and invisible, hoping not to be noticed, but listening to each word. He imagined, because he had felt the same himself, that they were uncertain how to feel.

Were they silently cheering for him and praying for him as their hero? Were they angry because the revolt had caused them more trouble? Were they afraid to hope for freedom? Were they afraid to hope?

They were captive witnesses and no matter how they felt about him now, they would remember. They were captives, and he must do all he could to defend and deliver them. There was a family debt he owed.

Nat Turner looked at Trezvant. This was the trial that mattered. The play to come in the Jerusalem courtroom would be of little importance. The verdict there was already certain: Nat Turner would hang. But the fate of the captors was still uncertain.

Today, the captors faced judgment. Trezvant held the fate of the nation in his hands—mercy and peace, or judgment and war. Trezvant did not seem to understand, and his questioning always came back to the same thing.

The congressman shook his head. "You niggers bite the hand that feeds you. We did you people a favor bringing you here from your dark continent to teach you about Jesus Christ."

"How can you teach what you do not know?

"You do not believe. You do not love. How can you teach Christ when you think you are gods?"

Like earthly kings, they expected those they forced into slavery to serve gladly. Like evil gods, they felt it was their right to sacrifice the lives and dreams of others simply for their own profit and pleasure. God Himself does not force any man to be His slave. He is the Creator, but He gives each of us free will to choose if we will serve Him—as His friends and children. Those who choose to serve, serve with joy. God proves His greatness by giving all mankind freedom.

"But you force others to follow you at gunpoint. Whips and dogs and armies enforce your rule.

"So which of us is heathen and which is Christian, sir? The one who keeps men in chains, or the one who is kept? It is hard to know until harvesttime. God has judged."

Trezvant's eyes narrowed to slits. "Don't press me, boy. You speak too boldly. I have been patient with you. Always a smart, crafty answer. No doubt that is why you wear that scar on your head."

Nat Turner touched the scar on his temple while Trezvant shuffled his papers.

"Why? You still have not explained, to my satisfaction, why, Nat."

"It will never be to your satisfaction; you do not want to understand. We are peaceful men forced to fight for our lives, our liberty, our birthright."

"Men?" Trezvant laughed.

Nat Turner thought of Will, Hark, Sam, Dred, and the others, even young Davy. They had fought knowing the odds were against them. They had defended their families armed with little more than courage. "Yes, men. It is our solemn duty to defend our families, our women, and to obey God—both when He tells us to bow down and when He tells us to rise up!

"We are men—God's men, God's warriors, God's sons!" This was the reason that he was here. He could not back down now; he had to speak the whole truth. It was no accident that they were in this place just beyond Bethlehem on the way that leads to Jerusalem.

God had spoken to Nat Turner in the Great Dismal Swamp. He did not want to return to Cross Keys. He did not want judgment to begin with the house of God, the house his father built, Turner's Meeting Place. If he could have chosen where to begin war, it would have been with Giles Reese, who stole his family away.

But it was God's command, God's judgment. Here they were, and Nat Turner had to be obedient; he had to speak the whole truth. "You brought us here. You pay for your education, for your homes, for your wealth, by stealing our lives. We cut your roads through forests; we erect your buildings; we tend your children. In return for what we do, you give nothing. In return for our work, you steal our memories, our families, and you shame us, you humiliate us. You doom us to lives where our only worth is breeding more children for you to destroy."

What would happen to the generations born of the people, God's children, used for breeding, the generations forbidden to marry? Who would heal them, who would make them whole?

Trezvant's face was flushed with fury. He put down his pen and crossed his arms. Parker looked troubled.

"When you are done with us—if we live to be old and you have no more use for us—then you abandon us and tell yourselves you owe nothing, it is over. You reassure yourselves that you are good men."

No good fruit could grow from the seeds the captors planted. What would chained and beaten men, men forbidden to love, teach their children and their children's children? How could sweet milk flow from women treated as animals?

The captors left behind a debt too great for their children to bear, an evil inheritance like the firstborn sons of Egypt. Cursing them, they left their children to defend their forefathers' wrongs. "You poison us, you poison your own children, you poison the land. You poison the nation. You are Old Testament men, men without grace. How will you pay the debt for the trespasses you commit against the children, against the generations yet unborn?"

Trezvant's mouth set in a line. "I don't care how crazy you are, don't think that I'm going to sit here and allow you to malign this great nation!" His face tightened. "We are the sons of liberty, and I will not tolerate your blasphemy."

"It is a great nation. But it is also *our* nation. We are also sons of this nation we built together." Every acre, every field, every sip of liquor was purchased with captive blood. "Ours is a great country—how much greater would it be if its bricks were not ground from broken hearts, if they were not patched with the mortar of broken dreams?

"You don't want to share what God has given to all with your brothers. How much greater would our country be if you did not ask our Father to deny us?"

Trezvant's fists, resting on the table, were taut, his knuckles white. "Don't you dare presume to preach to me. I'm not one of you nigger field hands. What I want to know from you is why you did it. Why did you murder all those good white people?"

"We did not make war against all white people. You are the proof: You two gentlemen are white and alive. We did not murder; we executed God's judgment."

Trezvant leaned against the table. "The judgment of God? Over fifty white people are dead!"

"Judgment begins at the house of the Lord, but many more will die. You have judged others, now judgment comes to you.

"Millions of African men, women, and children are dead. Who

will answer for the lives taken? Who will answer for the generations stolen—fathers, mothers, teachers, sons, daughters, farmers?"

The captors stole and murdered millions but claimed innocence and righteousness.

There were families left without fathers. There were villages left with no young men to farm and no men to protect them. Teachers and mothers, babies were stolen, mothers left with empty arms.

"If you demand justice, first you must pay the debt you owe. Who will pay Africa for her children? If you do not pay, you leave the debt at your children's and your children's children's feet."

Panting and blotched with rage, though Parker tried to restrain him, Trezvant blustered. "Fiend! Liar!"

Nat Turner was bound to the truth. All that had happened—his mother's theft from Africa, Cherry's beating, Hark's death, even the death of his captor and friend Sallie—was for nothing if he did not speak the truth. "What happened the night of the sickle moon was not murder. It was revolt. First harvest. God's judgment. Not against all white men, but against those who lie and say they are God's people while rebelling against His will, against His love. They are evil, wolves in sheep's clothing.

"God's judgment began at the house of God—at Turner's Meeting Place. My father bequeathed me trusteeship there—"

"A trustee?" Trezvant slapped the table then, wide-eyed and grinning ear to ear. He gaped as if, finally, the prize for which he had been waiting had come. "You are a clown! At last, comic relief! You? A trustee?" Trezvant looked at the other white men present and laughed. "A nigger trustee?"

Nat Turner felt his face warming, like that of a smaller boy begging his taller brother for what was his, jumping for what was just out of reach. "I am a free man forced into slavery. My property, my rights were stolen. Then they stole my wife and son from me."

Trezvant was still laughing. "You are a high-minded fellow, aren't you? Everyone's stealing from you."

"I am a trustee and have the right to set forth judgment. It is against God's law to make your brother your slave, and the penalty for this disobedience, for centuries of arrogant disobedience, is death." No mercy could be given to those who gave no mercy. "'For with what judgment ye judge, ye shall be judged: and with what measure ye mete, it shall be measured to you again.'" There was no life or mercy for those who chose to live with cold, dead hearts.

The smile left Trezvant's face. "You are a murderous wretch! You killed children!"

Nat Turner's head and shoulders slumped. He heard Levi Waller's family screaming. He saw their faces. If they had gotten to the still earlier, Waller's family might still be alive. A tear stung his cheek. "I thank God that I feel this sorrow," he whispered to himself.

Then their faces and screams were replaced by those of the captives he'd known. He saw his mother's tears and her shame. He saw and heard the witnesses, and he saw Misha and her baby floating away on the water. He felt their heartbreak, their humiliation, their shame. Nat Turner lifted his head, righted his shoulders. "How many children have *you* killed?"

In one swift movement, Trezvant rose to his feet and struck him. Nat Turner tasted salty blood as he toppled from his stool to the floor. Trezvant's boot moved in slow motion and Nat Turner felt bright, white pain across the bridge of his nose.

Harriet

Chapter 74

Harriet had thought she wanted to listen; she had thought she was ready. She had thought she had the courage to hear.

But she felt accused. She felt angry. She had done nothing wrong.

She had given her life and sacrificed her reputation working to abolish slavery. The guilt and anger she felt was not rational. She did not create slavery. She owned no slaves. She tried to help, had risked her life and reputation to help. But she felt guilt just the same, and Harriet wanted it to stop.

"How could you know this?" The anger in her voice surprised her. She felt it, but she had not wanted William to know. "You were in the Great Dismal Swamp, were you not?" She was embarrassed by the cynicism that laced her voice but not embarrassed enough that she could control it. "You were not there! How could you know this?" She did not call William a liar, but she wanted to believe he was. It would have been easier than feeling what she felt. She had done nothing, but she felt convicted.

William was calm. "There were others there. There are always those who go unnoticed—as long as they do not move too suddenly, as long as they are quiet. The truth is carried on whispers and birds' wings.

"There were even those in the courtroom who wanted the truth known."

Harriet thought of William Parker, the lawyer who acted as

Nat Turner's defense attorney, and she recalled the mysterious letter that had sent her on her most recent journey.

Harriet's hand shook when she lifted her teacup. Though she fought it, everything within her felt convicted. "I feel as though you are attacking me, Mr. Love." She rested the jittering cup back on its saucer. "All white people are not responsible. I did not create slavery. All white people are not evil."

"I only speak the truth of what happened."

"But Nat Turner was a murderer!" Harriet was surprised at the bitterness in her tone. "You try to paint him as a hero."

William nodded. "Why is it so hard for you to allow us a hero?"

"I hardly think 'hero' describes Nat Turner."

"Because he took up arms?" He shook his head.

It was the same thing she had felt before, a kind of quiet antagonism, as though William were angry with everyone. His aggressiveness and senseless anger sparked hers; she had done nothing to him. She did not deserve to feel guilty.

"You wanted to know the truth," William said.

Somehow she could not help feeling as if she and her family had played some part in forcing Nat Turner to be who and what he had become.

Now William reached out and touched her hand. Harriet was stunned by what appeared to be kindness in his dark eyes. "We can stop."

She pulled her hand away and then wiped at the tears on her face.

"It is not easy or pleasant for any of us. That is why we must work hard to end it."

"I didn't do it!" Harriet wept.

He nodded. "Still, all of us must work to clean up the mess. Part of ending it is facing the truth."

Harriet dabbed at her face. "Forgive me."

William shrugged and shook his head. "We may stop," he repeated.

"Continue," she said, and then braced herself.

Nat Turner

Nat Turner

Chapter 75

What must it feel like to sail, sailing away,
Watching the prow of a great ship cut through the water?
What must it feel like to stand, standing as master of the ship,
Riding the waves beneath you?
What must it feel like to step, stepping on sandy shores,
Dining on French pastries, drinking Turkish coffee?
What must it feel like to ride, riding in a grand carriage,
Bustling down the cobblestone streets of the capital,
Having men and women wave the flag and call you hero?
What would it be like to sit, sitting in a cabin before a golden fire,
Bouncing his son on his knee with his wife smiling at him across the
table?
What would it be like to see, seeing another spring,
Hearing the first robins and seeing apple blossoms?
What must it feel like to swim, swimming in the ocean,
Swimming until he disappeared from shore?

Nat Turner was choking now, water all around him. He bobbed in the ocean, great waves crashing around him, choking him. He was going to drown.

"WAKE UP, YOU devil!" Trezvant's voice reached him through the waves. "Wake up!" Then, "Douse him again!"

Come to, his face, hair, and shirt wet, Nat Turner sputtered and gasped for air. Trezvant's voice had a false pleasantness. "That's a boy. You must remember your place so you don't make me angry."

It was difficult to see; Nat Turner imagined that both his eyes must be swelling shut. Trezvant stared at him, seeming to admire the knot Nat Turner felt pressing the center of his face. "All right, Preacher man, let's try this all again."

Pounding the table one time and smiling another, it seemed to Nat Turner that all Trezvant's questions ran together. Outside, the leaves drifted and swirled softly, translucent against the late afternoon sun. His mind drifted away . . . he felt Cherry's warm hand on his face.

STANDING IN THE moonlight, he watched her walk the path that he had left for her. Still under the trees, she skirted in and out of the moonlight. *"I am black, but comely, O ye daughters of Jerusalem, as the tents of Kedar, as the curtains of Solomon."* In the darkness, secreted among the grass, the trail of stones glowed green and blue and pink. She collected them as she walked so that no one else could follow.

For months Nat Turner had been planning and planting and had managed to keep this secret in the woods to himself. Instead of tattered rags, he imagined Cherry in a white gown and shawl. When she stepped into the moonlight, her feet touched the carpet of rose of Sharon that glowed silver, like her gown, in the moonlight.

She saw him then and smiled but remained quiet so they would not be discovered. She waved at him with one hand and waved her skirt with the other.

When Cherry was close enough to see him clearly, Nat Turner stooped to release the jar of fireflies at his feet. Their lights gently flickered on and off around him, Cherry skipped toward him like a little girl.

Her smile broadened and she clapped her hands softly when

she saw the shining rocks that ringed the great oak. Within the stone boundary were the flowers he had planted for her. Vines heavy with white angels climbed the trunk and lower boughs of the great tree. Their trumpetlike, sweet-smelling flowers trembled in the summer night breeze, glowing where the moon shone through the translucent petals. In the garden were lilies of the valley and daisies he had planted for her, knowing this day would come. The blooms she lingered over most were the moonflowers. Their perfume was intoxicating. The blossoms were glorious in the moonlight, though the fragile blooms would be dead by sunrise.

Nat Turner placed a wreath of Queen Anne's lace in Cherry's hair, her beautiful black hair like sheep's wool. He held her so close he felt her heart beating. They swayed together beneath the moon and stars.

What needed to be said between them could be said without words. He stepped away from her into a small spot he had cleared. He would light the black powder mixed with minerals, the experiment he had placed there. He grabbed his small torch, touched it to the first of three piles. There was a puff and then a glow of red. Then another puff and a brighter flash of blue. Finally, a last puff followed by a brilliant flash of white. Still silent, Cherry smiled at him, leaping like a child.

NAT TURNER WOULD never see Cherry again.

Chapter 76

Trezvant had left his seat. Now he circled the stool where Nat Turner sat. "I hear you read and write and quote scripture. I hear you think you're some kind of Baptist preacher."

"Methodist."

"Eh?"

Trezvant and men like him knew so little about the world, but thought it was their right to rule it. "My mother was raised in the Old Oriental Church, but I was raised Methodist."

"Oriental?" Trezvant laughed. "An Oriental Methodist nigger? You are entertaining." Trezvant shook his head. "Murder is a funny business for a Bible-quoting preacher."

"What choice did we have? You stole everything, choking us, choking the life out of us."

"Well, I don't want to hear all the spiritual gibberish, Nat. More than fifty white people are dead, and I want to know why."

"What choice did we have? More of the wicked will die if you do not heed God's warning. More innocents will die because of you."

Trezvant reached across the table and hit him again, a stinging blow across the mouth. "You are a depraved, coldhearted black imp. Answer me straight, and no more about God!"

His face burned where Trezvant hit him, and Nat Turner tasted more salty blood in his mouth. "If it is not about God, then you have no right to hold me. You argue on one hand that your right to enslave me comes from God. But if it is not God's doing, then I have every right—every duty—to fight for my freedom." In court they would swear on God's Bible and wave the Constitution over him. The law, the Constitution, said all men were created equal. "Your Constitution says it is my duty to rise up against those who oppress me. Nothing more was done than what the law of the land requires."

"Don't quote the Constitution at me, Nat Turner. It was not meant for niggers! The Constitution does not apply to animals!"

"But I believe the words written in the Constitution come from our Father, and He intended them for all His children."

Trezvant shook the table. "Insane, uncivilized animal!"

The inside of his mouth felt raw, and Nat Turner felt his lips swelling. "Animal? If I am an animal, then you must free me. There is no natural law against killing. The strongest beast takes all— land, women, power. It is what animals do, what a lion or a dog would do. By natural law I have every right to take everything you have, to kill you if you threaten me or my family. Kill or be killed. If I am an animal, I may do anything to protect and gratify myself, my family, my land, and my community, my tribe."

"You are a monster! A crazed nigger!"

Chapter 77

Nat Turner was surprised at how calm he felt. The names had lost their potency. Perhaps he had been called so many names in his lifetime that they no longer had any effect. Maybe it was simply relief that this day had finally come. Maybe calm was a part of freedom, so free he would speak the whole truth. "A man buys my wife and misuses her so that his children are born from her. The captor, a thief, calls his children borne of her, as well as mine, his property. Slaves! He sells them. He abandons them. Or he sends them to work in the fields for him and then steals his own child's wages. The law supports him in what he does. The church agrees with him and calls him a godly man. Am I the one who is crazy?"

Trezvant made angry, grunting sounds.

"You expect me to agree, to bow down to wickedness. If I complain, I am beaten, tortured, sold away, or maybe lynched.

"I am threatened with torture and death if I run away. When I stay, the man says it is because I am happy and love him. Who is crazy?

"You say it is your individual right to own other men. You know it is wrong, but you want wrong to be right—to do wrong without consequence. So you lie and say God, who created all men, has commanded you to enslave others. You captors create wicked lies and write them into law to excuse your wrong.

"You say the state is sovereign and no nation can bully you and overpower your will. But you force me, an individual, to be a slave. You sing songs about your own freedom while you steal freedom from me and others like me.

"Who is crazy? Is it so difficult for you to understand? I am a man. A man! And I would rather die than be your captive!"

The captors could not humble themselves enough to consider that God's will might be different from their own. When God's will was different from theirs, they prayed against God's will. They were willing to lie and do wrong for the sake of what they thought right. They did not know how to submit. They were too proud and cowardly to submit. They shouted and stomped, pouted and demanded their way. Then the captors were surprised when rebellion rose among them.

They worshipped the wrong their fathers did and called it righteous. "You captors will shoot a starving man who steals an apple off your land. But you are surprised that a captive will kill so that you cannot steal his spirit, his humanity, his children, and his wife. You will draw blood for what you believe. You raised us; why should we be any different?" It felt good to speak the truth. It felt good to call the lie a lie.

Trezvant raised an eyebrow. "Captives? Why do you keep saying captives? You are slaves."

"Shakespeare was wrong."

"Shakespeare?" Trezvant looked at the other white men and laughed. "What does a jig like you know about Shakespeare?" Trezvant held his stomach as he laughed. He waved his hand for Nat Turner to continue.

Nat Turner would not let Trezvant's ridicule stop him from speaking the truth. "Shakespeare was wrong: Names do matter. You call us slaves because it soothes your consciences—it sounds as though that is what we were meant to be, as though we had no beginning without you, as though slavery is who we are. The name does not acknowledge that you stole us and keep us against our will.

"You call yourselves masters and not captors. You want the power and the authority without accepting judgment for how you claimed it.

"You call us slaves, but we are free people you hold captive. You use your guns, your armies, and your laws to keep us captive. All that you have is built on the backs of our stolen labor."

Nat Turner's voice cut through the increasing darkness. "Bend your knee before God and acknowledge who you are and what you have done. We are captives, like the Israelites. You are thieves— captors, like the Egyptians of old—and you hold us against the will of God."

"Why do you provoke me, Nat? We are not here to debate slavery."

"If not for slavery, we would not be here."

Trezvant looked to his fellow captors for agreement. "We are here, Nat, because you are a murderer. Because you and your kind are thieves and wanted your masters' possessions."

"You are the thieves!"

"Shut your mouth!"

"God sees, He knows, He hears our cries. We are here because it is a man's duty to protect and defend his family. If he does not, he is not a man.

"You pretend not to understand because it does not suit your purses and it does not suit your pride. You dare to moan about what has been stolen? You steal men's families. You are the thieves, liars!"

Trezvant leapt from his chair again. Rage choked him and reddened his face.

His fists pounded Nat Turner like hammers. Heat swept through Nat Turner and he could not breathe.

Chapter 78

There was no woman more beautiful than Cherry, black against the midnight sky, sweet among the clover. How could he leave her? How could he say good-bye?

Nat Turner draped a garland of white honeysuckle he had braided around her waist. He was not a good singer, he never sang for others, but he hummed the tune he had heard drifting from the ships harbored in the Chesapeake. He whispered the words in her ear.

> O Shenandoah,
> I long to hear you,
> Away you rolling river.

Cherry pulled him to her and wrapped her arms around his neck. If he never saw her again, they would still have this moment. Her lips on his face were soft and sweet, blackberries.

How could he not have known all along how much he loved her? Why had it taken Hark and springtime to show him? He plucked a honeysuckle blossom from her garland and squeezed the sweet nectar into her mouth.

> O Shenandoah,
> I love your daughter,
> Away you rolling river.

How could he have left her those years ago? They swayed together with the great oak as their only witness. The moon and stars above them, the fireflies drifted around them, the moon garden glowed at their feet.

I'll not deceive you.
Away, I'm bound away.

When he was finished, they lay down among the tall grass and flowers. Nothing but death would make him leave her.

NAT TURNER AWOKE, choking, again.

"Wake up, you scoundrel! I warned you your life is in my hands."

The wooden floor beneath Nat Turner was soaked with water. Trezvant ordered a servant to drag him onto the stool again. Through his own swollen eyes, he looked at the servant's downcast expression. He felt the servant's arm about him, lifting him. He could not fail the captives. There was a family debt he owed.

He was not in the orchard with Cherry. There was no night, no fireflies. He would never see her again. This was the last good work he would do for her, for his son, for the other captives. The stool rocked beneath him, or maybe he was tottering himself.

Trezvant looked to Parker and Edwards. "This is a waste of time. He is a lying beast."

He would not be still. What good was living without freedom, without respect? "Why do you take me to court if I am a beast? You will take me to court because it is the will of God Almighty!"

"As though He would talk to you, a nigger! I will have you skinned alive!" Trezvant's eyes were feverish.

"God has made me free; it is you who hold me captive. God, who is love, loves us both. We are brothers, His children, and He does not want to choose one brother over another. But you give Him no choice."

"Don't you lie on God Almighty, Nat Turner—I am not your brother and He would never defend a monster like you!"

"You captors put lies in the mouth of God! You hold us against His will!"

Trezvant removed his hands from the papers and eased his left hand down to his side. From a scabbard, he removed a long-bladed knife. Casually, he wiped the blade on the tablecloth and then laid the knife on the table in front of him.

The movement was a threat, but Nat Turner could not stop. He could not live without freedom or respect. "You mistake God's patience. You think His long-suffering means that what you do is right.

"But He heard our cries. Our Father loves us both, but you gave Him no choice. We love you, but you gave us no choice.

"I had no choice; I was defending my flock, as any shepherd or even any animal would." He could not stop; there was a family debt he owed.

"You have raped our wives. You have starved our children; their feet bleed. What did you expect us to do? Did you expect us to dance? To sing for you?"

Trezvant leaned forward, his eyes flashing. He touched the knife handle. "Don't go too far, boy."

Chapter 79

What was too far? There had been too many threats in Nat Turner's life—they had lost their power. Nothing could be done to him that his Father did not allow. "You say what you do is a natural thing, but does the red rose serve the white rose? Does the night surrender to the day and the day not to the night?" Trezvant inched closer, his fingers wrapped loosely around the knife, but Nat Turner did not pause. "In God's plan there is a harmony. He loves us all. We are all blessed. But you are greedy and say all blessings are for you.

"It is all a lie and you teach the lie to your children, so that they are blinded and cannot find their way."

Trezvant lifted the knife from the table. "I warned you—"

"You have taken a whole race captive to work for, and even amuse, you and your families. Are you saying that God has given the wolf the right to protect its offspring, but not to my people?

"What would make you believe that you are great enough to own another man, woman, or child? You do not have money enough to pay for the life of my son. You cannot count high enough to reach a price worthy of my wife." Cherry, his beautiful Cherry. He would never see her again. How could any man have hoped to pay for such a woman? He could never have paid a bride-price worthy of her. Her love was the sweetest gift. "It is a lie."

Trezvant continued to finger the knife. "I could take your life right now and no one would care. In fact, everyone would cheer and call me a hero."

"My life is already over. Slice me here, hang me on the tree, slavery's slow death; it is all the same."

The two judges looked at each other.

"But you won't kill me. I am here because God sent me. I go to Jerusalem because God has chosen me to pick up the yoke of Christ."

"Madman, are you saying that you are Jesus?"

"No. I am no different than you, brother. He asks us all to pick up His yoke."

It would be over soon. He would not see his mother again. He would not see his family. But their freedom was worthy of his life. "Our Father has said you will not kill me now, neither will you repent or atone for your sins.

"God has sent me to warn you: War is coming.

"You will take me to Jerusalem. And there you will hang me because of a lie."

Trezvant sneered. "Oh, we will hang you! We will hang you and I will cheer!"

"You put yourselves first, above and never beneath. But Jesus said the one who would be master is the one who would serve his brothers."

"Then we white men have done you a favor, nigger." Trezvant snickered.

"You laugh, but you speak curses over your own head."

Trezvant looked at the other white men. "Listen to how he rambles. Who can make heads or tails of this?" He turned back to Nat Turner. "You are a lunatic!"

"We are not murderers. We are your brothers. We are heroes. We fight against armies with not much more than bare hands. You think I am mad, but I am only the first, the first to call the lie a lie. More will come. War will come.

"You and the other slavery men are fanatics and your foolishness infects even many of those who believe they are well.

"God called you to judgment because there was no other choice. He loved, but you murdered. We loved, but you murdered.

"You have murdered the land, you have murdered us, as the wisteria vine chokes the tender tree.

"And for what cause? For thirty more coins in your purse? For a title? To hear others call you 'master'?

"We are not thieves. You steal—you stole our lives, our future, our hope. Look with your hearts. You are the predators. Wealth and power without love breed mad, beastly men."

Knife in hand, Trezvant again leapt from his chair.

His sudden move jerked the tablecloth askew. Glass and fruit crashed from the table. Nat Turner's back slammed to the floor, bare bones and wasted flesh against hard wood, Trezvant's knee pressed Nat Turner's chest, making it difficult to breathe. His blade pressed against Nat Turner's throat. "You are dirty, stinking cowards, stealing upon people in the middle of night, murdering them as they slept!"

Nat Turner grunted, the knife pressing into his flesh. "Brave men. God's men." He squeezed out the words, hardly any air in his lungs. Trezvant's breath smelled of corn liquor and cigars. His sweat and spittle dropped onto Nat Turner's face. Trezvant pressed the tip of the blade so a crimson bead appeared. "Despicable cowards!" He breathed the words like fire, his face closer still.

Nat Turner grunted again. "It takes great courage to love those who hate you. Courage to fight against those you love. We had courage to fight. To fight those we loved!" He felt the burning slash of Trezvant's knife down the side of his face.

Chapter 80

His beautiful mother's hair was graying; her hands wrinkled and knotted from too much work. He bent and whispered in her ear. "Is it all true? We are people of Ethiopia? There is a God who loves us? There is another place besides here?"

So many years had passed since she had washed up on the shores of this New World. Nancie looked up at him and placed one of her warm hands on each side of his face. "We are Egzi' abher's children, His children from Ethiopia. We are sojourners in a strange Nineveh, but we know that He was, He is, and He will be."

Her eyes looked deeply into his and he felt that she was seeing his soul. She reminded him of all that she had taught him, of the saints, the churches, and the highlands. "Nathan, my Negasi!" She called him by his Ethiopian name.

"And you are Nikahywot, my source of life." She smiled at him, and when she looked at him he saw the highlands, he heard the roar of Tis Isat Falls. "I am your mother and I would not lie to you. Our Father is waiting to welcome us home."

NAT TURNER AWAKENED. He had drifted in and out of consciousness, in and out of his mother's embrace. He did not know how much time had passed. He could not recollect how many times he had been beaten. The cut on his face burned and his shirt was stiff now with dried blood. He had been at Peter Edwards's table for what felt like days but must have been hours. The sun would set soon.

Trezvant's questioning came back to the same thing: "Why?"

Nat Turner held a hand to his jaw. "Only a fool would tell himself this day would never come. You would not listen." His jaw ached and both his eyes were almost closed. "For thirty-one years I have bowed and obeyed. Thirty-one years—even as my child was sold, as my wife was sold, as my mother and my wife were raped. I have prayed the prayers, and worshipped God, and pleaded with you men to change your ways."

As Nat Turner sat at the table before Congressman Trezvant, he heard the sadness in Mother Easter's voice as she sang. He saw his mother shivering and all the cracked, bleeding bare feet standing in icy, muddy water—the boys, Davy and Moses.

The slavery men in the room with him knew nothing about suffering. They knew nothing about sorrow. Thirty-one years. "In all that time, against my own will, I have been obedient, a goodly servant to man. Thirty-one years, my hand trembled with anger rather than strike back when white men struck me. Thirty-one years I forced my feet and hands to stay in the furrows raising another man's crops, even when I wanted to run away." Nat Turner felt the rough wood of the plow handles in his hands, the splinters. Felt the hot sun on his neck, the sweat running down his face. He saw the oxen pulling the plow, felt the earth beneath his feet and the soreness in his strained muscles. "Thirty-one years I willed my tongue not to speak. Thirty-one years I allowed other men to steal from me—and served man as God told me to.

"So when God called me to render judgment, to do His will, I obeyed." Nat Turner allowed himself to smile.

"It is a sin to know the Master's will and refuse to obey it." The teeth loosened by Trezvant's fists ached in his mouth. "I obeyed my Creator. I defended my family, my community.

"God's will called me to war, to render judgment, and, being a humble servant, I obeyed Him. Unwavering obedience.

"For thirty-one years I have submitted, prostrated myself before man. For thirty-one years I have debased myself, watching as people I love were violated and dishonored. I have obeyed.

"When God commanded, I obeyed. I am still obedient, even unto death."

James Parker reached, touching Trezvant's arm so he would not leap again. "We must not kill him. Do not allow him to goad you. He is only a slave."

"I know who you are, James Trezvant. I know what you've done, trading lives for money. What was your share?

"But I also know who I am. I am God's son. I am my Father's son. I am your brother. You expect our Father to forget about me? You expect me to forget who I am?"

Trezvant gripped the table until his knuckles were white. Then, slowly, the agitation left his face. A smile replaced it. "I have asked that you leave religion out of this interrogation, but since you insist, I will put a question to you." Trezvant tented his fingers, raised one eyebrow, and struck a relaxed pose. "Slavery has existed throughout the world almost since the beginning of time. The Bible you speak of condones it. Slavery is part of life and common among mankind."

Trezvant nodded, waiting for Nat Turner's response, and appeared certain he was bringing the game to a close.

Chapter 81

Nat Turner saw the lie smiling from Trezvant's eyes. "You are proslavery men, except when the slave is you. When Barbary pirates capture you from the shores of Europe you are horrified. When the English bring their boots down on your necks, you are quick to take up arms. You support slavery of the rest of humanity, but not for those with white skin. You see yourselves as superior; you think yourselves equal with God."

"We are not gods." Trezvant looked at Parker and Edwards and chuckled. "Not quite. But God *has* made us to rule over you. We are naturally greater than you, and God created black men to serve us."

It was hard for Nat Turner to breathe through his nose. No doubt—it was broken. "All sin is common among men. Murder is common. Stealing is common."

Trezvant's eyes narrowed as he spoke. "But there are rules in your Bible, *Prophet*, for slavery. If God did not intend for there to be slaves, why would there be so much attention in the Bible to slavery?"

"Moses gave many laws about things that God hates. Moses gave rules for divorce, because it is common. Because there are divorce laws, do you say that God decrees we must all divorce?

"You lie, knowing that the law is clear: The penalty for mansteal-ing is death. You attempt sleight of hand to sidestep the penalty. You mock God with this foolishness, and God will not be mocked!"

Trezvant was not ready to surrender. He did not blink but went on questioning. Trezvant shook the pages at Nat Turner. The congressman looked around the room at the other white men. "You read. Haven't you read the story of Noah in your Bible? God commanded us to be masters over you. Your servitude cannot be blamed on us; blame it on your God."

Chapter 82

The days were shortening now and the sun was beginning to fade. Nat Turner was tired, tired of answering questions, tired of the game. But he knew it would not be over until Trezvant felt he had won. Not until Nat Turner hanged.

From the corner of his eye, Nat Turner noticed a movement. He lifted his head to see through his swollen eyes. It was a small slave boy with sad eyes hiding behind a corner drape. He endured for the boy, for other boys like him, and for Riddick.

He touched a hand to his swollen jaw. He had come to Peter Edwards's to deliver a warning to the captors. But he endured to give hope to his son, to his sons and daughters. Nat Turner did not want the others to notice the boy. But Riddick and the nameless boy were worth whatever he might suffer.

It was clear Trezvant thought himself a fox. His smile broadened. "God cursed the black man for eternity. Haven't you read the story? The words are right there in your Bible. God said it, 'Cursed be Canaan; a servant of servants shall he be unto his brethren.' Niggers are cursed forever." Trezvant's smile curled into smugness.

There was no doubt that Trezvant thought himself superior. He thought all power was in his hands. Nat Turner fought to hold the anger he felt.

"It was not God who uttered those words, but Noah," Nat Turner corrected. "God blessed the whole family of man. Instead of offering thanks, Noah drank and cursed." What kind of father would want to believe that his drunken, angry words would curse his grandson and descendants for all time? How could a righteous man want to doom billions of people for one son's foolish act?"You describe a monster, not a loving father.

"You white slavery men write race into the story. You twist Noah's story. You say he is white and Ham black—it justifies your wickedness.

"And is God a genie, granting every drunken curse or wish without consideration of right or wrong? Would you make the Almighty a slave?" Nat Turner spit the words at Trezvant. "You are a liar, sir.

"Emmanuel walked among us, teaching the truth to untwist men's lies. He loved all mankind. He taught that none of us are masters; all of us are servants of God and one another. He taught that we should love God first, and love one another as brothers—even the least among us."

Trezvant fingered the knife again, threatening. But it was too late. Nat Turner was free and he would speak the truth. He owed it to Cherry, he owed it to Riddick, to his mother, and to all the captives. He owed it to God.

"What Jesus taught does not suit you in your thirst for property and power. So you twist what He taught and scurry like rats to the Old Testament. You gnaw at it and tear away chunks to suit you.

"You lie on God, Emmanuel. You hang your greed and your hate on Him and lead others to hate the gospel."

If he died, he would die with the truth pouring from him. "God did not grant Noah's wish. Each one of us is loved and blessed by God to multiply and prosper on this earth. It is still a covenant between God and all people. The rainbow is proof.

"Jesus came to walk the earth and remind us that we are all brothers—we are all welcomed in the kingdom—all nations, and kindreds, and peoples, and tongues.

"The evil you preach is in your heart and mind, not God's. Why force your wickedness on God?"

Trezvant bolted to his feet.

Chapter 83

Nat Turner had been called names. He had been lied to. He had been beaten and cut before; there was nothing more to dread. Nat Turner looked into Trezvant's crazed eyes.

James Parker caught Trezvant about the wrist with his right hand and used his left arm to pull Trezvant back to his chair. Parker shook his head at Trezvant, as though to calm the older man.

Trezvant frowned, fuming like a dragon. He grabbed the crumpled pages, pressed on them to smooth them, crumpled them in anger again, and then smoothed them again. He exhaled. "I am a man of honor." The muscles at his temples spasmed. "I will not allow a mere field hand, a nigger, a wild beast, to get the best of me." He breathed several times, sheathed his knife, then nodded for Nat Turner to go on. He sneered. "Speak, Prophet."

Nat Turner felt blood trickling down his neck. None of it mattered now. He looked toward the window. He would not see many more sunsets. "God did not curse us. He blessed *all* His children.

"God gave Noah and his sons, to all of mankind, the whole world with all of its beauty and delights. All authority and power. His commands were few: Take care of and replenish the earth, be fruitful and multiply, and do no harm to one another.

"The true lesson of Noah is that we are all brothers—fathers, sons, mothers, daughters—and that God has blessed us all equally. He loves us and has given us the whole world, everything."

Trezvant clapped his hands, laughing at Nat Turner and mocking him. "Hallelujah, Preacher!" He laughed to Peter Edwards. "Where is the preacher's pulpit?"

Nat Turner continued, undeterred. "But instead of gratitude to our Father, instead of singing God's praises, we demand payment from our brothers and sons for small debts. Instead of gratitude, we want to steal what belongs to our brothers. Like Noah, we are drunk on the wine of this world.

"Yet God loves us. Still God keeps His covenant. God remains true; He offers His blessing to all His children. The proof is the rainbow, the sign of His promise, a sign seen all over the earth."

Trezvant applauded. He stood and bowed. "Listen to the preacher!" He whistled. "Someone get the nigger a frock coat and a collar!" Trezvant laughed.

"You are hard-hearted and refuse to hear. You think that God is made in *your* image. God is a spirit, but what will you do if He looks like me? Will you turn from Jesus if He has hair like mine, lips like mine, skin like mine?"

Trezvant doubled over with laughter, looking around at the other white men. "He really is mad! A coon god?"

"Will you forsake Him? If He is like us on Judgment Day, will you be frightened? Make excuses? Will you repent and grieve for what you have done?"

Trezvant sat back in his chair, waving his hand in a dismissive manner. "You have no argument with me, Prophet. Your argument is with the Bible. I know what the words say, they say that you and your kind are slaves and nothing more."

Parker's brow was furrowed. He scratched his head.

"You read something that is not there. Open your heart. Open your eyes. You have been deceived. You twist God's Word. There is nothing in the Bible that says Noah looked like you—with straight yellow hair, white skin, and blue eyes. The men who wrote the Bible looked nothing like you. They were from my mother's part of the world."

Trezvant would not relent. "If God loves you so much, then why are dark people slaves all over the world?"

"Because you have told this lie all over the world, passed like a disease from heart to heart! All over the world, men with wickedness in their hearts use the same lie you are telling to justify what they do—stealing, raping, twisting God's truth.

"Noah was meant to teach us. He was not created to be your hero or excuse for torturing others who are not like you. God is father to all. We are all created in His image."

Trezvant's smile froze. His eyes glittered. "He is not God to niggers! God is not a nigger! And if He was, I wouldn't serve Him!" His stare was feverish. "I would as soon curse Him and cast the Bible into the sea!" He sneered. "Ridiculous."

Parker flushed but said nothing.

Nat Turner looked at Trezvant, Parker, and Peter Edwards. "You have lived the lie so long that almost the very elect accept it as truth. The lie lives in your hearts. The real truth is buried. Blood is on your hands."

Nat Turner looked at the young ginger-haired man, searching for light in his eyes. "I sense, Mr. Parker, that you have good intentions, you still have a spirit that can discern right and wrong. You still have a living heart beating within you." He nodded toward Trezvant. "You have heard Mr. Trezvant's sentiments—he is ready to curse God, to curse our Father. Will you follow him to hell?"

Chapter 84

Nat Turner ran through the forest, holding his son's hand. Laughing, they came to a quiet clearing and rested. They searched the brush for sweet berries, finally finding some ripe blackberries.

As they ate, Nat Turner pointed out birds to Riddick. "Listen to their calls." He pointed to two nearby. "There is a blue jay. And over there, an indigo bunting." The tiny bird flitted about, showing off its plumage, and flew away.

He took his son's hand and then led him to his fishing stream in the Great Dismal Swamp. "Listen to the forest," he told Riddick, and they walked deeper within.

Nat Turner had hoped to one day share his Hebron, his place of refuge, with his son. He had hoped that one day they would be free together. He hoped that the captors would repent and there would be no need for war.

When he was discouraged, when he was tired, the dream gave him comfort. But that was before the eclipse, before the indigo sun. Before the war began. Before he surrendered.

Now he sat at Peter Edwards's table looking across at James Parker. The younger man had been silent for most of the inquisition, but now Parker's chin trembled and his face strained white as his knuckles. "Nat Turner, you accuse us of intending to do harm."

Nat Turner read hurt and indignation on James Parker's face. He smiled at Parker. The young man looked to be the same age as he. In another life, in another time, they might have been friends. "You are angry with me, but I say to you, thank God for those who trouble you. Be thankful for the thorns in your side. Fear the day when you no longer tolerate those who speak against you. Fear the day when you no longer feel at all."

James Parker was insistent. "I have no malicious intent. I intend to harm no one."

"You do not think evil, you only do evil."

"My family is good to you people! We are criticized for being too good to you! I won't stand here and allow you to dishonor us!" Parker continued his defense. "Perhaps life would be better for all without slavery. But who would farm the land? I won't allow you to accuse my family of evil. We intend no harm. We have done all we can do! What do you want from us?"

"The thief who steals without regret is still a thief. Your ignorance to the harm you cause does not mean that you are faultless. Right in front of your eyes are murderers, rapists, sadists, and thieves. You are among them, but you don't see it, you don't want to see. Pray to God that He will help you see.

"Wrongdoers who see and grieve are blessed indeed"—Nat Turner nodded his head toward Trezvant—"even though others might mock him for wanting to change."

Parker's face was still flushed. If Parker could not hear him now, maybe he would hear and understand the words later. "If your heart aches when you think of what you have done, then fall to your knees, turn from evil, and give thanks." Nat Turner looked deeply into James Parker's eyes, blue eyes, looking for the life within him. "I do."

Nat Turner sighed as he remembered Cherry and his son walking behind Giles Reese's horse after they were sold to him. He remembered the pain that brought him to life, the pain that helped him to hear God. "We must ask Him to help us to cry, to ache, so that we might repent and turn." Parker was trembling now, and Nat Turner could not be sure whether it was anger or deep sorrow. "I pray that you do not refuse the gift. Repent and turn.

"Haven't you read the prophecy? Our Father will be broken-hearted and long for His children who are taken captive and scattered all over the earth. When we return, He will welcome us home. Haven't you read the prophecy? Those you steal and sell into slavery will someday rule over you."

Nat Turner continued to focus on James Parker. "Soon will come the time of sifting. Do you have the courage to stand against the wicked ones, to stand with those who are your brothers in spirit?"

Trezvant snarled. "I will die before I see you niggers free. Your little insurrection has only served to unite all white men against you. Every white man, even the abolitionists, will stand with us."

Trezvant reached out his right hand and laid it on Parker's shoulder. "He is a wily serpent. Do not let the devil deceive you. If he is a preacher, he is the devil's preacher. Don't allow this serpent to poison your mind. God said the niggers were to be our slaves. God spoke the words, not you or I."

It was men like Trezvant, like Nathaniel Francis, who deceived. God said all nations, but men like them said only white. "You are the serpent, Trezvant. You seek to hide in the Old Testament, knowing there is no slavery under grace. But if you hide in the Old Testament, God's Old Testament judgment will find you.

"God did not curse us; He loves us all. All the law and the prophets hang on love. Every lesson, every truth in the Bible, like sunshine through the leaves, must be filtered through love. Only man would hang the law on something as meaningless as skin color. God's Word rests on love.

"God knows who His children are. Anyone who does not love his brother is not a child of God."

Nat Turner turned to look directly at Parker. "God says that we are brothers, one blood, adopted into one family. Trezvant says that you should only love white men. Who will you believe? Who will you follow? For the sake of skin color, will you follow him to hell?"

Trezvant stomped his feet and whistled now. "You are a slippery-tongued devil. But all your going on has not helped your case in the least. You will hang. Slavery will live!"

Chapter 85

Through the window, Nat Turner could see the early evening blue of the sky—turquoise blending into indigo. All the lives, all the suffering had led to this. He pleaded with the captors for mercy for his people and for themselves. The fate of the nation rested in their hands.

Things might have been different if the captors would listen, if their cold hearts melted. He might have sat beside his son, fishing now in the pond. Nat Turner closed his eyes and imagined Riddick smiling up at him. He wrapped an arm around Riddick's shoulders.

Whoa! His son yelled when his pole tugged, a fish on the end of the line.

Nat Turner opened his eyes. That was all a dream. There would be no fishing. He had been sent to deliver this message. There was a family debt he owed.

"You worship white skin, not God. You teach the lie to others. If they are not light, they hate themselves; they feel forsaken by God.

"Today you called me prophet. So I warn you like Ezekiel, like Jonah, like Moses. Today I speak judgment against Southampton, against Virginia, and against this nation. God has heard and seen your wickedness and He knows the coldness of your hearts. Our voices, along with those of Nineveh and the Queen of the South, speak against you.

"Turn! It is your only hope! Repent and set my people free!"

Trezvant giggled. "O Moses, where are your plagues? Where are the locusts? Where is the bloody river?"

"We are slaves, dressed in tatters. We have no uniforms or flags. But we are part of the Lord's army. God's glory is our banner. God loves us all, but He will not endure your wickedness against us forever. War will come!

"God will make black men stand side by side with you. Children of Africa, children of our two continents—Africa and America will become leaders among you. 'Princes shall come out of Egypt; Ethiopia shall soon stretch out her hands unto God.'"

"The only thing a nigger can do for me is tend my fields or shine my boots. No nigger will ever lead me." Trezvant mugged for Nat Turner and flapped his arms like a chicken. He bugged out his eyes, like a minstrel, and began to sing.

> And wen Zip Coon our President shall be,
> He make all de little Coons sing possum up a tree;
> O how de little Coons will dance an sing,
> Wen he tie dare tails togedder, cross de lim dey swing.

Nat Turner had seen it all before. "Would you choose whiteness over obedience to God? Whiteness over holiness?"

"Call it what you like, no black jig will ever be king over me. All your heads will be on poles before I let one of you be head over me."

"As great as you are, my brothers, you are not greater than God. If you choose to lose your lives rather than grant our freedom, it is your choice!"

"Never!"

"Then you will hand this lie down to your children as inheritance. Like the family of Abraham, Isaac, and Jacob, your children will no longer recognize their sin. They will wallow in sin, turning from mercy, turning from repentance. What God calls wrong, they will call right. They will point at evil in other places and not recognize it in themselves.

"As God blesses those they despise, they will be bitter, full of rage. They will be angry when God shows the world that your truth is a lie. In the end, whiteness will rule them. It will choose who they love and where they live. It will choose where they pray, their family and friends. The idol will control the choices they make.

"You will leave your children a bitter inheritance. In your hands is the power to stop it all now. Look to God and turn."

Chapter 86

Trezvant's face blanched. He looked wildly around the room at the others.

Nat Turner encouraged himself. This was the trial that mattered. He must find strength. He must finish. There was a debt he owed. "This is only a warning, only the beginning. Brother will take arms against brother and fathers against their own sons. You will slaughter yourselves. The rivers will flow red, blood will drip from the corn. The battle is already raging in the heavens. I have seen it with my own eyes. Death will come again to the Tidewater. It will spread across Virginia and across this nation. I have seen it.

"In the end, the captives will be free. Whether freedom comes now or after much bloodshed is your choice. It is for you to decide whether you will walk like Pharaoh in your arrogance or humble yourselves like the Great King Xerxes."

Trezvant mocked Nat Turner, waving his hands in the air. "O great prophet, spare me! O great One, have mercy on me! Save all of us poor white people from the darkies!" Trezvant shook his head and stuck out his tongue as he laughed. "I am going to laugh as you hang, nigger! My wife and I are going to dance when they hang you from that tree!"

Nat Turner would not allow himself to be distracted. "You will bequeath damnation to your children. Their blood will be on your hands. Look to God, my brothers, you only have to turn." He was brought to these shores for this moment. He would not die with their blood on his hands. "Turn from your evil ways. Live!"

Even as Nat Turner spoke the pronouncement there was a bitter taste in his mouth. Live? Life for them, forgiveness for them after all the people they had murdered, after all they'd stolen, after all the broken hearts? Mercy? Nat Turner tasted bile.

He had been spit up on the shores of a foreign land among people who hated him and others like him. He would never see his homeland. Never see his grandparents or his sister. He would never smell the wildflowers of Ethiopia or see the green hills. These people, people who stole land that did not belong to them, who stole men and had no sorrow for it—these were the people that God wanted to pardon? Was no one beyond God's mercy?

How could the Lord shower mercy on people like Trezvant? Nat Turner looked at the proud man sitting before him. How could people like Trezvant and Nathaniel Francis escape punishment simply by repenting—simply by uttering a few words? Simply by feeling sorrow in their hearts for their deeds? After all they'd done? It was not fair.

But God was Father to them all. He was the Father of Cain and Abel. He was Father of the just and the unjust, of Nathan and John Clarke, and loved them both.

Nat Turner would do what he had promised; he would be obedient—his would be the voice that offered the nation an opportunity to repent. "God is the God of mercy, your Father as well as mine. It is He who sends me.

"Congressman, you have desired to be a great man, to have the nation's attention on you. So, like King Xerxes, like Pharaoh, the fate of the nation is in your hands. You have the power to speak to the people, to the governor, to persuade them to turn. There is still time.

"Virginia boasts that she leads the South and the whole nation. If you turn, if you set the captives free, the others will follow. It is in your hands to stop the coming war. You have the chance to turn the nation. If you do not, the judgment is against you and against this nation, and the blood will be on your hands.

"You stand at a crossroads today, and it is for you two judges to warn the people. If you choose the way of Pharaoh, you will bring judgment on this nation, on yourselves, and on your children. This is the Word of the Lord: 'He that stealeth a man, and selleth him, or if he be found in his hand, he shall surely be put to death.' This is the right and sure judgment of the Lord!

"Open your hearts, open your eyes. 'He that leadeth into captivity shall go into captivity: he that killeth with the sword must be killed with the sword.'

"Only repentance can change your destiny. Your fate is in your hands!" It was done now. It was finished.

Trezvant looked at James Parker. "We rushed here for nothing. He is a bloodthirsty maniac."

Remembering his wealthy host, Trezvant rubbed his hands together as though he was finished and motioned to Peter Edwards. "I am done with this scoundrel. Take him away." He looked down at his glass. "I am famished. Bring me more refreshment."

Chapter 87

The sheriff arrived as darkness dawned, along with twenty-five strong and armed guards; they chained Nat Turner hand and foot. The heavy iron clanked as he walked and tortured his skin as he stumbled down the road.

His head ached. Except for his own blood, his mouth was dry.

Patches of cold night with yellow-flamed torches. Fists and jeers. Familiar faces turned strange. Words and fists pounding him. Women's hat pins; who knew they could be so painful? On his knees, then up again. Heads on poles. Knees on hard ground. Swollen eyes. Threats, kicks.

Dragged into houses along the way, his face was pressed to their souvenirs. Fingers without nails, legs without feet, heads without eyes and ears. How much worse would they do to him? The Road with No Name. Black Head Sign Post Road. Jerusalem.

"Devil!" "Murderer!" "Thief!" "Give him to us!"

Slammed against cold metal bars, against rough, moldy concrete. He was alone except for the hands, the voices, angry steel. Outside the jailhouse, crowds shouted his name. Kill him!

THERE WERE NOT many visitors to his cell, other than those who came to beat him. There was only his lawyer: William Parker. "There is not much I can do." There was nothing, really, that Parker could do. It was all in God's hands.

At night he dreamed of Cherry dancing among the moonflowers. He touched her hair; he kissed her lips and held her to him. In the blue-black night, underneath the stars, the flowers glowed and the moonlight kissed her eyes and teeth. Suddenly she pulled away from him. *Aren't you angry with Him, your God?*

Nat Turner didn't want to argue; he wanted to remember everything about Cherry and to hold her. *He is your God, too.*

Look what He has done to you. Look at our miserable lives! I know you are surprised at me. I know you are a holy man, better than me, and probably angry with me for saying this, but God took you away from me, the only man I ever loved. The only man who ever loved me. The only man who told me I was beautiful. Cherry wept then, and in the moonlight, her tears glistened on her face.

Cherry had stepped too far away, too far away for him to touch her. *He told us He would send us forth as sheep among wolves, Cherry.*

I don't want to hear this, Nat. I don't want to hear it, Nathan!

She and his mother were the only ones who called him Nathan. The sound of his name in her mouth was like rose petals brushing his neck. *Some of us are sheep in our family of wolves, some of us are sheep working among wolves, and some of us are sheep walking through a nation of wolves. They seek to devour us, but we must still love, Cherry. Some of us will lose our lives, lose our loves.*

But it is not fair, husband!

God is loving and just.

How can you say that? Look at you! Look at the chains! Look what they've done to you! How could a loving and just God allow that?

As soon as she said the words, Nat Turner felt the weight of the chains around his ankles and wrists. The iron bars between the two of them seemed colder. He felt the soreness, the ache from his head to his feet. The dried scabs around his mouth made it difficult to speak.

The silver moon made a halo in her hair. *Evil men did this to you! Is that love? How can that be just?*

He wanted to hold her. *God knew us before we were born into this world. I believe He asked me to leave my heavenly home to* come here. I believe He asked the same of you, of all of us, even if we are only here for a moment. I believe He told us we were needed here.

A lot of good we have done!

I believe He told us ahead of time that we would be sheep among wolves and that we would suffer to help others. She was so beautiful, his Cherry. She was a princess in the moonlight. I believe He told you there would not be much joy for you here—no fine dresses, no great houses—but He promised you flowers. He looked down at her feet covered in moonflowers; he smelled the honeysuckle. He looked up at the dark blue sky. Stars and the moon. I believe He promised you me.

That promise is broken!

I think He promised that I would sing to you.

Another broken promise. You never sing.

And I believe He told you that I would need you—that you would be my joy, that you would make my life bearable. He wanted to remember everything about her—her hands, her feet, her smile, her frown. I believe you agreed to come, Cherry. Even knowing that you would suffer. He heard her weeping. Her shoulders shook; she cried from her belly. I believe you agreed to come for me and to bear my son. I believe you agreed to come to help the world, to bring joy to the world.

But who have I helped, Nathan? What good has it all been? She came closer. Pressing herself against the cold bars, stretching, hoping to touch him, even if only with the tips of her fingers. Reaching. Reaching.

I agreed to come, Cherry. He told me that I would be beaten for His name's sake. Hated. I believe that He told me that I would be heartbroken, hated by the people I loved. He whispered her name. But not you, Cherry. Not you. He tried to smile.

I don't want you to die, Nathan.

He promised me a few joys—my mother, my son, the books. ... He promised me you, the love of my life, your love. He choked.

The tears surprised him, sudden and stinging. It was hard to talk through the tears. We all agreed to come. Don't you remember? Hoping we could make it better. Out of love; love for Him and love for them, even the ones who don't love us back. Don't you remember? We have to remember, Cherry.

We agreed to come. This world is so cruel and so hard, some only have the heart to come for a short time, just a flash, a hope. Some only have the heart to come close, but not to stay. But you and I agreed to come, to live in this world and sacrifice everything—just in hopes that we might help one person—sad Charlotte, Mother Easter, or maybe even Nathaniel Francis. Knowing that we will return to a better home.

All our lives matter, all our comings to this world. Sheep among wolves . . . it matters. He was quiet for a moment. He searched her face. He wanted to remember everything. I could not have done it without you. She brushed her feet through the flowers. He sang to her.

> O Shenandoah, I love your daughter
> Away, you rolling river
> O Shenandoah, I love your daughter
> Away, I'm bound away

I could not have done it without you. His voice failed him. He tried again. Tell my son . . . tell my son I did my best. Tell him I love him.

He knows.

I did my best. It was a beginning. Tell him the truth.

He knows.

We died as men. Tell him that we are all heroes!

I will, my love.

> Away, I'm bound away
> Cross the wide Missouri.

Chapter 88

Saturday, November 5th, 1831. Nat Turner repeated the date to himself. Saturday, November 5th, 1831. As the armed guard marched him into the courtroom, he looked at the faces—lies and anger in their eyes, countenances full of poison.

They were all slavery men and women, but maybe a tiny bit of mercy would still save them—a pig's foot, a shriveled potato, or an old, torn blanket.

The people screamed and cursed at him, and they cried. They would take him away and hang him themselves. There was no need for a trial; they already knew the truth. Claws grabbed at him. The judges ordered twenty-five more armed guards so the people wouldn't carry him away.

Nat, alias Nat Turner, v. the Commonwealth of Virginia. The courtroom was crowded, packed even with people from out of town. They had set extra chairs in place for the visiting judges. Ten judges.

> *And ye shall be brought before governors and kings for My sake, for a testimony against them and the Gentiles.*

There were no black faces in the room—at least none that were not passing as white—no Negro guards, no one. The armed guards around him were three men deep on all sides, except his front, which faced the judges.

Benjamin Phipps, invisible in the throng, was pressed against the back wall. Nat Turner saw his brother John Clarke Turner pointing at him, sitting near Nathaniel Francis.

It was difficult to see the crowd once he sat down, but Nat Turner felt them and heard them. He felt the anger, the hot blood-lust in the air around him. Nothing would satisfy them but death.

"You had us fooled before, nigger, with your reading and your bowing, but we got you now!"

"You gonna dangle from that tree, boy!"

When William Parker entered Nat Turner's "not guilty" plea, the crowd erupted with outrage. He was a murderer, they said, and they demanded his head.

There was not to be much to the trial. Nat Turner did not expect more. He was not allowed to speak in his defense. There was no one to speak in his defense.

There was only one witness against him: an eyewitness, Levi Waller.

Levi Waller spoke lies, drunken lies. He drank even as he gave his testimony. Then Levi Waller said one true thing.

A slip of the tongue, or the hand of God?

William Parker seemed startled, then quickly regained his composure. He paused momentarily. He sighed and then began to press Levi Waller. "My question is this: Where were you, Mr. Waller?" Parker sighed again. "You testified you were in your home, and then you testified you were hidden in the weeds. Now, today, you tell us you were hidden in the plum grove and then in the swamp. Is there a swamp close to your house?"

Levi Waller was silent.

Parker cleared his throat. "Where were you? Where were you, Mr. Waller?"

Levi looked at the judges but did not answer.

"You mentioned some other place I've never heard you mention before, Mr. Waller. You said the teacher came to meet you there. Where was it you said you were?"

Waller looked at Nathaniel Francis. He nodded at Levi to reassure him, but Levi's mouth began to tremble. He hung his head. "My still."

Waller did not see anything. He frowned as though the words hurt, as though they were being pulled from inside him. Waller did not see anything. He was at his still.

Nat Turner looked away then. He imagined those who had died because of Waller's perjury. Families left fatherless. Children without a mother. So many broken hearts. He thought he saw them among the martyrs, among the witnesses. Though the courtroom was silent, as before a tornado, he thought he heard their voices among those of the witnesses.

Who would pay for their murders? No one moved to charge Levi Waller.

Then, in the courtroom, the screaming and shouting began again. The crowd demanded Nat Turner's blood. Waller's lies, his failure, only intensified their need.

Nat Turner looked at the two judges, Trezvant and James Parker. Would they speak? Would they warn the people and encourage them to repent?

Then Congressman Trezvant smiled at the people in the courtroom, as though to reassure them. Then his face was solemn, sitting as a judge, now testifying as a witness, Trezvant began to speak. "Nat Turner is a religious zealot, a fanatic, carried away by the lust for power and money. He has confessed his guilt to me. Persuaded by zealotry, Nat Turner and his band were motivated by ignorance and greed—by the love of money," Trezvant said.

> But when they deliver you up, take no thought how or what ye shall speak: for it shall be given you in that same hour what ye shall speak.
>
> For it is not ye that speak, but the Spirit of your Father which speaketh in you.

"Nothing I have done has ever been for money!" Nat Turner shouted the words in the midst of Congressman Trezvant's impromptu testimony. Nat Turner had not intended to speak.

The words had gushed from him, pushed up from his belly. But the people and the judges did not want to hear him. Nat Turner was warned to be quiet.

He sat mute in front of the drunken, screaming mob. There was no deliberation.

Trezvant smiled as he delivered the verdict. "The Court after hearing the testimony and from all the circumstances of the case is unanimously of the opinion that the prisoner is guilty. It is considered by the Court that you be taken hence to the jail from whence you were taken therein to remain until Friday the 11th day of November, on which day between the hours of ten o'clock in the forenoon and four o'clock in the afternoon you are to be taken by the sheriff to the usual place of execution and there be hanged by the neck until you are dead." Trezvant struck the gavel thrice for show.

The congressman looked at the clerk and then at Nathaniel Francis. "The Court values the said slave to the sum of three hundred and fifty"—Nathaniel Francis objected and Trezvant changed the amount—"three hundred and seventy-five dollars." William Parker, relative to young Acting Judge James Parker, was allowed the sum of ten dollars for defending Nat Turner.

Chapter 89

Outside the jailhouse people yelled, pelting the jail with stones. Pounding the outer door, they threatened to take Nat Turner. Frenzy. His six final days Nat Turner spent alone without visitors, except for one visit by Thomas Gray.

None of his family, no black people could be seen in town; it was too dangerous. The white people of Cross Keys and Jerusalem were united now. All of Southampton County and their guests were celebrating; they had tied a black man to a horse and dragged him to his death.

Two days after Nat Turner's trial, Thomas Gray came. Gray was his friend. But Thomas would have to be both friend and family now. Nat Turner was comforted at the thought of him.

Tears filled Thomas's eyes when he saw Nat Turner. "I wanted to come sooner. But it has been too dangerous for me to see you. You understand?"

What did Thomas want him to say in response? Weren't friends born for times of adversity?

"Now they've asked me to come to you. They've asked me . . ."

They? It was so easy to read his childhood friend's thoughts and heart. It was what made him endearing. It was also the same trait that made him dangerous. It was always a game, a game Nat Turner could not win.

"With all the confusion in the courtroom, they've asked me to help clarify what happened. They've asked me to write, to create a sort of confession."

"A confession? What confession? I pled innocent, just like all the others. I have confessed to nothing. I am not guilty. I have offered no confession. The trial is over. There is already a record."

"They mean to re-create the record . . . the trial."

They meant to devise a lie. "Trezvant, Nathaniel Francis, Levi Waller? They want you to be their writer."

Thomas Gray bowed his head. Nat Turner thought he saw a tear slide down his friend's face.

"You don't understand, Nat. They threaten my family . . . me." He looked up and then down again. "I'm not as strong as you."

"What have you done, Thomas? What is your part in this?"

To save his own life, Thomas would offer up the private things the two of them had shared, their childhood—Nat's private thoughts, not Thomas's—Nat's dreams. "Will you write it alone? Will others work with you to create the lie? Trezvant, I suppose?" His sense of betrayal was worse than any anger he had ever felt. "What part will you tell in the story? Our childhood, the things I told you in private? I imagine Trezvant will add his fantasies to it."

"I am not the only one. John Clarke is involved, and Nathaniel Francis, and Levi Waller."

"I might have known. You trade men's lives for a few coins. What was your share?" Nat Turner looked at his friend. "They use you to plunge the blade and turn it; they use you to betray me." The drying scabs made it painful, but he smiled at his friend. "So, finally, you will write your novel."

"You don't understand." Thomas Gray wept.

Of course he understood. Everything Nat Turner had and hoped for in this world was lost. He was about to give up his life, and what would be left behind now, the story of his life, would be a lie. It was futile. He should have sailed away.

> *There is no man that hath left house, or brethren, or sisters,*
> *or father, or mother, or wife, or children, or lands, for my sake, and*
> *the gospel's, but he shall receive an hundredfold now in this time,*

houses, and brethren, and sisters, and mothers, and children, and
lands, with persecutions; and in the world to come eternal life.
 But many that are first shall be last; and the last first.

He could not sail away. He had promised and there was a family debt he owed.

For his surrender, for his service, he was promised an eternal reward. The first resurrection. What of Thomas? Nothing now, nothing hereafter. "Repent while there is still time. Ask God to forgive you and walk away from this thing, Thomas. Repent.

"They will do it, no doubt, but you don't have to be involved. Don't surrender your soul for this—for nothing." He looked at Thomas Gray, pleaded with him. "You are my friend."

"You don't understand. My life would be worth nothing."

There was no point. It was finished. It was over. "Go, my friend."

"I have no choice. If I did, I—they are forcing me."

"What you do, do quickly!" When his friend left, Nat Turner prayed to God to cauterize the spot where his heart bled.

Chapter 90

Nat Turner prayed for a quick death; that his neck would break and there would be little pain.

Friday, November 11, 1831, the guards marched him to the hanging tree as the crowd cheered. Children hung from nearby trees, laughing, sucking on sweets. Their parents pelted him with stones. Others threw apples, overripe tomatoes, and rotten eggs.

There were no black faces. Nat Turner did not expect to see any. The crowd would have turned on them, too.

Chains jangled around his ankles. It had been six years since his time in the Great Dismal Swamp, but today he remembered the earthy smell, the marshy ground that sprang back against his feet when he walked. He remembered the little stream near where he slept. He could have stayed there. Hebron. He could have sailed away.

> Obey me and then shall thy light break forth as the morning, and thine health shall spring forth speedily: and thy righteousness shall go before thee; the glory of the LORD shall be thy reward. Then shalt thou call, and the LORD shall answer; thou shalt cry, and he shall say, Here I am. If thou take away from the midst of thee the yoke, the putting forth of the finger, and speaking vanity; And if thou draw out thy soul to the hungry, and satisfy the afflicted soul; then shall thy light rise in obscurity, and thy darkness be as the noon day.

Sheriff Butts put the noose around Nat Turner's neck—rough, thick rope that scratched him—and told him to step up on the chair, the stool they used for hanging.

Hebron. He had called the place Hebron. He could have lived a quiet life in Hebron. Then Nat Turner saw before his eyes and heard in his ears the screams of the pregnant captive woman being beaten on Hebron's shore.

There was no quiet place for him. There was no place to be but here.

Let it be over soon, Lord. He had prayed that the witnesses would come to him, that they would be with him and console him, sing to him.

But he was alone. Would he be forgotten like the first snowfall, the first flower? *Let it all be for something, Lord. My wife.* Who would care for her? *My son.* Who would help him become a man? *My mother.* Who would she have now? She would be all alone. *Take care of them. Promise me you will take care of them.*

"Does the prisoner have any last words?"

The chair rocked beneath Nat Turner's feet. The rope scratched his neck. Nat Turner saw his brother John Clarke jeering at him, shaking his fist. His brother would never love him.

He spoke to the crowd. "The man you are set to hang is our brother whom you love. That girl you sell as a concubine is your beloved little sister. You put Father's beloved sons in chains. I am your brother, and I warn you." Nathaniel Francis, clad in a new expensive coat, smirked at him. "Judgment rests on you, on Southampton, on Virginia, and on this nation. I am only one of the first; others will come. The Lord will raise up an army. War will come and you will fight against yourselves, brother against brother. There will be blood on the corn.

"'Woe to her that is filthy and polluted, to the oppressing city! She obeyed not the voice; she received not correction; she trusted not in the LORD; she drew not near to her God.'" He was the hope of his people, sent to deliver this message.

"'Her princes within her are roaring lions; her judges are evening wolves; they gnaw not the bones till the morrow. Her prophets are light and treacherous persons: her priests have polluted the sanctuary, they have done violence to the law.'" He was sent to warn the captors.

"Shut up, you black coon!"

All the eyes were against him. "'Thou art the land that is not cleansed, nor rained upon in the day of indignation.

"'There is a conspiracy of her prophets in the midst thereof, like a roaring lion ravening the prey; they have devoured souls; they have taken the treasure and precious things; they have made her many widows in the midst thereof.

"'Her priests have violated my law, and have profaned mine holy things: they have put no difference between the holy and profane, neither have they shewed difference between the unclean and the clean, and have hid their eyes from my sabbaths, and I am profaned among them.'" Nat Turner looked at the faces jeering and scowling. He must deliver the message. Perhaps one heart would turn. He looked at the children laughing, swinging from the trees. Perhaps one child would turn.

"'Her princes in the midst thereof are like wolves ravening the prey, to shed blood, and to destroy souls, to get dishonest gain. And her prophets have daubed them with untempered mortar, seeing vanity, and divining lies unto them, saying, Thus saith the LORD GOD, when the LORD hath not spoken.

"'The people of the land have used oppression, and exercised robbery, and have vexed the poor and needy: yea, they have oppressed the stranger wrongfully.

"'And I sought for a man among them, that should make up the hedge, and stand in the gap before me for the land, that I should not destroy it: but I found none.

"'Therefore have I poured out mine indignation upon them; I have consumed them with the fire of my wrath: their own way have I recompensed upon their heads, saith the LORD GOD.'"

Nat Turner looked for a friendly face but could not find one. "You can be forgiven. There is still time. God takes no pleasure in vengeance. Open your hearts, my brothers and sisters, and turn."

The Spirit controlled his mouth then and Nat Turner looked at their faces. Gaping, twisted mouths and excited, angry eyes. Eyes filled with hate.

What about sweet Cherry? What about his little son?

Sheriff Butts kicked the chair. Nat Turner dangled, the rope tightened.

There was so much pain. He had prayed that there would be no pain. *So much pain, Father.* He choked, but there was no sound.

So much pain, Father. Let it be over.

He heard cheering, and then he thought he felt someone cut him. But he could not be sure because he could not look down. And there was pain everywhere.

There was only gray sky, bare branches, and the angry, laughing, hard faces of the children. Eyes full of rage and death.

So much pain, Father. Make it go away. The waves shifted, and he choked as the water threw him up and down. The water was filled with gray faces, faces full of teeth to devour him. All their eyes were against him. He wanted to be brave. *Forgive me, Father.*

The pain was lessening. It would be over soon. He wanted to sing now, to the eyes, to comfort them. It would be over soon. Nat Turner drifted on the waves. But no sound would come from his mouth. He would be brave for his people—all of them. He was a man of two continents, a warrior priest, and there was a family debt he owed.

He wanted to tell them they were forgiven, but he could not speak. He was choking. He saw past the anger, saw the fear, saw the wounded hearts. *So many wounded, broken hearts. Forgive them.*

The witnesses joined him then. They sang to him. Their hands touched his face.

Forgive me.

He struggled against it. He fought for light.

"Surrender," the witnesses whispered to him.

Everything dimmed.

Then blackness.

Harriet

Harriet

Chapter 91

Boston
1856

It was such a heavy burden and it was hard not to feel hopeless. The others joined her then. They called for the carriage and when they were seated, Harriet spoke to William again. "Will you, will your people be able to forget?"

William nodded. "When a woman is raped I have heard it said that she may forgive but the memory lasts her lifetime. When a nation is raped, when a people are raped, I think it is the same."

It was dark now. Not even the gaslights or the stars, not even the moon could stop its coming. Harriet looked across the carriage at Frederick Douglass and at her brother Henry. They would return to Brooklyn soon, and then she would depart for Andover. She needed her husband now. She needed the comfort of Calvin's arms.

William Love's hand rested on the window opening.

"I am not sure what I will write," Harriet said to him.

"A tree is judged by its fruit," he replied. "Don't judge him by what others have said—many of them were liars. Instead, use your heart. You have a good one. Judge the man by his fruit." There was a sudden twinkle in William's eye. "That is how I have judged you."

Harriet smiled. She looked across the coach at her brother and then back at William. "There were so many deaths and weapons."

"That is war. We celebrate our warriors and paint pictures of them with weapons in their hands. Can a Negro not be a hero, even a tragic one, because he bears a weapon?"

"We must away now," Henry said to her.

She looked at William. "Do you think there is hope? Are we doomed?"

"So much harm has been done," William said. "But I have faith that we can be healed, though we may always walk with a limp. And if we die," he added, "there is always resurrection."

Chapter 92

First there was blackness.

Then he heard voices, the witnesses. "'Alleluia: for the LORD GOD omnipotent reigneth. Let us be glad and rejoice, and give honour to him: for the marriage of the Lamb is come, and his wife hath made herself ready.

"'And to her was granted that she should be arrayed in fine linen, clean and white: for the fine linen is the righteousness of saints. . . . Blessed are they which are called unto the marriage supper of the Lamb.'"

He heard them but he could not see them. In the distance he heard drums, then singing, "'Blessed and holy is he that hath part in the first resurrection: on such the second death hath no power, but they shall be priests of GOD and of Christ, and shall reign with him a thousand years.'"

He saw a glow in the distance and walked toward it. A green field stretched before him. The sky was rose, gold, violet, turquoise—a rainbow. He heard a voice speaking, "'I will divide him a portion with the great, and he shall divide the spoil with the strong; because he hath poured out his soul unto death: and he was numbered with the transgressors; and he bare the sin of many, and made intercession for the transgressors.'"

Waist-high green grass dotted with wildflowers covered the hills. Leopards and elephants sauntered past, and overhead ruby- and emerald-colored birds of paradise spread their wings in flight. The drums were closer now, the rhythms of a place he knew but had never been.

Each step he took released the flowers' sweetness. Breezes blew the tall grass so that it swayed, beckoning him.

Beyond the field was a golden throne. A tawny lion, flicking its tail, lay down in front of the throne; seated above him on the throne was a speckled lamb.

There was a great tree near them. Its branches, heavy with leaves, reached high into the sky and spread wide enough to give them shade. Beside the throne, kneeling down, was a brown-skinned woman. She waved to welcome him. He thought he heard his name. *Negasi!*

Though he was still far away and he could not be certain, he thought she mouthed a word. *Welcome!* The sweet scent of the moonflowers burst beneath his feet and drifted up filling his lungs. His mother had told him about the tall grass, but he had not expected the wildflowers.

Even from the distance, he thought he recognized her. She smiled at him across the field of wildflowers, beckoning to him. *Come!* He breathed in the clean air, familiar air, and in the distance he heard a roaring, like a great falls.

He was Nat, Nathan Turner, Negasi, and at last he was home. Alive.

Chapter 93

"All right now, Jack Snappy. Down with you now. I have work to do." Harriet Beecher Stowe pushed the large cat from her lap. Both of them had dozed off together.

She had dreamed the dream before, the dream of heaven, Nat Turner, and the throne. In fact, all the dreams swirled around her, the resurrection dreams, indigo sun dreams, the Nat Turner dreams.

It was hard to piece together exactly who had told her what, but she had begun writing about Nat Turner. She was writing twenty pages a day. But tonight, before she returned to her writing, she must finish the letter. It was overdue. Harriet tucked her hair into her nightcap and sat down at her desk with quill pen, ink, and paper.

July 17, 1856

Dear Duchess of Argyll—
It has long been my intention to write you with respect to some of the persons whom I have been instrumental in assisting with the money kindly left in my hands by His Grace.
For some time after the receipt of that money, no opportunity of redeeming any enslaved family seemed to present itself. My feelings have become deeply interested in a slave man—a refugee in Boston named William, who receiving his liberty by the grace of God and his own ingenuity, declined my offer to ransom him . . . together with an only sister and her child— they are persons of such gentleness of temper and refinement of manners—with considerable natural polish . . .

*Some of the money in my hands I lent to assist William and
this woman to furnish a lodging house and business which
they are successfully carrying on in Boston. I offered to send
and pay for their redemption to the nominal owner but they
declined—with some natural indignation and said they had
rather the money were expended in this cause in some other
way . . .*

*Inspired by William, and the life of the rebel Nat Turner,
I have decided to title my book* Dred: A Tale of the Great
Dismal Swamp.

Nancie/
Nikahywot

Fellow-Countrymen:

At this second appearing to take the oath of the Presidential office there is less occasion for an extended address than there was at the first. Then a statement somewhat in detail of a course to be pursued seemed fitting and proper. Now, at the expiration of four years, during which public declarations have been constantly called forth on every point and phase of the great contest which still absorbs the attention and engrosses the energies of the nation, little that is new could be presented. The progress of our arms, upon which all else chiefly depends, is as well known to the public as to myself, and it is, I trust, reasonably satisfactory and encouraging to all. With high hope for the future, no prediction in regard to it is ventured.

On the occasion corresponding to this four years ago all thoughts were anxiously directed to an impending civil war. All dreaded it, all sought to avert it. While the inaugural address was being delivered from this place, devoted altogether to saving the Union without war, urgent agents were in the city seeking to destroy it without war—seeking to dissolve the Union and divide effects by negotiation. Both parties deprecated war, but one of them would make war rather than let the nation survive, and the other would accept war rather than let it perish, and the war came.

One-eighth of the whole population were colored slaves, not distributed generally over the Union, but localized in the southern part of it. These slaves constituted a peculiar and powerful interest. All knew that this interest was somehow the cause of the war. To strengthen, perpetuate, and extend this interest was the object for which the insurgents would rend the Union even by war, while the Government claimed no right to do more than to restrict the territorial enlargement of it. Neither party expected for the war the magnitude or the duration which it has already attained. Neither anticipated that the cause of the conflict might cease with or even before the conflict itself should cease. Each looked for an easier triumph, and a result less fundamental and astounding. Both read the same Bible and pray to the same God, and each invokes His aid against the other. It may seem strange that any men should dare to ask a just God's assistance in wringing their bread from the sweat of other men's faces, but let us judge not, that we be not judged. The prayers of both could not be answered. That of neither has been answered fully. The Almighty has His own purposes. "Woe unto the world because of offenses; for it must needs be that offenses come, but woe to that man by whom the offense cometh." If we shall suppose that American slavery is one of those offenses which, in the providence of God, must needs come, but which, having continued through His appointed time, He now wills to remove, and that He gives to both North and South this terrible war as the woe due to those by whom the offense came, shall we discern therein any departure from those divine attributes which the believers in a living God always ascribe to Him? Fondly do we hope, fervently do we pray, that this mighty scourge of war may speedily pass away. Yet, if God wills that it continue until all the wealth piled by the bondsman's two hundred and fifty years of unrequited toil shall be sunk, and until every drop of blood drawn with the lash shall be paid by another drawn with the sword, as was said three thousand years ago, so still it must be said "the judgments of the Lord are true and righteous altogether."

With malice toward none, with charity for all, with firmness in the right as God gives us to see the right, let us strive on to finish the work we are in, to bind up the nation's wounds, to care for him who shall have borne the battle and for his widow and his orphan, to do all which may achieve and cherish a just and lasting peace among ourselves and with all nations.

—President Abraham Lincoln, Second Inaugural Address,
March 4, 1865

Epilogue

June 19, 1865

Nancie walked the road that led to the Nathaniel Francis farm. She adjusted the bundle thrown over her shoulder, then felt in her pocket for the tatter. She reached deeper into her pocket for the folded letters. She could not read them, but the children had read them to her so many times. They were not the children that her son, her Nathan, had taught to read. The children of those children now read to her.

There were letters that mentioned places she had never heard of—like Antietam and Gettysburg. Others mentioned places more familiar, like Richmond and Petersburg. The letters spoke of people she had never met, like Abraham Lincoln, Henry Ward Beecher, Harriet Beecher Stowe. "President Lincoln said we could not have been victorious without the help of the Beechers," one letter said.

Most of the letters mentioned Frederick Douglass, how he fought for the Colored Troops, and how he labored with President Lincoln to help him understand the Colored man's plight. Frederick Douglass's own sons had fought at a place called Sumter with a unit called the 54th Colored Troops from Massachusetts. Nancie tried to imagine the places—Sumter, Gettysburg—but each time, she imagined her beloved Ethiopia.

One of the letters told her about the Emancipation Proclamation that freed slaves in Southern states that had seceded from the Union. Following the proclamation, many of the boys and men she knew had left to join the war.

Nancie still carried the tatter. She felt it in her pocket with the letters. She removed the one that had been read to her most. She had memorized it. They were no longer children, but adults her son had once taught to read. The letter was from one of them, a young man who'd run away to serve with the 116th Colored Troops at Petersburg.

It is just as Prophet Nat warned us, blood among the corn, brother against brother. It was a hard battle, but we routed the rebs.

She looked down the road toward the farm. The division of the nation had split Jerusalem in two. Major General William Mahone, whose father ran Mahone's tavern, had served the Confederacy; while General George Thomas, the "Rock of Chickamauga" and nephew of Clerk of the Court James Rochelle, distinguished himself with the Union Army. Brother against brother.

Nancie looked back at the letter.

Colonel Woodward, who is himself a fine colored gentleman, says we owe much thanks to Mr. Frederick Douglass for convincing President Lincoln to allow us to join the battle. The colonel often quotes him, "Once let the black man get upon his person the brass letter, U.S., let him get an eagle on his button, and a musket on his shoulder and bullets in his pocket, there is no power on earth that can deny that he has earned the right to citizenship." We have done him proud here at Petersburg. I am assured that the war will soon be over and you will be free.

Nancie replaced the letter, knocking on Nathaniel Francis's front door. She smiled when Easter answered. There were not many old ones left. There were not many who remembered. "Make my way to Norfolk. Come." The American words were still bitter to her; they swelled her tongue, but she had learned to use them.

Easter looked over her shoulder. "Norfolk?"

"Nobody to stop us now."

Easter pulled at her shirtsleeve, then scratched at her arm, still looking back over her shoulder. She scratched her head. "I don't think I can."

Nathaniel Francis appeared at the door, now a stooped, gray-haired, toothless man. He was a bitter old man who had lost two sons in the war. "Norfolk? You two old mothers? Why, you'd die before you got there." He snickered and rubbed his hand over his worn leather belt.

She fought to keep tears from filling her eyes. She fought not to snatch it from his waist, knowing that such a move would land her in the white man's jail. The belt was all that was left of her son—it was a sign of what had once been, like the tatter she kept with her—and the cruel man kept it about his waist. No, Nathaniel Francis was not a man. He had lost all traces of manhood long ago.

Nancie stared at him, a look that would wither a fig tree, then back at Easter. "Coming?" Nancie was determined. She would make the journey alone if she had to. She would not let Nathaniel Francis's wickedness keep her bound to him. "Nobody owns us. Captivity turned. Free now. Old man owns no one!"

Nancie spit at Nathaniel Francis's feet. She was old, but there was enough spirit and strength still in her; she would pounce on him like a lioness.

"Oh, go on if you want to! Who needs you? I am wasting food feeding you."

Easter clamped her hands to her mouth. Giggling, she ran inside, like a schoolgirl, to get her few things.

Nancie heard Lavinia complaining inside. "You cannot let her go. My daddy will be furious!"

"Oh, good riddance," Nancie heard Nathaniel Francis say.

THE TWO OLD women traveled for many days. They followed the road to Portsmouth. It was foreign to Nancie, just as the road had been, long ago, when she had followed the Ethiopian road to Gondar. The roads were rocky and dry. There were places along the way where the ground seemed to be an open wound—places where green grass was torn away and red clay was fringed with a scab of brown grass. Signs of war.

It had all happened as Nathan had said. There was war—blood spattered on the corn—brother against brother. And in the end, black men had taken up arms, black men fighting against white men.

Occasionally, at a distance, the two women passed a wounded veteran or a family of refugees crowded with their goods into a ramshackle wagon that looked as though, at any second, it might fall apart.

Most of the way, Nancie and Easter walked in silence. Two old women now, their feet ached and their backs begged them to sit down. At night they stopped to stare at the stars. Easter had thought to bring a flint, so they made a fire and ate small portions, old women's portions, of the food they carried with them.

They traveled by sunlight, trying to stay beneath the shade of the trees. The heat tried to convince them to rest, but the two traveled on. Birds flew overhead and led them toward water, finally leading them to the edge of what must have been the Great Dismal Swamp.

She fought back tears. There was nothing left for her. His enemies, like Nathaniel Francis, had all that was left of her Negasi. She had lost him and she had lost her home. This place was not Ethiopia; it was not paradise, *ghe net*. But the greenery was lush. It called to her, but Nancie reminded herself that, though they were tempted, they could not remain. It offered refuge, but they must make their way to the water.

As she and Easter walked along the edge of the swamp, stopping sometimes to eat and sleep, Nancie tried to imagine her Nathan there walking in the woods, sleeping on the forest floor, and sailing on the waterways. She caught glimpses of flowers that reminded her of home.

Nancie and Easter walked along the forest edge, making their way toward Norfolk. But they were brittle now and each step made itself known in their hips, and feet, and knees. There was not much left for them. Not even Cherry and Riddick were with them. For years, to stay alive, the two had hidden themselves among the Cheroenhaka Nottoway Indians.

Easter pulled an old rag from her pocket and wiped her forehead. "You think we will ever get there, Nancie?"

Nancie nodded to her old friend. "Soon."

Easter stopped. Nancie watched as Easter looked at her feet and then at her gnarled hands. She dusted them against her old frayed skirt and gently touched her knees through the fabric. "Who will want us? Not much left of us now."

Nancie lifted her head and squared her shoulders. Her feet and knees were sore, but she would not surrender. "Plenty left. We will make way." She touched her gray hair. "Wise now." She touched her heart. "God here." Then her head. "Here." She nodded. "Egzi' abher Ab still with us."

Limping sometimes, the pair made their way farther along the edge of the Great Dismal Swamp, a place where they fed on fish they caught and drank brown, healing water. They rested there beneath the trees, while their feet cooled in the water and minnows flitted around their toes.

Nancie saw her reflection there. The years and the loss rested deep in her eyes. In the water, she saw her mother's face, and her daughter's. She thought she heard her husband, Josef's, voice calling to her from the stream. Nancie thought she saw her cousin Misha drift by cradling her baby in her arms.

Nancie sighed then and realized that she was crying. She turned to see Easter with her skirt hem pressed to her face. Nancie put her arm around her old friend's shoulders and sang to Easter the song that her daughter, Ribka, sang to her in Ethiopia.

I *am black but comely,*
O *ye daughters of Jerusalem. . . .*

THE NEXT MORNING they rose and began the final leg of their journey. The day stretched out before them. The longer they walked, the farther it seemed they had to go.

Finally, Nancie walked over the gray, gravelly sand and stepped into the cold waters of the Chesapeake Bay. Ships waited at the wharf, their sails billowing in the sun. Overhead, birds flew almost high enough, it seemed, to touch the clouds.

Nancie caught her breath. It was as Nathan, her Negasi, promised. Chilled. She touched her hand to the tatter in her pocket.

She was wrong. The tatter was not all she had. Her son was not with her, but she had her memories. And he had not died in vain.

Born beneath the blood moon, he had been the first to fight, but not in vain. Her Nathan—a man of two continents—had borne the family debt. He sounded the warning; he foretold the war and struck the first blow. But as he had promised, others had followed him into the battle, and they had marched and fought until all were free. She had more than the tatter; Nathan had left her a gift.

Negasi! Leaping like a child, she screamed his name into the wind. She turned and held out her hand for Easter.

She introduced herself to her old friend. "I am Nikahywot," she said. She giggled and then wiggled as though she were still a young girl with a king's pillow behind her.

She looked east, toward the falls, toward the highlands. The breezes kissed her hair and ruffled her skirt. Still holding Easter's hand, she lifted hers and spoke to those far away.

"Free!" Nikahywot said.

Acknowledgments

I am grateful to so many, like Karen Ball, Virelle Kidder, Deni Williamson, Sara Fortenberry, and Don Jacobson, who helped open the doors of publishing to me. Thanks to writer friends like Neta and Dave Jackson, Marilynn Griffith, Claudia Mair Burney, Stanice Anderson, Victoria Christopher Murray, Dr. Gail Hayes, and Karen Kingsbury, who have been sources of inspiration and wise counsel.

Thanks to the editorial team members at Howard and Simon & Schuster like Julee Schwarzburg, and especially to Dave Lambert, whose editorial insight and belief in me and this project helped it come to fruition.

Thank you to my agent, Mark Sweeney.

Faced with what seemed to be only closed doors and no budget, I am more than grateful to people who stood in the gap: Stanice Anderson and her son, Mike Tucker, who stepped out on faith and became Anderson & Tucker Agency—Publicity, Marketing & Promotion Architects. What you've accomplished has been remarkable. Thank you also to Dee Stewart, Marina Woods, and GoodGirlBookclubonline.com, Tia Ross and the Black Writers Alliance, Shana Adams and the Durham Arts Council, Ella Curry and Black Pearls, Linda Beed, Yango Sawyer, Joe Madison, Michael Eric Dyson, Monique Greenwood, Kam Williams, Regina Gail Malloy, and to the Washington Association of Black Journalists for beating the drums and helping spread the word about Nat Turner.

Thank you to all the warriors I have known, to those in my family and to those with whom I've worked. Blessings and love to my former Pentagon and DINFOS coworkers who have faithfully supported me, especially Lisa, Carol, Mark, Kenneth, Neil, Cody, John, Glenda, Robert, Tammi, and Edie. A special thanks to Marshall Dobson for sharing the psychology of battle.

Thank you to the host of librarians who have supported me through the years, like Jan Morley, Erica Holmes, Sharon Barrow, Saundra Cropps, and Sheryl Underwood. A special thank-you to those librarians who provided research assistance: Ann Southwell and Regina Rush at the Albert and Shirley Small Special Collections Library at the University of Virginia; Elizabeth Burgess, collections manager at the Harriet Beecher Stowe Center; Katherine Wilkins, assistant librarian at the Virginia Historical Society; and Chris Kolbe, archives research coordinator, Special Collections, Library of Virginia. Thank you also to Gary Vikan for sharing his knowledge of ancient Ethiopian art.

I am indebted to the descendants of Nat Turner, like Bruce Turner, and the rebellion's victims for sharing their stories. I owe a special debt of gratitude to local historians, James McGee and Rick Francis. Mr. McGee and his lovely wife, Lavenia, welcomed my daughter and me into their home. He shared his artwork, memories—like his recollection of a lamp shade fashioned from Nat Turner's skin—and the history of Southampton County. He left me with a charge: Find the truth and teach. I hope that I have met the challenge.

Mr. Francis, the great-grandson of Nathaniel Francis, was incredibly generous in sharing his time, local history and lore, and resources. It was he who confirmed the location of Nat Turner's trial records. In between serving as Southampton County Clerk, spearheading the drive for the Nat Turner Trail in Virginia, he responded to emails, calls, and met with me when I came to Courtland seeking answers. Thank you for your openness, your courage, and your commitment to truth.

Thank you to Chief Walt Brown for sharing the history of the Cheroenhaka Nottoway, the significance of the Artis surname, and their connection to the Turner revolt.

Thank you to preachers and ministries who have taught me and prayed for me, like Bishop Walter S. Thomas and First Lady Patricia of New Psalmist Baptist Church of Baltimore; Rev. and Senator James Meeks and First Lady Jamell of Salem Baptist Church of Chicago; Mary Williams and the Bible Witness Camp of Pembroke, Illinois; First Lady Norma McLauchlin, Patricia Davis, and the Lady Lifers of New Life Church in Fayetteville, North Carolina; and to the inspiring Daily Guideposts family. Thanks to Dr. Wendy Campbell, Carl Prude, and my other brothers and sisters from East St. Louis.

Thank you to wonderful teachers like Mrs. Cannady, Miss Basin, and my beloved Mrs. Wachter. Heartfelt thanks to Dr. Evie Adams Welch, professor of African American studies and South African literature, who believed in me when I was a struggling, newly married, and pregnant freshman at Western Illinois University. She planted the seed for this book more than thirty years ago and whispered songs of Ethiopia. Thank you. Thank you to my Gashe Getachew Haile—curator of the Ethiopian Study Center, Regents Professor of Medieval Studies, and cataloguer of Oriental Manuscripts, Hill Monastic Manuscript Library at Saint John's University—for sharing ancient Ethiopia with me.

To my friends and family, thank you for loving and believing in me, even when I struggle to believe in myself. Thank you Glenda, Theresa, Margaret Ann, Darlene, Mary, Joji, and many, many others. I am grateful to my father, brothers, nieces, nephews, cousins, and especially LaJuana. Lanea and Chase, there would have been no Nat Turner without the two of you. Thank you for your prayers, inspiration, friendship, and your impeccable editorial judgment. Thank you for covering me.

Now unto Him that is able to keep you from falling, and to present you faultless before the presence of His glory with exceeding joy, to the only wise God our Savior, be glory and majesty, dominion and power, both now and ever. Amen. Thank you, Lord.

Bibliography

A brief list of resources for further study and entertainment.

For more information and resources concerning Nat Turner, visit *www.theresurrectionofnatturner.com*.

Books

Applegate, Debby. *The Most Famous Man in America: The Biography of Henry Ward Beecher*. New York: Doubleday, 2006.

Aptheker, Herbert. *Nat Turner's Slave Rebellion*. 1966. Reprint, Mineola, N.Y.: Dover, 2006.

Brown, William Wells. *Clotel*. 1853. Reprint, Mineola, N.Y.: Dover, 2008.

Clarke, John Henrik, ed. *William Styron's Nat Turner: Ten Black Writers Respond*. Boston: Beacon Press, 1968.

Douglass, Frederick. *Narrative of the Life of Frederick Douglass: An American Slave*. Boston: Anti-Slavery Office, 1845.

———. *The Heroic Slave*. 1853. Reprint, Mineola, N.Y.: Dover, 2008.

Floyd, Governor John. *Journal–Original*. Richmond: Johnston Family Papers, 1779–1891. Personal Papers Collection. Richmond: Library of Virginia.

Greenberg, Kenneth S., ed. *Nat Turner: A Slave Rebellion in History and Memory*. New York: Oxford University Press, 2003.

Haile, Rebecca G. *Held at a Distance: A Rediscovery of Ethiopia*. Chicago: Academy Chicago Publishers, 2007.

Hedrick, Joan D. *Harriet Beecher Stowe: A Life*. New York: Oxford University Press, 1994.

The Kebra Nagast: The Queen of Sheba and Her Only Son Menyelek.

Translated by E. A. Wallis Budge. 1992. Reprint, Charleston, S.C.: Forgotten Books, 2007.

"Southampton County Court Minute Book 1830–1835." Southampton County Courthouse, Courtland, Virginia. Also now available online: http://www.brantleyassociation.com/southampton_project /southampton_project_list.htm#Court_Minute_Books.

Stowe, Harriet Beecher. *Uncle Tom's Cabin*. 1852. Reprint, Mineola, N.Y.: Dover, 2005.

———. *Dred: A Tale of the Great Dismal Swamp*. Edited by Robert S. Levine. 1856. Reprint, Chapel Hill: University of North Carolina Press, 2006.

———. "Letter to Duchess of Argyll." Andover, Mass. Albert and Shirley Small Special Collections, University of Virginia Library, June 17, 1856.

Styron, William. *The Confessions of Nat Turner*. New York: Vintage Books, 1966.

Tragle, Henry Irving. *The Southampton Slave Revolt of 1831: A Compilation of Source Material*. Amherst: University of Massachusetts Press, 1971.

Turner, Benjamin. Deed Book, Turner's Meeting Place Deed to Nathan Turner, et al. Southampton County, Virginia. 1810.

———. Will. Southampton County, Virginia.

Turner, Nat, and Thomas Gray. *The Confessions of Nat Turner (1831) by Thomas R. Gray, Nat Turner, et al. DigitalCommons@ University of Nebraska–Lincoln | University of Nebraska–Lincoln Research*. Libraries at University of Nebraska–Lincoln. http:// digitalcommons.unl.edu/etas/15/. Official court records indicate that Nat Turner pled innocent, offered no confession, and that William Parker was his defense attorney. Neither William Parker nor Thomas Gray read a confession in court. According to the official record, Levi Waller and James Trezvant offered testimony in court against Nat Turner.

Vikan, Gary. *Ethiopian Art: The Walters Museum*. Surrey, U.K.: Third Millenium Publishing, 2001.

Wilson, Harriet E. *Our Nig: Sketches from the Life of a Free Black.* 1959. Reprint, Mineola, N.Y.: Dover, 2008.

Online Resources

"Art of Writing—Henry Ward Beecher." *Old and Sold Antiques Auction.* June 4, 2011. http://www.oldandsold.com/articles12 /writing-1.shtml.

Beecher, Rev. Henry Ward. "Moral Courage: Extracts from a Sermon Delivered on Sunday Evening." *New York Times,* 1860. http://www.nytimes.com/1860/04/10/news/moral-courage -extracts-sermon-delivered-sunday-evening-rev-henry-ward -beecher.html

"Black Soldiers." Virginia Western Community College. http:// www.virginiawestern.edu/faculty/vwhansd/HIS269/Exhibits /BlackSoldiers2.html.

Blight, David. "Africans in America, Part 4: David Blight on William Lloyd Garrison." PBS. http://www.pbs.org/wgbh/aia/part4 /4i2980.html.

Brooks, Jennifer. "Black Soldiers Celebrated as Civil War's Forgotten Heroes." *Tennessean,* May 31, 2011. http://www.tennessean .com/article/20110531/NEWS01/305290095/1969/NEWS.

Brown, Chief Walt. Cheroenhaka Nottoway Indian Tribe Official Site. Cheroenhaka (Nottoway) Indian Tribe Tribal Council. http://cheroenhaka-nottoway.org/.

Challinor, Elizabeth. Peace Research Institute Oslo. "A History of Cape Verde: Centre/Periphery Relations and Transnational Cultural Flows." http://www.prio.no/private/jorgen/cvmd/papers /CVMD_Chall in or_Elizabeth.pdf

Davis, Paul. "Projo.com Digital Extra." *Providence Journal,* 2006. http://www.projo.com/extra/2006/slavery/day1.

"Documenting the American South—Fighting Slavery with the Pen: Harriet Beecher Stowe's 196th Birthday." http://docsouth .unc.edu/highlights/stowe.html.

Drewry, William S. *The Southampton Insurrection.* Washington, D.C.: Neal, 1900. http://www.archive.org/details/southamptoninsur 00drew. Born in 1867, Drewry's account of the 1831 event makes allegations without attributions and, because of racial bias, is difficult to read. However, it does provide surviving local lore.

E. Bruce Kirkham Collection, Harriet Beecher Stowe Center, Hartford, Conn.

EH.net—U.S. Agricultural Workforce, 1800–1900. http://eh .net/databases/agriculture/.

Early Negro Convention Movement. http://www.gutenberg.org /files/31328/31328-h/31328-h.htm.

Ethiopian and Egyptian Art at the Walters Museum. http://www .tadias.com/07/12/2009/ethiopian-and-egyptian-art-at-the -walters-art-museum/.

Ethiopian Orthodox Tewahedo Church. http://www.eotc.faith web.com/.

Ethiopian Orthodox Tewahedo Church Faith and Order. http:// ethiopianorthodox.org/english/indexenglish.html.

"Family Accused of Forcing Homeless into Farm Labor." *Orlando Sentinel,* July 29, 1993. http://articles.orlandosentinel.com/1993 -07-29/news/9307290604_1_homeless-people-farm-labor -north-carolina.

Floyd, Governor John. Proclamation Concerning Nat Turner. September 17, 1831. http://www.virginiamemory.com/online_classroom /shaping_the_constitution/doc/turnerproclamation; http://www .virginiamemory.com/docs/Nat_Turner_trans.pdf. "Frederick Douglass." PBS. http://www.pbs.org/wgbh/aia/part4/4p1539 .html.

"Frederick Douglass—Abraham Lincoln." *Abraham Lincoln's Emancipation Proclamation & 13th Amendment.* Lincoln Institute and Lehrman Institute. http://www.mrlincolnandfreedom .org/inside.asp?ID=69.

"Frederick Douglass & Talbot County." Historical Society, Talbot County, Md. http://www.hstc.org/frederickdouglass.htm.

Gondar Ethiopia Travel Photos. http://www.galenfrysinger.com /gondar_ethiopia.htm.

Greene, Ronnie. "Fields of Despair—2000s—MiamiHerald.com." *Miami & Ft. Lauderdale News,* 2003. http://www.miamiherald .com/2003/08/31/56963/fields-of-despair.html.

A Guide to the Johnston Family Papers, 1779–1891 (includes Governor Floyd's diary). http://ead.lib.virginia.edu/vivaead /published/lva/vi00706.document.

Guide to Speech and Photographs Related to Nat Turner. http://ead .lib.virginia.edu/vivaead/published/uva-sc/viu01760.document.

Haas, Christopher. "Ethiopian Icons—Early Christianity." Villanova University. http://www29.homepage.villanova.edu /christopher.haas/ethiopian-icons.htm.

Haile, Getachew. "Ethiopian Study Center and Curator." Hill Museum & Manuscript Library, St. John's University. http://www .hmml.org/centers/ethiopia/emml_curator.html.

Harden, J. M. "J. M. Harden: An Introduction to Ethiopic Christian Literature." 1926. Christian Classics Ethereal Library. http://www.ccel.org/ccel/pearse/morefathers/files/harden _ethiopic_literature.htm.

Harriet Beecher Stowe Center. http://www.harrietbeecherstowe center.org/.

Ifill, Gwen. "Exhibit Shows Slavery in New York: January 25, 2007." PBS. 2007. http://www.pbs.org/newshour/bb/social _issues/jan-june07/divided_01-25.html.

Historic Civil War Sites, Heritage Trails. http://www .hallowedground.org/.

"How to Hitch a Horse to a Cart." http://www.ehow.com /how_2101069_hitch-horse-cart.html.

Hubbell, John T. "Abraham Lincoln and the Recruitment of Black Soldiers. Papers of the Abraham Lincoln Association, 2." History Cooperative, University of Illinois Press, on behalf of the Abraham Lincoln Association. June 4, 2011. http://www .historycooperative.org/journals/jala/2/hubbell.html.

"The Birth of Isabel." 2003. *National Geographic Magazine.* http:// ngm.nationalgeographic.com/ngm/0508/feature4/multimedia 2.html.

"Industrial Revolution and the Standard of Living, by Clark Nardinelli: The Concise Encyclopedia of Economics." Library of Economics and Liberty. http://www.econlib.org/library/Enc1 /IndustrialRevolutionandtheStandardofLiving.html.

"Irish Potato Famine: Before the Famine." *The History Place.* http://www.historyplace.com/worldhistory/famine/before .htm.

The Irish Potato Famine. Digital History. http://www.digitalhistory .uh.edu/historyonline/irish_potato_famine.cfm.

Kahn, Carrie. "Modern-Day 'Slave Farms' in Florida." NPR, July 14, 2005. http://www.npr.org/templates/story/story.php?story Id=4753236 (accessed June 4, 2011).

Keyserlingk, Ela. The Weavers Hand: A Tablet-Woven Treasure; The Gondar Hanging. http://weavershand.com/cci.html.

"Lalibela—Lalibela, Ethiopia." *Sacred Sites at Sacred Destinations.* June 4, 2011. http://www.sacred-destinations.com/ethiopia/lalibela.

Leifert, Harvey. "Lightning Spurs Hurricanes—Link Shows Storms in Africa Can Cause Havoc in the United States: Nature News." Nature Publishing Group. 2007. http://www .nature.com/news/2007/070511/full/news070508-12.html.

Lincoln, Abraham. "The Avalon Project: Second Inaugural Address of Abraham Lincoln." Avalon Project, Yale Law School. http://avalon.law.yale.edu/19th_century/lincoln2.asp (accessed June 4, 2011).

"The Lincoln Presidency: Last Full Measure of Devotion." Division of Rare and Manuscript Collections, Cornell University. June 4, 2011. http://rmc.library.cornell.edu/lincoln/exhibition /question/index.html.

"Looking Ahead." *Lincoln at 200.* Newberry Library and Chicago History Museum. http://lincolnat200.org/exhibits/show/thefierytrial /pressed/lookingahead.

"A Lot of Hurricanes Start Out Over the Ethiopian Mountains." *Ethiopian News and Daily News from Ethiopia*. http://nazret .com/blog/index.php/2006/08/16/a_lot_of_hurricanes _start_out_over_the_e (accessed June 4, 2011).

"Martha Washington: A Life." Article reporting interview with Ona Judge Staines. http://marthawashington.us/items/show/4.

———. George Washington to Oliver Wolcott. http://martha washington.us/items/show/7.

———. Letter Whipple to Wolcott on His Attempt to Capture Staines. http://marthawashington.us/items/show/21.

Maxwell, Bill. "Columns: Slavery Alive in Florida Agriculture Industry." 2002. http://www.sptimes.com/2002/07/03/Columns /Slavery_alive_in_Flor.shtml.

———."Modern-Day Slavery Museum Reveals Cruelty in Florida Fields." *St. Petersburg Times*. 2010. http://www.tampabay.com /opinion/columns/modern-day-slavery-museum-reveals -cruelty-in-florida-fields/1081253.

Mystery of the Nile. Dir. Jordi Llompart. Perf. Gordon Brown. Egami, 2005. DVD.

"New York Divided: Slavery and the Civil War." New-York Historical Society. http://www.nydivided.org/VirtualExhibit/T2/G3/.

Newton, John. "Thoughts upon the African Slave Trade." 1788. Open Library. http://openlibrary.org/books/OL24362998M /Thoughts_upon_the_Afr ican_slave_trade.

———. "Conditions on the Ships" (audio). Abolition Project. http://gallery.nen.gov.uk/audio78744-abolition.html.

Nottoway Indian Tribe Met to Discuss Tribal Lands. 1821. Library of Virginia. Virginia Memory. http://virginiamemory .com/docs/10-27-1821_trans_ck.pdf.

Official Records of the Civil War—Chamberlain at Gettysburg. http://www.civil-war.net/searchofficialrecords.asp?searchofficial records=Chamberlain Gettysburg.

Pendygraft, John. "Slavery of Migrant Farmworkers Continues in the U.S. to This Day." *St. Petersburg Times*. May 30, 2010. http://

www.tampabay.com/features/humaninterest/slavery-of-migrant -farmworkers-continues-in-the-us-to-this-day/1098420.

Petition from "females of the County of Augusta" to the General Assembly, January 19, 1832. http://www.virginiamemory.com /docs/AugustaPet_trans.pdf.

"Petition from the Pennsylvania Society for the Abolition of Slavery, February 3, 1790." http://www.ushistory.org/documents /antislavery.htm.

Potter, Ned. "The Real Home of Hurricanes: Ethiopia?" ABC News, July 25, 2008. http://abcnews.go.com/Technology/real-home -hurricanes-ethiopia/story?id=5450407.

Proceedings of the Radical Abolitionist Convention, New York, 1855. http://medicolegal.tripod.com/proceedings1855.htm#p15d.

Raffaele, Paul. "Christmas in Lalibela." *Smithsonian*. 2007. http:// www.smithsonianmag.com/people-places/christmas_lalibela -200712.html?utm_source=relatedarticles.

———. "Keepers of the Lost Ark?" *Smithsonian*. 2007. http://www .smithsonianmag.com/people-places/ark-covenant-200712.html.

Randel, William Pierce. "The Humor of Henry Ward Beecher." *Studies in American Humor*. http://www.compedit.com/henry _ward_beecher.htm.

Reddington, Amelia. "News with State's Nod, Indians' Spirits Can Walk Free." *Virginia Gazette*, May 9, 2010. http://www .vagazette.com/articles/2010/05/09/news/doc4be68bb507 e39790421078.txt.

"Senamirmir Projects: Interview with Dr. Getatchew Haile." *Senamirmir Project*. http://www.senamirmir.org/theme/5-2001 /gh/cup.html.

"The Sermons of Henry Ward Beecher: In Plymouth Church, Brooklyn." http://www.archive.org/details/sermonsofhenrywa00beec /T2/G3/.

"Sermons and Studies by Godly Men: Fruits of the Spirit," ser. by Henry Ward Beecher. http://www.bibleteacher.org/hwb_1.htm.

Slavery in America: *Uncle Tom's Cabin* Unit of Study. Frederick

Douglass and Harriet Beecher Stowe Lesson Plan. http://www
.slaveryinamerica.org/history/hs_lp_utc-douglass.htm.

Slavery in New York Exhibit. http://www.slaveryinnewyork.org
/about_exhibit.htm.

Slavery in the North. http://www.slavenorth.com/slavenorth.htm.

Southampton County Court Records Online. http://www
.brantleyassociation.com/southampton_project/southampton
_project_list.htm#Court_Order_Books.

Southampton County Historical Society. http://www.rootsweb
.ancestry.com/~vaschs/.

Southampton Insurrection of 1831, Overview, Documentary. Perf.
Kitty Futtrell. Produced by the Southampton County Historical Society, 1990, on videocassette.

Stowe, Harriet Beecher. Letter from Harriet Beecher Stowe to
Frederick Douglass. 1851. http://www.harrietbeecherstowecenter
.org/stowedocuments/Letter_from_Harriet_Beecher_Stowe
_to_Frederick_Douglass.pdf.

———. *Libyan Sibyl*. Sojourner Truth Institute, 1853. http://
www.sojournertruth.org/Library/Archive/LibyanSibyl.htm.

"Teamed up with PAS: Black Images of Philadelphia." http://
www.hsp.org/node/2956.

Tiffany, Joel. *A Treatise on the Unconstitutionality of American Slavery*. 1849. http://medicolegal.tripod.com/tiffanyuos.htm.

Tupac, Hacktivists. "African Lightning Stirs U.S. Hurricanes." *Dis-
cover Magazine*. 2008. http://discovermagazine.com/2008/jan
/african-lightning-stirs-u-s-hurricanes/?searchterm=hurricane.

US Coloredtroops.org. http://uscoloredtroops.org/.

Vikan, Gary, and Leonard Lopate. "The Leonard Lopate Show:
Ethiopian Objects of Worship—WNYC." March 23, 2007.
http://www.wnyc.org/shows/lopate/2007/mar/23/ethiopian
-objects-of-worship/.

Washington, Booker T. *The Story of the Negro*. Garden City, NY:
Doubleday, 1909. http://openlibrary.org/books/OL7067786M
/The_story_of_the_Negro (accessed June 2, 2011).

Weidman, Budge. "Black Soldiers in the Civil War." National Archives and Records Administration. http://www.archives.gov /education/lessons/blacks-civil-war/article.html.

Whitman, Walt. "Leaves of Grass." 1856. Walt Whitman Archive. http://whitmanarchive.org/published/LG/1856/index.html.

"World's First Illustrated Christian Bible Is Discovered at Ethiopian Monastery." *London Daily Mail*, 2010. http://www.dailymail.co .uk/sciencetech/article-1292150/Worlds-illustrated-Christian -bible-discovered-Ethiopian-monastery.html.

Zip Coon song. New York: Thos. Birch, 1834. http://memory.loc .gov/cgi-bin/query/h?ammem/mussm:@field(NUMBER+@ band(sm1834+360780)).

Discussion Questions for *The Resurrection of Nat Turner, Part 2: The Testimony*

1. What made Nat Turner different from his peers? What made him more likely to embrace rebellion?

2. Nat Turner describes the other captives (slaves) as heroes. Why?

3. What is the difference between the words captive and slave? Captor and master?

4. What relationship or relationships in the book most surprised you? What relationship or relationships most pleased you?

5. Captives were not allowed to speak their native language. Why? Captives were not allowed last names. Why?

6. Who were "the witnesses" who spoke to Nat Turner?

7. According to local lore, Nat Turner and the other slaves met outside the local church. Though they were not welcomed inside, why would they continue meeting there?

8. In his original handwritten diary, Governor Floyd describes the August 1831 "indigo sun." Why might it have caused excitement? Would it cause excitement today?

9. Modern-day scientists say many Atlantic hurricanes begin over the highlands of Ethiopia. According to NASA, Hurricane Isabel began in Ethiopia, making its way to the Chesapeake Bay. An "Act of God" beginning in Africa may have triggered one of the deadliest hurricanes in American history, the Great Barbados Hurricane of 1831, and Nat Turner's revolt. Discuss.

10. As he is questioned by Trezvant, Nat Turner laments slavery's legacy for captives and captors. Describe that legacy.

11. In both parts 1 and 2, Nat Turner refers to a "family debt" that he owes. What do you think he means? How did he pay for that debt?

12. What made it easy for American slave owners to justify their behavior? What makes it easy for modern-day slave owners to justify their behavior?

13. Harriet Beecher Stowe, her brother, and others, such as Benjamin Phipps and William Parker, seemed to feel frustrated and hopeless in the face of slavery. Why?

14. Southampton County, in particular the Jerusalem area, was home to two very famous Civil War generals. General George H. Thomas, nephew to County Clerk James Rochelle, was fifteen at the time of Nat Turner's revolt. Thomas became a famed Union general known as the "Rock of Chickamauga." General William Mahone was almost five at the time of the revolt. Son of tavernkeeper Fielding Mahone, he became a famed Confederate general known as the "Hero of the Crater." Though they were from similar backgrounds, what might have caused the two men to go on such divergent paths?

15. The court records contradicting the original *Confessions of Nat Turner* have existed for 180 years. Why do you believe that evidence has remained hidden?

Author Q & A
A Conversation with Sharon Ewell Foster

1. In *The Resurrection of Nat Turner, Part 2: The Testimony*, we get a unique vantage point into the unrest that ultimately resulted in the Civil War. What was the most difficult part of re-creating these moments on the page?

There were a couple of things that made the process challenging. First was giving myself permission to tell a new story.

We all have stories that we own, stories that we've been told, and those stories are part of who we are. Civil War stories and antebellum stories are part of our American heritage. There are people vested in this history, in the way this story has been told. I'm an African American, but these narratives were taught to me, too. I am an American and the American narrative is my own.

I realized, as I was writing, that most of our Civil War stories tend to be more sympathetic to the South. For example, part of our national story is that we feel sorry for the South because Atlanta was sacked. That's one of the themes of *Gone With the Wind*—that this great way of life was torched, good people were torched. We feel sympathy for Scarlett and Atlanta. So we have this beautiful, poignant literature rising from Atlanta's ashes and bemoaning what happened.

But what isn't part of our national narrative is that instead of Atlanta, Philadelphia might have burned. That's what Gettysburg was about, to keep the South from reaching Philadelphia and destroying what was the North's financial heart.

Part of our national narrative, part of what helps us cope corporaly and psychologically with the foulness of slavery, is a story that says everyone believed in slavery. No one thought it was wrong. No one spoke against it, except for a few fanatics. Of course, this narrative negates the efforts of abolitionists like Harriet Beecher Stowe and Frederick Douglass. It also negates the patriotism of people like Benjamin Franklin, Bishop Richard Allen, and everyday people from Philadelphia, Boston, New York, and other towns across America, who risked their lives to speak out against slavery.

Part of our national narrative, because to think otherwise is painful, is that slavery wasn't so bad. Most slave owners were good people and the slaves were content. All slave owners were kindly. I can't think of one account of a slave owner who called himself cruel. No one wants to be that person.

I had to give myself permission to consider and embrace a new story, a new narrative, before I could even recognize the facts in front of me. There were other heroes, there were voices crying in the wilderness, and I gave myself permission to sing their songs and to sing songs about the beauty of cobblestone streets, ships, and immigrants of northern cities. I had to give myself permission to sing the songs of brutalized slaves who had no voices . . . and also one of cruel masters.

As I researched, I had to finally accept that I would never know everything; then, I had to give myself permission to take the creative leap so that I could tell the story. I had to give myself permission to tell the story through my own eyes—a different story of the time before the war.

2. What prompted you to intersect the stories of Harriet Beecher Stowe and Nat Turner, two of the most famous figures in the American abolitionist movement? How do you think their very distinct personalities inform our current view of African American history? I wonder if you know what a leap you have made with the question you've posed. The narrative surrounding Nat Turner has been that he was a monster, not an abolitionist or a freedom fighter. Your understanding is significant.

But, to answer you, I had a few unresolved questions while researching that I think were answered in a letter that Harriet Beecher Stowe wrote to an English duchess.

Long ago, I was a pre-broadcast screener at PBS—I screened programs before they were aired nationally. One of my favorites was called *Connections*—the host would find unexpected connections between seemingly unrelated historical events. The linking of Stowe and Turner was a *Connections* kind of thing.

In preparation for writing the book, I read everything I could get my hands on that mentioned Nat Turner, including other novels. Stowe wrote a book called *Dred: A Tale of the Great Dismal Swamp*, a novel which she said was inspired by Nat Turner. Though she is most well known for *Uncle Tom's Cabin*, whose protagonist is a long-suffering, passive slave hero, the hero of *Dred* is a fiery, revolutionary refugee slave ready to take up arms against his oppressors. There is a chasm between Tom's and Dred's responses to slavery. I wanted to know what inspired Stowe to make the leap.

As part of my research, I also visited Southampton County, Virginia, and talked to local historians. One of them told me the story of Will, one of the slaves involved in the rebellion. Will was counted as dead, but his body was never found. The mystery of it piqued my interest. "Aha! Will got away," I thought.

Some months later, I visited the Harriet Beecher Stowe Center in Connecticut looking for some hint as to what might have inspired her point of view in *Dred*. I wanted to know what might have inspired her to write about Nat Turner, who, by then, was already much vilified. There I came across reference to a letter in which Stowe mentions writing *Dred*. Upon obtaining a copy of the letter, I learned that in the same letter she mentions being inspired by a runaway slave named William. My eyebrow lifted higher when I read a novel, published around the time Stowe was writing *Dred*, by African American author William Wells Brown. Out of nowhere in his novel, Brown begins to write about Nat Turner and Will. Brown describes Will just as the local historian described him—very dark with a prominent scar on his face. That is part of how Stowe describes Dred in her novel. Hmmmm. Also, online, there is a letter from Stowe requesting that Douglass help her meet a refugee slave who might tell her more about slavery.

The connection was made for me and I wrote Stowe into the novel. But her role as the "tour guide" who helps readers through the story and history was inspired by the first editor who worked on the manuscript, Dave Lambert. Harriet was a section in *The Witnesses* at the time of his review and he suggested that I place her story more prominently among the other witnesses. His feedback was so insightful: He questioned whether the story, as it was, had enough arc. Lambert's comments reflected a doubt I had. As I mulled his notes, I soon realized that Harriet's journey to write *Dred* could be the bridge that tied things together in my own story. His comments helped make this a better book.

In response to your second question, I don't think of this as only an African American history story. What I see in Harriet Beecher Stowe is a person willing to learn from others and adjust her views. I see her as a symbol of hope for people who struggle with racism or any other kind of response to others that is based on ignorance. Her life and understanding says that change is possible. To me, she says that we should encourage positive change and acknowledge growth when we see it.

Generally speaking, I don't think that Nat Turner is part of our national view of African American history. While many know of Stowe and her contribution, far fewer have ever heard of Nat Turner.

Stowe is a much more acceptable hero. She was courageous. She fought with the weapons available to her—her pen, her words, and her faith. She had the benefit of formal education. Turner did not. There were no publishing doors open to him. He used the weapons available to him. His war against slavery was much more violent. People—men, women, and children—died.

Of course, as a nation we sing songs about the violent overthrow of oppressors. It is our patriotic duty to take up arms against tyrants. The fourth stanza of our national anthem says:

> *Then conquer we must, when our cause is just,*
> *And this be our motto: "In God is our trust"*
> *And the star-spangled banner in triumph shall wave*
> *O'er the land of the free and the home of the brave!*

Nat Turner's story challenges us. The questions are troubling. Does a person held against his will have a patriotic duty to take up arms? What defines a hero? What if that person is of another hue? Were we once a nation who wrote tyranny into our national laws? Were our national heroes also villains?

I think it's because the questions are so difficult that we have not really had a national debriefing on slavery. We have not had the discussion. We don't ask these questions of ourselves or of our children.

But I think we're ready, we're mature enough as a nation. I see Harriet and Nat as two people, courageous people, who can help us have a discussion of our past and our present—a discussion that involves and unites people who are as different as Stowe and Turner.

3. Nancie finds it imperative to drill her line of Ethiopian ancestry (all the way back to King Solomon) into Nat's head. How do you think the American sense of heritage has evolved in the past few centuries? And why?

Many of those who came to America came poor; came in chains, stolen or sold away; came from prisons; came wearing cloaks of rejection and disgrace, banished from their homelands. Some were forbidden to remember their past, their names, their languages. Others, I can imagine, simply reinvented themselves.

We are now, I think, the children of our national heroes. We are the children of Washington and Jefferson. Some of us are the children of Abraham Lincoln and others the children of Jefferson Davis.

This is problematic for many of us because many of the national heroes were slave owners, oppressors. The heroes made patriotic speeches, but their cruel words of oppression taint them. African Americans were the slaves and rejected children of these heroes. For so long race has influenced that connection; African Americans were the lesser children, America's bastards.

That's why *Roots* was so important—Alex Haley's book gave us a pre-American, an African forefather. Haley's work made Kunte Kinte a national hero, but still he was hero to African Americans. He is viewed like Frederick Douglass and Harriet Tubman, not as an American hero, but as an African American hero.

We are the children of national heroes. I think it's time that our connection to national heroes transcends race.

That's why the Martin Luther King statue is so significant—he is a hero for all the people. His words resound:

And so even though we face the difficulties of today and tomorrow, I still have a dream. It is a dream deeply rooted in the American dream.

I have a dream that one day this nation will rise up and live out the true meaning of its creed: "We hold these truths to be self-evident, that all men are created equal."

I have a dream that one day on the red hills of Georgia, the sons of former slaves and the sons of former slave owners will be able to sit down together at the table of brotherhood.

Beautiful, right? An American hero who welcomes us all.

4. Class and race often seem inextricable in the novel. And yet both Harriet and Nat are able to remember a time when the lines of class and slavery did not take race into consideration. Why do you think Harriet finds this knowledge both comforting and horrifying?
You can't see me, but I'm laughing uncomfortably and cringing because I find the notion comforting and horrifying, myself.

It is comforting because it proves that we are able to find ways to connect that transcend race. It is terrifying for me, as it was for Harriet, because it illustrates how easily we can be swept up into divisions. So much so that we are willing to turn away from our core beliefs and our faith—to chase after the gods of greed, superiority, and dishonesty—in our allegiance to misguided associations of class and race.

5. For which character did you find the voice hardest to write? Which came most naturally? Why do you think that is?
Nathaniel Francis was the most difficult to write. To write a character, you must surrender to him. His thoughts must be your thoughts. He invades you. You must believe as he believes. You must love him.

I didn't want to love Francis. I did not want to experience his viewpoint of the world, a viewpoint that would find me inferior and inhuman. I did not want to be a person who, I believe, conspired to have others murdered simply for money. I do not want to think that I am capable of that behavior.

I kept fighting him. He turned my hair grayer.

I did not want to be sympathetic to him, but in order to tell the story I had to give in to him. I surrendered to him because he was the only one who could tell me what happened in the courtroom. I had to be him in order to learn the truth.

I also resisted Easter because I had personal issues with the thought of slave women who loved the master's children, as in *The Help*, who would take an oppressor's child to her breast when she could not nurse or keep her own. But Nat Turner's character whispered to me, like a melody to a composer, that they were all heroes. All the slaves were heroes, like prisoners of war, even Easter.

Easter taught me about the power and complexity of love, love that even transcends chains.

The easiest characters for me to write were Harriet and Nat Turner's mother. They were both mothers of sons, as I am.

Many of Harriet's struggles to understand in the book are my own. As I wrote, I felt her. In the same way, I felt Nat's mother calling to me to find the truth, to clear her son's name.

6. Nat and Thomas clearly have an intimate, yet complex, re-lationship. Both care for the other, yet can't seem to keep their lines of communication open. How do you think this informs the debates that were raging between the North and the South at the time?
These are such deep questions. You've got me working here. I am grateful for your analysis.

I think that their relationship was like many present-day relation-ships: We make compromises so that we can remain friends. We are afraid to test the strength of our relationships. So it was with the North and South. There was a bond forged by common struggle and ideals, but as a new nation they were afraid to test the strength of their union.

Slavery was the issue. Right made a deal with wrong—many of those who knew that slavery was morally and legally wrong com-promised because they doubted that there was another way to hold the Union together. Those who knew better excused their friends' wrongdoing. They sacrificed millions of lives—because the North and the South were afraid to test the union, or to trust that they could survive disunion.

Those compromises—which were inscribed into our laws, words that remain to testify against us—were made out of fear, not faith or love. We made compromises with evil because we were afraid to test the depth of our relationship or trust God to resolve what seemed impossible. We are still living with the legacy of those compromises.

7. Nat can almost taste Ethiopia as he stands in the Chesapeake Bay, and yet the shrieks of the beaten woman resound loud enough around him to make him stay. What do you think Nat gave up when he decided to return? What did he gain?
He gave up what might have been. He gave up personal gain, his family, and peace, temporary peace, for a more lasting peace.

8. Harriet finds the murder of the Waller family the hardest to stomach, and the sentiment cannot help but echo in the reader.

Yet you still manage to keep Nat a sympathetic character. What was the hardest part about writing this scene?

The most difficult part, as the writer, was being Nat Turner. When I write, I sit in the characters. I felt everything. I experienced everything. I'm serious when I tell you my hair is grayer. (I think I'm going to invest in some dye.) I felt his agony. I smelled the blood.

It has made me very grateful to those who paid the price for my liberty. Most of my working career I have spent among military people, so I thought I was grateful before. But now I realize that we don't fully appreciate what we do to them and what they sacrifice having to make life or death decisions in order to secure and protect our freedom.

9. On page 188, there is an apple tree that has been overtaken by a beautiful, flowering vine. Nat "would prefer to allow both to live—the apples were sweet, fragrant, and might fill his stomach; the wisteria flowers were beautiful to behold." Do you think Nat would consider the vine in the same way as he carries out his mission in Cross Keys?

Exactly. You got it!

He loved both the captives and the captors. God loves both the oppressed and the oppressor. But there was no choice: Unchecked, the wisteria choked everything in its path.

10. Nat's relationship to God becomes most pronounced in his ongoing conversation with Trezvant in the jailhouse. How do you think religion both divided and united the white and black population of the early nineteenth century?

The conversation actually takes place in Peter Edwards's home before Nat Turner is taken into custody. Nat Turner was a preacher and I think the conversation about race and slavery would also have been about religion.

I think Christianity, in particular, was dealt body blows by slavery and race. Ruthless people, liars, used religion to justify superiority, slavery, greed, etc. They painted God as the white God of white people. There were many who professed religion even as they did ungodly things.

It's hard to trust people who say they are God's people when there has been a history of religion being used to manipulate, control, and oppress others. Mistrust was planted then and I believe it remains today.

That lie still causes many to turn away from Christianity. The lie still causes some to feel superior and others inferior. There are some who still preach, teach, and believe this foolishness—they're also slavery's victims.

Yet, at the same time, throughout history and even today, we find diverse people who are bonded together by faith. The abolitionist movement was undergirded by faith. For example, many of the leading abolitionists were courageous people of faith, both white and black—like Henry Ward Beecher, his sister Harriet, Harriet Tubman, Frederick Douglass, William Lloyd Garrison, and Bishop Richard Allen of Philadelphia—who worked together. In a previous novel, *Abraham's Well*, I wrote about Native American, African American, and white preachers who risked their lives to preach together to the Cherokee and the people of African descent who walked the Trail of Tears.

There are people today who find the courage to reach across color lines—despite all the barriers that would prevent it. If we are willing to do the difficult work of looking at ourselves, faith can help us. It can help us begin to judge people and choose friends and leaders not by skin color or by who they say they are but by the content of their character.

I guess if race and slavery dealt Christianity body blows, then I guess you could say that faith won't surrender. Faith, hope, and love keep fighting back.

11. Thomas Gray's decision to write a false confession for Nat is one of the strongest betrayals. Where does testimony figure in the novel? How does it inform your role as an author?

This second book really is Nat Turner's testimony. I never intended to write from Turner's perspective. I tried to avoid it.

But he whispered to me, insisting that he must speak. He told me that they, all the slaves, were heroes: When we teach school-children about slaves we should tell the children that they were American heroes.

He talked to me about the Great Dismal Swamp, about his love for his wife, Cherry, and his son. He told me about the heart-break and frustration, and about the witnesses. I suppose you could say he gave me his testimony, and it was my job, as author, to deliver it.

12. At the end of the novel, Nancie declares herself free when she can finally reassume her Ethiopian name, Nikahywot. Do you find a similar power in names?

Names open and shut doors. Names confer privilege and take away power. When you take someone's name, when you take their heroes, their God, whatever makes up their identity, you diminish them. You begin to destroy them and re-create them in your own image.

My mother was a schoolteacher. The first year of my life was spent on a Navajo Indian reservation in Arizona.

As a child, I remember my mother talking about our time there. She spoke with wonder. But then her voice would become a whisper and I thought I heard fear in the voice of a woman who showed no fear. "They take the children away from their families," she said. "They cut their hair." She shook her head with sorrow. "The children cry and the families cry, but they don't care."

I could imagine the faceless, nameless "they" who did these things. It was a reservation and these things were done by federal mandate.

My mother showed pictures of the Navajo children clinging to her as though she was their mother. "They won't let them speak their language," she said of the children. "They make them change their names."

I knew what she was telling me. It was a violation so great that it could not be spoken out loud. But Nancie reclaimed her name.

I needed to free my readers. I needed to give them hope; it is who I am. It is what I believe.

I needed to lift the lamp, to tell the tired, discouraged, and poor not to give up. We should not be deceived: No matter the circumstances we can wrestle back our power.

Nikahywot's name was like a light, a beacon to all of us, and she reclaimed it. Thirty years later, centuries later, it is never too late. It was restoration and, I suppose, I also did it for the Navajo children and for my mother.

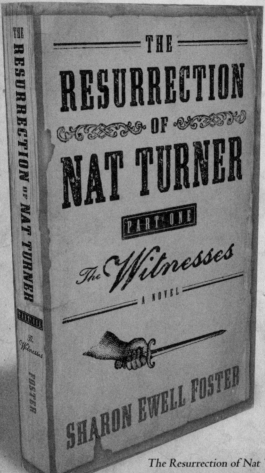